TO
HAVE
AND TO
HARM

TO
HAVE
AND TO
HARM

DEBRA DOXER

For everyone who loved *Keep You from Harm* and
reached out to tell me.
Thank you.

May you never appeal to Heaven in prayers so hopeless and so agonised as in that hour left my lips; for never may you, like me, dread to be the instrument of evil to what you wholly love.
—Charlotte Brontë, *Jane Eyre*

ONE

Lucas

"**I**T'S *me. My father knows we're looking for him. He sent someone to get me. We had the wrong name, Lucas. We were never going to find him ourselves. My father says he can heal me, but that I need to come to him alone. And I need to go right now. I'm so sorry I have to leave this way...without you, without saying good-bye. But please don't worry. I'm going to be fine. I love you. I promise to never stop loving you. All my heart is yours, Lucas. It belongs to you.*"

I pull the phone away from my ear and stare at it, like it knows more than it's telling me, because this has to be a fucking joke. Raielle left the message less than ten minutes ago.

"You're dripping water all over the floor," Liam says from the doorway.

Ignoring him, I try her again. When I get her voice mail, I try again. And again. Growling in frustration, I hurl the phone at my bed, but it slides across the blanket and hits the floor with a thud.

Liam scowls, retrieving it and checking its condition. His lips are moving, questioning me, but I can't focus on him.

I start pulling on my clothes, even though I'm still soaked from the shower. The T-shirt and jeans stick to my skin as I move around the

1

room, planting my feet in my shoes and grabbing my keys off the dresser. I can be at her house in five minutes if I hustle, because I know she'll be there. There's no way she left. She wouldn't do this to me.

"Boarding passes for you and Raielle?" Liam asks. "You're going to Los Angeles? Is this what you wanted to talk to Dad about?" He lowers himself onto my bed, eyeing the passes I printed out earlier, two pieces of paper that represented a lifeline to me just a few minutes ago, yet may be completely irrelevant now.

"Sorry, Liam. Can't talk."

I grab my phone from his hand. Then I'm out in the hallway, down the stairs, and through the front door.

I peel out of the driveway, adrenaline pushing my foot down hard on the gas pedal. My hand slams against the steering wheel as her message repeats in my head. *A voice-mail message?* I put my phone down for five minutes to take a shower, and she leaves me a message like that?

After passing a slow-moving minivan, I blow through a red light. I'm driving like a maniac, but soon I'm approaching her neighborhood. Chloe's car is pulling into the driveway just as I reach the house. Not bothering to turn off the motor, I jump out of the truck, run up the walkway, and try the front door. The knob turns and I push inside, ignoring whatever the hell Chloe is saying to me.

"Ray?" I yell down the stairs as I'm taking them two at a time. "Ray?"

When I get to the bottom, I look around the dark, quiet basement room, and I know. She's not here. My harsh breathing is all that interrupts the silence.

"Lucas, is something wrong?" Chloe calls down to me.

I turn to see her watching me from the top of the stairwell. "Is Raielle up there?" I ask, even though I already know the answer.

As Chloe begins to shake her head, I walk farther into the room, looking around the small space Raielle carved out for herself. When I spot her phone sitting on the nightstand beside her bed, my eyes close as its significance settles over me. If she's really gone, so is the only way I have to reach her.

I sink heavily onto her bed and scrub my hands over my face. *Maybe*

2

it's not true. Maybe she's coming back. But then I recall the way her voice sounded on the message. This isn't a joke. The anxiety clutching at my chest knows this is no joke.

Picking up the phone, I scroll through the list of missed calls. They're all from me. Why the hell would she leave her phone behind? I grip it tightly in my hand. Now what? Do I start running around looking for her? I could hunt through airports and bus stations. I could call Kyle and the police. I could reveal the fact that Raielle gave herself Penelope's disease, a secret she begged me to keep, all in an effort to find her. But what would be the point in that?

She said her father sent for her, that he's going to help her. Finding her father was our plan. A plan that was never going to succeed based on what she said. But why like this? Why would her father make her leave this way? Did he force her to go? She didn't sound like she was being forced to leave me that message. She sounded despondent, but not scared or coerced.

"Lucas?" Chloe asks from behind me. "Is everything all right?" She blinks at me with wide, worried eyes, like she actually cares, like her husband's long-lost sister was ever more than a means to an end for her. She wanted her daughter cured, but she never really wanted Raielle here. She'll probably throw a party when she figures out she's gone.

I slip Raielle's phone into my pocket. "No, it's all wrong," I say. Then I walk past her without another word.

Getting back into the truck and pulling away from the house, I operate on autopilot, running on anger and confusion. It feels like I've been sucker punched.

I don't know where I'm going, I just need to move. My eyes scan the sidewalk, peering inside passing cars, uselessly searching for her. My heart belongs to you, she said in her message. She'll never stop loving me. *Yeah, right.*

She was telling me good-bye. I could hear it in her voice, the bleak resignation, the finality of her words. What the hell was happening when she said those things? She should have found a way to see me before she left. Or she should have fucking called back five minutes later.

I don't know how long I've been driving when the sun begins to sink and the trees cast long shadows across the road. But somehow I end up at the bridge. I'm torturing myself coming here, making it that much worse by purposely immersing myself in memories. I think about the night I nearly made her mine. The night I found out that she was slowly dying, and she never intended to tell me.

From the first moment I saw her, she's been making me crazy. I knew I wanted her, and she made me work for it. She never stopped making me work. One minute, I think I've gotten through and all her walls are down. She's right there with me. Then the next, they're built back up again, and she's lost behind them. One step forward, two steps back. But now I'm so far back, she's completely out of reach. Was it hard for her to leave me? Did it tear her heart out, the same heart she promised was mine forever just seconds before she ripped it away?

I groan as I lean back against the truck and sink down to the ground, running my hands over my face, trying to keep my shit together. Then I reach into my pocket and pull out her phone. I'm not sure why I took it; I just wanted it. I begin searching through it, looking for a phone number I don't recognize. Maybe her father called her. But right off, I can see that he didn't. I mostly see my number, and the numbers of her only friends here in Fort Upton, Myles and Gwen. Then, because I'm a glutton for punishment, I open her texts, and read over the conversations we've had. Next I start looking through her pictures. She doesn't have many, a couple of Penelope at the park, and one of her and Gwen mugging for the camera. But it's the last one that stops me cold. Everything inside me stills.

It's of us dancing at the prom.

Swallowing against the growing thickness in my throat, my eyes greedily travel over every part of the photo. I take in her long blonde waves flowing down her back, curling over my hands, which are pressing her close to me. I remember the satiny feel of that blue dress, and the soft tickle of her hair against my fingers. My eyes travel up the long line of her neck to the small smile curving her lips as she looks at me.

This was taken before I told her that I loved her and she said it back.

But I can see it in her expression, because it mirrors mine. Even then, we were already in deep. She's not trying to mask it or deny it here. Her eyes are shining with it, and I can't hold back the emotions tumbling through me. I know Raielle. I know her heart. She wouldn't willingly walk away from me like this.

Looking at us together, everything becomes clearer. When I left her in the schoolyard this afternoon, she told me she loved me, and I know she meant it. She intended for us to go to Los Angeles together to find her father and somehow, someone convinced her to go without me. I was letting hurt cloud my judgment because I know my girl would only leave me this way for one of two reasons. Either someone was holding a gun to her head, or she was trying to protect me from something.

Anger overtakes the hurt, and I start to feel calmer. Anger is familiar. It's driven me most of my life. It's constantly simmering inside me, just waiting for something to provoke it and bring it to a boiling point. My thoughts are focusing. My brain starts to work again. Sitting there on the side of the road, a face coalesces in my mind. We had the wrong name. That was in her message, too. Alec gave us the wrong name when we asked him what he knew about Raielle's father. *Alec.*

Just the thought of him has me gritting my teeth and clenching my fists. He's caused Raielle nothing but pain. He had her mother killed to bring her here. Then he played on her emotions to manipulate her. He's the one who should be dying from Penelope's disease, not Raielle. That was the deal. It was supposed to be his fate, one he absolutely deserved, and he had the gall to smile when he found out he'd escaped it. He was the only one who knew we were leaving to look for Raielle's father. Soon after we talked to him, her father came and took her. There's only person who could have told him. *Alec.*

Before I can second-guess myself, I'm back in the truck. The drive takes too long and I'm about to jump out of my skin by the time I pull up to his house. When I see the driveway is empty, I worry that Alec's not here. But then I spot him, sitting on the steps leading to the front door. He's watching me. It almost looks like he's waiting for me.

I get out of the truck and stalk toward him as he stands, eyeing me with a neutral expression. Calmly, he watches my approach. "I've been expecting you. We can talk inside." Then he turns and goes in, leaving the door open behind him.

When I understand that he knows something, the pounding in my chest doesn't lessen. It builds, its rhythm moving up inside my head and roaring in my ears. He was waiting for me.

I follow Alec inside and slam the door closed behind me. It wasn't intentional, but I may not be in complete control of myself at the moment. I watch as the sharp sound pulls him up short. He turns around and tenses. He should be tense, because I'm not leaving here without the information I came for.

His hands go up. "You need to calm down, son."

I waste no time. "You gave us a bogus name and sent us on a wild-goose chase."

Alec closes his eyes and takes a breath. "No. The name I gave you is the only one I've heard Raielle's father use. But after you left here, I did what you wanted to do but couldn't. I helped her."

I take a step toward him. "What did you do?"

He clears his throat. "I'm not in touch with Raielle's father, but I do know how to get in touch with him. I sent a message when you told me about her condition. Despite what you think of me, I never wanted Raielle to be hurt. I wanted to help her. It was unlikely you would find her father, but you were right about him. He's her only chance. He's probably the only one who can cure her, and I made sure she found her way to him."

I can see that the explanation sounds perfectly reasonable in his own warped mind. He almost looks proud of himself. "If you wanted to help her so badly, why didn't you tell us this when we came to you?"

"I couldn't. I had to check with him first. I also didn't want to give you false hope in case he refused to help." He slips his hands into his pockets and just watches me, so in control again, and such a two-faced prick.

"Why would he refuse to help her?"

Alec shrugs. "It's complicated."

"It's complicated?" I ask incredulously. "Is that why he had to take her like this? Make her disappear without telling anyone where she went?"

Alec seems to be weighing his next words. "He has to be careful. He's made some enemies." Then his jaw sets, letting me know that he doesn't intend to tell me more.

I tilt my head at him, trying to figure him out. "Why are you in touch with her father anyway? Raielle's mother left you for him."

He swallows and leans back on his heels. "He contacted me the first time a few years after she went with him. Since Angela and I were still technically married, he wanted me to take her in with Raielle in tow. He was in some trouble, and he thought they'd be safer here."

He removes his hands from his pockets and grips them together in front of him. Then he shakes his head. "But I'd already moved on. Having Angela back in my home wasn't a possibility. Since I was still her husband, I helped him admit her to a treatment facility in California. She already had a drinking problem by then. Once that was done, I tried to divorce her. But she wouldn't sign the papers. Then she disappeared. That's why we've had reason to be in touch from time to time. Both of us were looking for her."

And that's probably when Raielle landed in her first foster home; neither Alec nor her father were willing to take her. My thoughts are spinning, connecting all the dots. He's been in contact with Raielle's father for all these years, but he never bothered to tell Raielle that. He turned his back on Raielle's mother and eventually had her killed.

Eyeing his perfectly combed silver hair, his Polo shirt, and his neatly pressed khakis, I think this suburban grandfather facade is barely hiding the putrid pile of shit that exists beneath the surface. And I know one thing with certainty. He either knows where Raielle is, or he knows how to find out.

"If you really want to help Ray, you'll tell me where she's going. She needs me."

He grins mockingly at me. "You mean, you need her."

His words play on my fears. I try not to show it, but he's right. I do need her, more than she ever needed me. "Just tell me. It makes no sense to keep us apart. I'm no threat to him."

"I can't." His back straightens. "But I will tell you this—if you want to find her, stick to your original plan."

My eyes narrow. "Our plan? You're talking about going to Los Angeles? That's where she's headed?"

"Yes."

Watching his placid expression, I don't know whether to believe him or not. "LA is a big place. I need something more specific. I need to know how to contact her."

"I told you. I can't say any more." He appears resolute.

"You might as well have said nothing. I can't find her with what little you've told me." My hands fist at my sides as I take another step toward him. He sees something in my expression that makes him take a step back.

"Go to Los Angeles," he insists, his patience slipping. "Once you're there, I'll let her father know. Then it will be up to him to decide if you can see her. That's your only option for finding her."

But I can't accept that. I'm trying to figure out how else I can persuade him before I give up and do something I probably won't regret, when a thought occurs to me. "If you can contact Raielle's father, why didn't you ask him to help Penelope?"

His gaze flicks down to the floor, hinting at the answer.

"You did ask him, didn't you? You asked him and he said no?"

He says nothing. There's no denial.

"Why would he do that?"

Alec sighs, shifting away from me. "He said she couldn't be cured, not without extraordinary measures. I understood what that meant. That's when I decided to offer myself so that he could give her disease to me. But he refused, and he wouldn't be persuaded. I had to go to Angela for help next. She, of course, refused, too." Alec is scowling now.

"Ray was your last hope. Jesus," I mutter, but I'm stalled on what he said before, knowing what it means. "Then her father can't cure her either. He can only give her disease to someone else, a blood relative, if he can find one. A relative that he doesn't mind killing." My eyes begin to burn. The stark reality is that even with her father's help, Raielle may not live through this.

Alec eyes me carefully, sensing my change in mood. "I'm sorry, son."

"I'm not your fucking son." I am seething. My eyes squeeze shut as I turn away from him. I have to get to her; she can't go through this alone. I look back at Alec. "I'll go to LA, and you'll convince her father to let me see her. You have to. She saved your granddaughter's life. You owe her."

"I'll do everything I can," he says.

I bite back my frustration and the impulse to keep pushing him for more. Looking at Alec's sympathetic eyes and his downturned mouth, I know this is all there is, and I have no choice but to believe him.

TWO

Raielle

AS the land flattens out into endless fields of burned grass and straight, uninterrupted highway, pressure builds behind my eyes. Punishing sun beats down on the car, and even with the wraparound sunglasses Apollo offered me back in Missouri, it's fueling my headache, causing me to shift in my seat and exhale my misery.

"Can we stop for more aspirin?" I finally ask, leaning the side of my head against the window, squeezing my eyes shut.

"You've already downed a whole bottle and it's done shit. We could stop at the next town. I could try to find you something stronger."

I'd shake my head at him, but it would hurt too much. "Forget it. Just keep driving," I whisper.

The fact that Apollo has been working with my father all this time, watching over me for years, long before my mother and I moved into the apartment above him in San Diego, is still so hard to comprehend. I keep thinking over all my interactions with him, and I never thought he was more than a common criminal who for some reason was nice to me. Now I know the reason. Now I know so many things I didn't before.

Trying to block out the pain, I think of Lucas, remembering the sound of his voice and the bliss of being held in his strong arms. Just the thought of him calms me, allows me to breathe through the hurt, and not sink down in it. After a couple of days on the road, this horrible disease living inside me has decided to launch a full-scale attack on my nervous system. If I were anyone else, I'd be dead by now. But I've been able to control the growth of the worst tumors, just not the piercing pain that's become a part of me. I would undoubtedly give up if I didn't have hope of seeing Lucas again. If I didn't keep the vision of his face and his beautiful dark blue eyes in my own mind's eye.

"Why on earth didn't we fly? How much farther is it?" I complain, rolling my forehead against the glass, trying to ease the pressure.

He sighs, and I hear him shifting in his seat. "Just hold on, kid. No more stops. I'll drive all the way through. We'll be there before you know it."

"We're going back to California, aren't we? To Los Angeles. He still lives there."

"Yeah, he's still there."

I've asked this question several times, but Apollo kept refusing to answer. I must look pretty pathetic if he's finally giving that information up.

I lean away from the window to rest my head back against the seat again. My skin is drenched in sweat. The pain has a strange kind of heat to it. It's only tolerable when I don't move. So I keep to this position, eventually drifting off, allowing the car's steady speed to lull me into semiconsciousness. My limbs gradually become lax and I sink deeper into the seat, sighing at the loosening of my tense muscles.

I stay this way, slipping in and out of awareness, until the numbness in my right hand seems to spread, moving up my arm to my shoulder, and then drifting across my torso. The numbness is slowly taking over my body. I should be terrified by this gradual disappearance of feeling. But instead I register it in a neutral way, hoping that it will travel up to my head and douse the heat singeing me from the inside out.

When I try to draw in my next breath, my body seems to forget how to do this simple task. I try again, but my muscles won't respond. My eyes pop open as a sense of panic finally erupts, making me buck forward and gasp for air. I can hear the whistling in my chest as the remaining oxygen is expelled. I hear Apollo questioning me, calmly at first, and then more frantically.

I'm flung toward the dashboard as the car screeches to a halt. My door is yanked open, and I can feel Apollo shaking me and saying my name again. A moment later, he has me out of the car and down onto the grass beside the road. The edges of my vision are fading as he puts his mouth to mine and blows air into my lungs.

As his breath flows into me, the panic eases. My eyes are able to focus. Apollo is leaning over me, drops of perspiration forming on his upper lip and forehead. He frantically tugs his phone out of his pocket.

When the air runs out and I still can't draw more in, my back arches as I gasp, and immediately Apollo's mouth is on mine, giving me his breath, giving me life.

My eyes are locked on his as he leans back and brings the phone to his lips. "This road trip is over. Get me a plane with some goddamned paramedics. She can't breathe. She's dying on the ground in front of me right now!"

I tremble as I absorb his words. We're in the middle of nowhere. We're not near an airport. How is a plane going to appear out of thin air? I'm not going to survive this. I'm going to die here on the side of the road. Tears spill over the sides of my face, and I close my eyes against them, stomping my foot on the ground. It can't end this way, with no answers gotten and no explanations given. I can't leave Lucas like this. I won't do this to him.

My air is used up again. Apollo's attention is on his phone, not me. I can feel my body struggling, and I roll over onto my side. The numbness has taken the pain away, but this slow suffocation is a different kind of torture. To get his attention, I kick my legs out at him, the only muscles I seem to have control over. Immediately, he rolls me onto my back again and brings his mouth to mine. Then he puts his phone away and eyes me stoically. I want to question him, but I can't form the words. I can't ask him if he somehow managed to get us a plane, or if he thought of calling an ambulance. And he's not offering up any answers. He's just watching me, waiting for me to need him again, and when I do, he's there.

"I could keep this up all day. How about you?" he asks. His dark eyes bore into mine, silently telling me to hang on.

I'm staring at Apollo's face, but now it's Lucas's voice I'm hearing in my head. *You're going to be fine. You have to believe that. I love you.*

As the day gradually darkens and chills, it's those words that keep me going when hopelessness threatens to drown me, when the idea of giving up becomes stronger than my will to continue this painful struggle. Even in his absence, Lucas is keeping me going. He's saving me by just existing.

CAN you hear me, Raielle?"

I swallow against the dryness in my throat and peel open my lids. When the bright light burns my eyes, I squeeze them closed again.

A hand lightly touches my forehead and smoothes back over my hair. "It's time to wake up."

The voice is low and gentle, deep and soothing, just like the hand.

"Wake up," the voice whispers.

I force my eyes to open again, prepared for the glare this time, blinking rapidly, trying to bring my surroundings into focus. I can feel that I'm lying in a bed, and my muscles are relaxed, free of pain.

Then I remember.

Suddenly frantic, I drag in a breath as I see flashes of Apollo hovering over me. I try to sit up, but the hand moves to my shoulder, applying pressure, easing me back.

"Lie still. You're fine now. You're perfectly fine."

I blink, and his image begins to gel, allowing me to put a face to the soothing voice. I see a man with clear green eyes and thick wheat-colored hair, combed to the side, arching over his ears. A wide, kind smile greets me. "You're safe with me," he says.

I can feel the way my body is absorbing the sound of his voice, calming under the steady, confident cadence of his words.

"I'm not dead," I whisper.

He laughs. "No. You're certainly not."

If I'm alive, then this man whose energy is flowing into me can only be one person.

I swallow again, trying to moisten my dry throat. "You're my father," I manage to say.

He grins and nods.

"You healed me?" I ask, my voice raw and rough.

"Yes," he says, his eyes intent on me.

Glancing around, I can see that I'm in a luxurious bedroom, tucked beneath the covers of a canopy bed. The walls are covered with art, the kind of art that has ornate frames with attached lights.

"You sent a plane?" I ask, trying to remember. As I study my lavish surroundings, it seems completely possible.

"A helicopter, actually. The plane couldn't land where you were."

"Oh," I reply, like this is a normal conversation. "Thank you."

He smiles briefly. "You're welcome." Then he stands. "I'll have some food brought up to you. You must be hungry."

My eyes travel over his lean frame, and in a detached way, I register that this is *him*. This is my father. We share the same genes, the same blood. When I used to see other children with their fathers, I'd wonder what mine looked like. And here he is, standing right in front of me.

The remaining fuzziness in my head fades, and I take stock of myself. I can feel my hand now. I fist it and turn it over. My back and head no longer ache. I feel like myself. Then the next logical question bubbles to the surface.

I sit up. "How did you do it?"

He eyes me curiously. "Do what?"

"I know I was dying," I say carefully as a small amount of relief sets in. What I'd hoped all along appears to be true. My father is so powerful that he can beat death. "Don't the rules about not interfering with death apply to you?"

His lips turn down. "What rules?"

I search his expression, wondering if he honestly doesn't know what I'm asking. "I was afraid I'd gotten too close to dying to be healed."

"There's a way around that," he says simply. "A trade. A life for a life." Then he shrugs, like he's talking about the weather.

No. My throat grows tight. "How? I mean, who? Other than you, I have no relations here." I think of how my mother mistakenly moved her boyfriend's death into his own son and how Lucas wanted me to transfer my death into my grandmother. But I refused to do it. I wouldn't save my own life by taking another's. *When death comes, it won't be denied.* Knowing that, I still hoped there was another way. Now I understand that I was fooling myself.

He watches me closely. "Relatives aren't necessary."

"Tell me how you healed me. Please," I whisper.

The bed shifts beneath his weight as he sits down again. "I just told you," he states. "A trade. A voluntary one."

"My life for someone else's?" I ask as my hands fist in the sheets.

He tilts his head at me, studying me for a moment, seeming interested in my reaction, before he slowly nods.

The breath rushes out of me. "Who?"

His expression doesn't change. "That doesn't matter."

"Tell me." My body starts to tremble as I watch his face, confused by his calm, seemingly unfeeling manner in the face of my obvious emotion.

"There's no need to get upset, but I can't tell you." Then he stands and says something else, but I'm no longer listening. He frowns at me as my vision blurs with tears and I lie back down, rolling onto my side away from him. A moment later, I hear the door open and close again.

Once he's gone, regret pools inside me and my stomach starts to cramp. "No," I whisper, turning my head into the pillow. I curl in on myself, wanting only to sleep again, wanting to disappear, because deep inside I knew. I hoped my father was so powerful that he possessed some magic ability that would heal me. But that was a fantasy, wishful thinking. Even as I was fighting for my life by the roadside, I knew it would take either a miracle or a sin to save me, and there's been no miracle.

I let this happen rather than letting go. I allowed someone else to die for me, and don't know how I'm going to live with that, or if I even deserve to.

THREE

Lucas

'VE been in Los Angeles for eighty-six days, and I haven't seen her. Today marks the start of day eighty-seven.

When I first got here, I sat in a hotel room and waited. I harassed Alec with phone calls, and he kept promising me she was fine. He said he'd spoken to his contact. He knew I was here, and they'd let me see her soon. But weeks passed and nothing happened. The waiting was driving me crazy. I hollered at my father, who told me I was throwing my life away, and I ignored Liam, who in his own quiet way suggested that I give up.

At first, my fury fueled me. Then it was my fear of losing her that drove me. Now it's the routine that keeps me going, waking up each morning, remembering it all again, and trying not to let the hopelessness get the best of me.

A few weeks ago, I moved out of the hotel and into an apartment, answering an ad in the paper. Then I started at UCLA to keep busy. I put in an application at the end of last year when I knew Raielle wanted to go there. I didn't tell her, because I wasn't sure if I'd go through with it.

But in a desperate attempt to feel close to her, I'm taking classes now.

17

She's probably not here, but she was supposed to be, and I couldn't sit around anymore just waiting. But the more time that goes by, the more I realize that Alec was probably full of shit, and I believed him because I wanted to so badly. I've been deluding myself, assuming if she were able to, nothing could stop her from reaching out to me. I figured that when her father told her I was here, wild horses couldn't have kept her away. That's how it would have been with me. But maybe I need to finally wake up like everyone says, because she's still gone.

I find myself hoping that she's perfectly healthy, and I'm just an idiot pining away for a girl who doesn't want me anymore. It's better than the alternative, that I've heard nothing from her for months because she isn't okay. That's not a possibility I can accept. It's a nightmare that I keep pushing away while I continue to wait, not admitting that I'm beginning to lose faith.

Meanwhile, I have my new roommate, Cal, trying to prop me up. He's a psychology major, which is too ironic. I was hoping for a roommate who minded his own business, but we had a few drinks one night and Cal dragged my story out of me. I revealed just enough for him to think that my girlfriend callously dumped me with no warning, leaving me crushed and unable to move on. Yes, that's all true, but it's not the whole truth, and I can't tell him the rest without betraying her. He probably wouldn't believe me anyway.

The club Cal is dragging me to is called Johnny Red's. It's a short walk from my new apartment. He's insisting I go out tonight. He thinks that I keep to myself too much, that I'm a loner who's missing out on the college experience. But he's wrong. I'm more like a ghost.

Johnny Red's has a line around the corner, and we walk to the end of it. Cal starts working the girls around us right off. He's got a nerdy, artsy look going with his black-rimmed glasses and messy blond hair pushed back behind his ears. Tall and thin with a slightly hunched-over posture, there's a certain kind of girl who seems to go for him, and the ones he's talking to now aren't that kind. He shrugs, unbothered by their lack of interest.

It takes just over half an hour to get inside, and when we do, I want to turn right back around again. It's too hot and too crowded. I don't know what the hell I'm doing here. Ahead of me, Cal sees some friends by the bar, and they're motioning to him. I decide that as long as I'm here, I could use a drink. One drink, and then I'm gone.

Nodding at Cal, I push my way up to the front and start chatting with the bartender, hoping he doesn't card me. He hardly glances in my direction when he slides over the beer I ordered. This must be why Johnny Red's is so popular at the moment. Once the police get wind of this, its reputation as the "in" spot will be over.

I down half my drink in a few long pulls. Then I finish it and look around, watching people talking, laughing, and dancing. They're living their lives, unlike me. I'm in some kind of purgatory, and I have no idea when or if I'm ever getting out. *What if this is it? What if this is just the beginning of a lifetime of missing her?*

Turning away from the crowd, I signal the bartender. He finishes serving the group in front of him, and when he looks my way, I order two more drinks—another beer and a double shot of vodka. I'm through the shot and well into the beer when a girl with dark blonde hair comes up beside me, brushing her hip against my leg. I pull in a sharp breath because for a long, piercing moment, I think it may be her. My heart leaps into my throat but then it plummets down to my stomach. My fingers tense around the cold glass as I take in the details I wanted to overlook at first. She's too short. Her hair isn't the right shade. She's got more curves, and they're all on display in a tight red dress that Raielle would probably never put on.

I'm still staring when she turns and smiles up at me. I mentally shake myself because she looks nothing like Raielle. She says something to me, but I turn away, draining my glass and going in for another. From the corner of my eye, I see her disappear into the crowd, but then she comes back again, sidling up beside me. When she sees me notice her, she slips her hand into mine. I look down into her big blue eyes, which are watching me from beneath heavy lids. Her head is tilted with a silent question. I don't answer her. I don't do anything except stand there and start to feel numb.

19

She tugs on my hand and begins to draw me away from the bar. I find myself following, letting her take me wherever she's going. Cutting through the crowd, she makes a turn down a long, empty hallway that leads to the bathrooms. When we're far enough away from the noise to be heard, she stops, turning to face me. "You can kiss me if you want," she says with a smile. Then she moves closer, taking my hand and placing it on her waist.

I stare at her uplifted face and feel a familiar dark hole yawning wide inside me. That's when I decide to pretend for just a while. I imagine those eyes belong to another girl. When her hand reaches around my neck and she smiles coyly, I fantasize that it's someone else's hand touching me. As she pulls my head down and her lips tentatively brush mine, I let myself fall into the dream of being with Raielle again.

My fingers dig into her sides as I pull her closer. I slide my tongue against hers, still pretending. With a groan, I edge her into a dark corner and piston my tongue in and out of her mouth. She makes an approving sound as her hand slides between us and she reaches her fingers beneath my shirt, brushing them against my skin.

Breaking away from her lips, I kiss my way down her neck to the beginning of her cleavage. Then I dip my fingers just inside the top of her dress. When she doesn't stop me, I push in further and slide my hand beneath the cup of her bra. She sighs and leans her chest more fully into my palm.

My eyes squeeze closed so I won't see her face. But it's not working; I'm still numb. I don't know this girl. She's not who I want, not even close. My whole body goes rigid as I realize what I'm doing.

Breathing hard, I push away from her. Just then, the bathroom room door swings open behind us, and she glances down to make sure her dress is in place as two girls walk past, giggling at us as they go by.

Once they're gone, she blinks at me. Then she grins. "Want to go somewhere else?"

I look down, raking my hands through my hair. When my gut starts to churn, I shift away from her and start heading back down the hallway.

"Hey!" she yells. "Wait a minute." She catches up with me. "Where are you going?"

I stop long enough to answer her. "I acted like an ass just now. I'm sorry." Then I keep moving fast enough for her to know not to follow me, and I don't stop again until I'm home.

Raielle

MY father told me I wasn't dead when we met. But I'm not alive either. I'm something in between. My heart beats and my blood flows, but my essence is gone and my thoughts are singular, focused on one goal—redemption.

Listlessly, I move through my days. Apollo has organized my new life, and I let him steer me through it, doing things by rote, like going to class and doing schoolwork. Those things are familiar and they settle my errant thoughts. But really, I'm waiting. My father is the key to my redemption, and I'm waiting to see him again. In the meantime, when the memories of what I've lost start to eat at me, I run. Well, actually, I drive—fast.

I'm going close to a hundred miles per hour when I exit the 405 onto Sunset. The tires squeal their reluctance as the back of the Porsche 911 Carrera slews to the left while I careen through a curve, rushing to nowhere along the winding road that hugs the back of the UCLA campus. The dead of night is the only time I allow myself to push this outrageously expensive vehicle, the cost of which could have paid our rent back in San Diego for the rest of our lives.

But tonight, I'm not taking it back to the condo on Wilshire I'm supposed to be sharing with my brother, Shane. The fact that I have yet another older brother would be comical if he wasn't such a pain in the ass. He couldn't be more opposite of Kyle. He has no manners, no tact, no feelings, and no morals. He's a train wreck, and I'm supposed to be sharing a two-bedroom condo with him and the harem that trails after him like a slutty exclamation point.

I lean into the turn that will take me to my home away from home, an apartment just off campus belonging to my one of my only friends here, someone unexpected from my past. Nikki and I were never close when we knew each other in San Diego. She was in and out of the system just like I was. We'd crossed paths, and we knew of each other, but one morning at the bus stop when she asked if I "had anything on me," I started keeping clear of her.

Little did I know that Nikki was smart and ambitious, and she'd always planned on going to college here, too. We stood stock-still that first day in the study lounge at Ackerman Union, shocked to see each other. Now Nikki and her boyfriend, Jason, are my only friends in Los Angeles, and I'm probably taking advantage of that fact.

Staying at Nikki's apartment is another way for me to run. It's the place where all her friends congregate. It's noisy and cluttered and there's always someone home; unlike the condo, which is often quiet and empty. It's nearly impossible for me to think at Nikki's place with the constant activity to distract me. It's a perfect place to hide.

When Nikki wordlessly handed me a key to her apartment last week, I realized how much I impose on her and Jason. I tried to refuse it, but she shoved it into my pocket and said the subject was closed. When I offered to pay them rent, her response was a silent scowl. She doesn't pry. She knows I have secrets; she has plenty of her own. She never talks about it, but I remember the bruises that marred her pale skin far too often. As for me, she knows my mother is dead, and that I only just met my father. She knows my father is wealthy, that he gives me cars and clothes and a fancy apartment, even though I want none of them. But she never asks questions, and that's one of the main reasons we've become friends. We don't push each other. We just are.

Using my key, I quietly let myself inside. Nikki and Jason's place is a typical cramped one-bedroom student apartment with a galley kitchen and a living room containing a worn-out couch and a widescreen TV. The building itself smells of stale beer and mold. Music and voices drift through the thin walls. In the darkness, I make my way to the couch. Not bothering to change out of my clothes, I lie down and pull an afghan over myself.

It's nearly three in the morning when I finally close my eyes and let the painful thoughts I block out during the day rush over me. I dream about Lucas every night. I'd rather not think of him at all. It would be easier that way. But I can't control my dreams. He stars in them. Sometimes they're wonderful. We're together at the bridge. He's bare-chested, draped over me like a warm blanket, making me tremble with need. Sometimes they're nothing but raw pain as he accuses me of willfully leaving him, of never really loving him, and the anguish in his eyes rips me in two.

Since I can't stop him from haunting my dreams, I indulge my thoughts of him during this quiet time before sleep overcomes me, and I let the sweet pain wash over me.

"HEY, man, are some of those for me?"

"Get your own fucking doughnuts."

"Come on. It's not like she's gonna eat them."

Their voices startle me awake. I pull in a harsh breath and reluctantly drag my eyes open, squinting against the dim light filtering in through the shaded windows. It takes a moment to remember where I am, to put faces to the voices, and a location to the moldy odor. It's the smell that finally connects it for me. I'm on the couch in Nikki and Jason's apartment. My heart sinks as I push my face into the cushions, not ready to start another day.

A hand lands on my shoulder, gently shaking me. Reluctantly I turn to see Apollo's looming form. He's holding a grease-stained box. "Morning, kid. Rise and shine. You need to eat and get yourself to biology class."

I shake my head at what he's become. Apollo was once a tough, coldhearted street thug, and now he's been reduced to playing mother hen to me. When he crouches down in front of me and holds out the box, I ask the same question I always do. "How is he?"

"He's fine," Apollo says patiently. That's what he always says. Apollo knows more about Lucas, but I never ask for more. It's his job to keep track of everyone who knows about me and what I can do. It's his job to keep track of me, too. Turns out, it always has been. But as long as I know Lucas is fine, I can make it through another day. He's at Columbia by now. I hope he's moving on. I hope never hearing from me again made him angry enough to want to move on. Even though the thought of that crushes me, I want him to be happy. He has to be. I couldn't stand it otherwise.

"I got your favorite, chocolate," Apollo says, gesturing to the box.

I grimace at the greasy cardboard. Since he saved my life that day, he's decided he needs to keep doing it every day. "Thanks. Just leave them on the counter."

He scowls. Then he opens the box, pulls out a doughnut, and holds it out in front of my face. "Take one fucking bite for me."

The sweet odor makes my stomach roll, but I know he won't give up. I narrow my eyes at him before biting into the doughnut. I chew it slowly, forcing it past the tightness in my throat that never seems to ease.

"See?" Jason smiles, stepping into the room. "There's more than enough to share."

Jason is on the football team, and his beefy chest and arms are testing the limits of his Bruins T-shirt. On weekends, he often consumes the entire contents of the refrigerator.

Apollo stands and points at him. "I don't like you."

Jason laughs, unbothered. "But I love you, doughnut man."

"Stop baiting him," Nikki snaps, coming around the corner already dressed for school. Jason dwarfs her narrow petite frame. Nikki says she remembers Apollo from "back in the day," and she hasn't shaken the fear he used to inspire.

But for me, he'll never be threatening that way again. Something happened between us out on the highway when he spent hours breathing life into me, never tiring, never speaking, just staying silently strong for me. I feel tied to him now. I don't mean in a romantic way, and not in a brotherly or friend sort of way either. In the way two people who have gone through a traumatic experience together feel, inexplicably linked.

"I'm not baiting him," Jason says.

Apollo takes the doughnut box into the kitchen and drops it onto the counter. "Your friend here is wasting away to nothing. But don't let that fact keep you from eating her breakfast. You're a real considerate guy. You caught a good one, Nikki."

Jason's eyes widen. "I was kidding. Come on. No one here can take a joke."

Nikki pats Jason's arm reassuringly and positions herself in front of me as I reluctantly stand up.

"I haven't wanted to say anything, but he's right," Nikki says, catching my eye to reinforce her point. "How long is this going to go on, Raielle? I hate to tell you, but you're looking kind of rough."

I bend down to neatly fold the afghan. "Nothing is going on. I'm fine."

Nikki sighs and shrugs at Apollo, silently saying, *Oh well, I tried.* "I've gotta run. I'm about to be late again. Play nice," she tells Jason as he practically bends himself in half to reach her lips and kiss her good-bye.

"I'm going, too." I reach down to grab my bag off the floor.

"I'll take you by the apartment to clean up, and then I'll drive you to school," Apollo offers, heading for the door after Nikki disappears through it.

I shake my head. "I'll take my car."

He turns and points a long bony finger at me. "No, you won't. You left it in a no-parking zone with the keys still in it. I had it moved back to the condo."

My hand goes to my hip. "Since I don't actually have a license, the fact that I keep bringing it back in one piece should impress you."

Apollo glances at Jason before stalking over to me, taking my arm, and escorting me out into the empty hallway. "You do have a driver's license."

I stubbornly stop moving. "A fake one I didn't earn. I also have a high school diploma, even though I never graduated."

Apollo faces me now and leans in close, invading my personal space. "You need to get this chip off your shoulder. It's getting fucking old."

I try to turn away from him, but his hand tightens on my arm. "Goddamn it, Raielle. You didn't die. Stop acting like you did."

My eyes widen at his bluntness. He's never been so direct with me, and I give him directness right back. "But someone else did die. Another person's life ended because of me."

His eyes darken and he shakes his head. "You have to find a way to make peace with that. You were barely conscious, for Christ's sake. No one asked your permission. I don't understand why you keep beating yourself up about it."

"Make peace with it? Are you kidding me?" I yell. "There is no peace. There will never be any peace!" My body flushes with heat, and I feel my face burn.

He drops my arm and takes a step back. "Shit, Raielle…"

I stand there stiffly. "Let's just go. Please."

"Fine," he says. His eyes are downcast, unable to meet mine. I wonder, not for the first time, if he knew what it was going to take to save my life, to heal my withered body so completely. He claims he never lied to me, but I think he did lie about that.

The car ride back to the condo is awkward and silent. When we arrive, Apollo decides to wait outside. The valet and doorman both nod as I walk by on my way into the lobby. I'm still not used to the opulence of this place, feeling uncomfortable every time I have to make my way in and out of the building. I'm just a college student, and Shane does nothing at all as far as I can tell.

Yet, inexplicably and unnecessarily, my father has us living in one of the high-rises along the Wilshire Corridor. There's a twenty-four-hour concierge, a pool, and a gym here. This place costs millions, and Shane alternates between treating it like a brothel and a clubhouse for his juvenile friends. He's the same age as Kyle, but in terms of maturity, they are worlds apart.

I use my key card to call the elevator. Then I ride up to the twenty-second floor. After stepping out into our private entryway, I unlock the door to our apartment. Once inside, my eyes immediately go to the wall of windows across the living room. The view from up here is impressive, even if there does seem to be a permanent haze floating above the city. Sometimes I feel like I need sunglasses when I walk in here. The muted light makes the polished hardwood floors gleam. The walls are painted white and are bare of any pictures or photographs. The furniture is off-white. The open kitchen is white, its starkness broken up by black counters. The overall feel is glaringly bright, not even close to cozy or welcoming in any way.

"The head case is back." Shane startles me as he shuffles out of his bedroom wearing only a pair of threadbare sweatpants.

I flip him off in response as he runs a hand through his thick black hair, causing the top to stick straight up. Despite his dark mop of hair, his skin, the skin that isn't covered in ink, is shockingly pale, making me wonder if he dyes his hair that jet-black color. He'd be vain enough to do it. Not surprisingly, a barely dressed girl trails out of the bedroom behind him, wearing only a tiny tank top and a thong. Shane is pulling cereal boxes down from the kitchen cabinets, tasting their contents, and then discarding them one by one as the girl comes up beside him and runs her fingers over his abs.

Shane is tall but scrawny compared to most of the posers here in LA, and Shane is definitely a poser. I watch as his pale, narrow chest is caressed by this girl who saw me when she entered the room, but obviously doesn't care that I'm witnessing her display.

I wrinkle my nose as I turn away from them and head toward my room.

"You've got an appointment tonight, little sister. Seven o'clock. Don't forget," Shane calls out to me, knowing how much I hate it when he calls me *little sister*.

Ignoring him, I walk past the table that houses his collection of cell phones and tablets. I have no idea why he needs so many. I'm pretty sure he switches out parts and then does something illegal with them. As quickly as I can, I disappear inside my bedroom.

My room is cavernous, also decorated in beiges and whites, with a separate sitting area and a black and white marble bathroom that could comfortably house a family of four. I've slept in this bedroom a few times when Shane wasn't home. From what I can tell, Shane has lived here for almost a year now. I'm not sure why our father insists that I stay here with him. At first I thought it was so Shane could babysit me, but he's on a downward spiral just as much as I am. The only difference is, he's so good at being a screw-up, no one notices how truly fucked up he is. And because he's such a bastard, no one really cares.

I strip off my clothes and drop them in a pile as I walk into the bathroom. Purposely avoiding the mirror, I run the shower, waiting for the mist to thicken before stepping inside and wincing as the scalding water pours down over me.

When I finally left my father's house, inside this shower was where I put the remaining jagged pieces of myself back together. After standing under the spray until the water ran cold, I realized that I couldn't wash it all away, and I understood that wishing things were different was a waste of time. But once upon a time, this was my dream. Now that I'm finally here in Los Angeles, attending UCLA, I understand that the goal I've worked toward all my life didn't require any work at all. My father and his vast wealth and connections could have gotten me anything I wanted. I could be at Harvard, if I'd only shown an interest.

Tears roll down my cheeks, mixing with the water flowing over me. This is the only place I let myself cry anymore. Everyone got tired of me and all the tears I shed when I first woke up. I got tired of me, too, and I knew I had to do something to drag myself out of the hole I was trying to disappear into. I can't change what happened or the reason why I'm here. But I can try to give it some meaning.

Making it right is what keeps me going now. It's all I have left. I've lost Lucas. He wouldn't want me like this anyway, because I've lost myself, too. The girl he knew is gone, and I hardly recognize the one who's standing here now. My old ambitions are meaningless. My own wants are unimportant. I'm unimportant. My spirit is broken. Everyone always told me how strong I was, but they were wrong. I'd never truly been tested. Now that I have, I know what a failure I am.

Sinking down onto the tile floor, I let the tears flow freely, wondering what he's doing right now, trying to remember the sound and feel of him. My eyes squeeze shut at the memories, understanding that my happiest times were with him, and knowing I'll never get them back again.

FOUR

Raielle

THERE'S a sharp bang on the door. "Come on!" Shane yells. "You know it's time to go. Stop hiding in there like a pussy."

I yank the door open and glare at him. "I'm not hiding, I'm studying. As in doing schoolwork. As in having a purpose beyond eating, fucking, and sleeping. I know that doesn't compute with you."

His mouth twitches. "Damn right it doesn't. Fucking comes first."

I roll my eyes. "Last and always. Yeah, I've heard your motto." Turning my back on him, I search for my shoes. "Just go without me. I can drive myself."

He steps into my bedroom, his boots clomping heavily on the hardwood floor. He's in his usual "out to be seen" getup, a black T-shirt and threadbare blue jeans, with leather straps on his wrists, silver rings circling his fingers, and a stud in his eyebrow. His hair is a shiny mess, sticking up all around his head, but in a way I know he worked hard to achieve. His tattoos, spiraling dark designs that don't seem to have any particular shape or identifiable figure, snake around his arms and peek out just above his collar. He spends far too much time decorating and admiring himself.

"I'm driving you. Those are my orders," he states, glancing at my duffel bag on the bed. "You going to unpack one of these days?"

Pulling on my boots, I ignore his question. "I'm driving. You can ride with me if you want."

He barks out a laugh. "No fucking way. You drive like a kamikaze pilot."

I grab my purse and keys up off the nightstand. But before I can turn, his fingers circle my wrist, moving my hand back over the table. "Drop 'em, Speedy Gonzales. I mean it."

Turning my head, I look him in the eye. He has the darkest eyes I've ever seen, even darker than Apollo's. It's almost like he has one big pupil. "What will he do to you if you don't follow orders?" I ask.

Shane leans in close, close enough for me to catch a whiff of his sour hangover breath. "You don't want to know. Drop the keys."

I release them, mainly because I'm going to hurl if he doesn't get out of my face soon.

He smirks condescendingly. "Now, let's go get you humiliated."

"Screw you." I scowl at him, because I can't help but respond this way to Shane. He's a convenient and deserving target for all the anger twisting inside me.

"They always do." He smiles, strutting out of the room, knowing I'll follow. Shane thinks I'm a fake, and he tells me every chance he gets. Apparently, there's been talk about my power and how strong it is. Transferring Penelope's disease to myself is something I've learned most healers can't do, even though it wasn't my intention. Shane told me that he doesn't believe I actually did it at all.

My nerves make an appearance as I ride silently in the elevator beside him. His eyes are glued to the moving numbers on the panel above the door. It feels like he's doing that on purpose so I won't try to talk to him, but he doesn't have to worry. My thoughts are otherwise occupied. There's been a big buildup to tonight in my head.

Apollo told me that it's my father's intention to make me a part of his team. "They do a whole lot of good," he said. "Once you see that, it might help you crawl out of this funk you're in."

I've judged him harshly so far because of how he cured me. But that's always been one of my flaws. I'm too judgmental. Everything is black and white with me. My mother told me that enough times. But if my father truly helps people, I need to be a part of that. I have to be. I just don't know if I can accept the other things I know he does.

Once we're down in the garage, Shane hands me a helmet and pulls his own on as he swings a leg over the strangest-looking motorcycle I've ever seen. It looks like Batman should be riding this thing.

"It's a special-edition Ducati," Shane explains. Lust, like he's staring at a naked woman instead of a hunk of metal, gleams in his eyes.

"Uh-huh." I shrug with disinterest, mainly to piss him off. But he just shakes his head at me, laughing at my ignorance.

I climb on the back and reluctantly place my hands on his sides, gripping the bike with my knees so that I don't have to grip him any tighter than necessary. He mumbles something before grabbing my hands and yanking them forward, placing them over his stomach. "Hold on, for fuck's sake!" he yells, just before the motor growls to life and the bike begins to vibrate beneath me.

I tighten my hold on him. I have no choice as he flies up the ramp and out onto the street. He could take Sunset and possibly get us there on time, but instead he heads down Santa Monica Boulevard toward the 101 Freeway, which means we're going to hit a ton of lights and traffic that will probably make us late. I figure he's doing this on purpose. He grudgingly falls in line, but he likes everyone to know he's doing them a favor when he shows up.

Afternoon warmth lingers in the air as the sun drops below the horizon, and dark blue and violet color the sky, making me think of Lucas, of his beautiful eyes, and the tenderness they once held for me.

Pushing away the memory, I concentrate on the stop-and-go motion of the bike, feeling it each time Shane puts a foot down to balance us, before lifting again and shooting us forward. I feel the pull of his muscles with each move he makes, and I get the impression of his ribs beneath my hands. From what I've seen, he eats nearly as much as Jason, yet he never puts on a pound.

I lean forward and open my eyes again as Shane turns onto the 101, heading up into the hills. It's nearly dark now, and I catch a glimpse of the Hollywood sign in the distance before he jerks the bike toward the exit. We're close, and we may not be too late, after all. This is my first time being back here since those first terrible days when I woke up and understood what happened to me. The closer we get to the house, the more tension I feel.

I glance around as Shane stops the bike in front of a closed wrought-iron gate. He leans over to a stone post and presses a button. When static sounds, he yells something unintelligible and the gates slowly part. We wind our way up the driveway, which is more like a small road, dark and shadowed by a canopy of trees. Soon a soaring glass-and-wood-beam structure comes into view, looming atop the hill we've been climbing. Shane maneuvers the bike around a driveway that circles a bubbling fountain. I stare up at the four-story square house with its sharp edges and straight lines. Each floor has a balcony and is rimmed with tinted windows. The house is shadowed by tall trees that grow all around it. It's simple and beautiful, but staring up at it is making my stomach flip as anxiety washes over me.

Shane pulls off his helmet and turns back to me, cocking his head at my hesitation. "Come on."

The ornately carved wooden doors open, and a dark-haired woman steps out, smiling at us.

I pull off my helmet and reluctantly follow Shane up the stairs toward her.

"Welcome back, Raielle," the woman says with a slight accent.

I frown at her familiarity. She's a beauty by anyone's standards, elegant with her dark hair pulled back into an intricate twist, and her long, flowing sundress. She looks to be in her fifties, but her heavy makeup makes it hard to be certain.

"You don't remember me," she states.

"She was practically catatonic the last time she was here," Shane says. Then he looks at me. "You don't even remember this house, do you?" He doesn't wait for an answer before he kisses the woman on the cheek and disappears inside.

Despite Shane's rude behavior, the woman's smile doesn't dim when she turns it on me again. "I'm Nyla, John's wife."

When I have no reaction, she explains. "John is your father."

"Oh," I reply, embarrassed, hating that Shane's rude remarks may have been on target. I've forgotten so much of my time here, erasing some on purpose. But the inadvertent holes frighten me.

"Come inside." She turns and waits for me to precede her through the open door.

I walk in cautiously, and my shoes immediately begin clicking on the tiled floor.

"It's just us today. We've given all the staff and the office workers the day off."

My gaze wanders over the vaulted ceiling and the giant chandelier that hangs from it. "Office?" I ask.

She comes up beside me, all elegance and poise. "Yes, the office is down the hall. It takes quite a lot of people to run this operation. We work with people and governments all over the world. You'll learn about that. Right now, your father is waiting for you. Come with me."

I follow her down a long wood-paneled hallway until she stops before a door. She opens it slowly and light pours out.

"Go on in," she tells me, urging me inside.

My palms grow moist as I step inside. The first thing I notice is a rectangular window through which I can see dark, dense woods.

"Raielle," a familiar voice says.

I turn to see him rising up from behind a desk and coming around it, toward me. Like everything else, I have only a dull memory of him from the time I spent here. After I first woke up, I'm not sure I even saw him again.

He stops in front of me. He's a few inches taller than I am, and I catch a strong whiff of cologne. When I meet his eyes, they're startling, such a deep green color they almost look like emeralds shining out at me. Dressed in a crisp white shirt with the sleeves rolled up and perfectly pressed black slacks, he looks like he's going to a business meeting.

"I'm glad to see you're doing better," he says. Then he smiles and the skin around his eyes and mouth wrinkles deeply, causing his age to show for the first time. Without those telltale creases, he could pass for someone in his thirties, which must be a good twenty years younger than his actual age.

I notice there's an odd energy surrounding him. I felt a similar energy when I was near my mother, but his is much stronger.

He gestures toward a chair. "Please sit down." Rather than go back behind his desk, he remains standing. "I know you have questions, but first I'd like you to meet someone."

Before I can say anything, the door opens, and Nyla ushers someone inside. It's an older man with a bent posture, and he's shuffling slowly toward us. I glance at my father, who smiles warmly at me before turning back to the man.

"Hello, Peter," my father says.

The man glances up, seeming surprised at being addressed. When he spots my father, his eyes light up. "Hello. I didn't know I was going to be seeing you today."

I stand, wondering what's going on.

"Peter," my father says, placing his hand on the man's shoulder, "can you please tell this young lady why you're here?"

Peter turns watery brown eyes on me, appearing hesitant.

"It's all right to talk about it," my father encourages.

When Peter turns back to me, he says, "I'm dying."

My gaze widens and travels over him.

He gives my father a grateful smile. "John is going to help my son and his family." Then he begins to tremble with emotion. "I'm so grateful," he says, his bottom lip quivering.

"It's okay, Peter. It's all going to be fine." My father moves beside him and whispers something in his ear. Then he pats Peter on the back and tells Nyla she can take him out.

I watch as she gently leads him from the room, and I feel shaken by the man's declaration. "You're going to cure him?" I ask once we're alone again.

His lips tighten. "Sit down, Raielle."

Once I'm seated again, he sits across from me and says, "Peter has stage-four colon cancer. He can't be cured."

I swallow, feeling heartbroken for Peter. "Why is he here then? How are you helping his family?"

I levels a serious look at me. "He's a volunteer. He doesn't have much time left, and he volunteered to be a part of our program. Once we use him, his son will get a very generous payment."

"Use him?" I ask, even as understanding makes my mouth go dry.

He leans in toward me. "We're going to cure another client of ours by giving his disease to Peter. The healing takes place tomorrow."

I tear my eyes from his and grip my hands together in my lap. "I see. You're going to kill Peter."

"He's dying anyway, and this client is very wealthy. He's going to pay me a great deal to help him, and Peter's family will benefit from that money."

"And so will you." I look up at him again.

He nods. "Yes, that's how one part of my organization works. That part funds the many charitable healings we do where no money is exchanged."

"But you won't cure Peter because he can't pay you?" My stomach clenches at the thought. Alec's idea to sacrifice himself for Penelope wasn't a unique one. This is how things work. This is…common. "What is Peter to this wealthy client?"

John grins. "His savior."

I blink at his flippant answer. "They're not related to each other. Are they? You don't need them to be. You told me that." That's the one thing I do remember clearly.

His lips twitch with amusement, just like they did the first time I asked this question, and I begin to realize that even the things I thought I knew about my power are wrong.

He looks at me, and much to my surprise he no longer holds it back. He laughs out loud. "No, Raielle. That's only necessary when the healer isn't strong enough. A powerful healer can move death into any receptacle, not just the easiest match."

My mouth opens, but no words come out as I remember the feeling of trying to move Penelope's disease into Alec, and how impossible it was.

"I know that happened more than once to your mother. And it happened to you," he says softly. "But that's not why I wanted you to meet Peter. I brought Peter in here to help you understand how you were cured. Apollo tells me that you're still bothered by it. But you shouldn't be. Someone similar to Peter volunteered and that's how I healed you. We have hundreds of Peters, Raielle."

I will away the tears that want to fall. I have too many questions to let my emotions get the best of me right now. "How do you find them?"

"We have health-care workers all over the world who bring candidates to us."

"Us?"

Pride gleams in his eyes. "Yes, I have a group of healers who work with me. I find them or they find me. I have a very quiet, but effective network."

My thoughts go to my own family. "Is that how you found my mother?"

His expression subtly tenses before he offers me a sad smile. "Yes, I traveled to New York because I'd heard about your mother and grandmother. When I met them, I knew your grandmother wasn't powerful enough to work with me. But your mother was. I persuaded her to come back here."

I try to picture my mother as a young married girl being swept off her feet by John. With his good looks and charisma, it's not hard to believe. He also has a detached coldness about him that I can imagine my mother being drawn to. She didn't do emotions well, or at all, really. "Did you bring my mother here?" I ask. "Did I live in this house before?"

"No. I had a home outside of LA then. That's where we lived when you were born. My first wife lived nearby with our twin boys, Shane and Blake. You all played together when you were children."

My eyes widen at this. "Shane has a twin?"

He shifts in his chair. "Had. I wasn't as cautious then as I am now." A dark emotion passes over his face, but it quickly disappears.

"Oh," I say, too shocked to say much else, thinking of the danger Apollo alluded to back in Fort Upton when he was persuading me to come here.

His eyes are on me, and he knows I want to hear the story. I want to know everything I can about my mother, and now about my brothers. His gaze wanders toward the window as he rubs a finger across his brow. "When I first started, I didn't turn away people who came to me for help. I took them at face value." His eyes shift back to me. "That's a mistake I no longer make. It was a client. One who tried to manipulate me by making threats. When I wouldn't do what he asked, he took my wife and Blake. Shane only escaped because he was with me that day."

The green in his eyes seems to grow darker. "I agreed to their terms. But he killed my family anyway. Once that happened, others thought they could get to me the same way. I hired security, fired everyone in my organization, closed ranks, but they still tried to go after you and your mother. They were stopped. They never touched either of you. But your mother was terrified. She was scared to be with me. So, I let her go. I let you both go."

My idea of Shane as a spoiled, pampered rich boy starts to crumble just a little. As for my mother, I know the rest. Running never got her anywhere good. For so many years, she kept her secrets, more secrets than I could have imagined. She erased her entire past. Did she really believe that past would never find me? Shifting in my seat, I say, "My mother didn't do any better on her own."

He nods.

Since he's being so honest with me, I ask a question, wanting more. "Apollo told me that you hired him to watch over me. Why didn't you watch over her?"

A twitch beside his eye is the only sign that my question bothers him. He leans forward in his chair and clasps his hands together. "I didn't think your mother was any of my business anymore. I'm sorry about what happened to her. I was trying to be respectful of her, honoring her wishes to be left alone. Eventually, I moved on from your mother. But my children are different. I will always watch over and protect you and Shane."

I study his face, wanting to believe him, looking for some sign that he's telling me the truth, but his expression is neutral now, giving nothing away. Other than brief glimpses of emotion, he's mostly serene, unusually so.

He stands abruptly and reaches down toward me. "Give me your hands. I want to show you something."

I look up at him warily.

An encouraging smile appears on his face. "Please trust me, Raielle. You want to learn about your power, don't you? Let's have a lesson now."

I'm not sure where my hesitance is coming from because I do want that. I need to learn everything he can teach me, but I don't trust him, and I don't know if that's my fault because of my history, or his because he's being less than honest with me. But the only way to find out is to do as he asks. Ignoring my unease, I stand and place my hands in his.

His fingers close around mine, and the energy that always radiates from him is dialed up. I can feel the heat being generated by his body. As I watch him, his hands turn hot against my skin. Then his eyes grow round and a shock pulses through me. I flinch as my body absorbs his energy. It burns hot and then cold over my skin. His green eyes pierce mine, and I can't look away. Then, all at once, it stops and he releases me.

I stagger back, gasping.

"Are you all right?" His hand lands on my shoulder, and his expression is a mixture of interest and concern as he bends to catch my eye.

When I straighten, I feel strange, more awake and alert than I was just a few minutes ago, like I pounded a couple of energy drinks. "What was that?" I ask breathlessly.

He laughs at my reaction. "When you learn to harness your power, you can use it on a subject whether they're injured or not, and you can use it on yourself to strengthen your own body. I just used my energy to take away your weariness and to probe your power to test its strength. I can see that you've grown stronger recently. Maybe you were able to heal yourself when you couldn't before?"

I nod, thinking of the way I was able to shrink the tumors when Penelope's disease first started affecting me.

Noticing the question in my eyes, he explains. "For some of us, as we mature, our powers grow stronger. Since you've hidden your ability for so much of your life, you really have no idea what you can do. But it's like exercising any muscle. Once you start using it more, it will become stronger. Already, your power is greater than most of the healers I have working with me now. With some practice and training, you could help a great many people. I would like you to work with me, if that's something you want to do."

His expression is both gentle and encouraging. I want to believe in him. It feels like he's throwing me a lifeline. Healing is what I've always needed to do. Even when I was suppressing it, it made me physically sick when I didn't use it, like it was telling me how wrong it was for me to ignore it. But I don't know enough about my abilities to use them without fear and without screwing it up. I need what he's offering me. It's something I can't get anywhere else. This is my chance to finally learn about my power, to have all my questions answered. But if I'm going to accept, there is one thing I can't do. "I want to work with you, but couldn't kill one person to save another," I say.

He looks at me for a long time before saying, "You think it's wrong. You would refuse the life Peter is offering and let someone else die? What if it was a young girl, and you could save her using Peter? Would that be less wrong?"

I glance away from his intense gaze because I know what he's doing. This is the same dilemma Alec presented to me, and I did agree to it, but I was wrong. I let my mother's murder cloud my judgment. It's not something I would ever do again. But I can see how he justifies it, and I'm sure there are people who would agree with him.

"Perhaps you could do other things," he concedes when I don't respond to his question.

I turn back to him, wanting to ask the question that's been waiting on my tongue the whole time I've been here. "Tell me about the person who died for me."

His mouth curves downward. He seems disappointed. "I can't do that. We promise them anonymity."

I swallow against my frustration. "You could make an exception. It might help me move past this if I knew the circumstances." As the words leave my mouth, I know they're not true. In fact, knowing may make things worse, but that doesn't change the fact that I need to know.

He shakes his head, and his eyes grow cold and flat. "There's nothing to move past. No one has done anything wrong. Everyone has benefitted. Especially you. Don't ask me this question again, Raielle. I won't make an exception for you."

A chill runs through me at the sound of his clipped words. He killed someone, and he has no emotion about it whatsoever. He believes the dead person somehow benefitted. He should at least believe it was a necessary evil, or even a terrible shame that a life was extinguished, but he doesn't. There is no remorse. There are no feelings involved for him. I begin to wonder why he agreed to save my life. He got nothing from it. Nothing that I can see.

FIVE

Lucas

"HEY, Diesel, there's someone here for you!"

I toss the rest of my clothes into the bag as my shoulders tense. Most likely, it's the brunette from history class who's there every time I turn around, or Cal's new girl, who thinks she's going to get some on the side from me. These California girls are seriously aggressive.

"Diesel!"

"Yeah, I'll be right there." I zip my bag closed and heave it over my shoulder. I've got an eleven o'clock flight back to New York.

My head is so messed up right now that I can't think straight anymore. I need a break, just for a little while. I have to go home for a few days to explain myself to my family and get my dad off my back. I have to make sure Liam is okay, since Mom isn't doing so great again.

"There's a scary-looking tall dude out there waiting for you," Cal says, interrupting my thoughts. He gestures toward the door, his eyes wide, indicating there's something off about the guy.

Curious now, I step outside, and I can see why Cal looked a little freaked. He's tall. I'd put him at six foot six or so, and there isn't an ounce

41

of fat on him. He's all tendons and leathery skin. Dressed in black, his dark eyes are filled with attitude as they take me in. He couldn't look more out of place on this bright palm-tree-lined street if he tried.

He takes a step toward me. "Raielle needs you."

I stare at up him. My heart stops. Then it starts pounding in my ears. "What did you say?"

He grins. "You heard me." Then he looks at the bag in my hand. "You going somewhere?"

My pulse races even faster because I did hear him, and if he'd shown up five minutes later, he would have missed me.

"She's okay?" I ask. My voice sounds strained. The chaos going on inside me makes it hard to stand still.

He hesitates, watching me, and then he nods. "Physically, yes, she's okay."

She's okay. His words sink in, and I take the first deep breath I've managed since I listened to her voice-mail message.

"Psychologically, though, she's not so good. She's in a bad place, and I haven't been able to get through to her. I'm hoping you can."

I drop my bag to the ground, wondering what the hell that means and who this guy is to her. "I've been here for months," I say accusingly.

He nods carelessly. "Yeah, I know that, but she doesn't. She thinks you're at Columbia. She asks me how you are every day. Those are her first words in the morning."

The fact that he hears her first words in the morning freezes me in place.

His hands go into his pockets and he chuckles, noting my reaction. "You got me wrong. I'm only there in the morning, not at night. I work for her father. It's my job to keep tabs on everyone who knows about her. To keep her secret safe. That's why she asks me how you are. She knows I'll have the answer."

That means he's been outright lying to her. "So when you're telling her about me, you leave out the part about my not being at Columbia?"

He shifts his weight from one foot to the other. "Look, this isn't anyone's fault. Her father's only lasted this long doing what he does because he insists on secrecy. The conditions were that she leave with me immediately and that she tell no one. When she insisted that she wouldn't go without you, I let her know that wasn't an option. She was willing to stay and risk her life for you, but I convinced her that you wouldn't want that. I made her believe that she'd be putting the guilt of her death on you if she did that. That's the only thing that finally convinced her to go with me."

I glare at him. It is his fault. He took her away. He convinced her to go, and he's kept her from me all this time.

He glances down at my bag on the sidewalk. "Were you finally giving up and going home?"

My jaw clenches. "I want to see her now."

"And we're back to why I'm here," he says, oblivious to the darts my eyes are shooting at him. "Let's go then." He starts down the sidewalk. "My name's Apollo, by the way," he throws over his shoulder.

"Wait a minute. I'll drive myself. I'll follow you." Because if I see anything I don't like, I'm leaving, and I'm taking her with me. Actually, I'm probably doing that anyway. Then this guy can go fuck himself.

"Fine with me." He shrugs. "I ain't no chauffeur."

We leave my apartment, and I stay close to his BMW convertible, which are a dime a dozen out here. Every asshole seems to have one. He's got the top down and at his height, I have no idea how he crammed his legs into that thing. I crank up the air-conditioner in the truck because my temperature is skyrocketing at the thought of seeing her again after all this time. I'm afraid to really believe it yet.

Within minutes, we're on the other side of the neighborhood, parking in front of a squat brick building. I get out of my truck and stare up at it. Has she been here the whole time, less than a mile away?

"She doesn't live here," Apollo says, seeming to read my thoughts. "She likes to stay here, though." He walks past me, holding a box of doughnuts.

"Does she go to school?" I ask, since mostly UCLA students live around here.

When he nods, I can hardly believe it. How have we never run into each other? It's a big school, but still, I wonder how close we may have come at times without ever connecting.

I follow him toward the entrance and watch as he shakes his head at an illegally parked Porsche. Reaching inside, he yanks the keys from the ignition and pockets them. "Treats this baby like shit," he mutters.

"Is that yours?" I ask, wondering if he's stealing those keys.

He shakes his head. "Not exactly."

He keeps walking, and I follow him inside the run-down apartment building in the student slum section of campus. As we head up the stairs, my hands are clenching open and closed. None of my fears were true. She's not dead, and she's not staying away because she doesn't care. She thinks I got on with things after she left. That I went about my business like we never happened. How could she possibly believe that? I haven't even seen her yet, and the hurt over how easily she gave up on me is nearly as stifling as the steamy air in the staircase we're climbing.

At the top, Apollo exits into the hallway and pauses by the first door on his left. He barely knocks before walking right in.

I'm behind him when a short redhead strolls by, not at all surprised to see him. "She's sacked out on the couch, as usual," the redhead says. "Good luck dragging her ass to class today, I think she only came in an hour ago." Then she spots me in the doorway, and her eyes widen. She glances at Apollo. "Who is...?" But Apollo places a finger to his lips and shakes his head, stopping her in midsentence.

With the girl's curious eyes on me, I follow him farther inside the cramped apartment and pause at the entrance to the living area. Apollo walks around a couch that's facing away from me and positions himself in front of it. By the expression on his face, I know she's lying there, just out of sight.

I pull in a slow breath as my heart hammers against my ribs. Now that we're finally in the same room, I realize I'm not just anxious, but I'm nervous, too. What if she isn't happy to see me? What if I exaggerated what we had, and she thinks I'm crazy for even coming here? When Apollo leans down, my hands are still by my side and my eyes stay pinned to the couch.

"Rise and shine, sleepyhead," Apollo says with fake cheer before turning to pull open the curtains, flooding the room with light.

I hold my breath as the back of her head gradually appears, and she pushes herself up. Then I smile at her bed head and at the achingly familiar dark blonde waves that cascade over her shoulders. Her hand reaches up to push the hair off her face, and I catch the delicate lines of her long fingers.

"How is he?" she asks, her voice soft and scratchy from sleep. Based on what Apollo said, she's asking about me. The fact that she cut herself off from me, yet still thinks of me when she first opens her eyes each morning, makes my chest grow tight.

Apollo looks my way, and I move into the room. "He's here," Apollo says.

"What?" she asks quietly, not turning to follow his gaze.

"Behind you, kid," he says gently. "He's standing right behind you."

When she slowly starts to turn her head, I stop, waiting to see those pale blue eyes again. As I watch, her profile comes into view. Then slowly her eyes come up and find me.

Our gazes lock, and it feels like I've been jolted with electricity. I can see her mentally shaking herself, wondering if I'm real. When her eyes begin to shimmer, I break out of my stupor, rounding the couch quickly and stopping directly in front of her.

Looking at her now, something inside me shifts, and I recognize the pull between us, the palpable attraction that sparks when we're together. When she licks her lips, I know she feels it, too. Bending down before her, I reach out my hand to brush her cheek, and when she leans her face into my palm, I gather her in my arms, burying my nose in her hair, drawing in her sweet fragrance. "Ray," I whisper, and I feel her arms come around my neck.

"You're here," she says, sounding as though she doesn't believe it even as she's pressing herself against me. Her soft voice stirs something deep within me. My memories did not do this justice. Nothing feels as perfect as this. My arms tighten around her, and I can hardly process the fact that I'm holding her again. I was starting to think this would never happen.

45

"Lucas." She says my name, and the caress of her warm breath on my skin combined with the husky tone of her words has me pulling back just enough to look at her, needing to take in every detail. My hands cup her cheeks, and I realize she's trembling. Her translucent blue eyes, the ones that I've pictured every day since she left, are wide with shock and uncertainty. I swallow back a curse. Whatever happened to her this summer has taken its toll. Her cheekbones are too sharp, and her skin is too pale. She's covered by an oversized sweater, and it's hot as hell in here.

"How are you here?" she asks with a wariness I don't like.

"Where else would I be?" I ask simply.

Her bewildered reaction isn't lost on me. She didn't think I'd come. "Are you okay?" I ask, thinking of her health, because in every other way, she's drowning. Anyone can see that. This is what Apollo meant when he said she was in a bad place.

She nods at me.

"No, you're not," I say, watching as her eyes widen even further.

She takes a deep breath, shifting away from me and running a shaky hand through her hair. The relief I felt when I first saw her begins a slow retreat.

"Why aren't you at Columbia?" she asks. It's a harsh whisper, like she's afraid of what my answer will be, and she doesn't want to hear it.

I glance back at Apollo. "Could we have some privacy?"

He nods and walks out into the hallway, taking the redhead with him, ignoring the questions she fires at him about who I am.

Once they're gone, I erase the small distance she put between us, purposely crowding her, wanting her to get used to my being near her again. "Did you really think I would write you off and go on my merry way to college?" I ask, unable to contain the bitter resentment in my voice.

Tears begin to spill onto her cheeks. "That's what you should have done," she says as her hands cover her face, hiding herself from me. "You shouldn't be here, Lucas."

I take her hands down. "Do you honestly want me to leave?" I ask, daring her to lie to me.

Her eyes show fear now, wondering if I'll really go, and I can see the wheels turning in her head.

"Stop thinking. Just tell me the truth."

She blinks her eyes and more teardrops fall. "No. I don't want you to leave, but you shouldn't stay."

Despite her words, she's not pushing me away. She's drifting closer. "Yes, I should," I whisper, my lips nearly touching hers. She shifts her face up toward mine, and I move in, gently pressing my mouth to hers. Anticipation holds me in place, waiting for her to kiss me back and take what I'm offering.

Then I feel her fingers slowly inch their way into my hair, and she applies soft pressure to my mouth. My whole body seems to sigh at the contact. Taking her cue, I kiss her gently, loving the way her hands feel on me, indulging the craving that's gone unsatisfied for so long. I pull her in close and open my mouth to her, needing more, but she turns her head away.

I lean back to look at her. She's crying even harder now. My hands automatically reach up to smooth away the wetness on her cheeks. "What is it?" I ask.

She gives me a wobbly half smile. "I'm so happy you're here." Then she wraps her arms around my neck and squeezes me tightly. The pressure in my chest eases as I hold her against me. I run a soothing hand up and down her back, slipping under her curtain of hair to rub the nape of her neck. A sliver of worry slices through me as my fingers move down again to skim over her too-prominent ribs, and I begin to wonder if she's not completely cured, if there's something she isn't telling me.

We hold each other for a long time, until her trembling begins to subside. I wait for her to break our embrace because I can't seem to let go first. When she finally unwinds her arms and we're face-to-face, I ask, "Did your father heal you? Is the disease completely gone?"

She nods.

"Your hand," I add, reaching for her right hand, uncurling her fingers and wrapping my own around them. "Can you feel this?"

"Yes." Her fingers grip mine, pulling my hand toward her, grasping it tightly. She's so brittle and defeated, not at all the strong, opinionated girl who knocked me on my ass when we first met, and I know there's something else, something more going on with her. "How did your father heal you?" I ask.

She tenses as her gaze shifts downward, away from mine. My heart sinks, knowing this must be the root of things. This is why she's such a mess.

"Can you tell me about it?" I ask carefully.

She withdraws into herself and pulls her hand from my grasp. "No."

I reach for her. "Look, I know how you felt. But—"

She drives her fingers through her hair, and her eyes won't meet mine. "But nothing. I can't..." Her lips twist as she shakes her head.

Gripping her shoulders, I try to get her to look at me. I need to know what happened if I'm going to help her. I need to know everything. "Ray..."

"You haven't changed." She laughs harshly. "Always pushing. Never letting anything go."

She's the opposite, I'm thinking, wanting to ignore anything that's too hard to deal with, keeping it all to herself, suffering in miserable silence. "Please," I say, hearing the plea in my voice.

"What?" she snaps.

My hand smoothes over her hair, trying to calm her down.

She's silent as her chest rises and falls. I decide to table this for now, thinking she isn't going to talk to me, but then she straightens. Her head comes up, and she gives me a defiant look. "On the way here it got worse, a lot worse." Her eyes move away from mine. "Everything hurt. My head was pounding. I was burning up, and then finally I went numb. It was such a relief until my body started to quit on me. I fought, though," she continues softly. "I fought for hours. I don't know how many. By then I couldn't breathe anymore. I couldn't move. I'd black out and Apollo would bring me back." Her face crumples, but she fights off the tears. "I should have died so many times that day. But he kept bringing me back...again and again."

"Ray..." I breathe out, clenching my fist as my chest starts to constrict.

I knew she was sick and that she was getting worse, but I never imagined the nightmare she's describing.

"Then the last time I woke up," she continues, "I was in my father's house, and it was done. I was cured."

She sounds so miserable that she didn't die, and I'm too shaken by how close I came to losing her to respond at first. My feelings are so different from hers. But I hear the defeated tone in her voice, and I desperately want to erase it. "You're blaming yourself when it was out of your control."

"But it wasn't." She grimaces. "It was in my control…to give up, to let go."

The words stagger from her mouth as though they hurt her, like they're coated in needles. I'm shocked by how little she understands herself. "You're wrong. You don't have it in you to give up. You're supposed to be here. I'm so fucking happy about that fact, you have no idea."

She has no reaction because she doesn't believe me. She doesn't want to. "Come here," I say, taking her in my arms again, wishing I could say something to ease the pain in her eyes, and wondering why she feels the need to suffer alone. "Why didn't you call me?" I ask softly beside her ear. "You should have called me." Even though I can see how broken she is, the fact that she didn't reach out to me hurts. "Did they tell you not to contact anyone? Did they threaten you, Apollo and your father?"

Raielle stiffens for a moment before slowly shaking her head. "No. No threats. Just warnings about my father's enemies and exposing anyone I care about to them. I couldn't risk it, and I didn't want to. I would never drag you away from everything you worked so hard for and get you involved in this. You deserve better. But I missed you every day, Lucas. I ached for you every minute. I never stopped thinking about you."

Her words burn into me. Apollo may have taken her away, but she decided to stay away, and that cuts so deeply I don't know if I can get over it, even though I reluctantly understand it. She's selfless to a fault, willing to martyr herself at my expense as well as hers, and far too willing to let me go when she thinks it's for my own good.

I don't know what I was expecting when I found her again, but it wasn't this, not the broken girl I'm holding now. I thought we'd both be fighting like hell to get back to each other, but I was the only one fighting. It didn't occur to me that she'd give up on us because I know she loves me. Now I have to make her understand that loving me is more important than saving me.

Raielle

WE'RE going to be a team now," Lucas says, giving me a serious look.

But I'm too distracted to listen as I drink him in, noticing the way my body craves his touch. That hasn't changed or lessened over time. His hair is longer than I remember, the sides falling over his ears and the back curling into his collar. He probably hasn't bothered with a haircut since I last saw him. He looks slimmer, too, still muscular and strong, though. I can't believe he's here. I don't deserve him, and I should be sending him away, but I can't. I'm not strong enough to do that when he's right in front of me.

He's been suffering, too. I see that now. I did him a terrible disservice believing he was better off without me, that he would go to school as planned and move on. He couldn't move on any more than I could. Pushing him away now would only hurt him.

"Which means you need to be a team player," he's saying. "Ray?"

I rein in my wandering thoughts. "What?"

Lucas's brow furrows in frustration. "I'm saying that you need to be a team player, and I'm the captain of the team, which means I'm in charge now."

My eyes narrow. "What are you talking about?"

He blows out a breath and runs a hand through his thick hair. "Back in Fort Upton, I listened to you far too much."

"What?" I bark out a laugh.

"I'm serious. I think I was a little in awe of you. I mean, look at you. You're gorgeous, and you have these kickass healing powers. Let's face it. You're not the average girlfriend."

I can feel the smile lighting my face.

"But your judgment sucks."

My grin falls away.

"You have no sense of self-preservation. You don't think you're deserving of anything. That's why you need me to run the show until you're back on your feet again and thinking clearly. Then we can revisit a more equal distribution of power in this relationship."

I just stare at him. "You can't be serious."

Lucas folds his arms over his chest. "As a heart attack. How much weight have you lost?"

Turning away, I begin searching the floor for my jeans.

"How much?" he repeats, wrapping his fingers around my arm and making me look at him.

"I get your point." I scowl.

In the doorway, Apollo clears his throat. "Sorry to interrupt, but you've got to get to class, Raielle."

"No class today," Lucas states firmly. "We need to finish this conversation."

My jaw drops. I look at Apollo, waiting for him to chew Lucas out. But he just nods easily and walks away.

Lucas grins. "See? He knows who's in charge."

"Unbelievable," I whisper, shaking my head. "You're taking advantage of the situation."

"What situation?"

"The one where I feel like crap for what I did to you, but I can't bring myself to get really pissed because I'm too happy to see you."

"Oh. That situation." He smirks. "Yeah, I'm using it."

Nikki strolls into the room, shifting a curious glance between us before her appraising and obviously appreciative eyes settle on Lucas.

I clear my throat. "Um, Nikki. This is Lucas."

"Her boyfriend," he adds, his tone indicating that I should have said it myself.

Nikki's gaze grows wide.

"Lucas, this is Nikki." I begin pulling my pants on in front of everyone, since I don't have much choice.

Nikki's eyebrows crawl up toward her hairline. "You've been holding out on me. Do you go to school here?" she asks him.

I'm about to answer no, when he shocks me with a yes.

"What?" I gape at him.

He seems abashed as he runs his hand over the back of his neck. "Can we talk about this later?"

"No." I answer, his strange reaction making it impossible to wait. "It's your turn now. Talk to me."

He shoots a quick glance at Nikki, who's still standing there looking extremely interested, before turning hooded eyes on me. "I applied here back in the spring."

"In the spring?" I repeat as my face wrinkles in confusion. But then something clicks in my head, a memory. "You mean all those trips to the school office that you wouldn't explain? The *stuff* you had to take care of? You were making plans to go here?"

Lucas looks at Nikki, obviously uncomfortable that she's hearing this, before hesitantly nodding.

"Stalker," Nikki coughs out, leveling an amused gaze at me.

"Could you excuse us?" Lucas finally asks, his tone even despite the way he's glaring at her.

She frowns. "This is *my* apartment."

I shoot her a pleading look.

"Fine." She sighs, bending to pick her bag up off the floor. "Call if you need me."

Once she's gone, I stare after her, shaking my head in disbelief. "You didn't mention this, not once."

Before he can answer, Jason comes back in. He looks between us. "Forgot something," he mumbles. Then he heads for the bedroom.

Lucas mutters to himself before reaching for my hand. "Let me take you to your place. We can talk there. Okay?"

I don't answer because I'm too busy thinking back over that time. I can feel him watching me with a guarded, assessing gaze when a conversation we had one night in his truck pops into my head. He asked me why I wanted to go back to California, and I gave him a simple "I just do" answer because my real reason was too complicated to get into. His reaction was a silent, almost sad smile, like he was accepting the fact that we would be saying good-bye to each other soon. But I must have misread him because he hadn't accepted it at all. He was secretly making plans to go with me.

I'm feeling so many things right now, I can hardly think straight. I do know that Nikki doesn't get it. She can't understand. Lucas is used to giving up what he wants for the people he loves, and that's what he did for me. A part of me is overwhelmed by it. But another part feels hopelessly sad for him. I don't want to be another person he has to make sacrifices for. Especially since I'm not a good bet. My life doesn't have happy endings, and every time it seems like something good is happening, it all crumbles to dust. Lucas can't fall with me when the next sinkhole opens up beneath my feet.

His warm hand lands on my shoulder, and I look up into his concerned eyes. "Where do you live?" he asks gently, seeming to know how unsettled I'm feeling.

I clamp down on my thoughts, knowing they're not going anywhere good. "Nearby. On Wilshire," I reply.

He waits while I gather my things. Then he holds my hand as we leave the apartment and head downstairs. Having him beside me is surreal, and I keep wondering when I'm going to wake up. On the one hand, it feels like we've been apart forever. On the other, it seems like just yesterday that I told him I love him. I can picture him back in Fort Upton so clearly, but I never pictured him here.

He walked away from everything to come after me. The fact that he did this is staggering. My insides feel scrambled. The world as I know it could never produce someone like him. I don't know what to do with all the emotions crashing together inside me. So I concentrate on the firm warmth of Lucas's hand surrounding mine. It grounds me, and I start to let myself believe that he's here, and that he may stay.

When we get outside, I squint against the sunlight, waiting for my eyes to adjust. Then I notice that the Porsche is gone. Apollo probably took it home again. Beyond it, I see Lucas's truck. "You drove all the way to LA?"

Lucas nods, following my gaze. My skin starts to tingle as I recall being pressed against that truck while his hands traveled over my body.

When I look at him, the heat in his eyes tells me he's remembering, too. Right then, a noisy pack of students strolls by, just like that night. Lucas grins at me, breaking the sudden tension as he opens the passenger door for me to climb inside. His hands splay across my hips, unnecessarily lifting me up to place me on the seat. Then his fingers skim across my stomach as he releases me. He's hardly stopped touching me since he showed up, like he's reassuring himself that I'm really here the way I keep doing with him.

When he climbs in on the driver's side, I keep my eyes straight ahead. His scent surrounds me, and I sink down into the leather seat as memories of our times together assault me. I grow warm remembering all the places he's touched me and kissed me. But as he pulls out into traffic, the question he asks rips through my thoughts. "Do you want to know about Kyle?"

I don't answer, not sure whether I want to hear this or not. But I can feel his eyes on me.

"Do you want to hear what happened after you left?" he asks.

I blow out a breath, knowing he's not going to drop it. It seems that Lucas wants me to face everything I've been avoiding all in one morning. Steeling myself, I turn to look at him. "Apollo told me that my father sent him a letter saying he was taking custody of me. He said there was a court order along with it so Kyle couldn't do anything." I hesitate. "Once I was gone, did you tell him what really happened to me?"

He glances at me. "No. I promised I wouldn't. He just thinks your father found you and you left without a word."

Relief filters in as I try to ignore the familiar guilt. I finger the worn seam on the side of my jeans, wondering if Penelope has grown at all, and if she asks about me. "I have another brother," I say, thinking of Kyle and Shane, and how different they are.

His head snaps in my direction. "What?"

I nod. "Another half brother."

His brow creases. "This is by your father?"

"Yeah. He was married before he met my mother." I glance out the window as he turns onto Wilshire. "It's this building right here." I point.

Lucas's gaze travels up the length of the glass-and-concrete structure, and he releases a low whistle. Once he pulls into the circular entrance, the valet appears to greet him. Lucas hesitates before handing over his keys. As I move beside him, his eyes grow wide, taking in the luxurious lobby.

"Hey," he whispers, touching my shoulder, "isn't that the guy from *Mad Men*?"

I smile at him. "Yeah. I think he lives here when they're filming."

"No way," he says, seeming starstruck.

"There's always lots of celebrities around. You're going to look like a total tourist if you gawk at them."

"He's the first really famous person I've seen. Although, I think I spotted Freddy Krueger at the Westside Pavilion. He was buying an ice cream."

I giggle as he turns his head and gestures outside. "I still can't get used to all the palm trees. Every street is lined with them."

"It's a lot different from Fort Upton." I press the elevator button for my floor.

Lucas watches me, looking uncharacteristically cheerful all of a sudden. "I know. All the colors are brighter, and the people seem happier here. Like all the sunshine goes to their heads or something."

I smile, amused by his reaction to LA. The truth is I can't take my eyes off him. In the elevator, I lean my body against his, still in shock that I can touch him, and realizing that the last time I smiled and laughed was when I was with him. He only turned up an hour ago, and he already has me grinning again. It's like when he found me, I found some long-absent part of myself. A part I tried to bury and have been mourning the loss of ever since.

The doors slide open, and we step out into a small hallway. Beside me, I can feel Lucas looking around. "Yours is the only apartment on this floor?"

"It has a private entrance that's monitored. It's more secure that way." I unlock the door and head inside, hoping that Shane isn't here.

"Nice," Lucas says, eyeing the floor-to-ceiling windows that line the living room.

I glance around, seeing it through his less jaded eyes. "Yeah, I guess it's nice."

"Someone likes white," he adds. "Why don't you like to stay here?"

Right then, Shane's door opens, and he stumbles out shirtless with bedsheets piled in his arms. The beige sheets have red stains on them that look like blood, lots of it. When he glances up and spots Lucas, he pauses halfway into the living room. His eyes narrow as they scan the apartment, and his brows launch upward when he notices me.

"Hey," he mumbles.

I stare pointedly at the sheets. "Are you okay?"

A slow smile slices across the severe angles of his face. "I'm perfect."

Then a half-naked girl appears in the doorway behind him. "I still have scars, Shane," she whines. "Will the scars heal on their own or do we need to do it again? Because I wouldn't mind doing it again." She giggles.

My gaze travels over both of them as I wonder what they've been doing.

"Shh." Shane holds a finger to his lips. "No sex talk in front of my little sister."

She whips her head in my direction. "So that's the sister I've been hearing about?"

Now that she's facing me, I can clearly see dried blood at the top of her chest and along her thighs. Suddenly I get it, and my stomach rolls. "Jesus, Shane," I mutter.

He cocks his head at me, questioningly. "What? You've never done it?"

My eyes widen at the suggestion.

"You're missing out. Fucking and healing," he says, feigning a faraway blissful expression. The girl smiles condescendingly at me, pleased at my shock. "You should try it," he says. "Seriously, you have no idea what you're missing."

I look at Lucas. Somehow he manages to appear unfazed. "This is Shane," I say flatly, scowling at my half brother. "Shane, this is Lucas."

Shane directs his gaze at Lucas. "You're with her? You deserve a fucking medal for that." Then he walks toward the kitchen and begins dumping the sheets in the washing machine. The girl twirls her hair around her finger before turning and heading back into Shane's bedroom.

"So that's your brother," Lucas comments, beside me now.

"Yeah."

"He can heal, too?"

"Apparently."

"Your brother doesn't like you much," he says thoughtfully, seeming to have no feelings about it.

"It's mutual." I shoot another glare in Shane's direction.

Lucas is quiet as he stares at me for a moment before taking in his surroundings, examining my new life.

"My room is this way." I have no idea what he's thinking as I turn and head into my bedroom. Dropping my bag on the bed, I watch Lucas as he walks in and begins looking around, poking his head into the bathroom, examining my belongings on the dresser, briefly picking up my copy of *Jane Eyre*.

His long fingers rifle through the pages of my favorite book before he sets it back down again. While he's preoccupied, I let my eyes travel over the black T-shirt that stretches across his muscled back and outlines his broad shoulders. It's loosely tucked into faded jeans that sit low and hug his narrow hips. Watching the confident way he moves causes warmth to pool inside me.

He turns and looks up, his navy-blue eyes catching mine. After a moment, they narrow, like he knows what I'm thinking, and I feel my face grow hot. My hands are itching to touch him, and despite my better judgment, in spite of the fact that I'm not going to be good for him, I allow his gaze to pull me in, and I close the distance between us. He doesn't move or reach for me as I hesitantly lay my hands flat against his chest and breathe out the warmth I feel when I'm close to him. He remains still, seeming to wait for me, letting me decide what I'm doing here. But I have no idea what I'm doing. I only know that I want to be close to him.

My fingers lightly brush over the soft cotton of his shirt. When I move lower, flattening my palms against the hard surface of his stomach, he exhales, tickling my face with his sweet breath. My hands work their way up again, over the bunched muscles of his shoulders, and farther upward to the scruff of his cheek.

"I missed you," I whisper before leaning up and pressing my lips to his. He's still standing there with his arms by his sides. This isn't what I'd planned on doing when we walked in here. My head is still a jumble of confusing emotions, but my body knows what it wants.

I push my fingers into his thick hair and slant my mouth across his, urging him to kiss me. When I lick his upper lip, he finally does, enveloping me in his arms, spreading his hands wide across my back as his mouth opens over mine.

He moves quickly from stoic restraint to passionate aggression as he meets my need with a harsh want of his own, fisting his hand in my hair, and urging my head back so he can plunge more deeply into my mouth. Every thought in my head flees as he takes me over. I only know the movement of his muscles as he caresses me and the strength of the arms that hold me. I grip his shoulders when he lifts me off my feet and lays me down on the bed. He covers my body with his, angling himself between my legs, which instinctively part for him.

"I missed you, too," he whispers in my ear and begins to trail warm, wet kisses down the side of my neck.

I'm completely lost in sensation when his name falls from my lips.

"Hmm," he responds, his low voice vibrating inside his chest.

I look at him, watching as his eyes slowly rise up to meet mine. They darken as his hand reaches out to brush my hair back from my face. Deep blue pools pierce me with their intensity, holding me in their gaze and not letting go. When his hand moves lower to brush against my breast, and he pushes his hips into mine, I gasp, arching up against him.

His nostrils flare in response, and he does it again, grinding himself against me, causing desire to flame deep within me. I hear myself moan softly before his mouth covers mine, capturing the sound as both his tongue and his hips push in on me in a persistent, even rhythm. We're still fully dressed, but I can feel the tension gathering in my muscles as I squeeze my thighs around him.

He watches the way I respond to everything he's doing as his eyes constantly capture mine. Soon the pressure inside me builds to an excruciating level and I groan, my head tilting back into the pillow, my breathing harsh in my ears. I remember this feeling from that night at the bridge and the initial fear of giving in to it, of losing control and falling over the edge. I didn't think things would go this far when I first kissed him. I only wanted to be near him, but he's bringing me back to life, and I'm shocked by how much I want him to.

"Go ahead, baby," he says breathlessly. "Let go."

And with those words, I do. I let the release happen, feeling my body arch up against his as my muscles tighten and my fingers dig into his shoulders. Heat courses through me, pulsing stronger with each wave until it crests into a sweet burn that singes and sparks behind my eyes. I hear Lucas's voice from far away. It sounds like a harsh grunt and suddenly his weight is gone.

I blink my eyes open, sucking in a breath as I regain my senses. My body feels cold as I realize I'm alone on the bed. Jerking myself up, I look around and say his name.

I hear him clear his throat. "Down here."

When I peer over the side, he's on the floor, gingerly lifting himself to a sitting position. "What are you doing down there?"

He runs his hands through his hair and shakes his head. "That's what I'm trying to figure out."

I lower myself down to the carpet beside him, trying not to laugh. "Did you fall off?"

He stares at me for a long moment. "Actually, I think you pushed me off."

"I did not push you." I can't help the giggle that erupts. But I quickly realize that his expression is serious. My smile begins to falter.

He rubs a hand against his shoulder and winces. "Didn't you feel it? A burst of energy came at me, and the next thing I knew I was flat on my back."

My grin completely dissolves.

His gaze sharpens. "What the hell was that?"

I swallow another denial. Unease prickles through me.

Lucas continues to stare at me. "It happened right when you were…" He motions his hand toward me.

Understanding his meaning, my eyes widen before squeezing closed.

"Hey, it's okay." He places his hand on my knee.

I shake my head as reality jolts me. He's not joking. He really believes my energy somehow pushed him off the bed. Is it possible that I unknowingly generated it? My eyes pop open, and I see him rubbing his shoulder. "I hurt you?"

He immediately lowers his hand. "I'm fine."

Guilt and confusion build inside me. "Let me heal it." I reach out to him, but he halts me, catching and lowering my arm. "I'm fine. Really."

I eye him, growing more upset by the minute, knowing I didn't feel it. I didn't feel anything but amazing.

"What do you think happened?" Lucas's concerned eyes search mine.

I run a shaky hand over my hair. "I don't know. I didn't even realize I'd done it." But I must have. His expression is so certain and so completely bewildered.

My chest is rising and falling too quickly, and I will myself to settle down. But my thoughts keep racing, trying to figure out how the hell that could have happened.

"Shh," he murmurs, reaching for the hand he just avoided. "It's okay."

"It's not okay. I have no idea what's going on."

"Calm down, Ray." His voice is low and even. He's calm, too calm, like he's faking it. He's freaked out, too. Of course he is. How could he not be?

SIX

Lucas

KNUCKLES wrapping hard against the closed door startle us.

"Raielle!" Apollo's voice shouts. "As long as you're skipping school today, your daddy wants to see you. I'm waiting on you. So hurry it up."

Holy shit. I'm keeping it cool for her benefit, but inside, I'm going crazy.

When she stands to open the door, I rotate my shoulder and hoist myself up. Obviously, this energy she talks about has gotten a hell of a lot stronger, and she can't seem to control it. It felt like I touched a live wire.

She's standing at the door talking quietly to Apollo when she darts a look in my direction. Then she urges him back and steps out of the room. Obviously, she doesn't want me to hear something. I want to barge out there and make sure she understands there are no secrets between us, but I need a minute to clear my head and calm myself down. I have no idea what just happened, and my thoughts are still reeling over the fact that I've finally found her.

When I woke up this morning, I didn't think this would be the day I would see her again. I was starting to believe we would never be together,

61

or that I might be disappointed when we were, because the heady experience of being near her must have been something I imagined. The potent attraction I remembered had to be an exaggeration of reality. That's what I'd begun to think. Then I saw her, and I knew it was all true. If anything, I'd underestimated how my heart pumps faster for her and my fingers itch to touch her. The way I need her levels me completely.

Their voices carry to me from beyond the door, and I wonder, not for the first time, if Apollo was Alec's contact to her father. That would make sense. He was the one who came to Fort Upton to get her when Alec reached out for help.

Apollo barges back into the bedroom past a protesting Raielle. "Look, Raielle's father wants to meet you, and I told him I'd bring you both over there. But she doesn't want you to go."

I notice the mutinous expression on her face. "Why not? Too soon to meet the parents?" I tease, trying to smooth out that little crease that forms between her eyebrows when she worries.

She folds her arms and tilts her head at me. "I don't want you involved with him, not if he has enemies that could be dangerous."

I make no attempt to cover my annoyance at her.

"We'll look out for him. Just like we look out for you," Apollo says.

I keep my thoughts about how well he looks out for her to myself. "I'll follow you again."

Apollo nods at me and once he's out of the room, Raielle eyes my shoulder with a frown. "Are you really okay?"

"I'm fine. Don't worry about it."

She huffs out a laugh. "Don't worry about it? Right. I'm a freak show."

I wrap my arm around her shoulder. "But you're *my* freak show."

Her eyes widen at me, before her lips twitch with a reluctant smile.

"So," I begin, wanting to get her mind off it as we head to the door, "tell me about your father."

Her long sigh indicates my subject change may not be a good one. I'm inclined to dislike her father as much as I hate Apollo. His complete absence from her life, his association with Alec, and the way he ripped her away from me are all good reasons to despise him. But he did save her life, and for that I feel indebted to him. For her sake, I'm hoping he's been kind to her, and that the reason he stayed away was to keep her safe.

"There's not much to tell," she replies. "I haven't spent much time with him." Then she glances away, saying nothing more about him. Her reluctance to talk about him tells me more than she'd like it to.

The drive takes nearly an hour due to the massive traffic jams that plague this town. I follow behind Apollo, watching curiously as we drive up the narrow, winding roads that lead into the Hollywood Hills. Then we get buzzed through a private gate and continue onto a wooded roadway. Once I pull to a stop behind Apollo, I try to get out of the truck before Raielle can climb down on her own. But I'm too late; I watch as her long legs slip out toward the stone-paved driveway. She smiles at me as I reach out to her.

Holding her right hand tighter than necessary, I find myself glancing at her wrist and forearm, grateful that there's no sign of the tumors that once grew there, thankful that she can feel my fingers surrounding hers. I'll never forget the stifling fear of watching her deteriorate while she put up a brave front. It was pure torture, even worse than coming home to find Liam bleeding at the bottom of the stairs. When Liam was hurt, there was something I could do; I could ask Raielle to help him. When she was suffering, I was completely useless to her. Hearing the story of her nearly dying on her way to find her father was like pouring salt on an open wound.

I tear my eyes away from her and take a look around. Based on the condo she's living in, I figured her dad had money, but this house is proof of it. It's a huge four-story looming mass of wood and glass. There's a lot of land and ostentation with the fountain and the carved-wood doors. Ironic that she's lived most of her life like a pauper.

I notice Raielle looking around the front of the house. "Who do all these cars belong to?" she asks.

"The office is open today," Apollo answers.

I shoot her a curious look, but her eyes are unfocused, and I can feel the tension in her.

"You okay?" I lightly shake her arm to get her attention.

She blinks at me and then nods her head. But she doesn't like being here. I can see that.

We follow Apollo up a short set of stairs and the front door opens just as he reaches it. A beefy guy dressed in a black suit nods at us as we file inside the house.

"I'll see you later." Apollo waves over his shoulder. Then he disappears down one of the many hallways that lead off the entryway.

Raielle seems nervous as she watches after him. Soon we can hear clicking heels echoing off the tile floor, growing louder. After a moment, an attractive brunette rounds the corner. She's dressed in tiny black shorts and a tight pink T-shirt. "Hi, Raielle," she says as she beams at her.

"Hi, um…" Raielle hesitates.

"Charlie," she supplies. Then her glossy pink lips grin up at me. "And who's this?"

I notice Raielle's jaw tighten before she answers. "My boyfriend, Lucas."

"Nice to meet you, Lucas." She reaches her hand out to me and I shake it, watching as the furrow on Raielle's forehead deepens.

"He's waiting for you both in the meeting room. Just follow me." Then she turns and begins an exaggerated sashay down the hall.

"Who is she?" I whisper in Raielle's ear.

"One of Shane's friends." She puts air quotes around the word *friends*, and I wonder why she dislikes Shane so much. It's not like her to be hateful toward people, even if her brother is a sadomasochistic smartass.

Charlie stops at the last door, then pushes it open and walks inside. I follow behind Raielle into what looks like a formal living room. Both our eyes go straight to the couch, where a frightened-looking kid is sitting.

"You must be Lucas?"

I turn toward a tall, uptight-looking guy who stands and approaches us.

"How are you doing, sweetheart?" He smiles at Raielle.

She seems surprised by the endearment and offers him a hesitant smile.

"I'm John, Raielle's father." His eyes, which are a strange shade of

64

dark green, focus on me again.

"Nice to meet you, *John*…" I say, letting the sentence hang, wanting to know what his full name really is after the bullshit name Alec gave us.

He stares at me for a beat, before replying, "Just John."

I nearly snort out a laugh. Just John, like just Beyoncé?

But he doesn't notice my reaction as he turns his attention to Raielle. "I'd like you to meet some people."

He moves in front of the couch where the boy is sitting. "This is Leo and his mother." At his introduction, the boy's round brown eyes dart between us nervously. I notice that he has thick gauze bandages wrapped around both his wrists. He looks to be around eleven or twelve. Beside him, his mother has her hands clasped tightly in her lap. She seems uneasy, too.

"They've come to us for help. Leo was just released from the hospital this morning. He tried to take his own life."

I can sense Raielle's surprise as she stares at the boy. Her feelings are the same as mine.

"Leo knows he made a mistake," John says. "And the stigma of what he's done will follow him forever. The scars on his wrists will never fade. His mother thinks he'll be able to move on more easily if those scars weren't there to serve as a painful reminder."

His words sound stilted, like he practiced them too many times. My shock multiplies. Her kid just tried to off himself, and she's worried about the scars?

John turns to Raielle. "I'd like you to do it, sweetheart, if that's all right."

She stiffens. "Why?"

"I want to observe you while you heal him."

The kid looks petrified, and it's horrifying that his mother would put him through this now, after what he just attempted.

John glances at me, but then looks back at Raielle again. "Please indulge me. When you heal him, I'll be able to take the measure of your energy. Then I can help you work on it. If not him, we can wait for another patient."

65

"No," the mother says, speaking for the first time. "I've already paid you. You said this would happen today before anyone can see what he's done to himself."

Raielle and I exchange mutually disgusted looks. There's no way she's going to agree to this.

Her father takes a step closer to her. When he speaks, his voice is low so only we can hear. "You can help him, and not just with the scars. Your healing can have a positive effect on his mental state, too."

She shakes her head. "No, it can't." Her eyes meet mine. She's thinking of my mother. While she was able to undo the devastation her grandmother caused, she had no effect on my mother's depression. That's still there, and it's still hurting my family.

"I think you can. It's worth trying. Don't you think?" John asks, his voice softly persuasive.

She bites her lip and glances at me. When I shake my head at her, her eyes flick back to the boy.

I reach for her hand. "You can't agree to do this." I can feel her father's gaze on me. "Have you healed anyone since Penelope?"

"No." Her eyes find mine again. "But what if I can help him? Maybe I should try," she says quietly.

I look at Leo again. He's shaking like a leaf. This is just plain wrong. Am I the only one who sees that? "Look at him. This isn't right."

Her eyes fill with compassion. "I already feel a connection to him. I want to try."

John smiles at her, pleased with her decision. My reaction is very different, but she's purposely not looking at me as she pulls her hand from mine.

John moves to the empty couch and sits down, giving Raielle the floor. I watch as she pulls in a breath, readying herself. She's nervous. I weigh whether I should try to stop her. I have no idea why she would agree to do this. But in the end, it's her decision, and I can't believe the way she made it.

"Do you mind if I sit beside you, Leo?" she asks the boy gently.

He glances at his mother first before slowly nodding at her.

With a warm smile on her face, she sits down on the couch next to Leo. "I knew a boy your age once," she says. "His name was Ritchie. He liked to play basketball. Do you play?"

Leo stares at her for a moment before slowly nodding his head. "You any good?"

He rubs his hands over his knees. "I beat my cousin Brian last time."

"You must be pretty decent then." She smiles, and he nods again.

Then she waits a moment before growing serious. "Leo, I'm going to hold your hands, if that's all right."

His round eyes flick up to meet hers.

"It's okay. I promise. Nothing I'm going to do will hurt you." Raielle meets his gaze, and I can see she's silently trying to convey her good intentions.

"Okay," he whispers.

With his permission, she gently takes his small hands in hers. I hear his breathing quicken. His wide eyes are pinned to her face as his hands appear to grip her harder. Then I can see the concentration in her expression when she looks down at his bandaged wrists and pulls in deep, even breaths. We're all watching silently, and in less than a minute, Leo starts to giggle.

"I can feel that." He grins, glancing back at his mother.

I remember the feeling, too, the exhilaration that filled me when she healed my broken arm and my bruised face. When my phone vibrates in my pocket, I ignore it, knowing there's no way I can cause a distraction now.

Obviously pleased at his response, Raielle continues. Leo's face is frozen in a grin as he stares up at her. We all continue to watch, wondering what's happening to his scars beneath those bandages. I glance over at John. He's edging forward in his seat, watching her more intently than he had been before. When I look at Raielle again, her expression is tight and her eyes are wide and fearful. My muscles tense. Something's wrong.

"Ray?" I take a step toward her, but her father stands and shoots his arm out in front of me, blocking me. *Son of a bitch!* I push by him, but before I can reach her, Raielle gasps, dropping the boy's hands and standing abruptly.

Once I'm beside her, I see that her eyes aren't focusing.

"Is it done?" the mother asks. "Are they gone?" She grabs her son's wrists and begins unwinding the bandages.

Raielle tenses and glowers at the mother.

The bandages fall to the floor. "They're gone." The mother laughs in happy disbelief. "They're really gone."

"You know why he did this? Don't you?" Raielle asks her.

Both Leo and his mother freeze.

"What did you see?" John asks quietly.

I can feel her body start to shake. "He's being abused," she whispers.

"You had a vision," John states.

She nods and swallows. "I saw it. He hasn't told anyone." She reaches out and grabs the front of John's shirt. "We have to help him."

For the first time since we walked into this room, John's calm expression slips. He seems almost pleased. "You did have a vision then?"

She nods.

"We'll help him. Of course, we will," he says. Then he goes over to his desk and picks up the phone. He says something quietly so none of us can hear.

When my own phone begins to vibrate again, I can't help the worry that gnaws at me as I ignore it for the second time.

Raielle turns back to the boy and his mother, who are standing now and looking anxious to leave. Raielle bends down in front of Leo. "It's going to be okay," she tells him. But he turns away from her, pushing his face into his mother's side.

The door opens and Nyla appears. "My wife will show you out," John says.

The mother nods, mumbles a thank-you, and ushers her son out the door. Nyla gives us all a curt nod before she leaves, closing the door behind her.

"Nyla has contacts at Social Services," John explains. "She'll make sure they're told."

"He shouldn't go home. I think it may be an uncle or some other relative." Raielle glances back toward the door.

"Leave it to Nyla," John says dismissively. Then he stares at Raielle for a long moment while she fidgets and looks like she wants to run after Leo. "How long have you been having visions during healings?" he asks.

She glances at me before answering. I notice that she has her hands clasped tightly together. "They started recently. Are visions unusual?"

He tries to fight a smile, but he's unsuccessful. "Yes," he finally says. "They're very rare, actually. I've only met one other healer who had visions. Sit down. Tell me exactly what you see and how you feel when it's happening."

When my phone vibrates again, I glance down apologetically at her. "I'm sorry. I need to take this." I bend in closer. "Are you okay? I don't want to leave you in here with him."

She smiles at me, but it's stiff and doesn't reach her eyes. "I'm fine. Go ahead."

She isn't fine, but now isn't the time to argue that point. I kiss the side of her head. Then I pull the phone from my pocket and step outside. I have three missed calls from Liam. My chest constricts with familiar fear as I call him back. The moment he picks up, I ask, "Are you okay?"

"Yeah. Sorry to call so many times. I'm fine."

"Jesus." I breathe out, relieved, and lean back against the wall.

"I'm really sorry. I didn't mean to worry you."

"Are you calling about Mom?" I ask, knowing it has to be about her.

He sighs heavily into the phone. "She hasn't gotten out of bed in three days. The depression is getting worse again. She won't talk to me or to Dad, and she says she's done with therapists."

I rub my hand over my face, knowing I should be there. "Where is Dad?"

"He's here. He wants her to go back into the hospital."

My eyes close. I hate the thought of her being in that place. But I can't deny that it helps her, even though it's always a temporary fix. "It sounds like that might be a good idea."

In response, I hear only the sound of his breathing.

"Liam?"

"I figured you'd say that."

"I'm sorry. Hang in there, okay?"

"Don't be sorry. I'm glad you found Raielle. I get that you have to be there now."

I shake my head at the empty hallway. He's taken my place. I never wanted to pass this torch down to my kid brother. I need to get back there soon, at least for a few days.

"Hey. Guess what?" he asks, trying to sound upbeat. "I'm going out with Abby Pierson."

"Abby Pierson? Isn't she the girl who keeps getting suspended for wearing her skirts too short?"

"That would be her." He laughs.

I can feel myself smiling. "So it's like that?"

"I have a pulse and a dick. So, yeah. It's like that."

"Shit. You're too young for that to be coming out of your mouth." I laugh out loud and wish again that I could be there talking to him in person. After a pause, I say, "Call me when it happens, okay? When she goes in."

"Yeah. Okay. Say hi to Ray for me."

"I will." We disconnect, and I close my eyes, hating how conflicted I feel. I was supposed to be there for him, for all of them.

The smell of perfume has my eyes opening again to find that girl Charlie standing directly in front of me, surprisingly close, unapologetically crowding my personal space. Looking downward, I see that her feet are bare. Gone are the clicking high heels.

"Hi, Lucas." She smiles up at me as her finger slides down my chest. "So, are you and Raielle exclusive?"

I stare pointedly at her finger on me. "I guess you and Shane aren't?"

She shakes her head, overdoing it so that her long hair flips around her face and shoulders. "I'm a free agent."

"Well, I'm not." I go to move around her, but she moves with me.

"Come on. Don't be that way." She eyes me from beneath her long dark lashes.

The truth is, she's beautiful in that too-perfect unreal Hollywood way that's so typical here. Not too long ago, I would have bought what she was selling, but like Liam said, I'm not anymore. "Excuse me," I say, moving from annoyed to pissed off when she blocks my attempt to get past her again.

"I could change your mind," she says coyly.

Before I realize what she's doing, a tiny blade appears in her hand. It comes up fast and slices down across my cheek. My face burns as my hand shoots out to grab her wrist, stopping the knife from coming at me again. I turn, pushing her back into the wall. "You're fucking crazy."

She only smiles at me. When I take the knife from her and step back, her other hand reaches out to grip my forearm. I feel a burst of heat travel into me. It runs up along my arm and then down the length of my back before it turns warm and soothing. Realizing what she's doing to me, I drop the knife and try to peel her fingers off me when the next sensation hits. My muscles loosen as the burning in my cheek fades. Then she presses herself against me and crushes her lips into mine. I fight the pull she has on me, bringing my hands up, grabbing her arms and shoving her away. She stumbles back, losing her hold on me.

Breathing hard, the blood pounding in my head, I watch as she retrieves the knife from the floor and stands, her eyes shifting behind me. When I turn, another girl is there. She holds out her phone and gives me a mischievous smile.

"See?" Charlie says, pointing to my cheek. "All better now." Then she turns and the two girls walk away together. I can hear them giggling as they disappear down the hallway.

My hand traces along my cheek as I glare at their retreating backs, and I know without a doubt that Raielle doesn't belong here.

SEVEN

Raielle

I OPEN the door to find him waiting in the hallway. Right away, I can see that something is wrong. His mouth is tight, and his eyebrows are a straight, harsh line. "Who was on the phone?"

Lucas says nothing until the door closes behind me. "Can we go now?" he asks.

I nod, worried by the look on his face.

Silently, he leads me out of the house and out to his truck. I watch his stiff movements, becoming more uneasy by the minute. "What's wrong?"

He shoots me a dark look. "Let's get out of here first."

We sit in silence as he maneuvers down the winding driveway and out onto the road. The soft hum of the motor is the only sound as he leaves my father's neighborhood and turns into traffic. After a mile or so, Lucas pulls into the parking lot of a Starbucks, but he makes no move to get out.

When he still says nothing, I get impatient. "Are you going to tell me what's going on?"

He pushes a hand through his hair, and I notice a smudge of red on his cheek. It looks like dried blood. He sees where my focus is, and his hand goes to his face. The same traces of blood appear to be on his fingers. Reaching for his arm, I ask, "What happened?" But I quickly sense that he's not hurt or cut anywhere.

He pulls his arm back.

My apprehension builds at his silence. I stare at him, waiting him out, wondering what his phone call could have been about to make him act this way, and begin to fear that something terrible happened.

Finally, he shifts his body in my direction and pins me in place with an ice-cold stare. "What are you still doing here?"

I blink in confusion.

"Do you know what this is?" he asks, holding his red-stained hand out to me. "This is blood from where Charlie cut me with a knife while I was standing out in the hallway."

I stare at him, running his words back in my head because they make no sense.

"She came up to me and asked if you and I were exclusive. When I told her we are, she pulled out a little pocketknife and sliced my cheek open. Then she healed it while she was planting a kiss on me."

My stomach clenches as I stare at the dried blood on his face.

"And also…" He cocks his head to the side. "One of her friends took a picture of it. No doubt, they plan to show it to you at some point."

I pull his gesturing hand from the air and clutch it in both of mine. I can hardly comprehend what he's saying happened. "Are you okay?" I ask, picturing Shane's bloody sheets and realizing that cutting and healing for the pleasure of it must be a common pastime around here. My own blood starts to boil at the thought of her attacking Lucas that way.

He takes a deep breath, and I can see him visibly trying to keep calm. "I'm fine, but I'm wondering what the hell you're doing. You've been here for months. You must know what it took me less than a day to figure out."

I clutch his hand tighter, wanting nothing more than to hunt down Charlie and hurt her myself, the same way she hurt him. I never wanted Lucas exposed to any of this, but I couldn't have imagined something like that would happen. Looking at his fierce expression, I try to find the words that will make him understand something I hardly comprehend myself. "I'm here to figure out who and what I am," I explain. "It's not like I can go to the library or search on Google to find those answers. In terms of teachers, my options are limited."

His lips draw together in a straight line. "You know who you are and so do I. You don't need these people for that."

Frustration and a sense of desperation build inside me. "Yes, I do. I almost got myself killed trying to heal Penelope, and look how I hurt you this morning. It's dangerous to have this power inside me and not know what the hell I'm doing with it. I don't want to just turn it off anymore. I'm like this for a reason. I have to understand how it works. And for the first time in my life, the answers are within reach. I need those answers. I can't leave here without them."

His eyes are intent on mine. I need him to understand, but then he shakes his head. "You're not seeing things clearly. When you were helping that kid before, I could tell something was wrong. But when I tried to get to you, your father stopped me. He wasn't worried about you. He was more interested in watching things play out."

I swallow the bitter disappointment in my father that I've felt from the first moment I met him. "I know that. He's not fooling me. He has his own reasons for why he does things. I have no idea why he saved my life or why he's offering to help me now. But I can't turn down his offer. I need him."

Lucas grips the back of his seat, and I can see that he wants to say something, but he hesitates. I watch him, hoping he's not going to keep trying to dissuade me. Finally, he leans forward and asks, "When your father saved you, who did he use?"

His question takes me by surprise, and I blink against the tears that always threaten when I think about it. "A stranger," I answer quietly. "He won't tell me who. He said that when a healer's power is strong enough, a blood relative isn't necessary. You can use anyone."

He nods as though it makes sense. "That's how he was able to do it. That's why you're sitting here now. Otherwise, he couldn't have…" When he stops, unable to finish the thought, I can feel his relief at how things worked out.

I turn on him. "Someone is dead because of me. You realize that, don't you?"

His mouth tightens, then his expression turns wary. "No matter how many times I tell you it wasn't your fault, that you didn't have a choice, it's not going to make a difference. Is it?"

His eyes bore into mine, like he's trying convince me of it again. But silence is my answer because I can't lie to him. Reluctantly, he tears his gaze away, runs a hand through his hair and slumps down into the seat, then exhales in what sounds like defeat.

I wait, but he stays quiet. I'd prefer him to yell and be angry. That I could deal with. Then I'd know what he's thinking. But I don't know how to deal with this. He can't make it better for me no matter how much he wants to, and I wonder if he's beginning to realize that. I wish his words alone could make a difference. I wish I could be different.

He shifts in his seat. "Would you like to know something about me?" he asks, staring straight out the windshield. But he doesn't wait for my answer. "I've never really gone after anything before."

His words pull at me, and I look at him curiously.

"Girls were easy. Well, except for you," he adds with a shrug. "Grades were easy."

I watch him, wondering where he's going with this.

"Money was easy. My dad always gave me cash and never cared what it was for. I was just biding my time, waiting until the day I could leave and take Liam with me."

"Things at home weren't easy," I point out.

He shifts to face me again. "But that was different. There was nothing to do there but withstand it. You're the only thing I ever wanted that didn't come easy. You're the only thing I've ever fought for. And the truth is, I don't know how to stop fighting."

I'm not sure what he means. "But you have me. You can stop now."

He tilts his head. "Do I?"

"Yes," I answer quickly, shifting under the weight of his uncertainty, shocked that he could misunderstand me so completely. I swallow, searching for the right thing to say. He needs to know how strongly I feel about him, but I can't paint him a pretty picture when one doesn't exist. Maybe he regrets coming here now. Maybe I'm not who he wants anymore.

Nerves make my hands shake, and I wrap them around my knees to keep them still. "I'm sorry for what I've put you through, Lucas, for what I'm still putting us both through." I pull in a shallow breath. "But I can't be the girl I was before, and no matter how hard you fight to bring her back, she's not coming back. But you can have the girl I am now if you want her, because she wants you. She still loves you." Licking my dry lips, I watch him for his reaction. My whole body feels poised for a crushing disappointment.

He shows no emotion at first. It feels like he's thinking about it, and that doesn't seem to bode well for me. His expression stays the same for an excruciatingly long time, but then gradually the ice in his eyes seems to melt. He blinks, and his focus sharpens on me. "Ray," he says softly, shaking his head. "I think we've both changed. After everything that's happened, how could we stay the same? But I still love you. That hasn't changed. No matter what happens, that won't ever change."

I swallow past the lump in my throat as his gaze stays on me, and it feels like we're being honest for the first time today. No more pretending. No going back again.

Everything is different now.

WE left the Starbucks parking lot with the air cleared and with a new understanding. Lucas hasn't said much since other than asking me if I was hungry. For the first time in a long while, I told him I was. Now my stomach feels like it's busting at the seams as we leave In-N-Out Burger. No one forced me to eat a Double-Double. But with Lucas here, the knots that have been twisting inside me are starting to loosen.

"I need to stop by my place first to get a few things," Lucas says as he turns down a narrow road he thinks is a shortcut to Westwood Village. I disagree, but I don't want to put a damper on his enthusiasm at saving a couple of minutes and probably less than a mile.

"First?" I ask.

"I'm staying with you," he states, rather than asks.

"Since you think you're in charge, you've decided this?" I tease, pretending the butterflies aren't fluttering in my belly.

"I don't just think it." He grins, but then his expression turns serious. "I'm not spending the night away from you. We don't have to do anything."

He glances at me, and all I do is swallow. I don't want to be apart from him either, but can we really be together all night and not fool around? If we can't, will I lose control of my energy again and hurt him? I jump when his finger touches my forehead.

"Stop worrying," he says. "It's just me. There's nothing to stress about."

I nearly laugh because that's exactly why I'm stressing out. He angles a look at me, and I know that despite his assurances of not doing anything tonight, his smoldering eyes tell me he has other ideas.

A smile plays at his lips, and he subtly shakes his head.

"What?" I ask.

He hesitates before his sly grin grows even wider. "You have no idea how sexy you are."

His words cause my cheeks to heat.

"I love how that embarrasses you," he says, amused by my reaction.

I look at my limp hair hanging down over my shoulders, and the oversized sweater that I've worn since yesterday because it's dark and makes me feel invisible. I used to turn heads, but not anymore. Now, I want to disappear most of the time. I guess love really is blind, because there's no way I look anything like sexy.

"See?" he asks before pulling up to an intersection and taking a turn that brings us to the back of campus. "Told you this was a shortcut."

My smile joins his because he looks so proud of himself.

A few minutes later, he passes Nikki's building and pulls to a stop in front of a three-story house.

"This is where you live?"

He nods, getting out of the truck.

"How long have you been here?" I ask, trailing behind him, wondering how I've never run into him.

"Only a few weeks. I saw an ad for this place just before school started. I share the bottom floor. Before this, I was in a hotel for most of the summer."

I'm following him up the short path to the front door, and my feet nearly falter at his words. "You were in town all summer?" I ask slowly.

After unlocking the door, he turns to me. "I came after graduation. Alec told me he'd get word to your father I was here. He implied that if your father approved, he'd let you get in touch with me. Since I didn't have a lot of other options, I came and waited."

"Wait a minute. Alec talks to my father?" I ask, feeling the bile rise in my throat at just saying his name. "And if you were here all this time, Apollo must have known."

He nods his head, and the skin around his mouth tightens.

I stare off at nothing as this sinks in. "He never said anything."

Lucas bends to catch my eye. "He purposely kept us apart."

My mouth opens, but quickly closes again because this may not be what Lucas thinks. I never asked Apollo for details about Lucas. I practically made it clear that I didn't want any. I thought it would be too hard to hear about his life, knowing he'd moved on without me. But he hadn't moved on. He was right here. Apollo must have realized I'd want to know that even if I never said as much.

Lucas goes inside, but I don't follow. My heart hurts, picturing him waiting for me all that time. And now he tells me that my father knew he was here because he talked to Alec. A sick feeling builds inside me as I walk into Lucas's apartment, finding him turning on lights and then disappearing into another room. Walking in behind him, I glance around his bedroom, noticing some clothes strewn over a chair and a pile of books on a table beside his bed. He has various electronics stacked beneath a small TV, but other than that, Lucas doesn't appear to have much here. In fact, he picks up a messenger bag and a backpack, and is ready to head back out again.

"You haven't unpacked?" I ask.

He looks around. "I guess I never got around to it."

There's movement behind me in the hallway. "Hey, Diesel. What are you still doing here?"

I turn to see a tall guy with black-framed glasses standing over me. He pushes his long blond hair behind his ears and eyes me curiously.

"This is my roommate, Calvin," I say. "Cal, this is Raielle."

Cal seems surprised. "You finally gave up on that other girl you were looking for?"

"No." Lucas clears his throat. "This is her."

His head rears back in shock. "You're the chick he's been so torn up over?"

"Um, Cal," Lucas says.

"What you did to him was seriously fucked up." He points a finger in my face.

Lucas mutters something under his breath as he turns me around and starts pushing me past Cal, toward the door. "Don't listen to him," Lucas says to me. Moving me in front of him, he leans back to say something to Cal, but it's too low for me to hear. Then he continues to propel me forward.

Once we're alone outside, I whirl around on him. "What did you tell him about me?"

He starts to walk past me.

"Lucas?"

Stopping, he drops his bags on the ground. "I had a few too many one night and said a bunch of stupid shit."

"What kind of stupid shit?"

Looking down, his hands go to his hips as he sighs. "I was missing you, and I was pissed. I told him the facts without any of the details. He drew his own conclusions, and I guess I let him, because how the hell could I ever really explain it? I'm sorry. Don't be mad, okay?"

But I can't find it in me to be mad. I told him I loved him, and then I left him in the worst way possible. He spent months waiting for me, not knowing if I was alive or dead, and I can still hardly believe he's here. Every time I think of what he's given up for me, I feel conflicted. I'm thrilled and saddened and weighed down by guilt. I feel so much guilt for all that's happened to both of us. "I'm not mad, Lucas. I'm just sorry…about everything."

He nods, looking both contrite and relieved, having no idea of the thoughts going on inside my head. He takes a step forward and kisses me on the forehead, letting his lips linger there. I lean into him, breathing in his scent, letting the heady sensation of having him close wash over me, and feeling exhausted from the tumultuous day we've had.

"Let's go," he says. Then he turns me with him and picks up his things.

EIGHT

Raielle

WHEN we get back to the condo, I'm relieved to see no sign of Shane. Despite what Lucas said earlier about not having to do anything tonight, there's electricity in the air between us. I feel it in the silence we've fallen into, and it only grows when we walk into my bedroom.

I busy myself with putting my things away and pulling out some clothes to change into. When I turn around, Lucas is standing in the middle of the room staring at me. The intensity of his gaze halts me as he slowly moves closer. My pulse starts to race, and the need to have him touch me is so strong, I feel weak with it.

But then I remember that I haven't showered or changed clothes in two days, and I avert my gaze, regretfully breaking the hold he has on me. It's been a while since I cared about my appearance, and right now I care a lot. "I'm going to take a shower," I say.

"Yeah?" His playful tone has me glancing back at him. "Can I join you?"

The breath stalls in my lungs.

A mischievous grin grows on his face. "Relax. I'm kidding. You go first."

I roll my eyes at him, turning away as my face grows hot.

Walking into the bathroom and closing the door behind me, I wonder why I'm feeling so skittish around him. I love him. I shouldn't be this nervous at the idea of being with him, of being naked with him while he's naked, too.

My whole body heats as I turn on the shower and step under the cool spray. The fact that it would be my first time is enough to give me jitters. But after what happened this morning, I don't want to lose control and hurt him again. I was so ready to give myself to him that night at the bridge. If he hadn't found those tumors in my wrist, my first time would be over and done with now. But that feels like a lifetime ago, and I don't remember feeling this nervous around him then. It's been a long time since anyone touched me so often or watched me so closely. It's been since I last saw him. Before that, it had been forever.

I shave before shampooing my hair, taking a long time, delaying. Then I towel off, not feeling any calmer, and realize that I forgot to bring my pajamas in with me. With this luxurious condo, you'd think the towels would be huge and plush, but no. There's not much to them, and this one barely hits the top of my thighs when I wrap it around me. I glance around the bathroom, searching for another one to use, before deciding I'm being ridiculous. Lucas has touched me everywhere. My nipples have been in his mouth. I need to get over myself.

When I pull open the bathroom door, he's standing in front of the window with his back to me. I can see his reflection in the glass as his eyes stare sightlessly into the night.

"Hey," I say when he doesn't notice my approach.

He glances at me sharply, like I startled him, before schooling his expression into blankness. "Be right out," he says, offering me a tight smile before heading into the bathroom and closing the door behind him, never once noticing me in the skimpy towel I was so worried about.

I stare after him, confused. I'd nearly forgotten about his quick-fire mood swings. When I hear the shower turn on, I look out the window at the streetlights below. Then I notice his phone lying on the chair, and I suspect it's the source of his sinking mood.

Turning away, I grab my Chargers T-shirt and some boxers, which are all I really have for pajamas. I've barely pulled them on when the shower turns off and the door opens, revealing a damp Lucas with nothing but a small towel wrapped around his waist.

"I forgot to bring my bag in with me," he explains, moving toward it.

As he comes nearer, my gaze travels over the smooth skin of his broad shoulders, dotted with water drops that are leading a path down his firm chest to his rippled stomach. The water is absorbed by the towel that's draped around his narrow waist, and my imagination fills in the blanks for the parts that remain covered.

When my gaze moves back up again, one side of his mouth tugs knowingly. But my embarrassment at being caught gawking is nothing compared to my growing need for him. He wants me, too. Desire is written there on his face. But there's also tension rolling off him. "Is everything all right?" I ask.

When he doesn't answer, and instead begins pulling clothing out of his bag, I move toward him and place my hand on his shoulder, feeling the muscle jump beneath my touch. "You can talk to me. You can tell me anything."

He stills before his eyes find mine. "I know. But not now, okay?"

My hopes sink, but I only nod at him, thinking whatever it is has something to do with his family. He only gets this way when he's hurting over them.

He reaches out and runs his hand up my arm. His face gradually relaxes, and he gets that familiar look in his eyes, the one that telegraphs his intent to kiss me. My whole body tightens as my pulse jumps. When he leans toward me, I wait expectantly, but he doesn't kiss me. Instead, he rests his forehead against mine. His warm breath spreads over my skin, and my chest rises and falls in anticipation. But he keeps us this way, just seeming to breathe me in before stepping back again and taking his things into the bathroom with him.

I stand there dumbstruck, staring at the closed door, and I understand that despite the way he looks at me, he doesn't intend for anything to happen tonight. Feeling both relieved and utterly disappointed, I shake off my warring emotions and slip into bed. But my body doesn't feel sleepy anymore, and I close my eyes, trying to find some calmness.

When the door opens again, I look over to find him standing there in a pair of cotton pajama bottoms and a white T-shirt. "Do you want me to sleep on the floor?" he asks.

I sit up, surprised. "Is that what you want?"

He walks toward the bed. "No, Ray. That's not what I want."

He's got that look again, like he wants something from me but he doesn't plan on taking it. "You can sleep in the bed," I say.

Then I watch as he turns out the light and walks back slowly, not really looking at me, as he lifts the covers and slides underneath them. The bed dips beneath his weight, and I find my hand reaching out to him. He grasps it firmly in his own, pulling me over so that I'm pressed against him beneath the blanket. I rest my head on his shoulder, and he places a kiss on my hair. "'Night, Ray," he whispers.

"Good night," I answer, but sleep still feels very far away. All my focus is on him and all the warm places where his body touches mine. I try to slow my breathing down and wipe away my thoughts, knowing how tired I am, but my awareness of him keeps me alert.

Sometime later, I'm staring into the darkness, and he's very still beside me, almost too still. When I absently move my hand to rest it on his chest, he pulls in a breath.

"We're not sleeping," I say.

He laughs softly. "No, we're not."

I shift to look up at him. His eyes are open, watching me, glittering in the darkness. We stay this way for moment, just looking at each other. But then he turns and leans over me. His face hovers above mine. I reach up to brush my fingers over his rough cheek before moving down to trace along his full lips. He presses a kiss to my fingertips. Then he brings my hand up behind his neck and dips down to kiss me again, on the lips this time. I kiss him back, reaching my fingers into his hair to keep him more firmly against me. He groans as he moves his body above mine, and his hand splays across my waist.

I love the feel of his weight pressing me down into the mattress. I melt beneath him when he seeks my lips more urgently, opening his mouth and giving in to his need. His hand slips under my T-shirt, making me shiver as his fingers dance across my ribs, rubbing back and forth before skimming up higher. Warmth gathers inside me, pushing away my nerves and tossing everything else aside to focus only on how he makes me feel. His scent surrounds me as our tongues collide, and soon it feels like kissing him so deeply isn't enough. I arch up against him, wanting more.

His other hand begins tugging the edge of my T-shirt up, but he pauses halfway and seems to regain his senses. "Tell me to stop," he says. "I told you we didn't have to do anything tonight."

My heart is jack-hammering, and I'm sure he must feel it. "Don't stop," I breathe. The thought of him stopping now is unimaginable.

A small smile forms on his lips, and I drink in the intimacy of it. The way he looks at me, his gaze heavy with desire, chases away any uncertainty. I lean back to raise my arms over my head. In seconds, the shirt is gone and cool air washes over my skin. I wrap my arms around his neck, making a low noise in my throat in response to the contact. His hands begin to knead my breasts, shooting warmth all the way through me, and his mouth fuses to mine again.

Our tongues meet, stroking against each other, and I'm struck by how much I want this. I've never needed anyone this way. From the very beginning, something inside me recognized something within him. My heart has been tethered to his ever since. Now that our bodies will be linked together, I remember the words he said to me back in Fort Upton. *When I'm finally inside you, I'll be your first, and I'll know that no one has ever done the things I'm going to do to you.* After all this time, he's about to make good on that promise.

When he turns away, I nearly whimper at the loss as I watch him reach down into his bag on the floor. He retrieves something from it before returning. I help him pull his T-shirt over his head, and then I look at him the same way he looked at me, admiring every line and dip of his muscled chest and stomach.

"You're so beautiful," he says as he angles himself above me and kisses his way down my body. I sigh, enjoying each sensation, giving myself over to him. His tongue dips into my belly button, and my stomach jumps. My hands slide into his hair as I watch him. Without breaking eye contact, Lucas slowly strips off my remaining clothes and then removes his own. When he leans up, I look at him, admiring all of him.

I reach for his face, making him look at me, wanting him to see how he makes me feel. I lock my eyes on his. "I love you."

He stills before whispering, "I love you." Then he takes my mouth in a slow, tender kiss. I run my hands over his back, loving the pressure of his hot skin against mine.

His hands move down to cover my knees, and he begins to part my legs. Watching me, he rolls the condom on. Then one of his arms comes down beside my head to brace himself. I feel him at my entrance. His eyes stay on mine as he starts to push in slowly. I breathe out while he slides in deeper, and I start to feel stretched. I'm watching him as the expression on his face becomes strained, and I realize that he's purposely keeping himself in check, trying not to hurt me.

"Don't be careful with me," I whisper. "Don't hold back."

He halts his movement, his eyes searching mine and hesitating before finally thrusting himself in. I gasp at the sharp pain, surprised by the intensity of it. Lucas presses his face into my shoulder, muttering, "I'm sorry, baby."

But even as he's apologizing, along with the pain I can feel the fullness of him inside me. Soon the hurt dulls, pushed away by the desire that's returning, and I move my hips, needing friction.

Lucas levels himself above me, watching my expression closely. He begins to rock into me, slowly at first, then faster as I move with him. Each stroke shocks my sensitive flesh as I shift beneath him, adjusting to the feel of him. I reach up, clasping my hands around his neck, keeping our gazes locked, watching every subtle change on his face. His eyes read mine, shining at me when I start to pant softly and turn my head into the pillow, anticipating the way I'm going to shatter beneath him.

He takes my hands from around his neck and places them above

88

my head, stretching me out, then shifts our hips up so he can push even deeper inside me, and hits a spot that makes my body catch fire. The muscles low in my stomach contract. I'm trying to hold back my climax, wanting to watch him unravel with me, but I can't stop it, and I begin to arch up off the mattress.

"That's right, Ray," he says, his voice low and husky. "Now, baby."

My muscles pulse around him. I hear him groan as waves of pleasure wash over me, drowning me in sensation. My body bows beneath his, but I still manage to see the way his expression tightens with his release. We're falling apart together, and I never knew I could feel this close to anyone.

Our breaths are in sync, and so are our racing hearts. When the room comes back into focus, my limbs feel heavy. Lucas's weight is on me, his moist skin pressed against mine. When he starts to roll to his side, my arms come around him. "Don't."

His face fills with concern. "Are you okay?"

I can't hide my satisfied smile.

He laughs softly. It's a deep, sexy rumble that I can feel vibrating inside him. When he does finally move onto his side, he takes me with him, keeping our bodies pressed together. His blue eyes bathe me in affection as his fingers lightly graze up and down my arm. "You're mine now," he says.

I revel in the possessive glint in his eye as I run my fingers through his mussed hair. I can't seem to get enough of touching him.

When the energy ignites inside me, I'm caught off guard. Closing my eyes, I will it away, trying to hold it in. But my growing anxiety only makes it worse. Afraid I might hurt him again, I frantically push myself back, breaking our contact.

His eyes widen in alarm.

Fisting my hands, I try to stop it. But then I realize that it's not flowing out of me. Instead, it's traveling down through my body and once it settles and the healing starts, I understand what's happening. "No," I mutter, sitting up. "No…" But I can't seem to stop it.

"What is it?" Lucas asks. I can hear the fear in his voice as he grasps my shoulders.

Wordlessly, I shake my head as my body finishes healing itself and the coil of energy retreats. He gently shakes me, his face a mask of worry. "Ray?"

My hands grip the sheets in frustration. I meet his gaze, not wanting to say it out loud.

"You're scaring me," he whispers hoarsely.

I let out the breath I'd been holding. "I healed myself."

His expression doesn't change.

My eyes close. "I *healed* myself."

When I dare to look at him again, he blinks at me, still not comprehending, but there's no way I'm repeating it another time. Then he narrows his eyes and understanding smoothes his brow. "You mean you…" He trails off and glances down at the lower half of my body, covered by the sheets.

"Yes," I mumble, feeling my cheeks burn, pulling my knees in and hugging my arms around them.

Lucas sighs heavily and falls back against the pillow.

"I couldn't control it. The energy started on its own," I explain, unable to look at him.

His hand slides down over my back. "You scared the shit out of me."

I can feel his relief, but I can't share it.

"At least you didn't knock me off the bed again."

I turn around to see one side of his mouth pulling up. He's trying to make light of it for me, but it isn't working. "Lucas, please. This is mortifying."

He sobers as his hand reaches up and pushes a lock of hair behind my ear. Then his eyes close and he mutters a curse. "It's going to hurt you again the next time," he says, realizing the ramifications. He shifts away. "What's going on? Why is this happening to you all of a sudden?"

I slump back onto the bed, pulling the sheets up over me. "I don't know. My father said that sometimes our power grows stronger as we mature. But I don't think this is what he meant." I laugh harshly, hating the tremulous sound of my voice. I can't stand feeling so out of control.

"Hey, come on." He moves beside me and pulls me close. My head tilts up at him, and there's an odd expression on his face I've never seen there before. I realize that he's completely thrown by this. Strong, arrogant Lucas is off-balance, and that makes me feel like I'm falling with nothing to grab on to.

"It was good, right?" I ask after a while, nervous that I've ruined it. "I mean, I thought so."

His eyes focus on mine, and he looks at me like I've just asked a really dumb question. "You were there, right? It wasn't just good."

Despite everything, I smile. "Better than good?"

"Yes, Ray, a lot better than good," he says, kissing me on the head. Then he exhales heavily. "Let's go to sleep. No staying up all night worrying about this. It won't do you any good. We can worry tomorrow. Okay?"

"Okay," I whisper, knowing it's unlikely that either of us can do what he's asking.

HOURS later, sleep is still out of reach. As I lie beside Lucas in the darkness, my thoughts won't turn off. He's sleeping but he's restless, constantly moving and pulling at the sheets.

As I slip quietly out of bed and relocate to the chair beside the window, I recall his sinking mood earlier. My gaze travels from the blackness outside to the person I love more than I ever thought possible.

My eyes squeeze closed in frustration and embarrassment at how I healed myself tonight. God only knows what Lucas is really thinking. He's so good at hiding his feelings, but he couldn't hide how completely out of his depth he felt when he looked at me earlier.

"Can't you sleep?"

Startled, I see his eyes are wide open and focused on me. I shake my head, watching as he pushes off the blankets and stands in the shadowed bedroom. His naked body is beautiful, sleek and sculpted in the moonlight. I'm transfixed by the way he moves, the roll of his hips and the pull of his muscles. He slides on his pajama bottoms and comes to the window to sit in the chair across from me.

"Are you still worrying about what happened?" he asks tentatively, like he's afraid to upset me.

I give him a small smile before glancing outside again, but all I see is both our reflections in the glass. "It's hard not to."

His gaze goes to the window also, meeting mine.

"Is everything okay at home?" I ask carefully.

His jaw tightens, and his gaze stays fixed for a moment before he turns back to me. He rubs his hands over his thighs when he says, "They had to put my mother back in a hospital."

My heart stutters at the pain I hear in his voice. "Because of the depression?" I ask, hoping it's not something worse, that she's turned violent again.

He nods stiffly.

"That's what those phone calls have been about, the ones that have been upsetting you?"

Not answering me, he runs a hand over the back of his neck, looking uncomfortable and restless now. Talking about this is still so hard for him.

"You should go home and be with them," I suggest, even though being without him is the last thing I want.

"I'm not leaving you. That's…" He pauses. "Not an option."

Slowly, I push myself off my chair and bend down in front of him, resting my arms on his legs. "If you want to go home for a few days, I'll go with you."

Surprise flickers in his eyes. "You'd do that?"

"Of course."

He watches me for a heartbeat before smiling sadly, and when he looks away again, I know he's not going to take me up on it. Setting me aside, he stands and walks over to his bag. "I have something to show you." He searches inside it, shifting things around. Then he pulls out a cell phone. After fiddling with it, he stills, looking intently at the screen.

I walk over to see, and I'm surprised to find that it's my phone, the one Kyle gave to me, and Lucas is staring down at the picture Gwen took of us at the prom.

He tilts it toward me. "I stole it from your room after you left. You never showed me this photo of us."

"I never got a chance." I take it in, admiring how handsome Lucas looks in his tuxedo, recalling the song that was playing and the feel of him holding me safe in his arms, even though everything in his life was such a mess. "I remember how I felt when I first saw that picture."

The weight of his gaze is on me. "I felt special. Because of the way you're looking at me."

He offers me a wistful smile. "I'm glad. You saw the truth." He tries to hand me the phone.

I shake my head. "That's not mine anymore."

His eyes narrow. "Do you have a phone?"

"No." I take a step back.

He holds it out to me again. "It still works."

I think of the people who could call me on that phone, the ones I walked away from without even saying good-bye. "I can't use that. Is Kyle still paying for it?"

"Looks that way." He shrugs. "He probably thinks you still have it."

"I can't take it. It's not right. What if…what if Kyle calls me?"

He closes the distance. "Then you answer it, which is the same thing you'll do when I call you. You need to have a phone. At least take this until we can get you a new one."

He has that stubborn glint in his eyes, and I know he's not going to give up. Reluctantly, I take it from his hand, holding it gingerly in mine.

"And there's something else." He reaches in his bag again and withdraws a rectangular box. "I know I missed your birthday, but I got you something."

I stare at it, shocked.

He takes my hand and places the box in my palm. "Open it."

"I can't believe you got me a gift." My pulse kicks up as I carefully lift the top. There inside, lying on a bed of cotton, is a delicate silver chain with a pendant made up of two intertwined rounded silver square shapes. Each square is completely covered in small blue gemstones.

"It reminded me of your eyes, and I knew I had to get it for you."

My vision blurs with tears. "It's beautiful."

"Let me put it on you." He withdraws the necklace from the box, and I notice how its delicate shape contrasts against his large hands, which handle it deftly as he raises it over my head.

I feel it come around my neck as he sweeps my hair over my shoulder to fasten the clasp. When the cool metal settles just below the base of my throat, my fingers reach up to touch it.

"Happy belated birthday." He smiles, moving in front of me to see how it looks. I watch the way his eyes crinkle at the edges. That's how I know it's a genuinely happy smile, when it reaches his eyes. My fingers smooth over the necklace, and my heart swells at his gesture.

"Thank you. I love it." I throw my arms around him and squeeze tightly. He doesn't realize that this is the first real birthday present I've ever gotten. He can't understand how much this means to me. The fact that he remembered and thought about my birthday would have surprised me enough, never mind giving me a gift.

"You're welcome," he whispers against my skin, tickling my neck with his breath, making me shiver.

Morning is still hours away when we crawl back under the covers together, and I lay my cheek against the warm skin of his chest. He begins absently running his fingers through my hair. I lightly trace over the edges of the pendant, a symbol of all the wonderful and unexpected things Lucas has given to me, most of which can't be seen or held in my hand.

As I finally fall asleep, the dull roar of catastrophe that always echoes at the edges of my life seems less real than the man lying beside me now. As long as I have him, it feels like I can get through everything else. I never thought of myself as lucky before, but I'm starting to feel that now, and I also feel thankful for the first time in a very long while.

NINE

Lucas

BANGING coming from the kitchen startles me awake. I blink at the muted light coming through the windows as I look around for Raielle. I find her already dressed, coming out of the bathroom and scowling at the door. "Shane is home," she says.

Her birthday present rests against her pale skin, and seeing it there does something to me. When I bought it, I wasn't sure if I'd ever get the chance to give it to her.

"Did you sleep at all?" I ask, sitting up and scrubbing my hands over my face.

"Some." She smiles at me before glancing away. She's still upset about what happened. I hate that our first time ended like that. I wanted more of her afterward, and less of the angst and confusion that seem to dog us. But I should have learned by now; Raielle is never what I expect.

She's still making faces at the noise beyond the door. "Why do you hate him so much?" I ask.

Biting her bottom lip, she looks as though she doesn't want to tell me.

"I get that he's not exactly a pillar of society, but has he done something to you?"

95

She sighs, absently fingering her birthday present. "When I first got here, I was"—her eyes meet mine briefly—"a mess, and he was just so awful. He's...I don't know, empty is what comes to mind. I don't feel anything good inside him. It's hard to explain. But he's had some bad stuff happen to him. Maybe it's not his fault."

"What kind of bad stuff?" I ask, wondering how awful he was to her, and starting to feel tense just thinking about the possibilities.

She begins sorting items on her dresser. "The kind where your mother and twin brother are murdered. It was a long time ago."

My eyes widen at that. "What happened?"

She turns to face me again. "It was to get back at my father when he refused to do a healing. Apparently that's one of the reasons for all the secrecy and the security, and he says that's why my mother ran away with me. She was scared for us."

Masking my automatic suspicion of anything her father tells her, I get up out of bed. "Well, you lost your mother the same way," I point out. "It doesn't affect how you treat other people. If your instincts are telling you he's no good, you're probably right to trust them."

"But yesterday you said my judgment sucks."

I move toward her and pull her in close. "Only when it comes to yourself and your own safety." Then I lean down to kiss her, smiling at the traces of minty toothpaste I'm picking up.

She trails her delicate fingers over my chest, and I groan at the sensation, knowing I can't follow through on what she's unknowingly starting. On that same topic, I'm wondering if I should bring up what happened last night again because I'm positive she won't. "You okay this morning?" I ask.

Her eyes flick down, away from mine, as she nods.

Hitching a finger under her chin, I make her look at me. "You sure?"

Pink tinges her cheeks.

I sigh, knowing she doesn't want to talk about it. "Are we going to classes today?"

"We probably should." She seems relieved with the subject change.

The door flies open and Apollo strolls through. His eyes bounce between us.

His interruptions are starting to get on my nerves. "There's this thing called knocking." I scowl at him.

His hands go to his skinny hips. "I see you got her to sleep in her own bed for a change. But I'm guessing there wasn't much sleeping going on."

I'm about to tell him to mind his own goddamned business when Raielle clears her throat. "Why don't you get dressed," she tells me with a pointed look. Apparently, she doesn't want me to get into it with him. Then she leads a smug Apollo out of the room, closing the door softly behind them.

I stand there for a moment, just staring after her, not understanding how she can tolerate him. She tells me that he saved her life, but that doesn't erase the fact that he took her away from me and kept us apart all summer.

Shaking off the nasty vibes Apollo gives me, I grab my stuff and head for the shower. Standing under the hot spray, images from last night flash through my head: her soft pale skin smelling so sweet, her delicate curves moving beneath my hands, her long blonde hair splayed across the pillow, the carnal sounds she makes when she begins to lose control, and the warmth of being inside her.

Everything about our first time was better than the hundred or so times I imagined it, that is, everything except the pain that flared in her eyes when I pushed into her. I would do anything not to hurt her that way again, and I scrub my hands over my face, still completely dumbfounded at what happened.

I think of all the shit that's gone down since I met her: the way she saved my family, the way she made me feel again, the many ways she tears me apart. Being with her is like going on that drop tower ride at the carnival where you slowly ascend to the top to look at the breathtaking view, and then wait in suspense for the stomach-curdling plunge back down to the bottom again.

From the first minute I saw her across the yard that night, she woke me up from a life I was sleepwalking through. I'd detached from the world so I could survive it. But suddenly there she was, and detachment was the last thing I wanted. I wanted to be close to her. Just a year ago, I didn't know someone like her existed in the world, and now I don't think I could live in a world without her. She says she's changed. She's worried I won't love the girl she's become, but she hasn't really changed. Despite everything, she's still my ray of sunshine.

After toweling off, I dress quickly, eager to check on her as I decide not to bother shaving. Then I head out into the living room to find Apollo waving a doughnut under her nose. "I didn't know you liked doughnuts," I say.

She wrinkles her nose. "I used to like them. Until they started showing up every morning."

"Come on. Eat it," I encourage her, hoping I'll have better luck than him.

She shoots me an annoyed look. But after an exaggerated sigh, she grabs the doughnut and takes a bite.

"Hallelujah," Apollo cries melodramatically, standing and jingling his keys in his hands. "I guess you are good for something," he tells me.

She frowns at his comment before taking another bite and reaching for her bag just as there's a knock at the door.

Shane strolls out of his bedroom bare-chested with a towel around his neck. "I got it."

We're ready to head out as Charlie strolls in with a tall, clean-cut guy by her side.

When Charlie catches my eyes and smirks at me, I tense, glancing over at Raielle. She's shooting daggers in Charlie's direction. But Charlie strolls in nonchalantly and plops herself down onto the sofa. Her friend is still by the door, and my jaw starts to clench at the blatantly appreciative look he's giving Raielle.

"That's your sister?" he asks Shane as he continues to check her out. But she doesn't notice. She's heading straight for Charlie.

Raielle stops in front of her, but Charlie hardly glances up. She knows Raielle is standing there, and she gets a satisfied look on her face.

"I hear you like playing with sharp objects," Raielle says to her, her eyes narrowed. There's no reaction. "Touch him again and you'll regret

98

it." Her voice is low and more threatening than I thought possible. I'm beyond shocked. Raielle is the least violent person I know. But she's harassing this girl for me, and I realize that I kind of like it.

Charlie clucks her tongue and lifts her eyes to Raielle's. "I don't like threats. Threats make me want to threaten back. I could probably hurt you right now with just a few words."

"Shut it," Apollo warns her, taking Raielle's arm and nudging her toward the door.

"Just three little words," she says in a singsong tone.

"Don't, Charlene." Her friend moves toward her now, looking worried.

I'm wondering what she's talking about and why everyone seems to know except us.

She stands up slowly, right in front of Raielle, who doesn't move, and leans in close to her. "Leo is dead."

I just stare at her, confused. Then it hits me. Leo. The kid from yesterday. I look at Apollo, and his tight expression confirms it. Raielle blanches and whispers, "What?" She seeks out Apollo, but he says nothing. He's glaring at Charlie now, who's puffing out her bottom lip in mock sadness over the news.

"When?" Raielle asks Apollo.

I move beside her and place my hand on her back so she knows I'm here.

"I don't know the details," he says carefully.

"He killed himself last night. Didn't botch it this time, though," Charlie calls over her shoulder as she saunters into the kitchen.

"But Nyla called Social Services," Raielle says, looking to Apollo for confirmation. "Didn't she call them?"

He hesitates. "I'm sure she did."

"Here we go again," Shane exclaims with his arms in the air. "She's going to curl into a fetal position and bawl her eyes out for the next month because she's a fucking head case. She belongs in a psych ward."

When I feel her stiffen beside me, all the blood rushes to my head, and before I realize it, I'm across the room getting right in Shane's face.

"You're a real piece of shit standing back here, calling her names."

At first he's shocked. Then his eyes narrow. "You planning on doing something about it?"

My muscles relax as I slowly smile. I was looking for a way to let off some steam this morning, and I can tell he's about to give it to me. "Open your mouth again and find out."

Behind him, Charlie oohs tauntingly. "Look at you two," she remarks. "She's suddenly grown a pair, and you're over here waving yours around. I'm impressed. Gonna whip yours out, too, Shane?"

He smirks at her. He's probably dumb enough to let her egg him on. When he looks back at me, his mouth opens wide. Then he shuts it again and starts chuckling to himself.

Disappointed, I shake my head and turn away. Maybe he's not as stupid as he looks, or more likely he's just a pussy.

"She's still a crazy cunt, though," Shane mutters.

When my fist collides with his face, he grunts and goes down in a heap. I follow him, landing the next blow to his nose. Suddenly, hands are on me, trying to pull me off. Someone manages to lock my arm behind my back, and I lose my momentum long enough for Shane to get to his feet and ram his fist into my gut. He hits hard for a skinny douche bag. But I hit harder. Blood gushes from his nose as he pulls his arm back, getting ready to clock me in the face. Just as I get free, Shane's eyes go wide and he's thrown to the side, knocking over an end table, hitting the floor hard as the glass top shatters over him.

The room quiets. I straighten and notice everyone's stunned expressions directed at Raielle.

"What the fuck was that?" Charlie whispers, breaking the silence.

Appearing just as shocked as everyone else, Apollo shoots me a strained look as he grabs Raielle's arm. "Let's go," he says tightly. I scowl because I'm pretty sure he was the one holding me so Shane could take a shot.

My side is already sore as I follow them toward the door. I have a feeling I know exactly what happened, and I can hardly believe she managed to do that to him.

Charlie levels a finger at her as we walk past. "Did you all see that? She touched him and he went flying across the room. What the hell is she besides a freak?"

Apollo has her out the door now, but not before she hears, and I want nothing more than to turn around and finish what I started. But I stay with Raielle. She's important. They're not.

"How long have you been able to do that, exactly?" Apollo asks her once the elevator doors close behind us. I'm surprised to see that he still looks shaken.

She doesn't answer. She's standing stoically, no sign of emotion, staring at her reflection in the metal doors.

I tilt my head down close to her. "Ray?"

"Don't worry," she says calmly, her eyes not moving from the doors. "I'm not going to fall apart." I feel her hand on mine, and out of nowhere a hot pulse runs through me. The pain in my side where Shane landed his only punch disappears. Before I can say anything, the elevator doors slide open and she steps out, walking purposefully through the lobby toward the exit.

"This is bad," Apollo says as we follow behind her.

He's right. I was ready for her to break down. But now I realize that the complete absence of a reaction is much more alarming.

TEN

Raielle

T'S Friday, and unlike most students who keep their schedules light today, I have three lecture halls in a row. School is still my refuge. Sitting with a pen in my hand and my notebook open in front of me is familiar. Burying my emotions as I absorb the lecture is like a habit, a good one I don't want to break.

Lucas checks in with me throughout the day. This is the first time we've been apart since he arrived, and I miss him, but I'm also relieved not to have him hovering over me. It wasn't easy convincing him to go to his own classes instead of babysitting me. He agreed eventually, but the acting it took to convince him I was fine exhausted me. Now my classes are over, and I'm sitting at a table outside, waiting for Lucas to finish his day. Then I don't know where we'll go. The condo is not an option right now. If I never see Shane or Charlie again, that would be fine with me.

My phone rings and I startle, still not used to having it. It's Lucas, of course. He tells me that he has a late-afternoon group meeting for his current events class and asks me to meet him at the library afterward. I can hear the concern in his voice, and I keep my own light so he won't worry and offer to skip it, which I can tell is on the tip of his tongue. I worry him far too much. Right now, that feels like all I do.

When Charlie so coldly told us about Leo's death, I could feel myself slipping under. It was Lucas's determination to fight my demons for me and the way he went after Shane that helped me to keep them back myself. I can't keep doing this to him. He deserves a stronger person by his side. I've already put him through enough. Keeping my focus now is important because I can't throw away this second chance with him. There's too much I want to do with it.

But first, I have to get control of the power inside me, although I still have no idea how. Sheer force of will doesn't work. I know the energy is tied to my emotions, but controlling those has proven nearly impossible lately. I used to be able to turn it all off. When I was shuttled between foster homes and let down by my mother time after time, I revealed none of the pain and disappointment I felt. But I can't seem to do that anymore. Now a sea of emotion is always churning inside me, far too close to the surface.

When Shane was going to hurt Lucas, I could feel the power surging. I touched Shane's shoulder and let it flow into him, watching as it propelled him off Lucas. In that moment, I felt strong and in control, but I doubt I could reproduce that without another big dose of emotional turmoil, or maybe an earth-shattering orgasm. I can feel my face grow hot at just the thought of that.

"What are you thinking about and how can I get in on it?"

I look up to find Nikki staring at me.

"You're all flushed and smiley. Never mind. I think I already know." She sits down across from me. "I met him yesterday. The secret hot boyfriend. Hey, you finally got a phone." She points to it on the table. Then she picks it up. "I'm putting my number in it for you."

"He wasn't a secret." I rub my cheeks, trying uselessly to erase the telltale blush.

"Uh-huh. Whatever. Your business." She seems insulted as she puts my phone back down.

I sigh. "It's a long story. I wasn't purposely keeping him from you. I honestly haven't seen him since I've been here. Not until yesterday."

"Based on what I overheard, that was your fault, not his."

I start gathering my things. "Like I said. Long—"

"—story," she finishes for me, watching as I get ready to leave. "So, I know I ask you this every Friday and you turn me down flat, but I'm asking again anyway. Want to go to Crossroads? Jason is working, and you know what that means."

"Free drinks," I reply with a grin, because we have this conversation on a weekly basis. Since I don't drink, and I know Shane tends to hang out there, I always turn her down. But when I glance at my watch and see that I have over an hour before I need to be at the library, I consider it. Nikki seems annoyed with me, and I hate the way she's expecting me to say no. So, I surprise us both when I say, "Okay."

Her eyes bug out. "Seriously?"

Her enthusiasm has me wavering. "Um, yeah?"

She hears my hesitation and links her arm in mine. "Well, let's go then. I'm not giving you a chance to change your mind."

Crossroads is the neighborhood dive bar. It's a hangout for both college students and locals who are mostly former students. I've walked past it and caught the pungent odor of beer and sweat drifting out, but this is my first time entering its dark interior. Glancing around, I notice how crowded it already is. I'm guessing this is typical for happy hour on a Friday afternoon.

"Hey!" Jason yells to us from behind the bar.

Squeezing through the crowd, I notice the melodramatic mask of shock he's wearing when he spots me. "Raielle. What brings you to this fine establishment today?" he asks as we press up against the scuffed, curved edge of the bar. "Or maybe I'm hallucinating?"

I try to hide my involuntary smile. "If you want me to never come back here again, keep it up."

Jason shakes his head at me like a scolding schoolteacher. "Shutting up now because you, my girl, need a drink more than anyone I've ever met." Then he turns to Nikki. "Tequila shots?"

She nods once and turns serious eyes on me. "You're doing a shot. No argument."

But I don't intend to argue as I turn to look around the room. When I spot a pair of nearly black eyes aimed at me, my chest tightens. I grip the edge of the bar as Shane cuts a path through the crowd. Of course there's no sign of the fight on his face, which is now perfectly healed. I wonder who did that for him, since I doubt he could manage it himself.

Once he's in front of me, he says, "No drinking, little sister. You're underage."

"And you're an ass," I reply.

He smiles. "Yes, I am. Nice to meet you. With introductions out of the way, I've got something to say to you." His finger pokes me in the chest.

I wince. "I have nothing to say to you except don't touch me again."

A hand lands on his shoulder, and I notice that the guy Charlie was with this morning is standing behind him. "Lay off her, okay?" he says. Then he moves beside Shane and extends his hand toward me. "I don't think we've formally met. I'm Grant."

At first glance, Grant looks like the typical laid-back California guy, built but still lean with spiky brown hair lightened by the sun, and coffee-colored eyes. Even though he's grinning at me, I sense that he has an edge to him, like the friendly demeanor he's showing isn't actually his natural state. I notice he has some small scars on his face, one on his forehead and two white slashes along his cheek. He's taller than most of the guys here, standing a head above the crowd, and his brown eyes are assessing, staring at me hard enough to make me uncomfortable.

Not wanting to seem rude, I finally place my hand in his. He grips it firmly and holds on. "Nice to finally meet you," he says softly, leaning in like he's conveying something more intimate than a casual greeting. I wonder if this approach usually works for him, because it's mostly just creeping me out.

I reclaim my hand when Shane bumps me lightly with his elbow, capturing my attention. "Tell me how you did that today."

"Did what?" Nikki asks, her eyes widening as they land on Grant. She's already had the misfortune of meeting Shane when she came by the condo once.

I shoot him a silent warning to keep his mouth shut, but his bloodshot eyes tell me he's already lost whatever inhibitions he may possess, and he doesn't seem inclined to drop it.

"Tell me," he whispers, leaning his face close to mine. I want to back away from both him and Grant, but the crowd around us is too dense.

When I notice Nikki turning to get the drinks, I shoot him an answer I know he won't like. "I don't know."

He scowls. "You're going to be trouble. I knew it the first minute I saw you. Just like your mother." The stench of his breath makes me cringe, but before I can push him away, Grant does it for me.

"You're drunk, and you need to shut the fuck up," Grant warns.

I really couldn't care less what Shane thinks about me, but I can't help wondering why he would bring her up. "What about my mother?" I ask him.

He shakes Grant off. "Your mother is the reason mine is dead. She kept him away from us. If we'd all been together that day, nothing would have happened to my family."

Or you'd all be dead, I think. "I'm sorry about your family, Shane."

"Yeah, sure. You know he's just using you, right? He doesn't care about you or else he would have tried to see you at some point in the last eighteen years."

His comment does what he intends. It hurts. It irritates the fissure inside me that existed long before he came along. But I can't argue with Shane, because I don't know that he isn't right. I don't understand what he means when he says my father is using me, though. If anything, it's the opposite. I'm the one using him. I don't feel anything for him. I'm not sticking around because I want to get to know him. But I do need him. That's the only reason I'm still here.

I'm pretty sure my father doesn't love me, and I realize how seriously messed up that is. Maybe he and I are more alike than I thought. Maybe cold and emotionless behavior is a family trait. That's why only one person in my entire life has ever broken through my walls and shown me any love. And how did I repay him? I disappeared and put him through hell.

When a lump starts to lodge in my throat and my energy starts to build inside me, I work hard to push it down. I'm so tired of all these emotions that keep assaulting me, but I can't manage to tune them out anymore.

After a moment, Nikki appears, holding a tequila shot under my nose. "Cheers," she teases with raised eyebrows.

Before I can think better of it, I take the shot glass and swallow the tequila in one gulp. Nikki's shocked eyes are on me as the burn kicks in, and I start to cough. When I can't seem to stop, I feel the pressure of a large hand at my back as Grant says, "Breathe, Raielle." And I do, pulling in a breath and glancing around the bar with watery eyes.

"That was good," I croak, and everyone, including Shane starts to laugh at me. As I'm watching them, the spark of energy burns out as an odd warmth loosens the pressure inside me. It's surprising how quickly one shot of tequila is affecting me, and I want more. I want more of this feeling and less of the intensity swirling inside me.

"Want to do another one?" I ask Nikki.

She gives me a skeptical look.

"Make it four," Shane says. "On me." He tries to hand some bills to her, but she waves his money away.

"Her boyfriend is the bartender," I explain to him.

He glances at me and then looks down at the floor. "I was kind of expecting you to bust my balls when I said that shit before. Why aren't you?" he asks, meeting my eyes again.

I shrug. "I can't get mad at you for telling the truth."

His jaw works for a minute before he meets my eyes again. "I shouldn't have said any of that. I'm sorry."

Tilting my head at him, I'm surprised by his apology. I don't know if it's sincere or if it's the alcohol talking, but it doesn't matter. Time will tell if he intends to stop being an ass to me.

"You know that most of us can't do what you did today," Shane says. Then he holds a hand up. "Strike that. No one can do what you did today."

I just look at him, understanding that even among people who are supposed to share my ability, I'm a freak, just like Charlie said. Maybe no one here can help me, and I'm fooling myself by thinking otherwise. I'm not exactly fitting in here, which means I don't really belong anywhere. Right on time, Nikki appears with another shot and I down it, waiting for my senses to dull even more.

"Let's start a tab and get a table." Nikki grabs my arm. "I think Jason is going to get in trouble if we cop any more freebies off him."

Before long, Nikki stakes a claim at a table by the door, and Shane offers to get us more drinks. Grant pulls out a chair for me. "You and I need to talk," he says once we sit down. Shane is at the bar and Nikki's attention is on a football game playing on the television mounted on the wall.

"Why? I don't know you," I say rudely, plopping down on the wooden chair harder than I intended.

"Sure you do. I'm Grant." He smiles innocently.

I squint up at him. "You know what I mean. Do you work with my father?"

"Sometimes," he answers vaguely.

I lean forward and rest my elbows on the table. "Okay, Grant." I stare into his light brown eyes, which are focused on me and lit with amusement. "On a scale of one to ten, how good a healer are you?"

His brow wrinkles.

"Come on," I prod as the lightness I felt after the first shot magnifies, loosening my tongue even more. "Some of us are stronger than others. I see your scars. So, I think you're closer to a one than a ten if you can't heal yourself."

He mimics me, placing his elbow on the table. "You think I'm not strong enough to heal my own scars?"

"That's exactly what I think. I could heal them for you." I think of Leo's scars and swallow back the regret, focusing on Grant instead and on trying to knock the cocky grin off his face. Boldly, I place my hand on his forearm while he watches me, but I frown as the energy once again betrays me.

He takes my hand in his large rough one. "First of all, I don't want my scars healed. They're mine and I want to keep them. Secondly, alcohol dulls your powers. I doubt you'd have much effect on my scars right now."

I take my hand back as a puzzle piece fits into place. "That's another reason why she did it."

"Who?"

"My mother. Why she drank." I glance up to find him looking at me oddly, but I focus on his scars again. "Why do you want to keep them?" I ask.

He doesn't answer at first. Then his gaze intensifies and he quietly says, "They're reminders of my mistakes."

My eyes travel over the tiny network of white lines that crisscross his cheek and brow. Before I can ask him about those mistakes, Shane appears with four more shots and some beers. I know I should probably stop now. I haven't eaten since breakfast, and it's becoming hard to focus, but I like the fuzzy way my brain feels. My worries seem far away, and I want to keep them there. So I do another shot and sit back, letting the burn flow through me, enjoying the numbness that continues to grow.

Jason is on a break. He's sitting with us now, and he has Nikki on his lap. Grant is sitting a little too close to me, but his attention has shifted to Shane. I'm watching them all through a haze and sipping the bitter beer Jason placed in front of me.

When my phone buzzes in my pocket, it takes me a moment to pull it out and remember how to answer it. When I finally do, I hear Lucas's voice in my ear. "Where are you?"

I glance at the clock on the screen, but I can't seem to read it. I guess I must be late, though. "Sorry, I lost track of time," I say, holding a finger to my ear to block out the noise.

"Where are you?" he asks again.

"Um…" It takes me a moment to remember the name of the bar. "At Crossroads," I finally reply.

"Crossroads?" he asks, his voice getting louder.

"Nikki's here," I explain. "And Jason, Shane, and Grant, too." At the sound of her name, Nikki glances at me and sticks her tongue out, making a funny face.

I giggle.

"Are you drinking?" he asks, sounding astonished at the possibility.

"Yes, a lot," I answer and laugh again. "I'm sorry I forgot about meeting you. I'll come right now."

"No," he says quickly. "I'll come to you. Just stay where you are."

I nod, but realize that he can't see me. Then I hang up and close my eyes, enjoying the way the room is swaying, and I imagine this must be what it feels like to be on a boat, something I've never done but always wanted to do growing up in San Diego. I'm not sure how much time passes before Grant's voice says, "Why don't you let me take you home."

I nod, thinking sleep sounds like a very good idea. He helps me up from my chair, and I bat his hands away. "I'm fine," I complain, but as soon as he releases me, the room starts to sway, or maybe I do. His arms come around me, holding me up easily, like I weigh nothing at all.

"Good night," he tells everyone, and I halfheartedly wave in their direction as I float past.

He secures me against his side as he maneuvers us to the door. Once we're out on the sidewalk, I inhale the cool night air and watch car headlights zooming past. Grant places his hands on my shoulders and turns me to face him. He's looking very serious as his eyes travel over my face. I know he's handsome, with his classic features and his tall build, but he does nothing for me. He isn't even a close second to Lucas.

When his hand starts to trace along my cheek, it takes a moment for me to recognize the look in his eyes and to understand that I shouldn't be standing here like this with him. But before I can move away, I hear my name called. Not my actual name, but the nickname that only one person has for me.

I turn to find Lucas walking toward us, his long legs eating up the sidewalk.

"Hey." I smile, so happy to see him.

"I told you to wait for me." He's stopped in front of me now, but his eyes are on the person beside me.

"This is Grant," I tell him. "He was going to take me home."

He directs a hard look at Grant as he reaches for my hand. "Well, I'm here now. I can take my girlfriend home."

I feel one of Grant's hands still heavy on my shoulder. "If she were my girlfriend, I wouldn't leave her on her own in a bar. I took care of her, though." His hand rubs my shoulder before releasing me. "You can count on me to be here when you're not."

I turn curious eyes on Grant, wondering if I heard him right. But he just smiles at me. "Good night, Raielle." Then he goes back inside.

Lucas's stormy gaze stays on the door for a moment before he begins moving us quickly down the sidewalk. I get the feeling he's angry with me. "I'm sorry I forgot to meet you at the library."

He says nothing in response. Silently, we walk along the quiet street with him pulling me by the hand. When we reach his truck, before I can get inside, he lifts me up and places me on the seat, shutting the door behind me.

It's hard keeping my eyes open, but they follow him as he walks around and slides in on his side. He doesn't say anything at first. The silence is heavy as he runs his hands through his hair. I watch the shiny locks slip through his long fingers. His eyes are dark when he turns them on me. "Have you ever been drunk before?" he finally asks.

I shake my head, and it feels like my brain is jiggling inside my skull.

He angles himself toward me. "Why did you drink tonight?"

I shrug. "Are you mad at me?"

His concerned gaze travels over me. "No. I'm not mad at you." He sighs and faces forward again. "Let's go home."

I lean my head back on the headrest, close my tired eyes, and correct him. "I don't have a home."

The low hum of the motor must have put me to sleep, because the next thing I know, Lucas is rummaging in my bag for the keys and then opening the door. "We won't stay here," he says quietly. "We'll just get your stuff and go back to my apartment."

I haven't had a chance to tell him that Shane apologized, and we don't have to feel chased off. But I'm too tired to form the words as I feel his arm wrap beneath my knees. He's carrying me across the living room and into the bedroom.

"I can walk." I laugh quietly at the way he keeps manhandling me, wondering if I'm really that far gone, or if he's being annoyed and impatient. Screw him if it's the latter, because I'm entitled to get drunk at least once in my life. The alcohol dulls my senses and my powers perfectly. But I'm not so wasted that I don't understand how dangerous it would be to crave this feeling too much. I've seen how that works out.

Lucas's strong arms jostle me as he pushes open the door to my bedroom. That's when something occurs to me. Alcohol dulls my power. I can't feel any energy burning inside me. This is the answer to my problem. We shouldn't miss this opportunity.

A moment later, I'm set gently down on the bed. When Lucas starts to step away, I wrap my arms around his neck and lean up to kiss him. As our lips meet, I feel a familiar shiver go through me. It seems that being drunk off my ass doesn't dull my reaction to him. If anything, it heightens it. Running my fingers through his hair, I pull him down to me, needing more of him. He groans when his arms wrap around me and his tongue slips into my mouth. This feels so good. I never want him to stop touching me this way, and kissing me so thoroughly. Reaching down, I begin to undo the button on his jeans. But his hand closes over mine, halting me.

"No," he says, his voice quiet but firm. "We can't."

He doesn't understand. I lean back to look at him. "We can. Alcohol dulls my power. Now is the perfect time."

His eyes search mine, and I can see he doesn't get it.

"My energy," I explain. "Alcohol lessens it. If we have sex now, I won't be able to heal myself afterward. Please, Lucas. I want to."

He continues to stare at me, but I can't tell what he's thinking. Then he starts to shake his head. "You've had too much to drink."

My eyes widen in disbelief. He's refusing me? Doesn't he understand? I grab his face again and press my mouth on his. Even as the room starts to spin and a wave of nausea hits me, I continue to throw myself at him, clutching at his shirt, trying to pull it off. But he's not cooperating.

"Stop, Ray," he pleads, peeling my arms away.

His expression is resolute, and I can't think of one good reason for him to say no. Why be a gentleman about this when I don't want him to be? Unless he doesn't want me. Maybe I've finally become too much for him to deal with. Maybe he spent the day regretting what we did last night.

I slump down onto the bed. "You wouldn't be taking advantage of me. I don't see why you have to make a big deal about this." I can feel the tears spilling from my eyes, and somewhere deep inside I know I'm making a fool of myself. That's when the nausea hits again, and I clamp my hand over my mouth.

"I'm gonna be sick," I mumble, brushing past him and dashing into the bathroom. I barely make it to the toilet before my stomach revolts against me. It's only alcohol that comes up. I've hardly eaten today. I retch again and again, feeling completely miserable when Lucas's hand pulls my hair away from my damp face and starts to rub my back.

"I'm disgusting," I say and then moan. "Please go away."

He chuckles behind me, but he doesn't leave. "Been here. Done this. More than once. When you get it all up, you'll feel better."

In answer to that, I throw up again. Lucas is being attentive, and mortification over my behavior is starting to settle over me. I'm not sure how long we stay this way, but I'm exhausted by the time my stomach stops clenching.

"I'm sorry," I say, wiping my mouth, groaning in misery as I sit back on the cool tile floor.

"For what?"

I stare down at the shiny swirls in the marble. "For throwing myself at you that way. To say I'm embarrassed would be a serious understatement."

He laughs, reaching out to lay his hand over my thigh. "Don't be embarrassed. Having you throw yourself at me is on my fantasy list."

My ears perk up. "You have a fantasy list? A list of fantasies that include me?"

He rubs circles on my thigh with his thumb. "I do. And when we get around to working our way through it, I want you to remember."

Feeling even worse, I glance away. "I only wanted…" Pausing, I try to find the right words. "I want to be with you again, but I don't want you to be afraid of hurting me, and I don't want to keep healing myself. What

114

I want is to be normal. I mean, this is ridiculous, right? I'm ridiculous."

Lucas's arms come around me, and I can't believe I'm losing it again in front of him after telling myself I was going to stop doing this. But his comfort helps. It always does, and I lean into him.

"Remember when we looked at the picture of us on your phone? Remember how you said it made you feel?" he asks.

When I don't answer, he replies for me. "Special."

"Special needs," I mumble.

His chest vibrates with his soft laughter, and I can't help it, I smile. "Thanks," I say when he stills again.

"You're welcome." He turns his face to mine, and I clamp my hand over my mouth. "I really need to brush my teeth and take a shower—a long one."

His eyes fill with amusement as he pulls us to our feet. "You sure you're okay for a shower?"

I nod, spreading my arms out to show him how steady I am on my feet.

"Okay. You pass. Don't be too long." He grins. Then he looks at me for a long moment before walking out.

Even though Lucas is being understanding, I still feel flushed with embarrassment as I slowly peel off my clothes. Then I gulp down a glass of water before spending at least ten minutes brushing my teeth and rinsing with mouthwash. Starting to feel human again, but no less humiliated, I turn on the shower and wait for the water to warm before stepping beneath the spray. After scrubbing myself clean, I just stand there for a while with my eyes closed, letting the drops pelt me as my mind reluctantly wanders over the evening, cringing at most of it, and surprised to find I can't remember all of it clearly.

When the shower door clicks, I turn, shocked to see Lucas standing there without a stitch of clothing on. My eyes travel down the length of his body, going back to his hand where he holds a condom between his fingers.

"I changed my mind," he says, stepping inside.

I blink at him, surprised, feeling my skin flush under his hot gaze.

"Why?" I ask.

He takes a step closer, letting the water hit him as his hand reaches out and brushes against my arm, causing my body to hum with awareness. "Because I want you, and I have an idea."

I'm suddenly apprehensive, confused by the combination of lust and determination I see in his eyes. But I don't have time to think about it before he closes the remaining distance and covers my mouth with his as his tongue immediately seeks mine. I feel his fingers running up my back to the nape of my neck. His other hand is at my hip, pulling me against him.

He begins to urge me backward toward the wall of the shower. When my skin comes in contact with the cold marble tile, he nudges my legs apart with his knees. My eyes widen in shock when he lifts me up, wrapping my legs around him. My breasts are level with his face, and his lips clamp down on one nipple. Pleasure swirls inside me as my arms reach up to tighten around his neck. He licks over my other nipple, causing me to sigh and arch toward him.

Warm water cascades over us, and he presses me into the wall, supporting all my weight while he runs his tongue over my skin, making me crazy with want. I don't know when or how he gets the condom on, but soon his eyes are burning into me, silently searching for something, maybe some cue that I'm ready.

I manage to pull in a quick breath of anticipation before he seals his lips to mine and pushes inside me. The pain is sharp again and I cry out, but he smothers the sound, his lips never leaving my mouth, and after a moment, he begins to move. The pain burns hot and only fades when he pulls out. But then he buries himself deep within me again and reaches a hand down to the place where our bodies meet, using his fingers to flood the hurt with a wave of desire. A soft moan escapes my lips, causing his other hand to grip me harder, digging into my skin as he takes control, grabbing hold of my hips and bringing me down on him in quick, successive movements.

There are no murmurs of sorry from him this time, no hesitance or fear of hurting me. I only feel his want and our need for each other overpowering everything else. He seems almost desperate, holding nothing back, and that fuels the fire inside me. My fingers fist in his hair, anchoring me as his rhythm spikes and the pressure builds.

He looks up suddenly, his eyes clashing with mine. Their intensity is devastating. When my climax rips through me, I cry out, clenching around him, tilting my head back into the wall as my muscles tighten. He groans and begins pulsing inside me. My eyes close as a sweet tension ripples through me, and I try to draw it out, feeling each sensation as it crests and wanes.

Listening to his ragged breathing, my grip on him begins to loosen, and I thread my fingers through his wet hair. The weight of his body pushes against mine as his head falls onto my shoulder. I'm exhausted and utterly boneless, like a rag doll in his arms.

My eyes flutter open when I feel him leaning back to turn off the water. "Keep your legs around me," he says.

Still holding me, he wraps a towel around us and walks us into the bedroom. After drying me off, he lowers me onto the bed, follows me in, and pulls the comforter up over us. My body is still tingling, and I can hardly believe what we just did. I want nothing more than to enjoy the after part where we hold each other. But I'm stiff in his arms. I feel sober now, and I'm anticipating the worst.

He seems to understand. "By the end of tonight, I'm going to solve this. I promise," he says against my ear.

Closing my eyes, I only nod. I don't know what he's planning, but I hope he's right. My body is sated and after a time, I begin to relax. I start to think it may not happen as his steady breathing comforts me. But just as I'm falling asleep, the unwanted warmth begins to build low in my stomach. Tensing, my eyes pop open.

"Shh," he says beside me as his hand moves down my body. I suck in a breath when I feel his fingers slipping between my legs. He begins a gentle massage and I curl toward him, pressing against his hand. When he shifts above me and slowly slides inside me, the energy threatening to spread is washed away by the growing tension. I'm still sore from the first time, but he manages to bring me to climax easily, whispering the sweetest words in my ear. I fall asleep in his arms, feeling cherished and loved.

When it happens again hours later, he's there filling me, rocking gently, building the pressure slowly, and loving me so tenderly it brings tears to my eyes. I don't know why my energy burst from me that first time or why the healing is starting on its own now. I only know that my power has gone haywire and Lucas's remedy seems to be working.

By morning, he has accomplished what he set out to. He took control. He made my body surrender to him.

ELEVEN

Lucas

'VE never seen anything like the raw pain that filled Raielle's eyes last night. She's always so self-possessed and in control, but she completely lost it. Does the fact that I liked it make me an asshole? She was being real with me for a change and letting me see all the crap she usually buries. Even though it took God only knows how many drinks to make her open up, I got a glimpse inside. When she cried about wanting to be normal, I felt like I'd been slapped. She's not normal, that's true enough. But who the fuck cares? How can she not realize how amazing she is?

When she was in the shower last night, I sat out in the bedroom with her words playing over in my head, and I knew I had to show her how much I want her. I thought I'd already done that, but when I turned her down I could see all her insecurities showing through. She's just waiting for me to get fed up and walk away. I think a part of her wants me to because she believes it's inevitable anyway. But she has to understand that's not happening.

I hand her a glass of water and a couple of aspirin, which she gratefully accepts. "Still good?" I ask, watching for any sign that her body wants to undo all my hard work.

"Yeah." She laughs, looking embarrassed, and hugs the blanket to herself.

After everything we did last night, she still feels modest around me. She's so fucking adorable.

I want to ask her how she ended up being drinking buddies with Shane, and who this Grant jackass is, but I don't want to wreck the nice morning-after vibe we've got going. Besides, she wouldn't have given Grant the time of day if she wasn't drunk. The fact that he was about to take advantage of her condition when I walked up on them outside the bar tells me a lot about him, and none of it's good.

"Let's drive out to the beach," I suggest. "It's the weekend. We deserve a day to just chill and enjoy the California sunshine."

Her smile brightens. "We can take the Porsche. The top rolls down."

"When did you get your license?" I ask, realizing that the Porsche Apollo took the keys out of must have been hers.

She laughs ruefully. "I never did. My father somehow got me one. I'm a good driver, though, despite what all those speeding tickets say."

I look at her, wondering if she's serious. Then I picture her in it. "Do you have any idea how sexy the idea of you driving a Porsche is?" I ask.

"Is that on your fantasy list?" she asks with a twinkle in her eye.

"It is now." I watch as she covers herself with a T-shirt and putters around the room, gathering her clothes.

"So what else is on this list? Is shower sex?" she asks, angling a look at me over her shoulder.

I grin at the way *shower sex* sounds falling from her lips. "Yup. Check." I make an invisible checkmark in the air.

Shaking her head, she smiles. "Tell me another one."

"Sorry." I turn serious. "I can't give you advance notice. That would lessen the impact."

She rolls her eyes at me as she grabs her hairbrush off the dresser.

Suddenly, it gets to me, us just being together doing regular things like getting dressed, making plans for the day, flirting. I like it. I want more of it.

She's about to head into the bathroom when she pauses and turns around to face me, pulling her bottom lip between her teeth and furrowing her brow, making that little crease form on her forehead.

"About my drinking last night," she begins. "I want you to know that I don't plan on making a habit of it. I'm not going to be like my mother."

I walk over to where she's standing. "Everyone needs to blow off some steam sometimes. I didn't read anything into it." I know she's the one who's worried about turning into her mother.

She nods, seeming unsure.

I tap her on the nose. "Hey, it's just you and me today. We're going to forget everything else. Promise me."

"I promise." She smiles at me before disappearing inside the bathroom.

Once I hear the shower turn on, I'm tempted to join her, but I have something else I need to do. We hadn't planned on spending the night here, but since we have, I'm taking this opportunity to talk to Shane.

Wandering out into the living room, I notice his bedroom door is shut. I knock loudly. Then I do it again until his muffled voice yells something from inside. A moment later, it swings open and he squints at me.

"What do you want? A rematch? Little sister and I talked. We're good now."

He's only got sweats on, and his skinny chest is covered in strange swirling black tattoos, reminding me of wrought-iron gates. "I want to talk to you about something else. But we can cover yesterday, too."

Shane smirks at me. "You know, I overheard what you two were up to last night, and as Raielle's big brother, it's my job to protect her innocence. So from now on, you're going to need my permission to have sleepovers."

I narrow my eyes at him. "Were you born this full of shit?"

He laughs and edges past me, going into the kitchen. "Look, like I said, Raielle and I are good. Don't say anything to me that's going to fuck it up. I wouldn't want to have to hurt you again."

I follow him. "Ray forgives too easily, and you weren't the only one doing the hurting."

His lips press together.

I'm standing across from him on the other side of the kitchen island.

"If you or your friends talk about her again the way you did yesterday, we're going to keep having problems."

He throws me an amused look. "Problems?"

Laying my hands flat on the counter, I lean in toward him. "You think I'm kidding?"

He shrugs, backing away slightly. "I couldn't care less, actually. I only know that what she did to me yesterday isn't normal."

The band around my chest tightens. Normal is exactly what Raielle wanted to be last night. Normalcy, and her lack of it, keeps getting thrown in her face. "Is there really no one like her?" I ask, getting to the reason why I knocked on his door in the first place, hoping he can answer me without being a complete wiseass.

He crosses his arms over his chest and studies me. He seems to be debating what he should say. Then his face relaxes and he goes back to hunting through the cabinets. "I don't know of anyone like her. That's the truth. Most of us are like me," he says, shrugging, pulling a box of cereal down, "able to heal cuts, broken bones, some diseases that aren't too severe, and that's about it."

I'm surprised that he's just admitted he's not that powerful.

"Others are like Grant. He can cure most anything, unless you're at death's door. Then he can trade your life for someone else's. He can heal himself, too, which a lot of us can't do. Now, my father, he's a step above Grant. He doesn't need someone to be hurt or sick for his power to kick in. He can shoot some energy into you at will, like a little charge just to make you feel good."

"What about Ray?" I ask, wondering where she falls on his scale.

Shane scratches his chin as he answers. "She's seems to be as strong as my father, only she's had no training and hardly any experience. Raielle has more energy inside her than she can handle, and that's dangerous. She's too powerful to be so emotionally unstable."

My eyes narrow. "She's not emotionally unstable."

"Po-tay-to, po-tah-to," he says indifferently.

I brush off my annoyance as worry pinches at me. "Can your father help her learn to control it or not?" I ask.

He throws some dry cereal into his mouth. "If it's in his own interest to do it, he can, and I think it is. He's getting older. Word is he's slipping and can't do as much as he used to. And if he can't heal the tough cases anymore, he's going to need her. If he wants her help, I'm betting he'll have to help her in return."

"Is he slipping?" I ask. I don't bother telling him that she'll take his help, but returning the favor is unlikely if I have anything to say about it.

Shane cackles as he pulls a carton of milk from the refrigerator and pours it into his bowl. "Like he'd ever admit it if he was. But I know the money isn't coming in like it used to. Since my dad's a greedy son of a bitch, I don't think he's cutting back his caseload on purpose."

The ripple of dislike I have for her father starts to multiply and spread. I wonder if he needs her more than she needs him. "Do you think your father would ever hurt her?" I ask.

He glances up at me, surprised at my question. But then the smirk appears. "No more than anyone else has." He takes the cereal bowl, walks past me, and disappears inside his room.

His answers do nothing to ease my worries; they have the opposite effect. Shane doesn't hold much affection for his father. You can see it on his face, in the grimace he wears when he talks about him. But it's hard to know what to believe with him or anyone else she's got around her right now.

I'm about to go back to the bedroom to see if Raielle is ready when two things happen at once. She appears, stepping out of the room in a light blue sundress that hugs her slim body and matches the necklace I gave her, and the front door bursts open as two big guys in suits come barging in, saying something about a lockdown. One of them has long black hair touching the top of his wide shoulders. The other one has a shiny bald head, and they're both eyeing Raielle.

I move toward her as my pulse rate rockets, but when Shane appears in his doorway, looking completely bored and saying, "Not again," I go from alert to suspicious.

"Let's go," the bald one says. "Your father wants everyone at the house."

"What's going on?" Raielle asks.

"Every few months, Dad claims there's some kind of threat. So he calls us all to the house where we have to stay until he decides it's safe for us to leave."

"What kind of threat?" I ask.

He rolls his eyes. "Oh, you know. The usual paranoid crap he's always going on about. Honestly, I think he's just lonely because he has no friends."

I look at the *Men In Black* wannabes. "So, there is no threat?"

Shane gets my attention back when he points to his head and makes tiny circles with his finger. "The old man is losing it. Getting high on his own juice a little too often. Didn't anyone tell you? Zap yourself too many times and it turns you loony tunes. Take that as a warning, kids," he says, aiming his finger at Raielle.

I reach for her hand. "Look," I say to the two guys filling the entryway, "is there a real threat or not?"

The bald one looks at me. "I don't know, and I don't care. One way or another, I have to get you to the house." He pauses. "Now."

"Is everyone getting a personal escort?" Raielle asks, and their impatience grows.

"No. You kids are special." The dark-haired one smiles tightly at her, and she edges closer to me.

"It's no use," Shane says, pulling a shirt over his head. "It's easier to go with them, enjoy the buffet and socialize for a few hours, until his control-freak moment is over and he lets us leave."

"Buffet?" Raielle asks, as if she couldn't have heard him right.

He nods. "Nyla always puts together a good spread for these things."

She starts to laugh. "So, we're being forcibly escorted to breakfast?"

Shane glances at his watch. "Actually, it's brunch."

I release a frustrated breath. For once, I'd like to make plans with Raielle that don't get all fucked up. "Should I stage a revolt?" I ask hopefully, not wanting to go along with this.

She shakes her head. "Let's just go with them. I need to talk to my father anyway."

Raielle

WE'VE met a lot of people since we've been here, and I can't remember all their names, but I know they're healers and they work with my father. They all seem to know me, and they're either wary of me or way too enthusiastic to meet me. Both reactions rub me the wrong way and make me uncomfortable.

Charlie and Grant are here, too. For some reason, Lucas stiffens and looks angry every time Grant talks to me. Since I probably look much the same every time Charlie throws a flirty glance Lucas's way, this is as far as we could get from the relaxing beach day we'd planned.

The room buzzes with conversation. It's interesting that most of the healers here are young like us. I wonder why there are no older ones. There must be older healers.

Shane is camped out in the corner with his own group of friends that he introduced to us when we first got here. There's Christopher with his blond faux-hawk and skinny jeans. Next to him is Jenna, a full-figured petite girl whose chest is getting most of Christopher's attention. Silently pacing behind them is a tall, willowy brunette who has barely spoken a word or cracked a smile all day. I've already forgotten her name.

It's been nearly three hours. There's no sign of my father, and I still want to talk to him. Lucas and I are sitting in a window seat inside the large living room. A deck of cards lies between us. He's been trying to teach me to play poker, but so far, I suck at it. My mind keeps wandering. I can't stop thinking about last night. It feels like I have a permanent blush on my face. The closeness I feel to Lucas, and the way we're attuned to each other, is making it hard to concentrate on anything but him.

Lucas is dealing out the cards again when raised voices catch our attention. Shane and Christopher seem to be arguing. Lucas pauses with a card in his hand and one of his eyebrows quirks up as he eavesdrops.

"Shut the fuck up," Shane snaps. "You don't know shit about her."

I watch them covertly, hoping they're not talking about me, as Christopher straightens in his chair, preparing to lob a comment back. "Neither do you. From what I can see, you don't know shit about anything."

I glance at Shane to see his reaction, but to my surprise he just chuckles. "I guess that's why you asked me to hook you up last week. Because I don't know shit about anything. Including the phone number that blonde told me to give you."

Shane is slurring his words. He and his friends must be drinking, although I haven't seen any alcohol around.

Christopher's eyes widen. "You serious, dude?"

Shane just stares at him.

"Come on," he pleads. "I was kidding around. I didn't mean anything by it."

Exhaling dramatically, Shane says, "Be nicer to me or I may have to cut you off."

"But I need to hear what's on the rest of that tool's fantasy list," Christopher whispers loudly. "Oh wait, I forgot. No advance notice." He bends over with laughter. "That shit was too funny."

Lucas's gaze clashes with mine. I watch as his expression hardens and his eyes ice over.

"Shh," Shane warns before he starts cracking up.

Lucas turns and Shane notices, averting his gaze, becoming overly interested in a painting on the wall.

Slowly getting to his feet, Lucas walks toward them. He seems to have the attention of everyone in the room. A wave of panic hits me, and I wonder if Shane's friends will come to his aid when Lucas makes good on the threat in his eyes.

"What are you two chatting about over here?" Lucas asks, keeping his voice low.

Shane looks up at him. "The weather, mostly."

Lucas's shoulders tense. "Have you been spying on us, you pervert?"

"Fuck," Christopher mutters.

Boldly, Shane faces Lucas. "Why would I want to spy on you? You're not that interesting." Then he turns to Christopher. "That's right, Ray. Now, baby," he says in a breathless falsetto voice that sends Christopher into juvenile giggles.

My mouth falls open. Lucas grabs Shane by the front of his shirt and pushes him up against the wall. "Just when I thought you might be decent, you turn around and show me what a little bitch you really are."

Rather than helping Shane, Christopher and the rest of their group back away. I get to my feet as my hands curl into tight, nervous fists. From the corner of my eye, I spot Grant with a couple of friends he's been talking to most of the day. They start trying to calm Lucas down. A part of me is hoping Lucas will punch Shane when the room grows quiet, and I see heads turning toward the door.

"Raielle, could you come with me please," Nyla says. Then her gaze goes to Lucas, still holding Shane by his shirt collar. Her eyes widen. "Is there a problem here?"

Grant clears his throat. "It seems Shane is still hiding cell phones in people's rooms and spying on them."

"You fucker," Lucas says, pushing at him again. Shane winces and scans the room nervously, looking for help, but not finding any.

My hand goes to my mouth. The thought of Shane listening to us this whole time makes me want to throw up.

"Maturity isn't Shane's strong point," Nyla comments. "Raielle?" She eyes me expectantly.

Since I want to be as far away from Shane as possible, I head toward her, looking back at Lucas to see if he's coming with me. He shoves Shane hard once more before releasing him abruptly and walking calmly in my direction. I watch as Shane sinks to the floor, yanking down on his wrinkled shirt.

"Just Raielle," Nyla clarifies.

"Just no," Lucas says glibly, and I can feel the residual anger radiating off him.

She glances at me, like she's waiting for me to convince Lucas to stay behind, but I don't. Finally she exhales an exasperated breath and turns toward the hallway, gesturing for us to follow.

"I can't believe he was listening to us," I whisper to Lucas.

He takes my hand, threading his fingers through mine. "You were right about him."

Nyla glances back at us, probably wondering what we're whispering about. "Did you call Social Services that day Leo came here?" I ask her.

Her face falls dramatically. "I did. But you must know, they don't work that quickly. We all feel terrible about it." Then she turns and continues down another hallway. Lucas squeezes my hand reassuringly. When Nyla reaches the end of the hall, she opens a door that leads to a steep stairwell.

"Where are we going?" Lucas asks.

"To the clinic downstairs. There's a patient Raielle's father would like her to see."

Lucas darts me a look, and I try to keep the anxiety out of my expression for him, even though I have no idea what we're walking into. After that scene with Shane, my emotions are all over the place. So is my energy, which I can feel flowing freely inside me, barely restrained.

Holding the banister, we all descend slowly with Nyla at the front and Lucas behind me. Once we reach the bottom, bright fluorescents light up a white hallway that has several doors leading off it. The place has an antiseptic smell, and I startle when a woman dressed in hospital scrubs steps out of one of the rooms and continues past us down the hall.

As we look around, Nyla turns to me. "These are our most critical patients. They have no hope but us. Their doctors have already told them there's nothing they can do. So we keep them here at the clinic, making them as comfortable as possible, until we're able to help them."

I glance sharply at her. "You mean until you find a volunteer to..."
She nods.

Eyeing all the closed doors, I ask, "How many patients are here now?"

"We have six who are waiting. Your father likes to keep them close so that when a volunteer is found, he can perform the healing as soon as possible. When a patient is too sick to travel, that causes problems. Your father prefers for them to come to him."

My hands clasp together and I begin to feel the tension building inside me. "I told my father I couldn't do these kinds of healings."

Nyla smiles again, calm and serene as always. "Don't worry. He knows. This way."

"Ray?" Lucas asks quietly.

I shake my head at him, cutting off whatever he intends to say as my nerves sprout wings. The reason I'm here is to learn from my father, and I can't do that if I refuse to take part in anything. At least I have to see what this is about.

Lucas's mouth is a tight, straight line as he watches Nyla disappear into one of the rooms. I follow, my pace slowing as I approach the door.

When I peer inside, I see my father standing beside a hospital bed, looking down at what appears to be a young girl swallowed up inside the blankets. Stepping into the room, I look closer and see that it's a child who seems close to Penelope's age. She has dark red hair that fans across the pillow. Her face is dotted with freckles, except below her eyes, where her dusky skin hints at illness.

I pull in a breath when my stomach drops and my energy sparks.

"Try to control it, Raielle," my father says softly.

My eyes meet his bright green ones, and he smiles at me. "Rein it in. You can do it, sweetheart."

I recall the times my mother said something similar when I was young and just starting to learn about my ability. I concentrate on holding back the power that wants to build. But then I nearly gag as the nausea hits. My power is turning on me. It wants to be used, and I'm denying it. Keeping my breathing steady, I try to push the sensations down deep inside. Finally, my stomach settles and it passes. When my eyes focus again, I realize Lucas has his arm around me, and my father and Nyla are watching me closely.

"Very good," my father says. "Now touch her and let it grow again."

"No," Lucas immediately says.

"I won't let anything happen to her," he assures Lucas.

"Tell me why I'm doing this?" I ask, understanding that this girl is too sick to be cured.

"Just trust me," my father says.

But I don't trust him, and he probably knows that.

"What's wrong with her?" Lucas asks.

"That's what I'd like Raielle to tell us," he answers evenly, his calm unbothered by our reluctant attitudes and questions. "I'm not asking her to heal this girl. I simply want her to learn about her power. That's all."

I want the same thing. So I nod my agreement.

Beside me, Lucas's frustration is palpable. I wait, but he says nothing. I know he understands why I need to do this, even if he doesn't like it.

After a moment, I approach the bed, holding the energy back as my eyes travel along her tiny frame. My heart squeezes just looking at her, and I feel nervous, almost jittery, no longer sure of myself or my power. But I push past the fear, hoping the energy obeys me and if it doesn't, that my father will step in.

Reaching out my hand, I place it on the bare skin of her wrist. Then I let go and swiftly the familiar coil unwinds. A calm settles over me as it grows and flows out into the little girl. It takes a moment for me to understand the darkness I find inside her. Breathing out, I push further. My energy is settling in her bloodstream, telling me that she has some kind of blood disease. It's cancer, I think, and it's advanced.

I wait for the coil to snap back, to resist my power, telling me she can't be healed. With Penelope, I didn't stop when that signal came, and I nearly died. But the resistance of my energy never comes. So I continue, not quite understanding what's happening because she's even worse off than Penelope was when the healing went so wrong.

"Raielle?" my father says.

But I don't acknowledge him, not wanting to break this connection yet. I push on, letting my energy eat away at the cancer inside her. I fan the flame within me, growing it and sending it out to her. My skin prickles as the euphoria that suddenly hits has me gasping. The room brightens around us, and I feel her disease responding to me as it begins to retreat.

"Stop. That's enough," my father's voice says from somewhere behind me.

I don't listen to him. I have to continue healing this girl, because something tells me that I can. I feel it so strongly that I'm completely lost to the flow of energy between us, when strong arms wrap around me and pull me back, breaking the connection, and causing the room to spin out of control.

"No!" I yell, frantic to get back to her.

"Ray, stop, please. Jesus, stop."

I blink Lucas into focus and realize I'm hitting him, pounding my fists into his chest. My eyes grow wide, and I start to shake.

My father's hand comes beneath my arm, lifting me up. Looking dazed, Lucas keeps his hold on me, too, standing with us.

"Why did you stop me?" I demand of both of them, trying to pull out of their grasp.

My father turns me to face him and his expression stuns me. He's trying to appear stern and disapproving, but what I really see there is restrained excitement. "You can't heal her that way," he says. "Haven't you learned anything?"

I shake my head, trying to understand because his words and his expression are at odds. "I could cure her. I felt it."

"You're wrong." His face fills with disappointment. The excitement I thought I saw there is gone now. "You don't understand your power at all, Raielle. Going any further would have been dangerous. There's only one way to help her. My plan for you today was to learn how it feels when someone is too far gone to save. So what happened to you before won't happen again. But you didn't feel it. Did you?"

Turning away from him, I try to get some clarity because I don't think I'm wrong, and I know what I saw in his face before. But maybe I'm misreading him. Maybe I'm misreading myself, too. My power has done nothing but betray me lately. I can't be completely sure of it or of anything it tells me.

I glance at the girl again and her eyes remain closed. There doesn't appear to be any change.

"That's enough for now. I was hoping this would go differently. We have a lot of work to do." My father shakes his head solemnly.

Lucas finally loosens his hold on me as a silent Nyla walks past us to open the door and lead us out. I fight the voice inside me, telling me not to walk away because I could end her suffering right now. But then I remember the way my body started to give out in that car with Apollo, and those horrifying hours of not being able to breathe, feeling sure I was going to die. My fears give birth to doubt, and that doubt wins as I allow myself to be led from the room.

I'm shaky and lost in thought as we walk out of the clinic, up the stairs, and out into the wood-paneled hall of the main house. Soon we're left alone, and I startle when Lucas's furious face appears before me.

"Every time. Every fucking time!" he whisper yells at me, so the voices in the room beyond won't hear. "I can't do this anymore. I can't stand there and watch you nearly kill yourself again. I won't let you keep doing this. We're getting out of here. This is over."

I've seen Lucas lose his temper before, but nothing like this. His expression is dangerous. His eyes bore into mine. I don't understand his reaction. I wasn't going to hurt myself. They stopped me. "Nothing happened," I say.

His jaw clenches briefly, but then his face smoothes out as he leans in close to me. "I just told you that I can't stand by and watch you do this anymore. Did that faze you at all? Because it sure as hell doesn't look like you give a shit about how I feel." With that, he walks away from me, disappearing into the library.

The pressure builds behind my eyes as I stare after him. I have no idea what just happened. He can't really believe that I don't care about his feelings. Can he?

"I never thought I'd get you alone."

I spin around as Grant steps out into the hallway. Pulling in a harsh breath, I rub my temples, wondering how long he's been there and how much he heard.

"We should talk," he says, and I vaguely remember him saying that at Crossroads, too.

I shake my head, not up for conversation.

But he doesn't leave. His expression is characteristically serious. He looks so intense all the time, even when he's trying to be casual. "Let's go out back. We can have some privacy there," he suggests, ignoring my response.

Grant cuts an imposing figure. I hardly know him, but I do know that

Lucas doesn't like him, and he could easily overpower me if he wanted to. "I don't think so."

At first he seems annoyed, then surprised. "I only want to talk. I would never hurt you, if that's what you're thinking."

"I don't know what to think…about anything." I sigh, shaking my head.

He looks up and down the hall, seeming frustrated that I'm not willing to go somewhere else with him. "Look, your father isn't the only one who can teach you what you need to know," he says in a low voice. "I think there's someone else you should meet."

I narrow my eyes at him. "Who?"

After glancing around again to make sure we're alone, he finally says, "Her name is Meera. She's been around a long time, and she's seen it all. She used to work with your father before he cast her out."

"Cast her out?" I ask, mocking his word choice.

He nods, unbothered. "She was a lot like you. I think she can help you. Let me take you to see her. What have you got to lose?" His eyebrows arch up.

I transfer my weight from one foot to the other, finding it hard to shake off everything that just happened and concentrate on what he's saying.

His expression turns strangely eager as he studies me. "Look, I couldn't help hearing some of that. Your boyfriend wants you to walk away, but he can't understand. It's hard for them to be with us. We always end up hurting them."

"Them?" I ask, curiosity focusing my attention.

"People who can't do what we can. Especially people we love," he says quietly.

I detect a note of regret in his voice. "You're talking from experience?"

His fingers graze the scars on his cheeks as he nods at me.

A part of me doesn't want to ask him what he's talking about, mainly because I can see how badly he wants to tell me. I get the feeling he intends to teach me a lesson that I don't want to learn. But I find myself asking anyway. "Who was she?"

He hesitates briefly. "My fiancée." Then he breaks eye contact, focusing on a spot just behind me. "She was in a car accident. She should have died, but I couldn't let her. John helped me. He found someone so that I could save her life." He slowly shifts his eyes to my face, looking for my reaction.

He's telling me that he killed a person to save his fiancée. Before I came here, I would have gasped or given him some kind of appalled and surprised response. But now I know how this works, how healers like him and my father do things. His eyes are daring me to react, though, to tell him that saving his fiancée was wrong. He wants me to think about what I'd do if it were Lucas before I judge him.

Grant's eyes darken when my expression doesn't change. "I didn't tell her what I'd done," he continues. "She knew I was a healer, but she didn't know that part. That's something John prefers us to keep quiet about." His mouth tightens for a moment before a humorless smile appears. "But then John let it slip to her one day, how she was saved. She didn't want to believe it. When she asked me, I couldn't lie to her. Once it sank in, she couldn't handle it. She blamed me. Eventually, she left me."

I can see the sorrow on his face, and the anger at my father for telling her. There's no question he told her on purpose. He's too composed to let something like that slip accidentally. I wonder why he would do that to Grant, purposely sabotage his relationship. "I'm sorry," I offer because he looks so upset by the memory. "And the scars?" I ask.

He absently runs his hand over them. "Fingernails. She lashed out at me before she left. I didn't stop her. If it made her feel better to hurt me, I wasn't going to take that away from her."

Now my eyes do widen. I think of all the misery I've seen, first with my mother and then myself. We've all suffered as a result of our power, Shane and Grant, too.

"You remind me of her." He eyes me with sympathy now, his gaze gently holding mine. "Your uncompromising sense of right and wrong. It's going to make things hard for you. It already has."

I can't look away from him, even though I want to. His sharp eyes see too much. Right now, they seem to see everything.

"That's why it's better to let him go," he says. "He's never going ⸱ understand you. You're going to hurt him. It's inevitable."

With those painful words, my eyes close, breaking the strange hold he has on me. I want to silence the nagging voice inside telling me he's probably right. But I know Grant didn't give life to that voice. It was already there.

"It's better to be with someone who's like you, who understands every part of you." My eyes open when his hand lightly touches my arm. "We could understand each other, Raielle. I feel like I've been waiting a long time to find you. We'd be good together."

I shake my head. My heart goes out to him and the obvious pain he's experienced. But I can't let him inflame my worst fears. He doesn't know me, and he doesn't know Lucas. He has no idea what we've already overcome to be together.

He smiles sadly at my silent refusal. "I know you're not there yet. But you will be. When that day comes, I'll still be here." Then he pushes his hands into his pockets and his expression changes. "In the meantime, I'd like to be a friend to you. Meera lives in Palm Springs. I can take you to see her tomorrow."

I blink at his change of tone. I haven't agreed to this, even though he's making it sound as though I have.

"We'll get an early start. Say around eight? Bring your boyfriend, if it makes you feel better. That is, if you two are speaking." He holds out his hand. "Give me your phone. You should have my number in case you need it."

Tilting my head at him, I try to see the sympathetic, slightly broken person that stood before me only a minute ago. But that person is gone now, replaced by the more familiar one that wears an easygoing mask, but radiates barely bridled tension from beneath it. I hesitate only a moment before pulling my phone out and giving in to my curiosity. "How do you know Meera will want to help me?" I ask.

He enters his number and bends to catch my eye as he hands the phone back. "How much has your father told you about how your power works? How much have you learned from him so far?"

y because we both know my father has taught me nothing

ıowingly. "I promise you, Meera's a great lady. She'll help you." Then he studies me for an uncomfortable moment before painting on a smile and walking back the way he came.

Standing in the hall alone now, I know I have to make things right with Lucas. We can't keep having this same fight. Learning about my power is not going to be like learning to swim or to ride a bike. The energy inside me can be dangerous. All I can do is try to mitigate that danger. But I can't give up and decide to go home every time things don't go the way I want them to, and Lucas can't keep insisting that I do.

TWELVE

Raielle

I STEP into the library and see Lucas sitting in a chair. He's leaning forward, his elbows resting on his knees. His hair is mussed from running his fingers through it, and his eyes are on the fireplace with the flames reflected in their depths. There's only one other person in the room, a girl curled up on a sofa across from him. She keeps glancing at Lucas, and I recognize the look on her face. It's only a matter of time before she works up the courage to start flirting with him.

Quietly, I walk farther into the room and bend down beside the chair to place my hand over his on his leg. He doesn't acknowledge me or move at all, and that sinking feeling I already had in my stomach bottoms out. "I'm sorry," I tell him quietly.

His chest rises and falls several times before his eyes finally find mine. But I don't see the hurt I'm expecting. The look in his eyes is passive. He's hiding his emotions now, and somehow that makes me feel even worse.

"I do care about how you feel, Lucas."

He leans back, watching me with an unreadable expression. Before I can say anything else, we hear loud cheering coming from the next room. The girl shuts her book and gets to her feet. "I guess it's over," she says, and smiles as she walks past us.

I'm relieved once she's gone so we can talk without an audience, but Lucas surprises me by standing and gripping my hand to help me up. Then he begins to lead me out wordlessly.

People are filing out the front door. "After-party at my place," Shane yells over his shoulder as he descends the stairs. I hear some catcalls and laughter behind him.

"I've just learned that you're John's daughter," an accented voice says from beside me. I turn to see a woman smiling up at me. Her graying hair is pulled back in a low ponytail. Her features are small and delicate. I politely return her grin.

"I'm Marion. It's nice to meet you," she says and begins to turn away.

"Are you a healer, too," I ask.

She nods.

"Can you tell me why you're the only…" I hesitate, not sure how to put it. "I mean, everyone is so young. I was wondering why there aren't any older healers. Not that you're old…" I add, tripping over my tongue.

Her smile falls, and I'm sure I must have offended her. "You don't know?" she asks, looking surprised. "There's a cutoff, a point in life where you really can't do it anymore."

I stop walking. "Why?"

"Because it takes something out of you every time," she explains, like it should be obvious. "When you begin to give more of yourself away than you can spare, it's time to stop."

This is new information and not anything I've heard before from my mother or anyone else. "I don't understand. What does it take out of you?"

She offers me a sympathetic smile. "It's the mind that tends to go first. So, knowing when to stop can be a tricky business. But I came late to the game. That's why I'm still here."

"What's the cutoff, and how are you supposed to know when you've reached it?" Lucas asks as my thoughts turn to my grandmother sitting in a nursing home now, nearly catatonic.

"Everyone is different," Marion says simply.

"My father hasn't stopped. How old is he?" I ask.

She laughs. "No one knows that for sure. Some say that he's nearly seventy."

My eyes grow wide. "Seventy?"

"Yes. The rules don't seem to apply to him." She glances around and lowers her voice. "At least, he makes sure that they don't."

I shake my head, finding this hard to believe. "How can he be seventy? He barely looks forty."

"Drinking his own juice," Lucas comments. "Just like your brother said."

He's joking, I think, but I turn to Marion, anyway. "Is that possible? Is he using his own energy to keep himself young?"

Her lips form a tight line. "I don't know. In all honesty, I don't want to know." She starts to move away. "It was very nice meeting you," she says, seeming regretful for stopping to say hello as she walks swiftly away from us, following the line of people returning to the cars that line the driveway. Lucas watches her, quiet again, before he leads us to his truck.

We follow slowly behind a line of cars, down the private road and then out onto the street. My mind is filled with everything that happened today—the sick girl, the uncomfortable conversation with Grant, and the strange words from the woman on the steps. But more important is the weight of Lucas's anger, which still permeates the air between us. He hasn't said a word since we got into the truck and neither have I.

Lucas keeps driving past the condo, heading into Santa Monica, and I realize that he's taking us to the beach, our original plan for the day. After parking by the sand, he says, "Walk with me," sounding more sad and wistful than angry now. My throat grows tight at his tone.

The beach isn't busy tonight. Some kids whiz past, rollerblading on the concrete path that runs parallel to the water. A few dogs and their owners jog by or linger at the shoreline. Lucas takes my hand when we meet on the sidewalk, and he begins to walk, his eyes on the water. The longer he remains silent, the more apprehensive I become. By the time he lowers himself onto the cool sand and brings me down beside him, I'm convinced of what he's about to say. "You're leaving, aren't you?" I ask.

When his eyes fill with hurt, I wish I could take back my words. "Lucas…"

"After everything, do you really think I would leave you?" he asks, appearing stunned.

Swallowing hard, I have to look away from his expression because I'm afraid the answer is yes as I recall his words. "But what you said back at the house…"

"Ray." He sighs, and when I glance back at him, he's running a hand through his tousled hair. "I never said I was leaving. I said that we were leaving, and I meant it."

I tense, seeing that he hasn't changed his mind or really calmed down at all.

"You still don't want to go," he states.

I shake my head. "Not yet."

He angles his body toward me and takes both my hands in his. "You didn't see what I did today. It was exactly the same as with Penelope. You had that girl lifted off the bed. The lights in the room all got brighter, and your body started shaking like a leaf. Your skin went pale and your eyes squeezed closed. I thought it was happening all over again."

The slight tremor in his voice shocks me.

"I know you need to help people and that you believe it's a part of who you are. I know you think you have to understand your power better in order to use it. But if you're being honest with yourself, you'll admit that you are coming to understand it. You just don't want to accept what you're learning."

I look away from his intense gaze and let my eyes wander over the expanse of ocean.

"Your power can hurt you. It works against you," he continues. "Maybe turning it off like your mother taught you is the best thing you can do."

My mind slams the door closed on that suggestion because there is one example that crushes it all to dust. "What about Penelope?" I ask.

His face tightens. "What about her?"

"She's a healthy, happy little girl. Knowing that fills me with such gratitude for what I can do. Refusing to help her was never an option. It's not a choice I ever would have made. What if there are more people like her that I could help? Like that girl today."

He scoffs at that. "Helping Penelope nearly killed you. The same thing almost happened again just now. What's it going to take to get through to you? Your healing always comes at a price, and you're the one paying it. I know you don't want to believe that the power you have could be something terrible. But you need to face that possibility. You need to open your eyes."

"My eyes are open, Lucas." When he tries to release my hand, I grip him harder. "I remember something else you told me back in Fort Upton. You said that power itself isn't evil, only the wielder of it."

He shakes his head. "I was wrong. I said that before you healed Penelope and before we knew why your mother was murdered. I said it before we met your father and your brother."

I pull him in closer. "You were right. I've always known that I was meant to help people. I let my mother convince me otherwise for a while, and I pretended that I didn't feel this need to heal those who are hurting. But I've been fooling myself. Now that my power is growing, I can't pretend it doesn't exist again. I can't suppress what everything inside me is telling me I'm supposed to do. My father has turned his power into a commodity, and he may be corrupted by it, but that doesn't mean I have to be. I have my own place in this. I just need to figure out what it is."

As he watches me, I can feel his frustration. When he tears his eyes from mine to look out at the water again, I follow his gaze to find swatches of gold stretched across the sky, bronzing the waves below. The beauty of it breaks my heart. We should be enjoying this view together, not arguing and missing a moment we could be sharing.

"What if you're wrong?" he asks quietly.

I watch a seagull dive down into the waves. "Then at least I'll know."

"No. You'll be devastated at best and completely broken at worst."

My breathing hitches when I look back at him. His gaze is on me again, and the tenderness I see there is overwhelming. But I have no words to reassure him, and I have no right to ask him to go through this with me. "Maybe," I answer.

He just watches my face as his throat works against his emotion, and somehow I know he's backing down, reining himself in. I wish things could be different, that I could do what he wants. "It won't always be this way," I say. "Once this is done, I'm going to make sure you get your life back. No more sacrificing your plans for me."

He gives me a strange look, like I'm way off base. "It's no sacrifice. That's not what this is about." He wraps his hand around the nape of my neck and leans his face close to mine. "No matter what happens, I'm not leaving you. Please believe that."

I nod at him, trying hard to hold back my tears. His words warm me even as something else, something bittersweet, claws at me, saying that I'm being selfish, that I shouldn't take what he's giving. But deep down I know that I don't have a choice. This is where I need to be now, and I need him, too.

He keeps me close as we watch the sun sink into the ocean together. More than anything, I want him to be happy. I want us to get out from under this dark cloud. Lucas needs to know there's going to be a light at the end of the tunnel because I believe there will be. Since he came back into my life, he's helped me to believe it.

I turn to face him and say, "The day might be over, but the night isn't. We can still do something fun. Let's drive out to Malibu for dinner. We'll take the night off from everything and pretend we're normal," I suggest brightly.

I can see that I've taken him by surprise. One side of his mouth hitches up. "Pretend we're normal?"

"Well, you are normal. So, I guess I'll be doing the pretending."

His eyes narrow, not liking my attempt at self-deprecation. "Normal is overrated. Malibu, huh? Someplace on the water?"

I nod.

He seems to think about it. "I could be up for that."

His arm comes around me as we watch the final remnants of the day disappear from the sky. Then we get back in the truck, and I give him directions. We start off with no real destination in mind, just open to finding someplace that catches our eyes. We turn off the highway and pass a few small restaurants and a bunch of noisy touristy places before the trees clear and a large expanse of dark ocean becomes visible in the distance.

"There," he says, pointing to a place that seems to cling to the cliff side. It's small and not too crowded. I can see orange lights strung along a balcony that overlooks the water.

Lucas parks and shoots me a familiar look when I reach out to open my door. "Oh." I smile, dropping my hand into my lap. Then I wait a moment until my door is opened, and he extends his hand to me. I'm grinning widely as he helps me down and pulls me in for a hug before taking my hand.

Once we get inside, we're seated out on the balcony we spotted from the road. What happens next feels like a dream. There's a gentle breeze in the air and our backdrop is the ocean, a dark moving mass glinting in the moonlight. The food is good, although I barely notice it. We keep the conversation light as our hands link on the table and our legs brush against each other beneath it. We prolong the evening, ordering dessert and lingering before paying the bill.

When my phone dings, I'm surprised. Lucas is the only one who calls me, and he's right here. I pull it out of my bag and see a text from Nikki the Awesome. It's the first one I've received since she put her number in. I grin at what she called herself.

"Anything important?" Lucas asks.

"Nikki wants us to meet her at a club." I glance up at him. My automatic response is always no. But I feel like going tonight. The idea of dancing close to Lucas and showing him off gives me a little thrill just thinking about it. "What do you think?"

He sits back. "Do you want to?"

I look down at my sundress. It isn't exactly club attire, but it will do. I smile and nod.

"Which one?"

"Johnny Red's. Do you know it? It's right near campus, but I've never been."

Lucas doesn't respond at first. Then he nods and gulps down the rest of his water. Before I can question his hesitation, he says, "Let's go for a walk on the beach first."

He points to a set of wooden stairs that lead down to the shore. Since the moon is nearly full, we're able to see our way to the sand. It's chillier closer to the water, but I shake my head when he asks me if I'm cold. There's no way the cold is going to stop me from taking a romantic walk on the beach with him.

We stroll silently hand in hand along the waterline. When Lucas stops and pulls me against him, my heart skips as I stare into his shadowed eyes. His thick hair gets tossed around in the wind, and his square jaw is even more pronounced in the dim light. Everything about him is achingly beautiful. My fingers trace over his shoulders down to his hard, muscled chest.

His hands sweep through my hair and then run over my back, making my whole body vibrate beneath his touch. I pull his head down to mine and nip at his full lower lip.

With his arms tight around me, he shifts his hips forward, letting the evidence of his desire rub against me. When I rub back, he breaks away breathlessly. "This is real nice and all." His voice sounds thick. "But let's go home."

"You mean go to the club. I already texted Nikki to let her know we'd be there."

"Right," he replies, his eyes closing.

"We won't stay long." I lean up for a kiss, smiling at what I know he'd rather be doing. "I promise," I whisper by his ear.

Before I know what's happening, he grabs my arm and brings it over his shoulder. Then he picks me up piggyback style and runs all the way up the steps with me giggling behind him.

It's nearly eleven thirty when we arrive. Lucas has to park a few blocks away, and then we have to stand in line to get in. It's after midnight by the time I text Nikki again to let her know we're here. Inside Johnny Red's it's dark, packed with people, and the air is thick and steamy.

Nikki finds us as we're pushing through the crowd. She's dressed in a sequined tank top with red leggings and black boots. She's breathless, and her face shines with perspiration. "We've got a table by the dance floor," she yells. Then she grabs my hand and drags me behind her.

I look over my shoulder to make sure Lucas is following. He's behind me, scanning the room, and I can't help but notice the girls who are noticing him. But Nikki is chattering away at me and pulling me along too fast for me to go back there and wrap my arm around him to let them know he's not available.

The table is full when we get there. I spot Jason's hulking form right away, but the rest of them are only vaguely familiar faces that I've run into at Nikki's apartment. She goes around the table introducing us, and we all nod at one another.

"We'll grab some more chairs," she offers, then she orders Jason to do it. He's halfway up when Lucas says, "Don't sweat it. We're going to dance first." His hands land on my hips and he shoots me a speculative look.

I smile my response. Then I drop my bag on the table and let him lead me through the sea of bodies on the dance floor to a spot with just enough room for us to squeeze ourselves in. He drapes my arms around his neck before his hands return to my hips, moving me in time with him as the lights and music pulse around us. This is exactly what I imagined when Nikki asked us to come. I knew Lucas would be a good dancer. He moves so fluidly when he does ordinary everyday things. We danced once before, at the prom, but that was just swaying to a slow song, not the rhythmic moving he's doing with me now. And I know female eyes are still on him, but his eyes are on me, and I feel a sense of pride and satisfaction. They all want him, but he's all mine.

The music is loud, and my body is already slick with sweat when Lucas lowers his lips to the crook of my neck and starts to suck lightly on my skin. I sigh, tilting my head to the side to give him better access. We're moving in perfect unison, and I'm so turned on right now, I can hardly breathe.

The song changes to a faster one, but Lucas keeps our rhythm the same. His hands move up and down my back now before his arms wrap around me and his leg shifts between mine. When his thigh pushes up against me, my eyes squeeze shut. Lust nearly makes my knees buckle, and Lucas's laughter rings in my ear as his arms bear my weight. Our dance is turning into a slow form of sensual torture. I endure it until I feel like I may explode or tear his clothes off right there on the dance floor. It's that last thought that finally wakes me up.

"Let's get a drink." I straighten abruptly and fan myself with my hand.

He shows me a satisfied, arrogant grin before taking my hand and turning to lead the way back. I'm following behind him, admiring the view, when someone steps in my path, making me lose my grip on him. Keeping the top of his head in sight, I push past the moving bodies in my way until I have a clear view of him again. Just then, a pair of female arms wind their way around his waist. As I'm watching, the hand attached to one of those arms moves lower and palms his ass. I stop in my tracks, frozen first in shock and then in outrage.

Lucas turns with a familiar sexy smile until he sees who owns the hand. Then the smile drops into a scowl. He takes her arms and returns them to her. I follow the line of those pale arms to a body clad in a tight black dress, dark blonde hair curling along the sides of hoisted-up, exposed cleavage. She's grinning at him with a perfect white smile. She's gorgeous, and she seems to think his ass is hers. I quickly unfreeze, intending to march up there and explain things to her, when Lucas looks back at me. I expect him to seem annoyed, rolling his eyes in exasperation or to appear smug, shamelessly shrugging at how irresistible he is. But his expression goes blank as he catches my eye, and something twists inside me. He knows her. If he didn't, he wouldn't be schooling his face so carefully.

He turns back and says something to her that wipes away the coy smile and has her sneering at him instead. I can read the words "the other night" on her lips before she flips him off and disappears into the crowd. The whole thing lasts a few seconds, but it feels like the ground just shifted beneath me.

Lucas's eyes are on me again, and their cool depths are cautious. I still haven't moved. When I don't come to him, he walks back toward me. He reaches for my hand and starts to pull me along with him. I hear Nikki calling us, but we keep moving past her table toward the door and then out onto the sidewalk, into the cool night air.

My ears are ringing from the noise inside, and my blood is pumping fast. I look at him standing beside me, just watching me, not saying anything, and I know I don't have a right to the sinking feeling inside me. I turn to go back in again.

"Wait." His fingers wrap around my arm.

I don't turn around. "I know you've decided we're leaving, but I left my bag in there, and I have to say good-bye to Nikki." Without looking back, I pull my arm away, and he lets it go. Then I catch the bouncer's attention. He allows me to bypass the line to go back into the club. I find Nikki's table again, grab my bag, and explain to her that we're going.

She winks at me. "I understand. You two looked pretty hot out there. Thanks for briefly gracing us with your presence."

I grimace.

"No, seriously." She laughs. "It's fine."

I make myself smile at her, thankful she didn't see the exchange between Lucas and the blonde. If she had, I'd probably be getting an earful about what a jerk he is.

Reluctantly, I push my way back toward the door again, but before going outside, I swallow my resentment. I left him. Therefore I have no right to be angry if he was with someone else during that time. And I have no right to the bile burning at the back of my throat at the thought of her touching him. I have no right to any of it.

When I get outside, he's just where I left him. "I'm ready," I say, keeping my expression as neutral as his.

His lips form a straight line as he starts to walk. We travel the three blocks back to his truck in silence. He opens my door, but before I can get in, he blocks the way. "Are you even going to ask me about her?"

I look up at him in the darkness. "No."

"No?" His eyes narrow on me.

My stomach jumps as I watch his expression grow fierce. I expected him to be relieved that I'm not acting like a jealous girlfriend.

"So what? You don't care?" Lucas is watching me closely. It looks like his feelings are hurt by my reaction, and I want to laugh at the irony.

"Did you sleep with her?" I hear myself asking, bracing for the answer.

"No. But I kissed her, and I thought about it." He says it bluntly, almost angrily.

I flinch and he notices, his nostrils flaring, his eyes challenging.

When I still don't say anything, he bears down on me. "I met her here a few weeks ago. Cal convinced me to come out with him and his friends."

I pull in a shaky breath. Cal again. I wonder if this happened the same night he got drunk and made Cal despise me. "Why didn't you?" I ask.

"What? Sleep with her?" He starts to laugh, and it's an awful sound without a trace of humor. "Because she's not you, and I wasn't drunk enough to forget that."

My hands grip the straps of my bag as everything I put him through over the past few months gets projected back at me through his wounded eyes. "Have you slept with anyone since you've been here?"

"Why?" He scowls. "I thought you didn't care."

When he makes that statement, the floodgates I've been holding back burst wide open. "I don't have the right to care! But that doesn't mean I don't. God, I cared too much. I wanted to punch that girl in the face when she grabbed you." I can feel the way my top lip curls up when I picture the blonde's hand on him.

His eyes sharpen.

"It made me sick to see the way she touched you. The idea of you being with anyone else…" I break off, unable to finish.

"What, Ray?" he asks softly. "Tell me."

"It hurts," I whisper.

In that moment, his harsh stance softens. "I'm sorry I hurt you," he says. "It happened, and you have every right to be upset with me. But I haven't been with anyone else since I met you. I promise."

I exhale slowly because I believe him. I trust him. He may be the only person I've ever really trusted. It scares me, how much I feel for him and how easily he can hurt me. Then I say what I'm thinking, realizing he'll like hearing me sound possessive. "Don't let it happen again."

He blinks. Then he slowly smiles. "I won't. That goes both ways, you know."

My head shakes at that possibility. "You have nothing to worry about. You're the only one who would put up with me."

Laughing now, he gives me an incredulous look. "Your cluelessness is cute. But it's going to get you in trouble one day."

"I'm not clueless."

"Says the clueless girl."

"Hey." I feign annoyance, but I'm glad to see the warmth back in his eyes. "By the way, what did you say to her back there? I saw her flip you off."

"I told her the truth." He shrugs. "That she was a stand-in for the real thing, but the real thing is back now."

"You did not," I reply, completely appalled.

His eyebrows inch up. "I can be a real bastard. You of all people should know that."

Swallowing, I kind of feel bad for her now. But not too bad.

"Ready to go?" he asks. "So we can finish what we started at the beach and then continued on the dance floor?"

I nod, wanting alone time with him, too, needing it even more now than I did back on that dance floor. Once we're in the truck, I lean my head back, realizing how tired I feel. Lucas's aggressive personality can be exhausting sometimes, the way he's all over me if he thinks I'm holding anything back. But the truth is, someone less sure of himself and more willing to let me stay in my shell would never make me feel the way he does. It's his willingness to challenge me and drag me kicking and screaming from the places I like to hide that have cemented him in my heart. He fills me with every emotion, and then he makes me confess to each one of them.

I wasn't being clueless when I told him that no one else would put up with me. I know I'm attractive, or at least I can be when I try, but I'm emotionally unavailable. My heart is cold. That's basically what every guy before Lucas told me, although not in so many words, and not always so nicely. I'm different with him, though. My heart was never cold. It was just in some sort of stasis while I was trying to survive each day. But it's not anymore. It pumps hard and fast for Lucas. He makes me feel so many things. My feelings for him are intense and persistent, and they root more deeply inside me each day. The fact that he's easy on the eyes and sexy as hell doesn't hurt either. And now he says he's never leaving me. No matter what.

"What's that smile about?" he asks, glancing across the seat at me.

"You," I reply, not realizing that I was smiling. I can see my answer surprises him as he flashes me a pleased grin.

"I marked you," he says, his eyes on the side mirror now, waiting for an opening in the traffic.

"What?"

He taps the curve between his neck and shoulder and then directs his eyes to the same place on me. My forehead wrinkles as I reach for the sun visor, pulling it down and pointing the mirror at myself. It's too dark to see it clearly, but it looks like there's a small red blotch on my skin. My temperature starts to rise as I recall the feel of Lucas's mouth on me there. "You gave me a hickey?"

His response is an amused wink.

After flipping the sun visor back up, my fingers skim over the mark. I haven't had one of these since I was fourteen and fooled around after school with my first boyfriend. Deciding to try something, I close my eyes and take a deep breath. My energy sparks inside me, and I send it up toward the broken blood vessels. Warmth radiates along the curve of my neck and then down over my shoulder. I flip the visor down to check again. "It's gone." I smile.

Lucas gives me confused look.

"I healed it. I wanted to see if I could."

He laughs under his breath and shakes his head. "Then I'll just have to put it back again."

Leaning back in my seat, I grin at the thought. "Maybe someplace less conspicuous."

"I can think of a few places like that," he says. When I glance at him, the humor in his eyes has faded, replaced by something more intense. He reaches out for my hand and holds it firmly for the rest of the drive.

When we finally arrive at Lucas's apartment, cars line the street and packs of people are milling around on the front lawn. "Fuck," he mutters. "Cal's having a party."

A huge one by the looks of it. The whole house is lit up, and I can hear the music pouring out from where we're parked almost a block away.

"Your place?" he asks hopefully.

My stomach clenches. "With Shane possibly eavesdropping again?"

"We can be quiet."

My eyes grow round. There's no way I could do that. I'd be too self-conscious and just plain pissed if Shane was anywhere to be found. "Can't we go to your room and lock the door?"

He runs a hand over his cheek and looks back at the party again. "If I had a working lock, which I don't. Anyway, Cal's probably got half the party in there using my Xbox."

"You've hardly unpacked anything, but you've got your Xbox set up?"

"Priorities," he says matter-of-factly. "Let's go to a hotel."

My hands twist in my lap as our little romantic bubble starts to deflate again. We don't have any of our things with us, and we need to be ready to leave early in the morning. Something I haven't even told Lucas about yet. "Let's just go to the condo."

He gives me a hesitant look. "You sure?"

I nod in defeat. "We'll be quiet." Then I try not to let him see how much I really don't like that idea.

He watches me for a moment as his jaw tightens. "Fuck it. I'll kick them out. It is my room."

Slumping into the seat, I stifle a yawn as I notice more people arriving. "You're tired?" he asks.

I am. We hardly slept at all last night. But I only shrug at him.

"You won't get any sleep here." He states the obvious, eyeing the party again. "Fine. We'll go to the condo. But I'm going to fucking kill Shane the next time I see him."

"That makes two of us," I mutter under my breath.

As we drive past the party, the romantic mood has faded for me, and with Shane possibly listening, we won't be able to discuss the plan for tomorrow morning once we get to the condo. I have no choice but to tell Lucas now. "By the way, Grant is taking us to Palm Springs in the morning. There's a woman there he thinks I should talk to."

At the sound of Grant's name, Lucas's fingers tighten on the steering wheel. "When did you talk to him?"

"Earlier, at my father's house, when you were in the library. He found me in the hallway."

He glances at me. "What did he say exactly?"

"That my father isn't the only one who can help me. He told me this woman used to work with my father, but she's on the outs with him now. He wants to take us to talk to her." I'm trying not to sound as anxious as I feel about this.

"Does your father know you're going to see her?" he asks.

"I haven't talked to him about it."

"Is it a good idea to go behind his back and start trusting Grant?" The way he grimaces every time he says Grant's name tells me what his answer to that question is.

I cross my arms. "This isn't about trusting Grant. It's about finding out as much as I can. If my father isn't my only option, that would be good news. Right? I figured you would think so."

A grunt is his only response. "So is that all Grant said?"

When I don't answer right away, his eyes sharpen on me. "What else did he say?"

I sigh, knowing he won't like that Grant is sharing personal stories with me. "He told me about his fiancée, and how she left him."

His expression turns skeptical. "No kidding? That's too bad."

But he doesn't sound like he feels bad, and I find myself defending

Grant. "It was a pretty messed-up situation, actually. He's had a rough time. I know you don't like him, but I get the feeling he's on our side."

Lucas bites out a laugh. "He may be on your side, but he's definitely not on mine."

THIRTEEN

Lucas

GRANT has a quiet confidence about him when he watches her, like he knows it's only a matter of time before she comes to her senses and dumps my ass for him. Of course, Raielle is completely oblivious to the predatory look in his eyes. I have a shit ton of worries when it comes to her, but despite what I said to her last night, other guys don't top the list. She wouldn't hurt me that way. But that doesn't mean I don't want to smash his face in for having those kinds of thoughts about her.

We slept here at the condo last night, and lucky for Shane, there was no sign of him. Since I doubt Raielle will ever live here again, I suggested we move her stuff to my place when we get back later today. Because she doesn't have much, that shouldn't take long.

"You ready to go?" Grant asks, his eyes only on her. I want to offer to drive because I'm pretty sure I know who he plans on having ride shotgun with him. But they've already got it arranged for him to drive, and since I don't want to look like the jealous, petty boyfriend I probably am, I keep my mouth shut about it.

We follow him downstairs and the valet brings his car around. My eyes widen when I see it's a black 1964 Pontiac GTO, a classic muscle car. He notices me admiring it. "I restored it myself," he says. "Found the parts for it all over the country. Took me nearly five years with all the traveling I do."

Grudgingly impressed, I run my hand over the hood. "Nice."

Raielle is eyeing me with an amused look on her face. Not surprisingly, when she starts to slip into the back, Grant says, "Why don't you ride up front with me?"

She raises an eyebrow in my direction, silently offering me the passenger seat, but I shake my head. What the hell. Only an asshole would make her sit in the back.

Once we're on the road, I lean forward. "So, why is this woman on the outs with John?" I ask. I place my hand on Raielle's shoulder and knead it gently. I feel satisfied when Grant's eyes flick briefly to my hand. *Yeah, I can touch her and you'd better not.*

"It might be best for her to tell her own story," he replies.

I huff out a frustrated breath. "Come on. It's a long drive. Give us something."

Raielle's hand comes up to touch mine as she, too, waits expectantly for an answer.

He watches me through the rearview mirror. "Meera and John were always reluctant partners. I think they joined forces because they were both desperate for an ally. We need each other to thrive. We need a common community to stay sane and safe. It's not easy to be alone when you're like us." He turns and meets Raielle's eyes when he says that, giving her a meaningful look.

Her own eyes widen at first, before skittering away from his. We both know he doesn't mean alone because she's not alone. He means without other healers, and specifically he means without him.

My hand tightens on her shoulder. "You still haven't answered the question."

Grant sighs, flexing his fingers on the wheel. "She's as powerful as John, but she has no agenda. I get the feeling Raielle is wary of her father. A lot of people are uncomfortable around him. He's like a block of ice, only no matter how hot it gets, he never melts. If Raielle wants to learn about her abilities, I thought she might feel more comfortable with Meera."

Again, a nonanswer. "If she's persona non grata, why are you in touch with her?"

He swallows and darts another look at me. "That's a long story."

"Really? Good thing we've got time then."

Raielle turns her head and narrows her eyes at me. Sighing, I decide to take the hint as I sit back to stare at the hazy mountains looming in the distance. But my attention is still on the front seat.

"Could you tell us how you came to work for my father?" she asks him.

He turns a smile on her. "It's not that interesting a story. I'm from New Mexico originally, and I moved out here after high school because I'd heard about John. That's how most of us come to him, because we're searching for answers about ourselves. He welcomes us in, lets us become a part of something, instead of feeling alone and different. A lot of us suppress our power because it's hard once people know what you can do. They want to use you and take advantage of you, or else they're just plain scared of you. After a few generations of disuse, I think the power atrophies. But some of us, like you and I, are too powerful to suppress it. We're compelled to use it, and we have to help people when we can."

After that explanation, Grant starts a more personal conversation with her, asking her what it was like growing up trying to hide what she could do. He's attempting to get to know her. But she hates talking about herself, and she's giving him only brief monosyllabic responses. When I see the look of frustration on his face, I feel satisfied and start to relax.

The conversation picks up when Grant decides to tell Raielle about his upbringing. Turns out, they have similar backgrounds with single moms who taught them to suppress their power. Grant is on a mission to win her over, and he's laying the groundwork. I wonder if she realizes that.

The drive takes about an hour and forty minutes. Grant pulls into the driveway of a sprawling beige stucco ranch with a red tile roof and glances at his watch. "Right on time."

I climb out of the car and stretch, looking around. This street has very few houses on it, only two others that I can see. The yards have no trees. They're mostly straggly bushes, dry dirt, and rocks. After all, this is the desert. Looming in the distance are mountains with the same landscape as the barren yards.

We follow Grant up the stone walkway to the front door. After he knocks, the lock clicks but the door opens only a foot or so. Standing there is a tall thin woman with dark hair cropped close to her head, and she doesn't seem happy to see us.

"I told you not to bring them." She scolds, looking down her nose at Grant. I can feel Raielle go rigid beside me.

"But your mother told me otherwise," he replies, unbothered by her cool demeanor.

"My mother is too nice. I don't suffer from that problem."

He takes a step toward the door. "Please, Adrienne. We came all this way. At least tell her we're here."

For the first time, the woman's eyes shift to us. "You brought John's daughter." She wrinkles her nose like she smells something bad. Then she shuts the door in our faces.

Raielle is obviously and justifiably shocked by her reception.

"Thanks for dragging us out here for nothing," I say, not wanting to stand outside like a bunch of unwelcome strays.

He holds his hand up. "Meera will see us. Just wait."

"Why is she so hostile?" Raielle asks.

Before he can respond, the door opens wide and the same woman stands there glaring at us. "She's in the back. You have thirty minutes." Then she turns on her heel and walks away.

Grant turns to us. "Sorry about that. Come on."

When he walks into the house, I see Raielle hesitate. "You don't have to do this."

She pulls in a breath and gives me a hesitant smile. "What do you think she'll do to us if we stay longer than thirty minutes?"

I shrug. "Beat us with her broomstick?"

Her eyes smile at me.

As she steps over the threshold, I give her a warning. "Watch yourself now. She's probably got a herd of housecats in here."

Elbowing me playfully, she continues on. I follow her to find Grant waiting for us. He leads us through an airy open main room that attaches to a bright kitchen with a sliding glass door to the backyard. As we walk through the house, I can smell the remnants of breakfast in the air, coffee and maybe some burned toast.

We step out onto a patio covered by a white awning. Even in the shade, it's hot as hell out here. It takes a moment for my eyes to adjust to the brightness, but when they do I spot a frail woman sitting at a metal table at the end of a concrete patio.

"Hello, Meera," Grant says, bending down to kiss the wrinkled skin of her cheek. Her thin hair is an artificial shade of brown, and she has it sprayed up around her head in what seems like an attempt to make it look fuller. A cotton shirtdress with a bright flower pattern hides most of her body. Her eyes are sharp, though, and they're fixed on Raielle.

"What's her name?" she asks Grant in a soft, thready voice.

"Raielle," he answers, motioning her over. "And this is her friend, Lucas."

She glances at me for an uninterested moment before her gaze returns to Raielle. "Raielle," she whispers. "Come sit down."

There are only two other chairs at the table. So I grab a deck chair that's sitting in the sun and bring it under the awning, positioning myself beside Raielle once she sits. Of course, Grant takes the other chair next to her.

"You look like your mother," Meera tells her. Then she rests her small, withered hands on top of the table with her palms up. She seems to be waiting for something.

"Give her your hands," Grant says.

For a long moment, Raielle doesn't move. Then, slowly, she extends her arms across the table. Meera's fingers shake slightly as she takes Raielle's hands in hers.

I keep a watch on Raielle, waiting for her expression to reveal any sign of trouble. But her face is calm, almost curious as she watches the older woman.

When she releases her hands a few moments later, Meera laughs softly and shakes her head. "Your father is playing games with you," she says. "I can feel his energy inside you."

Raielle pulls her arms back. "What do you mean?"

"He touched you," she says. "He gave you a jolt and your power has been out of your control ever since."

Raielle's mouth drops open, and she angles a quick look at me. I can see the mix of anger and relief on her face. "That's right," she says to Meera. "Ever since he touched me, my energy has been so much stronger, and it seems to have a mind of its own. I didn't connect what he did to me with that, though." She turns to me again, and I can see the thoughts racing behind her eyes.

"It's almost worn off," Meera says. "But he didn't make you stronger. That occurred naturally as you've matured, especially over the past few months. You should be back to yourself soon. Did you tell your father about your loss of control?"

Raielle shakes her head and Meera chuckles. "He's probably dying of curiosity by now."

"Why would he do that to me?"

She shrugs her narrow shoulders. "To see if he could. To see how you would react. I suppose it was a litmus test for your strength and independence. May I take your hands? I'd like to feel your power again now that I know what to expect." When Raielle hesitates, she adds, "I won't do what your father did. I promise."

My chest feels tight at the thought of what her father put her through. And he was just playing with her? I touch her arm, watching as she once again gives her hands to the old woman. When I look over at Grant, he appears fascinated by their exchange.

"Please release her," Meera says, and I realize she's talking to me. "You'll muddy things if you're touching her." She eyes my hand still on Raielle's arm.

Reluctantly, I remove it. Once I do, Raielle pulls in a breath. A small smile plays on her lips for the next few moments as Meera does something to her. When the woman finally releases her and sits back in her chair, Raielle's smile remains.

"What did it feel like?" I ask, curious about her expression.

She hesitates, searching for the words. "Like I was swimming in a pool of warm water."

Across the table, Meera smiles at her.

"She's pretty strong, right?" Grant asks. "As strong as John?"

"No." Meera shakes her head and Grant's face seems to fall. "She's stronger."

I glance at Raielle, but she doesn't react at all to this news, even as Grant is pinning his eyes to her, obviously intrigued.

Meera points in her direction. "You have visions when you heal."

"Visions?" Grant asks before she can answer.

Raielle licks her lips nervously. Then she nods. "Do you know why I have them? And why it doesn't happen all the time?"

I think of the vision she had when she healed my arm. She saw my mother with the baseball bat, and then she knew the secret I'd been keeping for so long.

Meera leans forward in her chair. "I don't know why some of us have them and others don't, but they occur when you're healing someone who has experienced a devastating trauma of some kind. Those types of events leave behind more than physical injuries. They cause mental pain and create emotional scars. You can't heal those, but your energy is still drawn to them. You still see them."

"You have them, too, then?" Raielle asks.

Meera nods.

I wonder what Raielle is thinking as her body seems to relax into the chair. She glances at me and despite her calm expression, her eyes are shining. Then it clicks for me. Here with Meera, she's finally found someone who understands her, someone who may be like her and can finally answer the questions she's had for so long.

"What about her father?" I ask. "Why don't you work with him any longer, and why does your daughter hate him so much?"

Meera sighs and looks out over the dusky mountains along the horizon. "We didn't believe in the same things. When I first met him, he pretended that we were alike. He said I was the strongest healer he'd ever encountered besides himself. He asked me to partner with him. When I realized how many people we could help together, I agreed. But once we became established and John had the channels in place that started bringing us more and more patients, he stopped pretending."

"Pretending what?" Raielle asks.

"That he cared. That he was in it for more than the money and the power."

Raielle swallows and blinks a few times before she says, "Grant said that my father made you leave."

Meera nods. "I wanted to help more than only rich people, and I told him so. John doesn't like when people disagree with him." Her hands disappear in her lap and she glances down at them. "He showed me the door." Then she looks up at Grant and Raielle. "I didn't go far, though. Because some of you still need me." She smiles at them.

"Does he know that you're here? That you're still involved?" Raielle asks.

"I'm not involved. Not really. As long as I don't cause trouble, he doesn't care about little old me."

Raielle bites her lip, and I can tell that she wants to ask something. I reach out and take her hand in mine, giving it a reassuring squeeze. "What is it?" I ask her.

She looks at all of us, still hesitant, before saying, "Can you feel it, Meera? When you're healing someone and they're not meant to recover. Do you always feel something different?"

"Yes." Meera nods.

"Have you ever pushed past that feeling and continued anyway?"

I watch Raielle's expression, knowing she's thinking of that girl in her father's clinic.

"No," Meera says vehemently, shaking her head. "You can't ever cross that line."

"But what if something was telling you to keep going?"

Meera's expression hardens. "You can't. You never push past that point. If death is there, it must take someone, and if you disregard that, there are always consequences."

Raielle swallows back her emotions. "But I felt something different yesterday. My father gave me a test using a sick little girl who he said didn't have much time left. He claimed that he wanted me to learn that stopping point, but I already know what that point feels like. I've felt that before and I made the mistake of pushing past it. But yesterday, when I should have felt it again, my energy told me to keep going. That I was strong enough to heal her."

"Your father was there with you?" Meera asks, leaning forward again.

"Yes. He stopped me. He told me that I'd failed his test and still had a lot to learn."

Meera looks thoughtful as she clasps her hands in front of her. "The way you felt was probably his doing. His energy was still working inside you. It was tricking you. It's likely that he wanted you to fail so you'd believe you need him more than you actually do."

I watch Raielle's face, wondering what she's thinking, trying to gauge how upset this is making her, but her expression doesn't change. "If Ray decided to walk away from her father, could you help her?" I ask. "Could you teach her what she needs to know?"

Meera's daughter appears in the open doorway. "She can't. If John's daughter tries to walk away from him, he'll come after her and he'll come after us, too."

Raielle shakes her head. "I don't want to cause you any trouble."

Adrienne steps out onto the patio. "Then you shouldn't come back here again. Especially considering what we've heard about John lately."

Meera and Grant exchange a look.

"What have you heard?" I ask.

Adrienne crosses her arms. "That he's suffering from what you all eventually fall victim to when you keep this up too long. He's losing it. His power is fading and so is his mind. Grant, you must have heard the rumors. They say that John is unstable and desperate. He's killing people without their consent now. He has more sick, rich people than he has willing bodies to trade for them."

Raielle directs a sharp look at Grant. "Is that true?"

"I don't know anything for sure." He shifts in his chair. "What is true is that he's losing some of his power. He's not as strong as he used to be. It takes him longer to recover after a healing, which means he can't do as many as he could before."

I think about what Shane told me, that the money wasn't rolling in so fast for the same reason Grant just said.

"Either way. It doesn't matter," Adrienne says. "We can't help you."

"Yes, we can," Meera counters.

Adrienne glowers at her.

"This is what I do, Adrienne. I help people. I don't turn them away."

Raielle stands stiffly, interrupting them. "I appreciate your kindness, but I don't want to cause you any trouble."

I take her arm. "Wait. She said she'd help you. Don't say no so fast."

Her eyes narrow, but before she can say anything, Meera says, "Why don't you think about it. I know I've already given you a lot to think about. If you change your mind, you know where to find me. When you do come again, I promise Adrienne won't give you any more trouble." She's looking at her daughter when she finishes speaking.

Raielle is on edge now as she thanks the old woman. Grant seems surprised by her refusal of Meera's offer. But he also seems a little in awe now as he watches her. I don't think he fully realized how strong Raielle is before now. He says his good-byes and follows Raielle through the door. I nod politely at a stoic Adrienne as she waits to shut the door behind me.

The three of us are quiet when we get back into the car, as though we don't have a million things to discuss after what we just learned. Once we're on the road, Raielle turns toward me in the backseat. "I know what you're going to say."

I give her a curious look, noticing the worried crease between her brows.

"That everything we learn about my father makes him sound worse and worse. That I should let Meera help me instead. But we can't put her at odds with him. We probably shouldn't have even come here today. You saw how afraid her daughter was."

"We could get you out here without your father knowing," Grant suggests. "You shouldn't dismiss what she could do for you so quickly. And you heard her; she's more than willing to help you."

I can't believe Grant and I are in agreement, but I take up his cause. "You heard what she said. Your father is playing with you. He's not teaching you anything. Look at what he's already put you through with that little test of his."

"But that girl…" she says softly.

"What girl? The one in the clinic?" I ask, hating that I'm sitting behind her and can't see her expression.

"Yes," she answers, looking at Grant, not me. "I just don't believe it was his power tricking me into what I felt with her. Now that it's fading, I need to know for sure. I want to try to help her again."

I sit back against my seat. "Christ, Ray."

She turns around to face me. "Meera said that when you know it's time to stop, you have to stop. But I never reached that point with her. There was no stopping point for my power. It was you who stopped me. What if I'm the only one who can help her? What if she dies in that clinic waiting for a volunteer? Am I supposed to just forget about her?"

I know there are no words I can say to erase the determination on her face. There's no talking her out of anything when she gets this way. "You can't try to heal her again," I snap at her, knowing that my ordering her not to do it is only going to make her angrier. But I don't know how to make her listen. "Meera knows what she's talking about. She knew about your visions and why your power was so out of control. You need to listen to her. Please, Ray."

I'm scrubbing my hands over my face when I see Grant reach out to her and gently stroke her arm. "You're not supposed to forget," he says gently. "That's not who you are. But we should think carefully before you decide anything. We should talk about it more."

When he directs a calm, reassuring smile in her direction, I want to yank his hand away from her and tell him to stay the hell out of it. He's not the one who encouraged her to heal Penelope, and then had to watch helplessly while she suffered from the horrific consequences of a disease she mistakenly gave to herself. I'll never get over the part I played in that, and I don't intend for it to happen again.

But when she grins back at him gratefully, my heart lurches. That's what she wants, support, not an angry asshole who keeps yelling at her because he's so afraid of losing her. I wonder if I have it in me to do what Grant seems to manage so easily. I can't even pretend to support something that could result in nothing but more devastation for her.

What he said to me outside Crossroads runs through my head. At the time, I took it too literally because I can see it happening now. True to his word, Grant is there for her when I can't be.

FOURTEEN

Lucas

GRANT drops us off at the condo so we can pack Raielle's things, but I don't want to go inside. With the way I'm feeling, I'll just get on her case. If Shane's home, it's likely I'll lose it on him, too. Her wary expression says she knows what's brewing inside me.

"Let's go for a drive," I suggest.

The sun is going down, and we're standing on the sidewalk. She looks at me like I'm nuts. "We just spent almost four hours in the car today."

She's right. A drive may not be the best idea. "How about we go get some dinner then?"

She glances up at the condo, obviously not wanting to go inside any more than I do. "We could go to the market. I'll cook you dinner at your apartment, and we can come back later to get my stuff."

At her offer, I feel some amount of relief. I can't pretend to approve of what she wants, but I can refrain from discussing it for a little while the way she seems to want me to. "You cook?" I ask.

She nods. "I cooked for my mom and me all the time."

I know Cal's working tonight, and the idea of the two of us alone at my place while she makes me dinner sounds too good to refuse. I dip down to kiss her. "You cooking for me is on my fantasy list," I say, wanting to lift her mood.

"It is?" She tilts her head at me. "Why is that a fantasy?"

"Because you're doing it naked." I grin when I see her cheeks redden.

"I don't think that's very sanitary," she says, wrinkling her nose. But I'm pretty sure she's feigning her reaction because she can't hide the gleam in her eyes.

"I'd be willing to risk it." I find the truck myself in the valet lot and get the keys from the attendant. Then I pull open the passenger door for her.

Before she gets in, she levels her gaze at me. "You know I'm not cooking you dinner naked, right?"

Leaning down, I say quietly, "What if I promise to eat it naked?"

Her eyes widen. "Umm…" Then she yelps in surprise as I lift her up onto the seat.

"Keep thinking about me naked." I shut the door, quietly laughing to myself, unexpectedly eager to temporarily put aside the issues hanging heavy in the air between us if it means we get to spend a nice night together.

Raielle is quiet beside me as I pull out of the parking lot. We drive through the outskirts of Westwood just as the colorful neon marquees for the various movie theaters so abundant to this neighborhood start buzzing to life. Once we're past all the shops and restaurants, I take a side road I discovered a few weeks ago.

She furrows her brow. "Another shortcut?"

"The last one worked out, didn't it?"

I'm heading through an intersection, and I can see her skeptical expression as she watches out the window. When I drive up the narrow hill that will bring us out behind the grocery store, I feel her eyes on me.

"Told you," I say smugly.

"Yes, you did." She laughs.

The market isn't too busy, and I have fun trailing behind her, watching as she chooses ingredients for a pasta dish she's decided to make. When I toss Ring Dings into the cart, she makes a face.

"You know you're gonna want a Ring Ding when you see me eating them."

"Doubtful," she replies over her shoulder.

I grin, feeling a sense of optimism creep in. Now that we know about Meera, her reasons for needing her father have disappeared. She can get what she wants and tell him to kiss off. But there are two problems with that. First, she doesn't want to put Meera at risk. Second, she can't forget about the girl lying sick in the clinic. I can probably change her mind on the first issue, but the second one is problematic.

The more I think about that girl, the more the situation feels manipulated to me. Her father found a sick kid exactly like Penelope to throw at her, like he knew the best way to pull at her heartstrings. If he manipulated her power to make her believe she could cure the girl, and then he stopped her from doing it, he had to know how obsessed she'd become with healing her. But why would he do that? To keep her close and make sure she had a reason to stay? Maybe.

We get the grocery bags into the truck and head back. Raielle is fidgety beside me. "Is Cal going to yell at me again?" she asks.

I wince, still feeling guilty over that situation. "He won't be back until late. I talked to him, though."

She says nothing in response, but her knee stops bouncing.

When we arrive at my apartment, I'm surprised to find the front door unlocked. *Shit.* Maybe Cal is home. I look around for him as I carry the groceries through the hallway into the kitchen. He doesn't seem to be here, but I hear Raielle calling my name. After dumping everything onto the counter, I find her standing in my bedroom doorway. Her face is pale as she looks at me. Then she takes a step back, and her eyes shift toward my room.

When I come up beside her and look into the bedroom, the naked girl lying on my bed grins at me. "Your roommate let me in," she says. "I didn't realize you already had company tonight." Then slowly, making sure I have time to enjoy the view first, she reaches down to pull the sheet up over herself.

My brows arch up in surprise. "And you are?" I ask, wondering if she's one of Cal's castoffs.

Her dark hair falls over her shoulder as she sits up more fully. "It's okay. I get it." She gives me a wobbly smile. "I'll go."

I step inside. "What do you get?"

She pushes her hair off her face. "I know you didn't make me any promises, Lucas, but please stop pretending. You're not fooling anyone."

My head reels when she uses my name. Then she looks at Raielle. "He told me he has a girlfriend, but that he doesn't mind screwing around on her. Is that what he told you, too?"

Raielle's eyes grow wide. I storm the rest of the way into the room. "Get the fuck out!" My head snaps back to Raielle, still standing in the doorway.

Her eyes bore into mine before she turns and starts to walk out of the apartment. My jaw clenches. If this is Cal's idea of a joke, I'm going to kill him. "This isn't fucking funny. Get dressed," I bark at the girl before going after Raielle.

I find her out on the sidewalk, waiting for me. Her expression is pained. It shoots a dagger right through my heart. "You know that wasn't what it looked like," I begin, pretending her hurt isn't written on her face. "She's lying. I have no idea who she is. Someone put her up to this." After everything we've been through, Raielle can't really believe I'm the one lying here. But her reaction makes me fear that all the trust we've built has just been obliterated.

She takes a shallow breath. "Why would someone put her up to it?"

My hands rake through my hair. "I have no idea. Please stop looking at me like that. If I'd done anything with anyone other than the blonde at the club, I would have told you about it last night. I've never even seen that girl before."

Her expression doesn't change.

I take a step closer to her. "Come on. You know me better than this." When she doesn't move away, my hand reaches toward her cheek. "Ray…"

She averts her eyes and shifts her weight. Then she starts to nod. "Okay. I believe you."

I let out a relieved breath and reach for her hand. But she steps back.

"Get her out of your bed first. Then come find me at Nikki's. I'm going to walk over there."

She won't even look at me. "If you believe me, why are you punishing me?"

Her eyes close for a moment, and she seems tired. "I'm not punishing you," she says. "It's been a long day. I don't want to go back in there right now. Just figure out what's going on. Okay?"

As she starts to turn away, I grab her hand. When she finally looks at me, I see how weary she is, and it's not just from lack of sleep, it's everything piled on top of that. She pulls on her hand and reluctantly, I release her, watching as she walks away from me.

FIFTEEN

Raielle

I MOVE to the side to let a group of girls pass. It's dark, and the sidewalk is uneven and cracked. I keep my eyes on the ground, trying not to trip and add injury to insult.

I know I'm abandoning him, but I don't trust myself or what I may say to him right now. After what happened at the club the other night, I thought the girl in his bed really knew him, and that she was waiting for him, which would mean he'd lied about not being with anyone else. It would also mean he gave up everything and followed me out here just to start sleeping around with other girls. That makes no sense; I know that. I guess I really do believe him. Does that make me an idiot?

Just now, I could see how my doubt hurt him. Could he blame me, though? If the situation were reversed, he would take it at face value, too. He wouldn't automatically assume my innocence when the evidence of my guilt was lying naked right in front of him. But who would set him up like this? Who would pull such a mean-spirited prank?

I keep walking, shaking my head at no one, trying to sort through my jumble of thoughts that are all tangling together into a knotted mess. I'm the one who found a naked girl in his bed, and he's probably mad at me now. What's wrong with this picture?

Because my eyes are cast down, I don't see Apollo's car until he rolls down the window and calls out to me. I startle, realizing that I'm already at Nikki's building.

"You okay?" His eyes narrow on me as he leans across the passenger seat.

"What are you doing here?" I ask, bending down to see him better.

"I was looking for you. You're not answering that new phone you told me you had."

It's actually my old phone. The one Apollo made me leave behind, but I don't bother correcting him. I pull it out of my bag and see that it's dead. I can't remember the last time I charged it.

Apollo pushes open the passenger door. "Get in. Your daddy said some girl you tried to heal took a bad turn, but whatever you did to her yesterday helped. He wants you to do it again."

I steady my hand on the door. "The girl in the clinic? I helped her?"

"That's what he said." He shrugs, indifferent to the news.

But my hopes flutter. "Why didn't he tell me?"

He gives me a disparaging look. "When you don't answer your phone, and you don't turn up at home, it's hard to tell you much of anything."

I look back the way I came. "I have to let Lucas know where I'm going."

Apollo reaches into his pocket. "Call him from my phone. I don't think there's much time. That's why I came looking for you."

I hesitate a moment longer before finally giving in and getting into the car. My reluctance is because I know Lucas wouldn't want me to go. But Apollo's words confirm what I already felt inside. I was helping her before I was stopped. I could help her again.

He hands me his phone, and it takes Lucas a long time to answer. He sounds out of breath when he picks up.

"It's me," I tell him.

"Ray? Where are you calling from?"

"Apollo's phone. My battery's dead. We're headed to my father's house. The girl in the clinic got worse and—"

"What?" he yells over the line. "You're going back there?"

Apollo glances at me as Lucas's raised voice carries to him. "I'm already on my way. My father says that I helped her. He wants me to do it again. Where are you? It sounds like you're in the car."

"Ray, no." I hear shuffling in the background. "I was headed to your condo but I'm turning around. I'll meet you at the house. Don't do anything until I get there."

I grip the phone tighter. Based on what Apollo said, there won't be time to wait for him. "Why were you going to the condo?" I ask.

"It was Shane," he replies, and I can hear the tension in his voice. "He paid that girl to act like I was fucking her. He helped her break in, and then he left her there. She told me easily enough. I think he wanted me to know it was him. I was planning on showing him what I thought of his little joke."

There's no love lost between Shane and me, but I never imagined he'd go this far to hurt me. "Why would he do that?" I ask, thinking of the planning and sneaking around needed to pull that off.

"Who knows? To make trouble. To break us up." He pauses. "Tell Apollo to bring you back."

My eyes close at the quiet plea in his voice. "I can't."

He says nothing in response, he just breathes out, and I imagine I can hear his disapproval over the line.

"I'll see you soon," I say quietly. Then I take the phone away from my ear and disconnect the call.

Apollo eyes me for a long moment, and I wonder how much he heard.

"You okay, kid?" he asks.

I grip my hands together in my lap. "I'm fine. I'm always fine, right?" I smile humorlessly.

He looks down his nose at me. "You always say you are."

We're stopped at a red light, and his eyes hold mine until I turn away first to stare out the window. My thoughts go to Shane and the malice he must feel toward me. He put that girl up to it? I can't understand it. Other than that one drunken moment at the bar when he apologized, he's shown me nothing but disdain and now he does this?

Apollo touches my arm to get my attention back. "I've been meaning to tell you, Lucas is okay in my book. You do better with him than without him."

My shock prevents me from responding at first. Apollo never likes or approves of anyone. But then I find my voice, needing to say something that I've been holding back. "You should have told me sooner that he was here."

The light turns green and his eyes go back to the road. "You're right. I should have told you," he says, still not looking at me.

He surprises me again by admitting that, and I watch his profile, dimly lit by the red dashboard lights, wondering if he's going to explain himself about why he kept us apart. When I realize that he's not going to say anything else, I turn back to the window, deciding not to ask. If he was going to tell me, he would have. Questioning Apollo never gets me anywhere.

Apollo may approve of Lucas, but the feeling isn't mutual. Lucas hates Apollo. After taking me away and keeping us apart all summer, Lucas believes I should hate him, too. But what he did for me the day I nearly died is not something I'll ever forget. He saved me as much as my father did. Even though I regret the way I got my life back, I don't blame Apollo for it. It's because of his actions that I'm alive and I'm with Lucas again.

Soon Apollo is turning into the long wooded road that leads up to the house. Once we pull in front of the fountain, I see Nyla standing in the open doorway, wearing a long, shimmery silk robe. My father appears beside her.

"Go on in," Apollo urges, apparently not intending to stay.

Smiling my thanks at him, I get out of the car and walk up the steps.

"I'm glad you came," my father says.

Nyla nods at me before quietly disappearing inside. Then my father motions for me to follow him. Once I'm behind him, he walks swiftly through the house, heading straight for the clinic door.

I thought I'd be nervous being here again, knowing what he did to make me lose control of my energy, and understanding that greed is probably his main motivation. He may want me here for his own reasons, but whatever they are, he's done nothing to indicate an intention to hurt me. He's played with me so far, just like Meera said. But my determination is giving me courage, and as far as I'm concerned, playtime is over.

His eyes travel over me as we walk. "She doesn't have long now, and we haven't found a volunteer," he says solemnly. "But after you left yesterday, she woke up and was able to get out of her bed for the first time in weeks. I ran a blood test and saw that her counts were better. You didn't cure her, but you did manage to reduce the amount of disease in her body. I'd like you to do it again."

I can feel myself smiling as I remember how it felt when I was healing her, and now I'm even more certain they shouldn't have stopped me. "I could do that, but I'd like to try to cure her again."

His head shakes dismissively. "You can't."

I stop walking. "But it felt like I could. I want to try again." Meera's words about my father tricking me into feeling that way echo in my head. If that's true, will he let me try? Because either way, I still need to know.

He pauses in front of the door and turns back to give me a harsh look. "If you're not strong enough, she has a mother or a sister it could travel to. Or even worse, you could give it to yourself. As I told you, when your power is strong enough, you can move an illness into anyone. But if it gets inside you, you may not be able to get it out again."

Feeling his doubt and even his condescension, I say, "I know the risks."

His lips press together. "I shouldn't let you do it. But I didn't think you could help her either and you did. Can I ask why you feel so strongly about this?"

I swallow hard, wishing I could explain. "It's something inside me, an instinct or a belief that I can't really put into words, not even to myself."

He looks at me for a long time. Then he nods. "All right. I'm going to let you try. If there's anyone who can do this, I have a feeling it's you. But if I see it's not working, I will stop you again. I can't let you hurt yourself or anyone else."

I nod my agreement, feeling the way my energy seems to spark with anticipation.

His expression gentles as he urges me toward the door. This is really happening. My heart races as I stay close behind him. I wonder how far Lucas is from the house, but I won't delay this and risk my father changing his mind.

We go down the stairs until we reach the brightly lit clinic with its sharp smells and white walls. Soon my father is standing in the doorway of her room. "You can change your mind," he says.

I shake my head. There's no changing my mind. "Can you tell me her name?"

"Kaylie."

Thinking how pretty that sounds, I ask him, "Where's her family? Do they come to see her here?"

"They come during morning and evening visiting hours every day," he replies, pushing open the door.

I hope they'll find a healthy Kaylie when they next see her. I pull in a deep breath and try to calm down. When I look at him, he seems to understand my nerves, and he smiles encouragingly. Once we step inside, I hear him shut the door behind us as I look toward the hospital bed.

The girl, Kaylie, appears much the same as she did the other day, except her red hair has a pink barrette in it now. Her chest rises and falls beneath the blankets with her steady breathing. As I approach the bed, I can feel the energy inside me wanting to form. I glance at my father and he moves to stand beside me.

"I'll stay right here, just in case," he says, his voice reassuring.

Nodding, I grip the bed rail. My eyes travel over her features, lingering on the sprinkle of freckles across the bridge of her nose, thinking how small and vulnerable she seems. Then I take a deep breath and reach for her small hand. Her skin is so terribly cold as I hold her fingers in mine. My plan was to send the energy out to her slowly, trying to monitor her reaction, but it bursts from within me, heating my skin and making my whole body tremble with its force. I can't hold it back as it streams through my arm and out of my hand into hers. Just like last time, I feel no resistance from the power that coils between us. I sense none of the forces that fought against me when I was trying to cure Penelope. Everything about that healing felt wrong while everything about this feels so perfectly right.

I'm watching her face as her eyes open and focus on me. When the euphoria bubbles up inside me, she smiles.

I'm burning through the disease in her body, ridding her of it with the heat my energy generates. She's growing stronger beneath my fingers. I can feel it happening.

"My God," my father whispers beside me.

My eyes close as my body hums with power. I've never felt anything like this. It's as though I'm lit up inside. My power knows exactly what to do. It feels strong and precise, and the healing is nearly effortless. But then just as I'm thinking that, it stutters. My eyes pop open as it starts to diminish on its own. But I know I'm not finished. She's not cured, and I dig deeper, trying to bring it back again. But it slackens quickly, and I feel a ring of pressure surrounding my arm. Glancing down, I see my father's hand gripping me tightly.

"Keep going," he says. His face is intent on mine as his fingers tighten painfully.

I don't understand what he's doing. I try to pull my arm away without breaking the connection to Kaylie. The energy is still moving between us, but it starts to tug on me, grating against my skin as it stops flowing toward her and changes direction. I look at my father, and I realize that he's drawing it into himself.

"What are you doing?" I cry, trying to wrench my arm away. But he grabs my other arm, breaking my hold on Kaylie completely. He's stealing my power, forcing it out of me and into himself. I struggle against his grip, but I can't get him to release me. Instead, I try to stop the energy. But somehow he's making it grow, and he's drawing it out in a steady stream. I can't get control of it, and it's starting to burn beneath my skin, like my blood is changing to liquid fire inside my veins. I hear myself scream as my legs buckle beneath me while my father forcibly holds me up by my arms.

From the corner of my eye, I see Kaylie getting down off the bed, watching us with a frightened expression.

"Stop, please," I beg. I can't hold back the tears as the room tilts and darkens around me.

I feel it when he drags me toward the bed and the energy finally begins to dwindle. His eyes are on me and their green depths are placid, a calm sea with nothing behind them.

"Is this what you wanted from me all along?" I ask weakly.

He lifts me up and lays me down as a frightened Kaylie tries to open the door to run out. I can't seem to move. My muscles are heavy and slack. It's a struggle to stay alert.

"I had no idea this was possible," he answers. "A plague is coming, Raielle. I have to be ready. I have to be strong. And you're going to help me. Just not in the way I initially thought."

His words flow over me as I struggle to move, to do something as simple as lift my head, but I can't. Lucas is on his way, and I don't know what he'll find when he arrives or what they'll tell him. My eyelids are too heavy to keep open, and I wonder if I'm dying, understanding too late how foolish I've been.

When sleep finally drags me under, I can feel the pillow growing damp beneath my cheek.

SIXTEEN

Lucas

I POUND on the button, but they won't open the gate. Then I pull out my phone and call the number Raielle dialed me from, but no one picks up and no voice mail answers either. It just fucking rings. Finally, I leave my truck on the side of the road and climb over the gate. I begin to walk, knowing that something's wrong, and I move faster, breaking into a jog when I hear the mechanical gate swing open behind me. The Porsche comes through. It's Shane.

"I need a ride to the house," I tell him, moving to the passenger door without waiting for his agreement.

He scowls at me once I'm inside. "I thought that was your truck I saw. Why didn't you hit the buzzer?"

I turn angry eyes on him. "Your sister is up there and they won't let me in. I don't suppose you know what's going on?"

He shifts his gaze forward as he starts to drive again. "Remember when you asked me if my father would ever hurt Raielle?"

All my attention focuses on his face. "You said no more than anyone else."

He glances at me. "I might have been wrong about that."

181

I go still. There's only the feel of my heart wanting to pump right out of my chest.

Shane shifts in his seat. "He heard an argument you two had during the lockdown. He knew you were trying to convince her to leave. At first he thought you'd be good for her. But he changed his mind. He decided to break you two up to get you out of the picture. My father gets what he wants and right now he wants Raielle for some reason."

My jaw locks up tight because I'm pretty sure I know what's coming next.

"That girl tonight was supposed to get Raielle to dump you, which I guess didn't work since you're here. Unless you've gone all stalker on her."

My hand slams against the dashboard. Then it does it again, vibrating all the way down my arm.

"Hey, watch the car," Shane complains. "Where did she find you anyway, anger management class?"

"You're making jokes?" My anger is about to combust, and he must realize that because without my doing or saying anything else, he gulps and his expression turns serious. "She said Apollo was driving her here so she could help a sick girl in his clinic. Is that the real reason?" I ask.

His hand rubs behind his neck. "I don't know why he brought her here. That's the truth. We could call Grant or Apollo. Maybe they know."

"Do it," I tell him. "Call Grant."

He glares at me. "I don't have to help you at all. I only told you all that because you're already on your way to the house, and he's just going to throw you out. You might as well go home."

"Call him."

Shooting me an annoyed look, he finds the number on his phone, and when he starts to talk, I grab it from him. "Grant?"

"You're with Shane?" he asks, surprised.

We're just pulling up to the house when I finish explaining all that's gone on tonight. Grant has been listening quietly, not seeming surprised, when he says, "John can be dangerous. Wait outside, I'm on my way."

I hand the phone back to Shane, and he gives me a once-over. "Are you going to do as he says, or are you going to charge in there and make everything worse?"

I grip the door handle. "I can't wait. What if he's hurting her?"

Shane rolls his eyes. "His bodyguards are in there. If he doesn't want you inside, you're not getting in. It makes sense to wait for Grant. He'll have more luck than you or even I will. I'll wait with you," he says. The keys jangle as he pulls them from the ignition.

My head snaps in his direction. "Why?"

"I don't know." He shrugs. "I wouldn't mind finding out what my dad wants from her. Besides, she's my sister."

"Yeah, lucky her," I mutter, staring out at the house as my knee starts to bounce with impatience.

Raielle

WAKE up disoriented with a dry mouth and a pounding head. It feels like I'm hung over again but ten times worse. I wonder if I dreamed that my father came after me like some kind of vampire. But once I realize where I am, I know it really happened.

I'm lying in the same bed Kaylie once occupied, looking at the quarter moon through a small rectangular window at the top of the wall. I'm waiting for my strength to return, for the ability to lift myself up and out of this bed, but I'm still weak as a kitten. I know the door to this small room has opened several times, but it takes me so long to turn my head, it closes again before I can see who's there.

It still seems unreal that my father would do this to me. I knew the image he projected wasn't really him, and I suspected he was agnostic at best when it came to right and wrong. When Meera's daughter told us the rumors she'd heard about him, I didn't dismiss them as impossible. Although, I didn't want to believe them. But I pushed all that aside for the little girl who was lying here. I needed to help her with a single-mindedness that wouldn't be deterred by the possibility of danger.

A plague is coming, he said. He's not just dangerous, he's crazy, too.

Gripping the bed rail for leverage, I pull myself up, hissing sharply when my brain feels like it's shifting inside my head. My hand starts to slip because it and the rest of my body are drenched in sweat. I'm trying to listen for the doorknob turning or for any other noise as I shift my legs over the side and just sit there, breathing hard, listening to the sound of my harsh breaths echoing in the room. I don't understand what's happening to me. When my father stole my energy, I wonder if he did something else, because it feels like I'm burning up with fever. Everything hurts.

Next I try to slide down to my feet, but gravity works against me and I hit the floor hard, my hip banging painfully against the tile floor. I turn toward the door, and I know I have to get to it. I don't know what my next move is once I'm through it, but the door is what I focus on as I struggle to pull myself up.

Lucas

WE'RE a restless group gathered in the library of the house waiting for John. The same place Raielle and I sat just the other day. When Grant arrived, he went running up the steps and we followed. Shane was right. The guards were ready to turn me away, but they hesitated when they saw Grant and in the end, they let us all inside.

Raielle would be surprised to know that she had us all here for her now, and that her father was behind the scene back at my apartment earlier. We've been kept waiting for nearly half an hour with the guards watching over us, and I can't wait a minute longer knowing she could be here somewhere hurting or frightened. Just as I turn for the door, John and Nyla come through it, their expressions solemn.

We're intent on them when John says, "You're all here for Raielle?" His curious eyes stay on Shane the longest.

"She told Lucas that Apollo brought her here to help the girl with cancer in the clinic," Grant says.

This seems to surprise John. He probably thought she wouldn't be speaking to me at all by then.

He nods at Grant. "I asked Apollo to find her. I saw a marked improvement in the girl after Raielle's healing. I hoped she could help her again. But Raielle got it in her head that she could cure her. She wouldn't stop when I asked her to." John's gaze meets mine. "Just like last time."

My breath halts at that possibility even as I'm narrowing suspicious eyes on him.

"She acted foolishly and I'm afraid she gave the disease to herself," John says stiffly. He looks like he's trying to feign being upset, but failing miserably.

Shane is the first to speak. "Can you help her?"

His lips press together. "I could, but she wants no part of what it would take to do that."

I don't believe a word coming out of his mouth. "I want to see her," I say.

John's green eyes shift to me again. "She's quarantined for now. Her immune system is compromised."

I take a step toward him. "I don't care. I want to see her."

His expression doesn't change. "You don't care about putting her in more jeopardy than she's already in? We're taking good care of her. If she improves tomorrow, you can see her then."

I take the three steps necessary to close the distance between us. Nyla's expression tenses, but John doesn't flinch. "I'm going down there now."

Finally his calm shifts to annoyance. "I told you—" John begins.

"I hear you perfectly fine, but I don't give a fuck." I start to move around him when he shouts out to his bodyguard. Feet pounding down the hall alert me to their fast approach.

"Lucas, step back," Grant says. When one of the guards appears and grabs for me, I dodge him just as I spot Grant moving forward with a handgun pointed at John.

"What are you doing?" John asks. His voice is calm despite the way Nyla is now clutching his arm.

Grant shakes his head. "The question is, what are you doing?"

"I'm taking care of my daughter," he states.

"No," Grant says. "I don't think you are." He glances at me briefly before turning and firing a shot. John goes down, his head jerking back before his body hits the floor. When the next deafening pop sounds, Nyla crumples in a heap, and before the guard can turn and run, Grant nails him, too, clipping the side of his head, just like the others.

My adrenaline is surging and my ears are ringing. "They'll heal," Grant tells me before turning to Shane. "Do I have to shoot you, too?" he asks.

Shane eyes the bodies on the ground before giving Grant a wry look and saying, "Nope."

"Let's go find her." Grant brushes past me, and I hear him firing again. I have to step over the carnage in the doorway to get out into the hall. For a moment, I'm sure I must be imagining this or having some kind of insane nightmare. But when Grant stops at the clinic door and glances back, I know Raielle is down there, and if they're going to all this trouble to keep us away from her, Grant is right. We have to do whatever it takes to get her back.

When Grant starts down the stairs, I'm right behind him, and I can hear him barking at the people in the clinic. Once I hit the bottom step, I see him aiming the gun at a terrified nurse. But I move past him, concentrating on the door to the room I know must have been her destination.

The moment my eyes land on the tiny square window at the top of the closed door, I can see that the bed is empty. But I go inside anyway. I don't even remember turning the knob or moving, but the next thing I know I'm staring down at Raielle lying on the hard tile floor. I bend to touch my hand to her cheek. It's cold and clammy. She has a sickly gray pallor to her face. "Ray?"

Her eyes flutter open. Their translucent blue color looks even more pronounced against her bloodless skin. She says nothing, just looks at me, and my insides splinter apart.

"We need to get her out to my car," Grant says from behind me. When he sees her, the concern on his face is clear. "Maybe John was telling the truth. If she gave herself the girl's disease, Meera can help her." He tucks his gun away and crouches down to help me lift her.

But I don't want any help, and I block her from him. A soft moan falls from her lips when I lift her up and cradle her against me. I can feel more cracks forming inside me.

Grant leads the way out. There's a door to the outside just beyond the desk where the nurse is still standing, stoic and quiet, her gaze moving with us as we walk past. Once we're out, I realize we're at the side of the house. The yard is dark with shadows as I hold Raielle close and follow Grant up a hill toward the front.

The black GTO is parked off to the side under some trees. Grant gets it started, and he's out again, holding the seat forward so I can slide into the back with Raielle. Before I do, I follow his gaze to the front of the house, where I see Shane standing in the doorway, watching us.

Grant nudges my shoulder, wanting me to get in the car, and I do, laying Raielle down on the seat before following after her. The fact that she's hardly stirred since I found her makes it hard not to panic. I rest her head on my lap and smooth my hand over her forehead, pushing the tendrils of hair away from her face.

"We're going back to Palm Springs?" I ask, looking at his eyes in the rearview mirror.

He nods as he turns onto the freeway.

"I can't believe she did this again," I say. Her chest rises and falls as she draws in each breath. My heart is still racing in the aftermath of what just happened. I stare at the back of Grant's head, thinking how easily he shot four people. "Why do you have a gun?" I ask.

He eyes me again in the mirror. "It's necessary sometimes," he says. Then he reaches over and turns on the radio, letting me know he doesn't want to talk.

SEVENTEEN

Raielle

"HE drained her energy. Feeding off her like a parasite. I had a vision of it when I started healing her. She suffered. He was ruthless."

I recognize Meera's voice along with the warm, peaceful, floating sensation she's giving me.

Gradually becoming more aware, I try to nod, confirming what she's saying, and I can hear someone moving toward us. Then a familiar hand finds me, brushing at my cheek, and another gently grips my waist. Tears slip from my closed eyes. He wipes them away, murmuring softly to me, telling me it's going to be okay.

I want to tell him I'm sorry, but I make no sounds. I'm afraid I've hurt him too many times, put him through too much. Until I feel the slightest pressure of his lips on my forehead before he's gone again. I only feel Meera's hands taking both of mine now. She fills me with her own energy until I'm finally able to open my eyes.

Meera is all I see at first, and I take in her kind face as she sits beside

189

my bed. Then I can make out Grant standing behind her. His hands are buried in his pockets, and his face is tight with worry despite the small smile he's giving me.

When Lucas touches my forehead, I turn and see him. My gaze stays on his lips and his strong chin, afraid to take in any more. Fearing what I may see in his eyes. I won't be able to handle his anger, even though I know that's exactly what I deserve. But when he bends down, forcing me to take in his expression, I see a potent mix of compassion and love. There isn't a hint of animosity there. I smile and his eyes grow shiny as he looks down at me.

"Thank you," he says, turning to Meera. When he leans back away from me, I pull my hand out of Meera's and reach for his arm. He seems surprised as I tug weakly on him, needing to be close to him, needing it like air. I reclaim my other hand and stretch it out toward him, desperately fisting my fingers in his shirt. As he lowers himself to sit on the bed beside me, I use my grasp on him to pull myself up. He meets me halfway, wrapping his arms around me, hugging me close. Silent tears trail over my cheeks as I wind my arms beneath his, pressing myself to him, drinking in the comfort he gives me. I cling to him, never wanting to let go. He holds me tightly, running his hand over my head and down my back soothingly.

When he leans back to look at me, I realize we're alone. Everyone else has left the room.

"He hurt you," Lucas says quietly, and when regret takes over his face, it nearly undoes me.

I nod and he continues to hold me, not saying anything else. When my grip finally loosens, I can see the questions in his eyes. I don't want to talk about it or even think about it, but he wants to know, and I need to tell him.

"He stole my energy while I was healing the girl we met." I swallow hard. "His hand was around my arm and the energy started to flow into him. I couldn't pull it back, and he wouldn't stop." I close my eyes because the blood starts to rush to my head. "I still don't know if I could have healed that girl, and he obviously cared nothing about her." As I look up at him, my next words are a strained whisper. "I watched him the whole time, and there was only emptiness in his eyes. He was erasing me bit by bit and he didn't care."

Lucas doesn't say anything as his hand strokes my hair.

"I closed my eyes to all the warnings, and I didn't listen to you. How could I have been so stupid? I don't know why you're not angry with me. You should be."

He seems regretful now. "I'm not, Ray. Not at you. I talked with Meera when we got here. I understand better now, I think."

I look at him, wondering what he means.

"She explained some things to me," he says. "She said that the need to help people is as basic to you as eating and sleeping. That it's not fair of me to ask you to suppress it, or to get angry when you become obsessed with helping someone. It's instinctual for you. Now that your power has grown stronger, you couldn't deny it if you tried."

I nod, realizing that Meera really does understand, and relieved that she was somehow able to make him see what I'd been unable to.

He smiles sadly at me, and I swallow against the lump in my throat as I begin to think of how my father nearly took this from me. If he'd had his way, I'd have lost everything. My father cared nothing for me, and he only wanted the power he could take from me. He took it all without mercy or any second thoughts for how he was hurting me.

Lucas's thumbs brush over my cheeks, wiping away the tears I hadn't even realized were there. "Stop, please," he whispers. "You're breaking my heart, Ray."

"I love you so much," I tell him, hating that I'm falling apart, that I can't just lock it away and stop what I'm feeling. But this is different. This is my own father trying to hurt me, and I don't know where to put all the pain I'm feeling.

Lucas lowers us to the bed and presses his forehead to mine as he continues to rub his hand up and down my back. I close my eyes while he tries to keep away the darkness for me the way he always wants to.

Lucas

'M shaking my head as I leave her room. She fell back to sleep in my arms. Her pain is so sharp, I can feel it cutting me. I watch as Meera leaves her own room down the hall and walks back into the guest bedroom where Raielle and I are staying. Grant has been sleeping on the couch.

Meera told us it could take days of healing sessions to undo what Raielle's father did to her. I'm beyond thankful to Meera and reluctantly so to Grant, too. If it weren't for him, she might still be there in her father's house.

I'm standing in the kitchen, and I can't keep still. My skin feels too tight. My anger is simmering beneath it, mixing with feelings of frustration and helplessness so strong I can barely contain them. They're like living things inside me, blaring in my ears and twisting me into knots.

I hear Grant calling after me as I push open the slider and shove out into the night. Then I run. I move mindlessly in the darkness, dirt and rocks crunching beneath my feet. My fury feels toxic, like it's poisoning me. And it's not only directed at Raielle's father, it's spilling over onto her, too. I can't protect her if she won't let me. The tighter I hold on to her, the more trouble she finds. Meera says that she can't help herself. I told Raielle that I understood, and I do. But I can't be expected to accept it. Not when shit like this keeps happening.

My lungs heave, and I can't see anything in front of me. I know the mountains are out there somewhere, but I see only blackness. Coming to a stop, I brace myself on my knees, pulling in gulps of air. Then I just stand there for I don't know how long, breathing hard, looking at nothing, before I turn around and start walking back toward the lights of Meera's house.

"Feel better now?"

I squint as I near the back patio. Grant is sitting there at the table, watching my approach.

"No." I drop down into the chair across from him, running my hands through the hair that's plastered to my damp forehead. "I want to thank you for what you did today."

Grant shrugs like it was nothing.

"I know you have your own agenda, but I'm still grateful to you."

He leans in, putting his forearms on the table. "My only agenda is to keep her safe."

When I say nothing because I don't quite believe him, he leans back in his chair again and looks out into the night.

Grant seems a little too relaxed for a guy who just shot a bunch of people and burned all his bridges. "You were pretty good with that gun today."

Rubbing a hand along his cheek, he says, "I travel to some rough places. John may have decided to only help rich folks, but I haven't."

"Do you have it on you now?" I ask.

He looks at me for a long moment before nodding slowly.

My eyes travel over his T-shirt, which he's wearing loose over a pair of jeans. I'm looking for a sign of it, but there is none. I'd never seen anyone get shot before other than on TV and in the movies, and it was nothing like that. It was so much worse; the harsh burst of sound, the wet *thunk* of the bullets hitting their bodies, the metallic smell of blood.

Grant senses my unease. "John's bodyguards carry weapons when they go out with him. We were lucky they didn't pull them on us today."

I'm not sure why he told me that, maybe to justify his own actions. "Are you sure you didn't kill John?" I ask. Not that I would mind.

"I clipped him, just enough to knock him out, real easy for him to heal. But I shot Nyla right between the eyes," he says, placing a finger between his eyebrows. "If John gives a shit about her, he'll have to spend time healing her. He'll be distracted for a little while, at least."

"Distracted from what?"

He eyes me solemnly. "From coming after us. If he was able to take Raielle's energy and make himself stronger with it, he's going to want more. He's going to keep wanting it."

At first, I was relieved when Meera explained that Raielle hadn't given herself the girl's disease like John said. But when she told us what really happened, my relief was short-lived. "Why Raielle?" I ask. "Why can't he just siphon off power from Shane or from you or one of the others?"

He shakes his head. "I don't know. I guess it's because her power is as strong as his, maybe even stronger. Taking it from one of us might not do him as much good."

I think of that sunset we watched together on the beach the other day. I thought things were turning around for us. I thought the worst was behind us.

Grant stands and walks to the door. Before he goes in, he turns back to me. "Make no mistake, this is a deadly game we're playing now. John isn't happy when he doesn't have control, and we've just shown him how out of control he is."

When he disappears inside, a shiver runs through me. This is why her father wanted her here. Everything that's happened so far led to that moment in the clinic when she finally saw him for who he really is. And now Grant says that he won't give up. As long as John wants her, this will never be over.

Raielle

"YOU can trace our kind all the way back to ancient times." Meera smiles, her thoughts far away. "For most of our history, we kept to ourselves, insulated and safe from the rest of the world. We lived that way for centuries, generation after generation, keeping each other healthy, living long, happy lives. But we couldn't stay that way forever. Some of us were lured away with the promise of money and fame. Others simply wanted to leave. Little by little, the old ways disappeared, and we were scattered across the globe."

She shakes her head. "But we discovered that we can't live that way. We need each other. Eventually, we came back together in smaller groups in different places, but it was never the same. What we used to be is gone, and what we are now is something very different."

"How many of us are there?" I ask.

"There's no way to know exactly. We have communities all over the world."

"Where do we come from? Why are we this way?"

She shrugs carelessly. "I suppose we're a mutation or an adaptation, like every other creature on the planet."

"So, we don't have some kind of alien DNA inside us or something?" I chuckle, not admitting that actually occurred to me as a possibility.

She laughs, too. "Not that I'm aware of."

It feels good to laugh, but my next question shrinks my smile. "Is my father very important?"

"No," Meera says quickly, as though that thought were too terrible to contemplate. "Not in the overall scheme of things, thank goodness. But he's important enough, for too many of us. He's always been more powerful than most of us. His father was, too. It was natural that he would assume a leadership position when his father died." She takes my hand in hers. "We've always wanted a leader, someone to be the center of our own little community. Usually, it's the most powerful among us who rises up to take that role. But it's always been someone with our best interests at heart, until your father. He pretends to be caring and kind, but we've come to see that he's not."

I glance down at her hand, gripping mine, remembering the look in his eyes when he was draining my power from me.

"I'm sorry to say that about your father," she adds.

But she needn't apologize for that. As far as I'm concerned, he's less than nothing to me. "What would he have done if Grant and Lucas hadn't gotten me out of there?" I ask.

Meera licks her lips before answering. "Waited to see if you got your strength back, and then drained you again."

"Would I have?" I ask. "Would I have recovered without your help?" I tense, waiting for her answer.

Her eyes turn sympathetic. "No. I don't think so. He took too much. If he had stopped sooner, you might have recovered on your own."

I nod and look down again, feeling the ugly hatred I have for him burning inside me. "Do you think he knew that?" I ask, my voice a hurt whisper.

Sadness weighs down her expression. "I don't know. This is new territory for all of us."

"How did they get me away from him?" I remember Lucas carrying me to the car, but not much before that.

Her thin lips turn up slightly. "Grant says they had to fight for you. They took you by force," she says, seeming impressed. "Your father wasn't about to let you go."

Fight for me? I swallow, trying to picture it. Then I realize what I should have known the moment I woke up here. "He's coming after me, isn't he?"

Without hesitation, Meera nods, and I understand the risk she's taking by helping me. "Thank you for everything you've done. I'm sorry if I put you in any danger."

She places her hand on my knee. "It's going to take time for your strength to return, Raielle. You're right where you should be."

Adrienne appears in the doorway. "Someone needs to stop John," she says flatly.

Meera tenses at her daughter's statement, but she doesn't refute it. I think of my father coming here, possibly hurting Meera and Adrienne or Lucas and Grant, when all they've done is try to help me.

"Could I do the same thing to him that he did to me?" I hear myself asking, the idea forming at the same time the words are leaving my mouth.

Meera doesn't answer, and I lift myself to an upright position to see her eyes narrowed at me.

"You mean take his power?" she asks carefully.

I nod.

She glances at Adrienne. Then she turns back to me. "Yes. You probably could." Then she smiles and laughs softly. "That would be a fitting end for him."

My gaze travels between them. "I'm being serious."

"So am I," Meera says, her smile disappearing.

My eyes go wide with understanding. Hers are steady and intent.

We all hear the front door open, and the spell is broken as Meera blinks and looks away. My shoulders fall, and my pulse echoes inside my head. Adrienne leaves and soon Lucas's and Grant's tall forms are filling the doorway. Lucas pushes past Grant and comes to sit beside me. "How are you feeling?" he asks.

I tear my eyes away from Meera and offer him a smile. "Better."

He gives me a skeptical look as he presses a finger into the crease between my brows that drives him nuts. "What's going on?"

I tense, knowing I can't tell him this, not yet. I need more time with it myself. "Meera thinks John is going to come after me," I reply.

He doesn't look surprised. "Grant said that, too."

Grant steps farther into the room. "He won't get near you. Don't worry."

I watch as Meera licks her lips, getting ready to speak. "Do you know how John came to have so much influence over all of us?" she asks. "He took it. Little by little. First, by using his power to gain our respect. When that respect waned, he used threats to maintain control. Now he uses fear. But power is a tenuous thing. It's easy to lose your grip on it, especially when your grip isn't as strong as it used to be."

Her eyes return to me on her last sentence. "Well," she says, looking away and clapping her hands together once. "I think Raielle could use some rest."

Lucas agrees with her and begins to usher everyone out of the room. When he closes the door behind him, his hand goes to the back of his neck and he just stands there for a moment before turning to face me.

When he asks, "What aren't you telling me?" while watching me closely, I'm caught off guard at first. Then my mouth falls open, and I wonder if I'm that transparent, or if he's fishing for information. My jaw snaps closed, and I know I have to tell him, that the time to mull this over on my own has already run out. But I also know what his reaction will be, and it seems pointless to walk knowingly into an argument I can't possibly win. He'll never agree to this, and I don't want to upset him.

"What is it?" he asks, walking back toward me with a look that warns me to be honest with him.

I sigh and brace myself. "I'm thinking about something Meera said before you and Grant came in."

He blows out a heavy breath as his suspicion is confirmed. "What did she say?"

My eyes are on his, ready for his reaction. "That it might be possible for me to take my father's energy the way he took mine."

Lucas frowns. After a moment, he asks, "And how exactly would you do that?"

"The same way he did it to me."

The skin around his eyes tightens. "Since you're never going near him again, that's not possible. Is it?"

My back straightens as I embrace the idea even more. "It would finally stop him."

His hands go to his hips. "You're not seriously considering this?"

My mouth goes dry as I nod my head.

He stalks closer to me. "Forget it. It's too dangerous, and it would be a temporary fix. When he recovers—"

"He wouldn't recover," I add quickly. "If no one helps him, he won't ever get his power back."

He stares at me, and I can see my words are registering. "You mean, what he did to you, you never would have... Jesus, Ray."

I watch his stricken expression. "This would stop him and make sure he couldn't ever hurt anyone else again."

Lucas runs his hands over his face. "In order to do this, you have to be touching him?"

"Yes."

He turns away and starts to pace. Finally, his face fills with determination and he sits down beside me. "Look, I'm glad you told me, but no. You can't go near him again. I mean it. I know you weren't asking my permission because you don't need it. But I'm asking you. Drop it. Put it out of your mind."

Sighing at his response but not surprised, I glance away, only to have his fingers land on my chin and turn me back to face him.

"Tell me you understand," he says.

Tension is radiating off Lucas, and I can feel the desperation he's bottling up inside. The truth is, he's hurting even more than I am because he doesn't put me through half the crap I dump all over him.

Bringing my hand to his cheek, I say, "I understand." And I do. As much as I want to stop my father, I won't do anything to hurt Lucas that way again.

EIGHTEEN

Raielle

WEAKNESS still weighs me down, but I feel stronger today than I did yesterday, and eventually, thanks to Meera, I'll be back to myself again. I need a shower, and I could use a change of clothes since I've been wearing these for two days straight.

Stretching my tight muscles, I move toward the door like a newborn chick taking its first steps. My body feels like I worked out for hours, even though I've mostly lain in bed. Hearing voices on the other side, I pull open the door to find that girl, Charlie, smiling at Lucas. Her hand is pressed against the front of his shirt as she swings her dark hair over her shoulder. His eyes narrow at her and then shift to Grant, who's standing by the door, making me think she's just arrived. My body tenses as I glance around, looking for others, looking for my father.

When Lucas spots me, he walks over. But my eyes are still on her. "What's she doing here?"

She tilts her head at me and crosses her arms. "You look like crap."

"Charlene's okay," Grant says. "She brought us some news and some things." He gestures to a couple of shopping bags sitting on the floor.

My eyes widen at Grant like he's crazy. "She's going to tell him where we are."

"I wouldn't tell him where the water was if he was on fire." She laughs.

"He doesn't have much loyalty among his followers," Grant says. "Recruiting help for our cause isn't exactly hard."

"What he did to you was way out-of-bounds," she says, losing the smirk. "It's not right and I didn't get into this to hurt people. Well," she amends, looking at Lucas, "unless they want me to."

Lucas narrows his eyes at her. "She can't be trusted, Grant. She shouldn't be here."

Charlie smiles at him. "You're just sore because you liked it when I healed you, and that makes you feel guilty."

Grant clears his throat, trying to break the tension and the death glare on Lucas's face. "She brought us some clothes. And she says John and Nyla and everyone else are fine. Scrambling to cover what happened, but they're healthy as horses again."

I recall Meera's words about them having to fight to get me out. "What did you do to them?"

Charlie shoots me a surprised look. "You've been keeping poor Raielle in the dark? Grant shot them all," she says casually.

Shocked, I look at him before turning back to Lucas. "Is that true?"

He nods. "He knew they could heal themselves. They weren't going to let us near you. He didn't have a choice."

"My God," I utter, not fully realizing how far they'd gone to help me.

"How are you, Charlene?" Meera asks, slowly making her way down the hall from her bedroom in the back, leaning heavily on a cane.

Charlie's expression brightens before she notices the cane. "I'm good. How are you, ma'am?"

"I'm fine. Just old." She chuckles.

"Meera and Adrienne are leaving," Grant announces. "They're letting us stay here, but I'm sending them to a safer place."

Guilt fills me at seeing how weak Meera seems this morning. "Is this because of me?" I ask.

"Yes," Adrienne answers for her, and Meera scowls.

I move beside her, looking for other signs of weakness. "I'm so sorry."

Meera shakes her head dismissively. "Don't be. This is how it works. I'll be just fine again in a few days and so will you."

"Charlie is going to take you to the airport," Grant explains. "Have you got everything you need?"

Meera nods. Then she turns to me and takes both my hands in hers. "You're a strong, brave young lady, and I know you'll be fine. Once you embrace your power and understand your purpose, the sky's the limit for you."

Beside me, Lucas's brow quirks up. I can feel heat coming from Meera's hands. "I don't know what you mean."

She eyes me knowingly. "Yes, you do. Your mother suppressed her power. Your father abused his. What will you do with yours? Will you bury it? Will you misuse it? Or will you listen to your heart and embrace your destiny?"

Beside me I can feel Lucas shifting closer to us. "Destiny?" I laugh quietly.

Meera gives me a wistful smile. Then she turns to Grant. "Despite what they say, you know it's not you," she tells him. "It's her."

His gaze travels over me. "I know," he says and his clipped response is unsettling.

Lucas stiffens at their exchange.

"You'll do fine," she tells me. Then she lets her daughter walk her out of the house.

"That was intense," Charlie mumbles. She air-kisses Grant and follows the two women out the door.

Once they're gone, I'm not surprised when Lucas asks, "What was that about?"

Grant sighs as he scrubs his hands over his face. "Come sit down. How are you, Raielle? Are you feeling stronger today?"

I lower myself onto the couch across from him, but Lucas doesn't sit. He stays where he is with his eyes on Grant.

"I'm good," I say, but really I'm waiting for what he's going to say next.

He lets out a heavy breath. "For a while, people have assumed that I'd take John's place if anything happened to him."

"Sounds like a plan to me." Lucas smirks.

"But I'd just be a substitute for you." Grant's focus stays on me. "It's your destiny, not mine."

Lucas scoffs at that.

Grant shrugs. "Deny it all you want, but Raielle's future is in her own hands. Not yours. It's up to her."

Lucas comes over and stands behind me. "She's eighteen years old. She's a freshman in college who deserves to have a life. You people aren't her responsibility, and I don't want you planting this shit in her head because knowing her, if she thinks you need her, she's going to want to help every last one of you."

"Lucas, please," I say, needing a minute to digest this. "Don't assume things about me."

He moves around the couch to look at me.

Grant stands and narrows his gaze on Lucas. "Meera said that you understood now, that she explained it to you. This is where Raielle belongs."

"No. That's not what she said at all," Lucas argues.

"You think I'm planting shit in her head? It looks to me like you're doing the same thing." Grant's lips form a thin, frustrated line.

Leaning forward, I hold my hands out. "This is a ridiculous argument. No one can plant anything in my head because I can think for myself, thank you very much."

Grant looks down at me. "I hope so," he mutters before walking from the room.

Once he's gone, Lucas seems to lose steam. "Sorry," he says. "You're right. I shouldn't make assumptions." He sits down beside me. "So tell me. What are you thinking?"

The truth is, I'm not thinking past my father yet. His threat looms too large to think about what happens after. I just want the after part. But I can't say that because Lucas will make more assumptions. He'll think that I'm not doing what he asked me to, that I'm not putting my idea for stopping my father out of my mind, and he wouldn't be wrong.

I eye the bags Charlie brought, still sitting on the floor. "I think I want to shower and change," I answer.

When he looks disappointed, thinking I'm avoiding the subject, I add, "One step at a time, okay?"

After a moment, he nods. "Okay."

LUCAS is taking his shower when I find Grant sitting on the patio, lost in thought. I've already showered and pulled on the jeans and T-shirt Charlie brought from LA for me. My phone charger was in that bag, too, along with Lucas's.

"You can't be angry with him," I say. "He's afraid for me. He's almost lost me twice now. I can't put him through that again."

When I sit down across from him, Grant leans forward and levels a serious look at me. "You think I want your father to hurt you any more than he does?"

The calm expression he wore so often in Los Angeles has been absent since we got here. I try not to squirm under his critical gaze.

Grant rests his arms on the table, bringing him closer to me. "I want John stopped. It's long past time for that, and I don't expect you to be involved in that part. But once he's gone, people are going to start looking to you. You heard them at the house during the lockdown. Your presence here has given them hope. Hope that things can be different, be better for all of us. Will you really turn your back on that?"

I might have heard them, but I didn't believe what I heard or put stock in it. "Why me?" I ask.

He grins. "Why not you?

I look down at my hands on the table.

"Don't play dumb with me," he says harshly.

My eyes flick up to him.

He leans in even closer. "There's no place for modesty here. You're strong. Even stronger than your father. You know that. Enough of us have told you that. Healers are an unruly bunch. We're full of ourselves. We can do things that most people can't. Superhuman things. Most of us are not going to follow a person like Shane or even me. We need someone we're in awe of. Someone who can do things none of us can do. Someone we're a little afraid of. Only a healer like that will ever be able to keep us in line. And believe me, we need to be kept in line."

My hands have moved down to my lap and are now clenched together under the table. "That's not me. No one's afraid of me."

Grant's head starts to shake, and he laughs. "You really have no idea. Your own father's afraid of you, Raielle, and everyone knows it."

It's hard to believe my father is afraid of me. But I can see that Grant believes it. He really believes everything he's telling me, but I don't know what to believe. It's seems ridiculous and overwhelming, and far too much to absorb.

"We've just got to get your father out of your way," he adds, rubbing his unshaven cheek thoughtfully.

Of everything he's said so far, that's the one thing we can agree on. "How do we do that?" I ask.

He leans back. "Fuck if I know."

I chew on my lip, not saying what's on my mind, that I could probably stop my father if I were given the chance. But then I do say it, because I can't stop thinking about it. I've tried, just like I promised Lucas, but if it's our best shot, how can I just forget it? "Meera believes I could drain his energy, leaving him powerless, the same way he left me."

Grant looks at me without commenting, but I can see his focus sharpening.

Clearing my throat, I glance away first. "Lucas thinks it's too dangerous."

"It would be dangerous."

I look back again when he doesn't outright dismiss the idea. But before I can say anything further, he changes the subject.

"John knows we're here," Grant says, surprising me. "That's why I sent Meera away. But he's not ready to come after you yet. In the meantime, we'll stay and you'll work on getting your strength back. Then you'll move on. We're going to pass you between us to keep you hidden. A friend of mine has agreed to take you in next. We'll keep you moving until we have a better option."

I shake my head. "I'm not doing that, hiding indefinitely, getting passed around from stranger to stranger. No way."

He says nothing.

"You know, you're wrong about me. I'm the least likely person to inspire awe or fear in anyone."

"No, you're the one who's wrong." Lucas's voice sounds from behind me.

I turn around to see him standing there. His hair is wet from his shower and all he has on are his jeans, sitting low on his hips. His shirt is bunched in his hands.

He steps out in his bare feet. "You're the strongest person I know. What I said before, it wasn't because you're not capable of it. It kills me to say this, but there's no question that you could handle it. Look at all you've handled your whole life. But I don't want you to be railroaded into this, or to do it out of guilt. You deserve to live the life you want, not one that's determined by them."

Grant's eyes snap with annoyance. "He's right about one thing. If you don't want to do this, you shouldn't. But don't let him or a misguided lack of confidence prevent you from doing what you know is right." Then he pushes his chair back. It squeals as the legs scratch against the concrete. He stands and looks down at me. "This is too important to let knee-jerk reactions make your mind up." We watch as he goes back inside.

"Dumbass," Lucas mumbles. "That guy likes to make an exit. Or maybe I just like driving him away. Am I right? He seems to leave the room when I enter it."

But I don't respond because Grant's words from before about my father being afraid of me, and Lucas's just now about how much I can handle, are hitting me like a bucket of cold water. "This is crazy," I say.

He gives me a lopsided grin. "This is Wednesday."

It takes a second for his words to register, but when they do, I huff out a laugh.

"Actually," he says, "I think we passed crazy and went straight to cuckoo for Cocoa Puffs."

I chuckle again and after everything that's happened, I can't believe

Lucas is making me laugh. I wanted to take back the word *crazy* after I said it. I've been careful not to use words like that around him because of his mother, but obviously he's not overly sensitive about it. He drops his shirt on the table and takes my hands, pulling me up against his warm skin.

"Did you hear what Grant said?" I ask. "That my father knows where I am? That they want to start passing me among them to hide me?"

"Yeah, I heard," he replies, and I can feel his deep voice vibrate inside his chest.

"We can't let them do that."

Lucas blows out a breath. "I don't like that plan much either. We could just leave. Get lost somewhere."

I look up into two dark blue pools and see my own reflection. "I don't want to spend the rest of my life running and being afraid of him."

His brow furrows as his arms tighten around me. "It won't come to that."

"Won't it? Hasn't it started already?" I look down and try to bite back the words before they spill out, but I can't. "What if I can stop him?" I ask. Then I dare to meet his eyes again. Predictably, they've turned hard.

"Ray," he says in a warning tone.

"But I might be the only one who can. I don't want to run or have to hide for who knows how long." After everything that's happened, I still don't think Lucas grasps the seriousness of our situation. I'm imagining a future where he has to give up even more for me, his family and his career aspirations. There's no way I can let that happen. I'm done with him sacrificing everything he's worked for because of me. "I want you to go to Columbia like you planned," I say.

He blinks at me, confused for a moment, then annoyed as he begins to refuse.

"And I want you to bring Liam with you, like you were going to before you met me."

"Ray, no."

Everything Meera said about my destiny feels unreal. Just thinking about it makes me uneasy. I add one more part to the plan. "And I want to come, too."

Lucas stills, and his eyes search mine. "Say that again?"

"I want to come to New York with you both. That's where you should be, and I want to be there with you." As soon as the words leave my lips, I know how right they are. I'm not chickening out or fooling myself, although I doubt Grant would believe that. I'm not interested in what he or Meera say is my destiny. Not by a long shot.

"What about UCLA?" Lucas asks.

I smile because that question tells me he's letting himself consider it. "UCLA itself was never important. It was a symbol, a goal to keep me motivated to get into college. But I can go to school anywhere. I can apply somewhere in New York."

He's still watching me, looking a little shell-shocked. "Are you sure?"

I grin at his stunned face. "Yes."

"When did you decide this?"

I hated the fact that he gave up Columbia for me the moment I found out he'd done it. I shrug at him, not really knowing the answer myself. Although I think the idea has been rattling around in my head for a while.

His hesitation is obvious. He wants what I'm suggesting, but I sense that he's mentally dismissing it. He's putting the pieces together and acknowledging the roadblocks. "This all depends on stopping your father," he finally says.

"Yes. He'll never let me go if he can prevent it."

Lucas lowers himself into a chair, and I sit down across from him. "Will Liam want to go?" I ask.

He shrugs his bare shoulders. "He'll want to go, but he'll beat himself up about leaving my mom."

"Just like you," I point out.

His eyes flick to mine before glancing away. "Yeah. He's too much like me."

"How is your mom?" I don't bring her up much because he's still so reluctant to talk to me about his family, and I'm trying not to feel hurt since I'm no better than him at opening up. But I'm trying. We both are.

"No change," he answers. "And my dad—" He breaks off abruptly.

I push off my chair and kneel in front of him, trying to see his expression. When he looks up at me, he says, "My dad keeps telling me, not so nicely, to come home."

Lucas may not like it, but of course that's what his father wants. I'm sure he doesn't like the fact that Lucas chucked Columbia and everything else to come after me.

"We'll go home," I say, even though it's not really my home. "We'll go back to Fort Upton once this is finished, and we won't come back. We can make the rest of our plans from there."

"You really want to do that?" he asks.

The truth is, the only bad thing about that place was Alec. Otherwise, I had family that cared about me and real friends for the first time in my life. "I'd like to see Kyle and Penelope."

"Kyle calls you on your phone at least once a week," Lucas says.

The familiar guilt I feel about cutting him out of my life prods at me. "I know." I saw the caller ID. And my message in-box is full, mostly because of Kyle, but I haven't listened to any of the messages. "You never answered it when it was him?" I ask.

"No. I don't have anything to say to Kyle." Lucas leans over me and slowly runs his hands up and down my side. "We'll talk to Grant. There must be a way to stop your father that doesn't involve putting you in the same room with him."

I smile up at him, because even though he hasn't said it, he wants his life back, and together we're going to figure out a way to get it for him. Then I do what I've been wanting to since he stepped out on the patio. I kiss him. He kisses me back as his eyes close. When they open again, he stands abruptly, pulling me up with him. "Apollo," he says.

I turn around and there he is, leaning back against the house, watching us.

He smiles. "Relax, will ya? I just came by to check on you."

Staring up into Apollo's dark eyes, I ask, "Does my father know you're here?"

His expression sobers. "Yes."

Lucas reaches for his shirt on the table and begins to pull it on.

"Do you know what my father did to me?" I ask, but it sounds more like an accusation. I've wondered if he knew what I was walking into when he took me to my father's house. An ache forms in my chest when I think of Apollo playing any part in this.

He nods. "I know now. But I didn't know when I left you there."

"For someone who's supposed to be watching over her, you seem to be conveniently absent for all the significant things," Lucas says.

Apollo goes still and slowly turns his attention to Lucas, but Lucas is looking at me, telegraphing his disdain for Apollo so strongly that it shocks me.

He's right, though. When I string it all together, thinking of the events that took place in his absence, especially one horrific event, I can't deny that Lucas has a point. I turn hurt eyes on Apollo. "Did you know my mother was going to be murdered? Did you let it happen?"

Apollo's eyes narrow on Lucas before meeting mine again. "I didn't know," he says flatly.

I can feel a knot in my stomach grow. "Are you lying to me?"

Something that resembles shame flits across his face. "I don't control my own life. I haven't since I met your daddy. I do what he tells me."

"Where were you that day?" I ask.

His jaw sets, and he looks away. I think back to that terrible afternoon, coming home to find her dead with her blood spilling across the table, and seeing Apollo's apartment door cracked open only an inch or so. I remember thinking that was odd. "You were home," I say quietly. "You were inside listening, weren't you?"

When his eyes reluctantly meet mine again, he nods. My stomach lurches, and my hand goes up to my mouth. I can feel the pressure of Lucas's fingers on my back, giving me strength. "You both let her die. You and my father," I whisper.

Lucas shifts restlessly beside me. "It goes even further. Doesn't it?" he says to Apollo before looking back at me. "Alec asked your father to heal Penelope first, and he refused because he knew Alec would go to your mother and you next. Your father wanted your mother gone. He wanted you to try to heal Penelope. He was watching you the whole time to see what you were capable of."

My eyes widen on him, wondering how he could know that.

Looking regretful, he says, "Before I came out here, Alec told me that he asked your father first. I would have said something sooner, but I didn't get the significance of it until now."

Apollo looks unsure as his eyes travel between us, but then he nods, confirming Lucas's words, and my knees grow weak.

"My father has been behind everything," I say. "He was working with Alec to kill my mother."

Apollo shakes his head. "Not exactly. Alec was convenient. He and your daddy had the same goal. Alec wanted his granddaughter healed, and your father wanted to see if you could do it."

I swallow back my tears. My mother was just part of some experiment for my father. For Alec, she was simply in the way. She was disposable to both of them, like her life meant nothing. I glare at Apollo. "How can you work for him?"

He tenses at my harsh tone. "I have no choice," he snaps. Then he purposely takes a breath and calms himself down. "He gave me my son's life back, and I gave him mine."

I stare at him. "Your son?"

He nods.

"You never told me you had a son."

Laughing quietly, he says, "It never came up."

"Where is he? What happened to him?"

Apollo's dark eyes zero in on me. "He's fine, nearly a teenager now. But he was only four when he got into my stash and swallowed a bunch of pills. He thought they were candy. I raced him to the emergency room and they pumped his stomach, but it was too late."

"Your stash?" I ask.

One of his shoulders hitches up. "I was a dealer, Raielle. Still am sometimes. You know that."

But I tended to overlook it because I thought he was a friend to me. "What about his mother?" I ask.

His eyes freeze over. "She was an addict. I took the kid from her when I saw how she was neglecting him. I'm not sure the bitch even noticed."

"And my father saved your son?" I ask.

"He was at the hospital that day. He approached me—collected me, I guess—the way he likes to collect people he thinks can help him. We made a deal, and he saved my kid." He says all this nonchalantly, like it's over and done, but I can see how rigid he's standing, barely hiding the resentment he feels. And I can also see how naive I was to think he was my friend. I never really knew anything about him at all.

Shifting his feet and looking uncomfortable with all he's just revealed, Apollo is eager to change the subject. "Besides checking on you, I'm also supposed to convince you to come back with me."

I stare at him in disbelief. "What could you possibly say that would convince me to go back there?"

"Convince or forcibly take back?" Lucas asks, crossing his arms.

Apollo places his hands on his hips, looking offended at the suggestion. "No one is here to force you into anything. Your dad says that he didn't know what was happening to you. He didn't realize he was hurting you. He just wants you to forgive him so he can make it up to you. That's why he wants to see you."

I laugh miserably. "Seriously? He said that?"

Apollo doesn't respond.

"You can tell her father that she's not coming back," Lucas says, putting his arm around my shoulder.

"No. Don't do that," I add quickly. "Tell him I'll come back when I'm ready, but he needs to give me time."

"What?" Lucas turns on me.

"How much time?" Apollo asks.

"A few days at least, maybe a week."

I can feel Lucas bristling beside me as Apollo arches skeptical eyebrows in my direction. As long as Apollo is here, I figure we may as well use him to our advantage. "I need time to think about everything. I'll come to him when I'm ready. Get me more time."

His eyes travel between an oddly silent Lucas and me. "Fine. I can do that. During that time, what will you actually be doing?" Apollo asks.

I try to look offended. "Just what I said."

Apollo stares at me, scrutinizing my expression. He takes a step closer to me, and then another. Lucas begins to block his path when I hold my hand out to stop him. An unimpeded Apollo doesn't halt until his face is only inches from mine. "I like you, Raielle. I always have," he says in a calm voice. "You're a brave kid."

I stand stock-still, listening. He's so close, I can smell cigarettes on his breath.

"I'll buy you time. But you'd better be careful. Make sure you succeed at whatever it is you're planning." His eyes drill into mine. "Because if you decide to run away, he'll send me after you, and I will find you." With that, he turns and walks back into the house. A moment later, we hear the front door close behind him.

I fall hard into the chair behind me, clasping my shaking hands together tightly.

"Sounds like he won't help us, but if we try something, he won't interfere. Should we fail, though, look the fuck out." Lucas is scowling toward the door. Then with a heavy sigh, he drops down into the chair beside me. "Are you okay?" he asks.

"They all treated my mother like dirt, like she was nothing," I manage to say.

I hear footsteps, then I see Grant lingering in the doorway. "I guess Apollo delivered his message," Grant says. "You know, he's just your father's go-between. I didn't think it would be a bad idea for you to hear him out. But, apparently, I'm on the shit list and not invited to Apollo's parties anymore."

Lucas turns to Grant. "So, how do we stop him? Ray wants to go back there to try to steal his power the way he took hers. I told her there has to be another way."

Grant shifts his weight as his eyes travel between us. "Well…" He hesitates. Then his eyes stay on Lucas. "That isn't a bad idea."

I blink my surprise before glancing at Lucas, and rather than flying off the handle, he's just sitting there not looking like he wants to wring

Grant's neck. The ticking muscle in his jaw is his only reaction. Just as I'm about to ask him if he's okay, he mumbles, "Shit," and runs a hand through his hair.

Grant shrugs. "I won't lie. That would be the most effective solution. We'd basically be neutering the prick. If we could get John alone, we could protect Raielle while she tries it."

Lucas stares up at him like he's trying to decide if he's serious. Grant bears it silently, his eyes pinned to Lucas's. They're having some kind of staring contest. Then Lucas asks, "How would this work? I don't think her father is letting you get anywhere near him again."

My head swivels between the two of them. Not only are they not trying to dissuade me, they're thinking about it themselves? "Are you two being serious right now? Lucas?"

Lucas slowly turns to me. His expression is blank, completely unreadable. "You heard Apollo. If we run, he'll follow. I want a life with you, Ray. Maybe it's worth taking one more calculated risk to get that. I'm willing to consider it if we could somehow guarantee your safety."

I nod, feeling my eyes burn with unshed tears. "I agree."

"We can do this and keep you safe," Grant promises. "I wouldn't attempt it otherwise."

The fact that they're finally agreeing with me does nothing to ease the way my body is shaking. With everything Apollo told us and the possibility of seeing my father again, the jitters take me over. They talk more, but then Lucas looks at me and stops.

"Come on," he says softly. "This has been a lot to take in. You should rest for a while."

I want to protest, but instead I let him pull me up and lead me to the bedroom that I've already spent too much time in. But when he eases me down onto the bed, I find my eyes starting to close, and I give in to it. If I'm going to go up against my father, I'll need all my strength back and more.

NINETEEN

Lucas

I **REACH** for my watch on the nightstand, but I know what it's going to say. Two thirty in the morning. I always wake up at two thirty. That's my witching hour, the hour when I first heard the piercing shriek of the fire alarm before my father began rushing us outside. There she was, sitting on the front lawn, calm as could be, watching the house and waiting. She was disappointed the fire trucks arrived so quickly because she wanted to watch the flames dance. My mother didn't seem to care that we were all in our beds asleep when she started the fire. She just wanted to watch it burn.

I close my eyes, hoping to fall back to sleep the way I normally would, but I know I'm too keyed up for that. Worry for Raielle and for my family, especially Liam, snakes inside me, slithering restlessly with nowhere to go. And the worry is caked with guilt. I feel guilty because I'm relieved to be out of my house and away from the daily grind of watching my mother's ups and downs, but even more so for lying to Raielle. That decision is sitting like a weight on my chest, making it tough to take a deep breath.

She agreed to drop the idea of stealing her father's power from him, but she didn't drop it. She never stopped thinking about it, and I overheard her bringing it up to Grant, too. I'd already warned him she might. He didn't like her idea any more than I did. That's one thing I can count on, the fact that he wants to protect her almost as much as I do. He agreed with me that she was unlikely to let this go, and might even do something stupid like go after him on her own.

So we came up with a plan, the three of us together, but it was bullshit. It was all for her benefit. Grant knows something has to be done about her father, but he also knows that she shouldn't be involved. When he gave me a pointed look out on the patio as he was talking about Raielle's plan, I followed his lead. I knew he was asking me to go along with it, and I knew he had no intention of following through. After she fell asleep, Grant and I discussed another plan, and we decided not to tell her about it until we had to. When she finds out, she's going to be beyond pissed. She's going to blow a gasket. But we need her to think we're all in this together so she'll cooperate until we're ready to lift the blinders from her eyes.

If I thought I could convince her to run away with me I would, but she's determined to stay and face her father. She's such a contradiction. She'll run from her feelings and from emotions that are too strong, but put her in a life-and-death struggle that would have most people heading for the hills, and she refuses to back down. I'm proud of her bravery. I even respect it. But I can't let her do it. Not this time.

Running isn't what I want either. The temptation of getting rid of that bastard is too strong, and the lure of a life together that doesn't include looking over our shoulders is too appealing to pass up. I want all the darkness out of her life once and for all. If I have to deceive her to make that happen, I will. She'll forgive me once it's done.

I shift restlessly in bed as Grant's words repeat in my head. Before we were done talking, he admitted to me that he loves her. He said he'd do anything to protect her. It felt like both a warning and a promise. I believe him, and that's the only reason I'm trusting him.

Raielle is turned toward the window with her back to me. I can tell by her uneven breathing that she's not asleep either. We have one more day left before we leave for Los Angeles, one more day for Raielle to get stronger and for Grant to put all the pieces in place. She thinks we're planning to let her father know we're coming back, pretend to believe his explanation and apology, and then wait for him to go after her again, to try to steal her power so she can turn it around on him.

She and Grant had an in-depth discussion about how that would work with Raielle taking hold of her father's energy just as he's grasping on to hers. Then Grant told her that he has friends who will let him and me inside without John and his guards knowing. Grant really seems to have her fooled. For a smart girl, she's too naive for her own good sometimes. She doesn't think we would deceive her this way or that I'd deceive her at all.

I'm breaking the trust I worked so hard to gain, a trust I know is tenuous based on how she reacted to finding that girl in my bedroom. But if this works, I'll have plenty of time to build it back up again. I'll devote myself to it.

Raielle

URING the few hours I slept last night, I dreamed that I wasn't strong enough to take my father's power from him. So he took mine again, and then he went after Lucas. I startled awake, covered in sweat, but beside me, Lucas didn't stir.

This morning when he got up, I pretended to be sleeping, feeling too shaken to face him. Now I can't stop thinking about it. My thoughts are racing, trying to find a way to keep him out of this.

When I finally slip out of bed, I take a long time in the shower, and then I dress slowly. My hands tremble as I button the white cotton blouse Charlie brought. The thought of seeing my father again literally has me shaking, and I fist my hands tightly, hoping Lucas and Grant won't notice.

After brushing my hair and pulling it back in a ponytail, I walk out into the main room of the house. Lucas and Grant abruptly stop talking.

"I hope we didn't wake you," Grant says. He looks tense and so does Lucas.

My eyes shift between them. "What's wrong?"

Lucas is sitting on the couch across from Grant. I move to stand beside him, but he surprises me by grabbing my hand and pulling me down onto his lap.

"Nothing." He grins. "Want some breakfast?"

Grant stands and heads into the kitchen.

"No," I answer, suspicious at their sudden mood change.

"Yes, she does," Lucas calls out to him, ignoring me when I shoot him an annoyed look.

Grant returns and hands me a bowl of what looks like Fruit Loops. I wrinkle my nose at it. "What is it with guys and sugary breakfast cereals?"

"It's about all I know how to cook." Grant shrugs.

I frown at him. "Last time I checked, a bowl of cereal didn't require any cooking."

"Which is why I'm so good at it."

Grinning at his answer, I will my hand to stay steady as I spoon some into my mouth because they're both watching and waiting for me to eat it. But my stomach is in knots and my dream lingers. "We need to talk about what happens if there's a problem tomorrow," I say, forcing the food down my dry throat.

"What kind of problem?" Grant asks, and I feel Lucas go still beneath me.

Glancing at Lucas, I grip my spoon tighter. "I mean, if it doesn't work. If I can't do it, do we have a backup plan for that possibility?"

"You'll be fine," Lucas says.

I turn back to Grant, feeling desperate about this, needing him to understand. "We have to have a plan. If I fail, he'll go after you two next. Our chances might be better if you're not both there in the house with me."

Lucas picks me up off his lap and sets me down on the couch. The cereal sloshes over the side of the bowl as he pushes up and walks past me, going through the kitchen and then out onto the patio.

I sit back and sigh. "Well, that went well."

Grant laughs. "You're not as subtle as you think you are. What kind of reaction did you expect?"

I look toward the door that Lucas disappeared through. "I don't know. A discussion of some kind." I turn back to Grant. "I had a dream last night, a nightmare actually. I have a bad feeling, and I don't think Lucas should come with us."

A strange little smile comes over him. "You can't cut him out now."

I put the bowl down on the table. "I can't let anything happen to him either. Help me. Maybe there's something he can do that keeps him away from my father."

"Lucas is a big boy. He can take care of himself." When I shake my head, ready to contradict him, his hand goes up. "Trust me, okay? It will be fine." He's not listening to me, and I can see by his expression that he doesn't intend to.

When I stand, deciding to find Lucas, Grant's arm reaches out as I walk past him. His fingers circle my wrist, stopping me.

"He's lucky to have you," he says simply, looking up at me.

"I'm the one who's lucky." I start to pull my arm away, but his fingers tighten for a moment, sending a warm wave over my skin. I inhale sharply before he abruptly releases me.

"I want to try something," he says in a light tone, dismissing whatever it was he just did to me.

Rubbing my wrist, I watch as he goes into the kitchen and withdraws a long knife from one of the drawers. My eyes grow round. "What are you doing?"

Lucas comes back inside and his gaze travels from my face right to the knife.

"I'm going to cut myself," Grant says calmly.

"What?" I exclaim at the same time Lucas asks, "Why?"

Grant ignores me and looks at Lucas. "So I can heal it and generate energy for her to absorb. I want her to see that she can do it. She's worrying herself sick about tomorrow."

My head shakes vigorously at his suggestion.

Lucas crosses his arms and gives Grant an odd look.

I move toward the kitchen. "Don't, I'm not—"

But before I can finish the sentence, Grant drags the knife across the tender skin on the inside of his forearm. His only reaction a slight wince.

"Grant!"

He turns serious eyes on me. "You ready?"

I'm outraged as I watch a ribbon of blood flow out of his sliced skin and drip down onto the floor. He's eyeing me expectantly, but I can't seem to move.

He tosses the knife into the sink. It hits with a metallic clank. "Raielle?" he asks, still waiting for me.

My eyes are on the cut when his skin starts to close and the blood flow tapers. He's already healing it. As I move closer, I can feel the warmth coming off his body. My own skin grows damp while I watch, fascinated to see the serene expression that takes him over as he heals his own wound. I glance at Lucas. There's a deep wrinkle in his brow, and his face is a strange mix of interest and irritation.

Wiping the moisture from my palm onto my jeans, I decide to try. I can't deny that I would be more confident about tomorrow if I knew I could do this, and Grant has already sliced open his own arm. With the decision made, I take a deep breath before reaching my hand out toward him. It shakes, and they both eye me with renewed concern. Ignoring their looks, I realize that the power is stronger near his face, and my fingers travel upward, finally pressing firmly against his cheek. I try to grab on to his energy, but I can't figure out how. It's like trying to grasp water or smoke. It has no substance.

"It's not working," I say, and I can tell that he's prolonging the healing, waiting for me. When I move my hand away, he looks at me sharply.

"Don't give up," he says. "Maybe I'm not generating enough. I want you to go again. This time I'll give you more, as much as I can."

I nod, taking a deep breath. Then I press my hand back to his face. After a moment, I can feel it again as the heat pouring off him grows. At first, there's no difference. I still can't latch on to anything. But then I feel his power increase and this time, at this elevated level, it seems to have some weight. Instinctively, I understand that if I make my own energy, it will connect with his, and somehow link to it. So I build it inside me, and when it's strong enough, I send it toward him.

His body jerks, and I can feel his shock. Then I pull it back to me, but I try to take his along with it. The moment it hits me, my eyes widen. My body seems to vibrate. I hear a low buzzing in my ears, and there's a strange bitter taste in my mouth.

Grant looks at me with a pained expression, and I know he feels what I'm doing. I know it's hurting him. "Good," he whispers. "That's good."

But it's not good. I can see that he's trying not to cringe but if he feels the same way I did, this must be excruciating for him. I start to pull my hand away when he covers it with his, holding my fingers firmly against his face. "Keep going."

Against my better judgment, I draw in more. I can feel it coursing through me, making me stronger, but I can also feel his pain. He can't take much more of this. Even though my hand is still on him, I end the connection between us, turning off the flow and letting it settle quietly.

I look down at Grant's arm and see that it's not healed. It's still bleeding. Before pulling my hand back, I send out a pulse to close the wound. Then I look up into his eyes, which are wide and focused on me.

"Why didn't you finish healing yourself?" I ask.

He seems far away as he blinks several times, trying to focus. "Once you started draining my energy, I couldn't do it," Grant says evenly, seeming to find that fact interesting. "I couldn't heal it. I didn't have enough power left."

They both stare at me, Grant looking tired, and a little shell-shocked. Lucas is looking pissed off at Grant for some reason.

Grant places a hand on the counter to steady himself before smiling at me. "You did it. That was—" He breaks off, laughing. "It was amazing."

I look at him like he's crazy. When my father did it to me, it was the most excruciating pain I'd ever felt.

Grant scratches his cheek. "Was John able to feed off your energy right away, or did he wait until you'd reached a certain level? It seemed like you couldn't take hold of mine until I had it turned up all the way."

"He waited," I reply, remembering now. He waited until I was lost to it, trying my hardest to heal the little girl.

"How do you feel now? Stronger?" he asks.

I nod. I feel none of the lingering weariness I had before, and I wonder if my nightmare was nothing more than my getting cold feet. It appears that I'm perfectly capable of doing this.

I glance up to see both of their gazes on me, watching me intently. This isn't the first time I've been stared at like a science experiment, and even though they don't mean to make me uncomfortable, I am.

They're quiet as my attention shifts between them. Then I clear my throat in the heavy silence and unceremoniously leave the room. Walking back into the bedroom, I go over to the window to stare out at the bright sunshine. I have a feeling Lucas is going to follow me. I hear him talking to Grant. His voice is low and tense. Then I sense him walking into the bedroom. I know he's here when the door closes.

"That was interesting," he says.

But I don't turn around. I can feel him coming up behind me. His warm hands cover my shoulders, and he begins to knead the tight muscles. "Grant is impressed. He's also tired as hell and can barely stand up."

"Yay for me," I say flatly.

His hands move down to circle my waist, and I automatically cover them with my own. Then he slides his fingers across my stomach, pulling me back against him. The feel of his body pressed against mine sends shivers through me like it always does.

"I thought you were mad at me," I say.

"I just needed some fresh air," he says beside my ear.

"Hmph." I grunt at him, not believing it.

"You know what I think?" he asks.

His question makes me want to smile. "Not usually."

He laughs quietly into my hair. "I think Grant wanted to feel close to you. That's why he cut his arm open. Extreme, but effective."

"No. What I did hurt him." I turn around and look up into his eyes. Based on the light tone of his voice, I'm surprised by what I see there. His gaze is heavy, filled with a potent mix of restrained fury and possessiveness.

"How can you not see it?" he asks as his arms tighten around me. "He wants you for himself."

But I do see it. I just hadn't realized Lucas did, too, and the jealousy I hear in his voice surprises me. "When you're in the room, you're the only one I see."

His eyes soften at my words, and he leans down, slanting his mouth over mine, drawing a deep kiss from me. Then he tilts his head back to meet my eyes. "Soon it will be just you and me. This will all be over," he says.

I want to believe him as I lean forward to lick at his lower lip before sliding my tongue into his mouth. Lucas groans softly, walking me backward until I'm pressed against the wall. Then his hands drift down my sides and over my hips, digging into my thighs. He deepens the kiss, and I melt. He hasn't touched me this way since we got here. I've missed this. I'm desperate for him.

I suck in a surprised breath when he lifts me up, wrapping my legs around him and aligning our bodies. He presses his groin into mine, making me gasp at the contact. When he pulls back and does it again, raw lust tightens my muscles and shivers race over my skin. I breathe out his name as my fingers fist in his hair.

"I need you," he says with an edge to his voice that has my pulse racing faster.

Nodding my face against his, I feel him release one of my legs. His fingers start working the button on my jeans. I reach out to free him from his, fumbling in my eagerness. As my fingers slip inside to touch him, he begins yanking my pants and panties down my thighs. My legs slip down his body as I use my feet to push them the rest of the way off.

When he reaches for me again, he stops abruptly, biting out the word, "Condom." Taking me with him, he pulls open the nightstand drawer. Once he locates what he needs, I figure he's going to move us to the bed, but instead his hand wraps around the nape of my neck, and he holds me in place as he begins to devour my mouth. It's hard to breathe, he's kissing me so deeply. His other hand slips beneath my sweater, pushing my bra aside. His warm, rough fingers brush against my nipple, causing me to exhale heavily into his mouth.

Lucas breaks the kiss, breathing hard as he hands me the condom. This is the first time he's asked me to do this. I realize I'm nervous as I try unsuccessfully to tear the wrapper. Finally, I just use my teeth, hearing him laugh softly at me. But the laugh disappears when I take him in my hand and begin to roll it on slowly, caressing him as I go. I glance up to find the look on his face is wild, like he's lost all control. His fingers grip my thighs again, and all I can do is hold on when he pushes me up against the wall and buries himself inside me all in one smooth movement.

We cry out together, piercing the silence with our mingled voices. His hand lands on the wall beside my head, and he begins to pump his hips. My legs are tight around him as I marvel at how perfectly we fit together, like our bodies were made for each other. His clean scent surrounds me, and the guttural sounds coming from his throat fill my ears. My own moans are growing embarrassingly loud, but they seem to egg him on. His pace quickens while my back thumps a steady beat against the wall. He's driving me higher, making his presence felt in every cell of my body.

"So good," he says in a strained voice. "You always feel so good."

All at once, my nerve endings flare, and my muscles ripple in response. I spasm around him, my nails digging hard into his shoulders. Fighting to keep my focus because I need to see him, I watch his face tighten before he drops his head into the crook of my neck, gasping hard against my skin.

In the sudden quiet, I listen to his breathing and feel the warmth of it drift across my shoulder. My heartbeat begins to slow again. Awareness comes back to me in pieces and tomorrow looms, threatening in the background. I love this man so much, the one wrapped around me now. I love him so fiercely it hurts sometimes. It hurts in this moment, and I know I can't lose him, no matter what happens.

We're still connected. Lucas groans in my ear when I shift my legs to slide my feet down to the floor. He leans back with a satisfied look in his eyes. His fingers reach up to touch the necklace he gave me, the one I haven't taken off since he fastened it around my neck.

"You're mine," he says, like he did once before, his voice husky with passion.

I nod my agreement, unable to talk, still catching my breath while my thoughts keep hold of my tongue. He lifts me up with one arm around my waist and carries me to the bed.

"Check," he whispers beside my ear.

I lean back to look at him, finding my voice again when I see a sly glint in his eyes. "That was on the list?" I ask.

He nods.

"Up-against-the-wall sex?"

His head shakes as he puts me down. "We checked that one off with shower sex. I guess shower sex was a twofer."

Smiling at his reasoning, I ask, "What fantasy did we just fulfill then?"

His blue eyes darken. "Possessive sex. The kind where I brand you and ruin you for all other guys."

My mouth forms a silent O, and he starts chuckling at me.

TWENTY

Raielle

WHEN I'm nervous, I can feel my energy bubbling beneath the surface of my skin. It makes me uneasy, the power I have inside me. It's grown so much stronger.

"Do you think it's strange?" I ask from the backseat as Grant takes the exit that will bring us to the condo within minutes. "That he didn't come after me. That he just sat in LA and waited me out."

Grant glances over his shoulder. "Not really. He's an egomaniac. He figured you'd be back eventually."

I look out the window, ignoring the nerves that are bouncing around inside me. "I want to go over there this afternoon," I state. The idea was to get word to him that I was back and wait for him to contact me, but I don't want to wait. I don't want to prolong this.

Grant and Lucas look at each other. "Let's settle in first and then see how you feel," Lucas suggests.

"I'm going to feel the same way I do now. I don't want to wait around for him to summon me like I'm one of his subjects."

Grant looks in the rearview mirror at me, and Lucas twists around, reaching his hand toward my face to brush a stray lock of hair behind my ear. "We'll talk about it when we get to the condo," he says. Then he smiles reassuringly and my nerves seem to settle, even though I know his evasive answer means he doesn't want it to happen today.

Grant exits onto Wilshire, and since I'm lost inside my head, it takes a moment for me to realize he's driving in the wrong direction. "The condo's that way," I say, leaning forward to see his face.

He glances sideways at me. "You're not staying there anymore. It's not safe. I've made other arrangements."

I look at Lucas, but he has no reaction. "What arrangements?"

Clearing his throat, Grant says, "You're leaving today and driving back east."

My eyes widen before my head snaps back to Lucas again. "What's he talking about?"

But Lucas doesn't turn around. He doesn't acknowledge me at all.

Suddenly something that didn't make sense, the ease with which they agreed to my plan, becomes all too clear. A sour realization takes hold. "What's going on?"

Lucas knows I'm talking to him, and he's ignoring me. My eyes shift between them as I begin berating myself because I knew it. Deep down, I knew they were up to something. "You were never going to take me to my father's house, were you?"

"No," Grant answers, his eyes on the road.

They've been planning something together behind my back. They've been lying to me. My stomach churns at their betrayal, and my eyes are burning holes into the back of Lucas's head.

"How could you?" I ask, hearing how hurt my voice sounds.

He still doesn't move.

"Lucas!"

His jaw clenches before he finally shifts around to face me. "This is what's happening, and you can be as pissed as you want, but it won't change a thing."

I rear back, shocked by his tone. Then I grit my teeth. Their obstinate replies are infuriating, treating me like I'm a child who has no say in her own life. "All that crap about me talking to you. That was bullshit, wasn't it, Lucas? You said that so I would tell you everything while you told me nothing."

"Did you tell me everything?" he asks. "You were going to forget about your plan to take down your father. But you wouldn't let it go. You kept bringing it up." He swings back around and sits there silently.

My mouth opens to argue, but then quickly closes again when he gives me the back of his head. They've been talking about me and making arrangements without me this whole time. I'm quietly imploding, realizing I have no choice but to sit here and see what they have planned, fuming at how they've gone about this and the way I've been lied to.

Grant drives us toward Venus Beach and pulls down a one-way road filled with narrow three- and four-story houses, all reaching upward to claim a view of the ocean. The mutinous fog in my head clears enough to start asking questions. "So we're running away? Is that what this is?"

Grant eyes me through the rearview mirror. "You and Lucas are leaving. Then you're going to wait for my call."

I glance between them. "Why? What are you doing?"

He doesn't answer as he turns into the driveway of a small white saltbox house.

"Whose house is this?" I ask.

"No more questions," Grant says. "Your stuff is packed and waiting for you in the car out back."

I feel panicky. I have no idea what's going on, and they're both shutting me out. Once Grant is out of the car, I grab Lucas's arm. He turns to me with a somber expression.

"What is going on?" I ask. "Why are we running? You know my father will never stop looking for me."

"He won't be looking for you," Lucas says evenly.

"Why not? Is Grant going to go back there with his gun and finish what he started?"

Lucas is trying to keep his expression neutral, but I don't miss his subtle flinch.

My eyes go wide.

He turns back around and pushes out of the car. I follow right behind him, scrambling to catch up. When I do, I grip his arm again. "Don't do this. Please. I can take his power away. Once it's gone, he can't hurt us anymore."

Lucas whirls on me. "You don't know that. You can't take that risk. I won't let you."

We're standing toe-to-toe now, and I search his face, trying to understand him. "Do you realize what you're doing? You're planning to murder someone."

Grant appears beside us. His expression is incredulous. "Are you two out of your minds talking about this out here? Get inside now. The both of you." With that, he turns and starts toward the house. I move up beside him, knowing this had to be his idea. "How could you involve Lucas in something like this?"

His expression hardens as he keeps walking. "Neither of you will be involved if you just fucking leave like you're supposed to."

"I hate him, too. But you're no better than him if you do this."

Grant bends his head close to mine. "Do you know how many people's lives your father has destroyed? Every rumor you've heard about him is true, and he needs to be stopped. Now, you're either going on your own or you're not. But either way, you're going." He turns and stalks into the house.

Once he disappears through the door, Lucas takes my arm. "You have to calm down."

I'm not sure why Grant is doing this, but I know why Lucas is, and I can't allow it. Killing my father is not the answer. This isn't Lucas, and I can't let it become him, especially not for me. "Stop. Just stop and think for a minute," I plead.

His mouth tightens as he backs away from me. "Go inside. Grant's right. We shouldn't be talking about this out here."

I plant my feet on the ground defiantly.

His eyes squeeze shut before opening again. "Please, Ray."

He sounds so desperate for me to listen that I find myself moving slowly, knowing that only more coercion awaits me in there. But I go anyway as my mind scrambles for the right words to convince them not to go through with this.

Grant left the door open, and I peer inside as I step over the threshold. The house is tiny, more like a small beach cabin. I'm barely in when a hand fists in my hair and yanks me to the side. I yelp as I'm twisted around and pushed face-first into the wall. I manage to turn enough to see the door, and I know Lucas is right behind me. But before I can yell out a warning, a hand clamps over my mouth. Lucas comes inside, and one of my father's bodyguards, the bald one, slams something against the back of his head.

A muffled scream tears from my throat as I watch him fall to his knees. I bite down on a finger, trying to break free, but my scalp burns when my head is yanked back. Lucas turns and tackles the bodyguard who hit him. The guard stumbles backward, giving Lucas time to get to his feet and charge him again. They both go flying back into the wall. The bodyguard grunts when his head hits hard, and suddenly I'm released as the one holding me goes to help his friend.

I look around the room, searching for something I can use as a weapon. That's when I see Grant lying unconscious on the floor behind me.

"Run!" Lucas calls to me. I lock eyes with him before the two guards work together to wrestle him to the ground.

I'm only feet away from the open front door, but I sink down onto my knees.

"Ray," Lucas whispers, his eyes closing in frustration.

The bald guard pulls out his phone. "Yeah. We're ready," he says into it.

"How did you know we were going to be here?" I ask them.

"I'm psychic," the dark-haired one smirks.

My eyes flick to Lucas. "My father wants me, not him. You can leave him here. There's no reason to bring him."

Lucas glares at me, but the bald bodyguard just shrugs. "I do what I'm told, which is to bring you all with us."

He comes over and yanks my arms behind me. Lucas twists uselessly within the hold of the other one. I glance back at Grant before I'm hauled outside, wondering if he betrayed us and why he would, since this doesn't seem to be going very well for him either.

T HEY took our phones and loaded us into their SUV. Now Grant is sitting beside me and Lucas is in the back. Every time I try to turn around and look at him, my hair gets yanked by the bald hulk sitting next to me.

Grant started waking up as they were loading him in, and now his expression burns with anger.

"How did this happen?" I whisper to him.

"I have no fucking clue," he replies. "I only told people I trusted."

I scoff at him. "Look around you, Grant. I'd say you're not a very good judge of character."

He shakes his head as his jaw moves back and forth. "I'm sorry, Raielle."

Turning away from him, I don't bother responding. I wanted this chance with my father, and now it looks like I'm going to get it. But thanks to Grant, he now knows I'm not coming willingly, and he's going to be ready for me. My stomach burns with an acidic mix of trepidation and rage. My throat is tight with fear, not just for myself, but for Lucas. I need to be stronger than my father, the way everyone thinks I am. I have to beat him, because the alternative is too horrible to contemplate.

We're mostly silent for the ride. Every few miles, Grant starts talking to the bodyguards, trying to convince them to let us go. They ignore him. Finally, as the car pulls to the side of the house where the clinic door is, I start to react. My skin breaks out in a cold sweat, and my stomach rolls with nausea as I recall what happened to me the last time I was here.

After the SUV comes to a stop, the bodyguards say nothing as they herd us all out. Lucas comes around and quickly closes the distance between us.

"You okay?" I ask. "Did they hurt you?"

He shakes his head and before they can separate us, I take his hand and send my energy out to him, finding a whopper of a bruise on the back of his head. I soothe it over, shrinking the swollen tissue, and eliminate the bump along with its accompanying headache.

He smiles sadly at me. "Thanks."

I stare into his eyes and despite his outward calm, they're filled with more pain and guilt than I can handle. Like Grant, he thinks this is his fault. "It's going to be okay," I say, looking away from his piercing gaze.

"Let's go," the dark-haired guard says.

Grant is nudged forward, and Lucas and I follow him. "Please don't do anything stupid," I whisper. "Let me try for the opportunity with my father that I need."

He squeezes my fingers. "I can't believe it's come to this. I did everything I could so that it wouldn't." His throat works as he swallows hard. "Don't you do anything stupid either."

When we step inside the clinic, the familiar ammonia smell hits me first, and in my head I'm dragged back to the room at the end of the hall. My breathing goes shallow as I try not to think of it.

The bald guard starts to lead Grant away before glancing at his friend. They're communicating something between them, and by the way their eyes are focusing on Lucas's hand tightening around mine, I get the feeling they're weighing the hassle of trying to separate us.

"Just put them both in the room John wanted her in," says the dark one, the one who seems to be in charge. Then the other guard pushes on Lucas's shoulder to move him forward. Lucas brushes him off and glares at him before slowly walking in the direction he indicated.

He's leading us to *that* room, and I swallow the acid my stomach is trying to push up. What happened to me in there will haunt me for a long time. The feeling of being drained, the agony of having my energy ripped from me against my will, was incomparable. Every part of me ached, right down to my bones.

My steps slow and Lucas glances at me. I take a deep breath, steeling myself, gathering my courage. If I'm going back into that room again, I'm going to overwrite that terrifying memory with a new one, one that finally ends my father's reign of terror over me and everyone else.

When we finally reach the door, it's standing open. The guard nudges us inside before closing and locking it behind us. Not even a second later,

Lucas pulls me into his arms. "Christ, Ray," he whispers.

I squeeze him tight, and I feel so much regret for dragging him into this. I should have left when he asked me to. He begged me so many times to go with him, and I stubbornly refused. If anything happens to Lucas, I won't be able to bear it.

He releases me and tries the door. Then his eyes go to the tiny rectangular window high in the wall, just out of reach. I watch silently as he stands up on the bed and attempts to get it open. It's futile, but I know he needs to try.

Once he's satisfied that he can't get us out, he begins pacing. I stand there and watch him. He's a restless combination of anger, frustration, and helplessness. Time goes by, and there's no sign of my father. The waiting is starting to take its toll on me as I listen for any sound that could signal his approach. When day turns to night, Lucas lowers himself to the floor, leaning back against the wall. He reaches a hand out to me and I take it, lowering myself beside him, resting my head on his shoulder. There's a perfectly good bed in this room. But I've already lain in that bed once. I want nothing to do with it now and Lucas seems to know that.

"Do you think you're going to like living in New York City?" he asks.

I look up at him, surprised, before a small smile turns my lips. He's talking about the future, and I find myself wanting to join in that daydream with him. "I've never been there before. But since you'll be there, I'm sure I'll love it."

He opens our hands and threads his fingers through mine. "Gwen's there, at NYU. You'd already have a friend to hang out with."

"If she's still talking to me after the way I dropped off the face of the earth."

"Don't worry. She'll talk to you. Once we're there, I'm going to take you on one of those carriage rides through Central Park. We'll go to the top of the Empire State Building. I'll buy you a hot dog from a street vendor."

Right on cue, my stomach rumbles. I press my hand over it, giggling softly. But Lucas doesn't laugh. "Hungry?" he asks. We haven't had anything to eat or drink in hours.

"A little."

He nudges me forward so he can reach his arm around me and snuggle me in next to him.

It's fully dark now and shadows move across the walls as the moonlight begins to stream in through the tiny window. We don't bother to move, and I can feel myself drifting off when I hear the sound of footsteps come down the hallway. My eyes pop open and my stomach jumps. Lucas's shoulder grows tense beneath my cheek.

The door swings open, and I squint against the bright light that pours in from the hallway. "I've got dinner," Shane states, looking down at us. "Don't you two look cozy."

Lucas starts to stand, pulling me up with him. "I shouldn't be surprised that it's you here," Lucas says. I see the long-haired guard standing behind Shane, and I wonder if Shane volunteered to bring us food so he could gloat.

Shane tenses before a smirk appears on his harsh face. "I'm in a better place than you are, my friend."

"If I'm your friend, how about letting us out of here?" Lucas suggests.

Shane gives him a condescending look. Before Lucas can get into it with him, I say, "So, you're a part of this? You're helping him do this to us?"

Sighing heavily, he sets the tray down on the floor. It contains two sandwiches and a couple of water bottles. "Shit, Raielle. He doesn't want to hurt you. He just needs you to cooperate with him."

I study his expression, trying to understand what goes on in his head, because despite his words, his actions have always had one goal in mind, to hurt me. "You know he's not capable of actually caring about you?" I say.

Shane doesn't respond to the question. "You should eat. You need to keep your strength up."

"Did you hear what I said?" I ask.

He scowls. "Yeah, I heard you."

I stare at him, stunned. "And what? You don't care? You like the perks, the money, and the girls? Is that why you're doing this?"

His gaze is all over the room, unable to meet mine. "What does it matter?"

"Is the money enough to help you close your eyes to it all? Or are you really like him, not caring about anything or anyone but yourself?"

For a moment he looks hurt before his eyes turn hard. "Say whatever you want to me. It doesn't matter. I mean, look at you." His gaze settles on me. "Did you really think that you could win? That you could suck his power right out of him and ride off into the sunset with your boyfriend?" His gaze moves to Lucas. "Or that Grant, the biggest jerk-off on the planet, would kill him for you?"

My jaw tightens, and from the corner of my eye I notice Lucas take a step toward him. "How did you know that, Shane?" he asks, somehow keeping his voice calm.

Shane's thin lips turn up into a huge shit-eating grin. "Oh, I don't know. Maybe the phone Apollo left under the couch at Meera's house told me. It stayed on for two days before the battery finally died." He shakes his head. "It's so simple, yet no one ever suspects it."

"Apollo helped you?" I ask more to myself than to him, nearly wincing at the pain of another betrayal by him.

Shane eyes me with contempt. "Apollo knows who his friends are."

"So does Raielle," my father says. I look up and see him standing just beyond the doorway. I tense and feel Lucas's hand gripping mine.

My chest tightens as my father steps into the room. He fingers the light switch on the wall and bright fluorescents buzz to life, illuminating his piercing green eyes. They drill into mine, making my stomach flip.

"You can go now, Shane," he says.

Shane glances at me before turning and leaving the room. We can hear his heavy boots moving down the hallway.

"You haven't eaten yet," he says, gesturing toward the tray. "Please, don't let me stop you."

But neither of us move or say anything.

He seems amused as his gaze travels back and forth between Lucas and me. Meanwhile, Lucas's hand is beginning to fist in mine, and I'm praying he listens to my plea about not doing anything stupid.

"I'm so impressed with you, Raielle." My father smiles at me, and if I didn't understand him so well now, I might miss the monster waiting patiently behind his grin.

"If things were different," he continues, "I'd be happy to have you by my side. I'm astounded by your power. I was stronger than my father, too, but not like you." Then he turns his eyes on Lucas. A moment later, the bald bodyguard appears. "Take him outside, please."

Lucas's hand grips my waist, pulling us both back when the guard comes toward him.

I turn on my father. "If you hurt him, you will never get my cooperation."

"Was I going to get it?" He smiles condescendingly at me.

Taking a deep breath, I step out of Lucas's hold. "If you let him go, I promise to do whatever you want."

I can practically hear Lucas bristling behind me, but he stays quiet.

My father looks at me carefully. "Do you know what I want?"

Swallowing, I nod my head.

He eyes me carefully. "I know you've seen Meera, and I know that Grant has been filling your head with stories about me. The truth is that my power has been weakening as I grow older. It's a fate that none of us can escape, although I've certainly tried. But it seems that everything has changed. Because of you, sweetheart. Your power makes me stronger. It's brought me back to life. So," he says, taking a step toward me. "If I do what you're asking and let your friend leave, then I bring you with me into any of the rooms here and ask you to heal one of my patients, you'll do it willingly, knowing that as you're healing, I intend to take your energy from you?"

I try not to let him see any fear in me when I nod.

"Jesus," Lucas mutters, placing his hands on my shoulders.

My father laughs. "I wish I could believe you, Raielle."

Lucas's fingers unconsciously dig into me while my father studies me calmly.

"I know that you have to be trying your very hardest to heal before I can drain your power," he says evenly. "What if you don't do your best to help a stranger? What if you hold your energy back from me so that I can't take what I want? A halfhearted attempt on your part does me no good."

Now that all the artifice is gone, the stark reality of who he is makes my insides squirm. It's hard not to rail against him and release all the fury I feel for him. Instead, even though I'm shaking like a leaf, I speak evenly. "I told you my condition for cooperating. I'll hold up my end."

He glances at his bodyguard before his eyes return to me. "I think there's only one way to be sure you're really giving it your all, using every bit of energy you have inside you."

His words accelerate my already racing pulse. When he turns to the guard and says, "In the heart," terror flashes through me. Instantly, I know what he intends. I go to move in front of Lucas, to block him, but my father grabs my arm and yanks me hard, pulling me to the floor. Time seems to slow as the gun appears, and Lucas tries to lunge for it.

I hear myself screaming just before the shot sounds, echoing inside the small room. Lucas jerks backward as a tiny dot of blood forms in the middle of his shirt. I'm already up and running for him when he begins to fall back, catching himself hard on his elbows just before his head hits the floor.

"Lucas!" I see the blood spreading over his shirt, pumping out of his chest. Instinctively, I place my hand over the hole, feeling the warm liquid seeping beneath my palm.

His eyes are glassy when they find mine, and he coughs, causing a trickle of blood to drip down the side of his mouth. "Shit, this hurts," he says as he winces.

I cry out his name again, shaking my head, not wanting to believe this is happening. I can almost hear myself shattering into pieces.

"This is your chance," Lucas whispers so softly I can barely hear it. His eyes squeeze closed before he struggles to open them again. "I know you can do this."

Looking at his pained expression, I feel the energy sparking inside me. But I know that as soon as I let it go, my father will begin to siphon it off. Lucas is hurt too badly. It's going to take all my power to save him, which is exactly what my father wanted. I think of Grant in the kitchen with the knife, and how he couldn't heal himself once I drained him. Instinctively, I know that I won't be strong enough to save Lucas once my father begins leeching my power from me, and I won't be able to take his power unless I divert my attention from Lucas. My father has outsmarted us, and now the only person who has ever loved me is going to pay a terrible price for it.

Lucas's mouth tightens in pain as he watches me, and I can see that he has no idea of the terrible thoughts running through my head. He's confused by my complete despair. I cry even harder, wanting to be strong for him, but failing miserably because my whole world is crumbling.

His eyes have a desperate hold on mine, and I see it when a glimmer of fear creeps into his expression. Maybe he is starting to understand. He swallows hard and licks his lips. "It's okay," he says. His voice is thready and weak.

"No," I whisper because it's the farthest thing from okay.

"I'm sorry," he rasps. His fingers whisper across my arm. "I'm so sorry, Ray."

A sob rips from me as I stare down into his beautiful face. He's apologizing to me. He's worrying about me when I'm the one who's done this to him. I have so many regrets, so many things I wish I'd done differently.

I take his hand and lean down to kiss him. He barely manages to press his own mouth against mine. I can't stand this. He's meant to live a long life filled with happiness. It's not supposed to end this way, and I won't let him go without trying. Even though I know what that will mean for both of us.

With his hand still in mine, I squeeze my eyes closed and throw everything I have into fueling my power, letting the coil grow hot and bright inside me, taking every ounce of strength and directing it to my center. It swirls beneath my skin, expanding and heating me from the inside out. I'm shaking with the effort, feeling as though I'm going to ignite at any moment. Then I let it unwind, traveling through me like a lit fuse sparking hotly into Lucas. His breathing hitches as I reach inside him to wind the coil around the raw wound mutilating his chest.

From the corner of my eye, I see my father moving toward me like a predator. I cringe away as his hand reaches for me. Does he know, I wonder? Does he realize that Lucas will die if he takes my energy while I'm trying to heal him? As his hand stretches out to touch my cheek, I reach up and pull it from the air, grasping it tightly with my free hand. He only grins as he starts to pull on my power where our hands meet. I try to yank away, but I can already feel it. It's like he's slowly dousing me with water, extinguishing my energy little by little.

I turn back to Lucas, watching as the light in his eyes dims. His pallor is gray now, and my heart leaps into my throat. *No!* His body is failing too quickly and without all my strength, I can't reverse what's happening. I feel it inside him, the shift that occurs when the coldness of death starts to grip him.

My hand tightens around his. I won't let this happen. I can't let him go, and there's something else I can do, something that worked when I was far less powerful. I did it with Penelope, and I hope that at the very least, I can take Lucas's death into myself.

Instead of using my remaining strength to heal his wound, I pull on it. My coil of power snaps back at me, making me flinch as it fights against me. But I push past it until I can feel each pulse of Lucas's weak heart echoing inside my own chest.

Gradually, it begins to work as the damage done to his body shifts into me, making my own heart sputter. My eyes skim down to the bullet hole, watching as the blood seeping out starts to slow. That's when I feel the hideous pain of what my father is doing to me, the tug on my power, the fire burning in my veins as he rips my energy from me.

Easily now, my father breaks my grip on him and his hand lands on my cheek, his fingers digging into the skin below my jaw. I snap my head in his direction and see that his eyes are closed. He's enjoying the flow of energy, and the hatred I feel for him is like a living thing slithering inside me.

When I look back over at Lucas, my chest starts to tighten. Breathing is a struggle as my heart skips unevenly, but I keep going, waiting for the color to return to his face and for the hole inside his chest to close completely. It's getting harder as my father takes my power, and I'm teetering on the edge, fighting for clarity as my vision darkens.

I'm running out of time when Lucas coughs harshly before pulling in a deep breath. I watch as the blood flows back into his face and relief pours through me. His lips and cheeks are taking on a pink tinge. The bullet hole is sealed closed, and little by little the rhythm of his heart starts to even out, growing strong inside his chest while my pulse slows. Pure joy makes me smile as I look at him. It worked. He's coming back. He's going to be okay, and at least one of us is going to walk out of here alive. Slowly, I pull my hand from his, severing our connection.

Then I turn on my father, fighting against the blackness that wants to swallow me. He's watching me now, feeling good, oblivious to my struggle as I gather the horror swirling inside me. I don't know if I can pass my death into him, but one way or another, I'm going to make him feel my pain. He doesn't expect it when I lunge at him. My hate-fueled scream shatters the silence as I grasp his wrists with both hands and slam the agony pulsing through me directly into him. It fills the stream of energy flowing between us. His eyes are wide, and he doesn't seem to feel it. He just thinks I'm fighting back. But soon his forehead wrinkles, first in suspicion, then in pain.

He tries to pull away from me. Astonishment breaks across his face, and I wonder what he thought I would do. I told him that I wasn't willing to trade one life for another, but did he really think that would apply to Lucas? Maybe he didn't believe I was strong enough to do this or that I would be afraid to try because of what happened with Penelope. Or maybe he thought I'd be scared to die, just like he is. But more likely, he's never cared about anyone in his entire life. He had no idea how far I'd be willing to go to save someone I love.

He tries to stand, but I throw my weight against him, pinning him down with all the strength I have left. I'd nearly forgotten the bodyguard who is still standing in the doorway, looking confused now, not realizing what's happening right in front of his eyes.

But my father can't talk. He can't call out for help as the color drains from his face. His struggling slowly diminishes as his head falls back to the floor, and his eyes silently plead for me to stop. Instead of stopping, I mercilessly push into him every last bit of death I've taken from Lucas's body until his eyes lose their focus. His arms go slack in my hands. My blood turns ice-cold when his heart gradually comes to a stop, and I collapse in a heap, right on top of him.

I lie there for a moment, shivering and breathing hard. When I'm able to push myself up, I try to stand, but the room tilts, and I slump down to the floor. The bodyguard slowly approaches us, trying to get a closer look. He says nothing, just stares at my father's lifeless form.

"Lucas," I call out. But my voice is a strained whisper, and I get no reply. Getting to my hands and knees, I crawl over to where he lies. His color is good, but he still hasn't moved. I lay my ear against his chest, listening for his heartbeat. It's there, I think. But my own pulse is throbbing in my ears, making it hard to distinguish his from my own. "Lucas," I plead, shuddering as my teeth chatter loudly.

Then I feel a slight movement before his fingers slide into my hair. I burst into tears, gripping his shirt in my hands. I turn to see his eyes staring up at me. They glitter with intensity. He winces as he levers himself up, still holding me against him.

"You're okay," I whisper, barely getting the words out between sobs.

Lucas's hand curls over the nape of my neck as his other arm winds around me, pressing me to him. "I'm okay, baby." He holds me close and I breathe him in, letting his warmth flow into me. Reaching up, I loop my arms around his neck, pressing my face into his skin, wanting to get closer because I can't seem to get close enough. His arms tighten around me, and I can feel him trembling. When my hand brushes his cheek, it comes away wet with his tears. We cling to each other until Lucas finally leans back to look at me.

"You did it. You took his power?" he asks, his eyes flicking briefly to my father lying motionless on the floor.

I blink away the wetness blurring my vision. "I took everything. He's dead."

His eyes widen as they stare at my father's body. When they focus on me again, I see relief and concern for me. His hands come up to cradle my wet cheeks. "Good," he says. Then he kisses my lips, and I know I'll never regret what I did.

TWENTY-ONE

Lucas

THE asshole that shot me looks like a lost puppy. "What now?" he mutters to himself, staring down at the body on the floor.

"Now you run," I say, rubbing the sore spot on my chest. "Before she does the same thing to you."

He blinks at us. Then the bodyguard turns on his heel and disappears faster than I figured a hulking sack of shit like him could move.

Raielle is still shivering beside me, and I'm choked with emotion. I'm so proud of her and so in love with her that I can barely breathe. I'm alive, thanks to Raielle, and other than feeling like an elephant spent most of the day sitting on my chest, I'm filled with renewed hope for us. But I can't even crack a smile because she looks like hell. She saved my life, but ended up killing her own father. I still don't know how that happened, and right now she isn't talking.

"Let's go," she says, tugging on my arm, leading the way out of the room.

As we make our way down the hallway, opening each door we pass because Raielle wants to find the little girl named Kaylie, we're surprised to see that no one is here. Her father was bluffing. The clinic is empty.

Finally, we open the last door near the stairwell to find Grant sitting on a bed with his head in his hands. He glances up at us, and his shock is apparent as he takes us in. We're both covered in my blood, and it's starting to dry, making my shirt cold and stiff.

"What the fuck happened?" he asks, getting to his feet.

Beside me, Raielle takes a deep breath and opens her mouth, but nothing comes out.

"John is dead," I say.

He looks to Raielle for confirmation. She nods.

"How?" he asks, his wide eyes traveling between us.

I'm about to tell him that it doesn't matter, when Raielle finds her voice. "He had a heart attack." Her tone is even, but the sound is nothing more than a dull rasp. She pulls on my arm and takes a step toward the door that leads outside.

Grant's face wrinkles in disbelief.

"He's in there." I point over my shoulder. "There's a lot of blood, but it's all mine."

His mouth works silently, as though he's going to say something, but he doesn't.

I lay my hand on Raielle's shoulder to reassure her because she looks like a trapped animal, desperate to get out of its cage. Then I turn back to Grant. "We're going home. Can you take care of things here?"

He wants to object, to hear more details, but as he studies her, worry wrinkles his brow and he nods. Then he points to the phone sitting on the nurse's desk. "I'll call you a cab. Here, take my shirt. You'll never get a ride looking like that." He pulls his gray T-shirt over his head and hands it to me.

I peel mine off, grimacing at the way it sticks to my skin. Then I pull Raielle's blood-stained sweater off her. The T-shirt she has on underneath is clean.

"I'll go upstairs and punch in the gate code for the taxi. We'll talk later," Grant tells me pointedly. Then he eyes Raielle again. She's just standing there, looking dazed. "Is she going to be okay?"

"She'll be fine," I reply, and I hope I'm right.

I lead her outside, securing her beside me as we climb the hill up to the driveway. Then we stand in the cool night air, waiting. She's silent as her body leans into mine. The shaking has subsided, and now she seems drowsy as she sways on her feet. I look around, scanning the area for Shane or those guards, but we seem to be the only ones out here.

Soon we hear the sound of crunching gravel. Glancing at my watch, I see it's nearly midnight. I practically have to pick Raielle up to get her into the cab. I give the driver my address and sit back, cradling her in my arms. She reaches around my neck and burrows her face into my shoulder.

I looked for it on the way in, but I check again now. My truck, which I left sitting just outside the gate, is gone. I didn't see it up at the house either. It probably got towed.

The streets are quiet, and we get home in no time. The driver tells me the fare has been taken care of, so I pick up a sleeping Raielle, push the door closed with my foot, and carry her inside. Since I have no money on me, no wallet and no phone, it's a good thing Grant thought of that.

It's a little tricky, balancing her and getting the front door unlocked, but she hardly stirs. I see that Cal's door is closed as I walk by, and I figure he's asleep already. When I finally lay her down on my bed, she whimpers softly before curling in on herself.

Stepping back, the sight of her lying there all alone breaks my heart. I planned to shower the dried blood off my skin, but I can't leave her for that long. I settle for changing into sweats and my own T-shirt before lightly tugging Raielle's jeans down her legs and crawling in beside her, pulling the comforter up over us. I hug her body in close to mine and bend her head into the crook of my neck, where she likes to rest it when we sleep.

The moment my eyes close, the night comes back at me in flashes. I recall the look on her face before she healed me. Complete and utter despair were all I saw. At first, I couldn't understand why she looked like she was losing me. But then I remembered how Grant couldn't heal the slice in his arm when she drained his power. That's what the desperation in her eyes meant. I had more than a slice in my arm. So I told her it was okay, even though it wasn't. I'd failed her. She was at the mercy of her father, and there was nothing I could do to help her.

My eyes squeeze tight at the thought of what could have happened. I shift restlessly, unwilling to go there, not wanting to give that nightmare substance because it didn't happen. Somehow Raielle managed to save us both. What will it do to her, though?

In the end, she did what she begged Grant and me not to. When she wakes up in the morning, how will she feel about it? I want to believe it's over. Her father is gone. This is what we needed to move on with our lives. But can she move on from this, or will she go back to being the ghost of a girl I found when I first got here? My hand goes to my chest and I rub at the spot that aches, knowing that ache will never go away if Raielle can't recover from this.

She shifts, curling into my side. I nuzzle my nose in her hair, listening to her quiet, even breaths as I start to think that running away to New York with me may not be the best thing for her. With her father out of the picture, she could finally be free to do all the things she's felt compelled to do her whole life. She doesn't have to hide anymore. She could become part of a community with others who are like her. I recall Meera's words about her destiny, and I think of how alone she's always been.

As much as I want the fresh start we talked about, I'm not sure that's right for her now. If she stays here, maybe she could feel normal for the first time in her life. Maybe she could find a way to be happy.

Raielle

I COME awake slowly, squinting at the light filtering through the blinds. My head feels fuzzy, as I try to figure out where I am. Lucas's hand touches my forehead and brushes my hair back from my face.

"Hey," he says softly.

My eyes focus to find him sitting beside me. Then all at once, I remember everything. I push up and look around.

"We're at my place."

My mind races over every detail as my heart squeezes tight. "He's…"

I begin.

"Gone," Lucas finishes for me.

I pull in low breath, letting the truth of it settle over me. Lucas is watching me closely. The weight of his thoughts sits heavy on his shoulders, and the remaining pain he still feels calls to me. Reaching out to him, I press my hand to his chest.

A brief smile pulls at his lips as he leans away.

I eye him curiously because I know it hurts. "Let me help with the soreness."

He takes my hand and holds it. "You still look wiped out. No healing today." His gaze stays on me. "How are you feeling?"

I know what he's thinking. He thinks I'm going to fall apart because of what I did to my father. But if I do fall apart, that won't be the reason. "I'm fine," I assure him. I'll be fine as long as I don't dwell on how close I came to losing Lucas.

His mouth turns down. I don't think he believes me. "Can you tell me what happened?" he asks gently. "I know you started to heal me, but after that, I don't remember much."

When I look away his thumb starts to rub over the top of my hand, and I wonder what to tell him. Once I moved his wound into my body, I didn't know if I could pass it on to my father. All I knew was that I had to save Lucas, no matter the cost. He said he was sorry as he lay there dying, but I'm the one who's sorry. I have so many regrets, I still feel choked by them now.

I look up into his eyes and offer him a bittersweet smile. "I out-monstered the monster."

He looks shocked. Then his gaze sharpens on me. "You're not a monster."

I don't bother correcting him. I have nothing else to say about what occurred in that room last night. I can accept the monster inside me, the one that killed her own father. But I know that same monster has been hurting Lucas, too. I turned his life upside down, and then I nearly got him killed. That's the monster I can't accept, and the one I won't be anymore.

He sighs at my silence, misunderstanding me. "No, Ray," he says simply, like it's an obvious fact that isn't worth discussing. Then he dips his head to kiss me. It's a soft, tender brush of my lips. He urges me back down and we hold each other the rest of the morning, dozing in and out of sleep until a knock at the front door wakes us. We hear Grant's voice.

Lucas blows out a heavy breath, running his hands through his hair. "We should talk to him," he says, looking weary but resigned. When I nod, he goes out to let Grant in.

I pull the covers off to find I have only my underwear on. So I stay in bed as Grant walks into the bedroom, looking pleased to see me. "How are you feeling?" he asks, his eyes scanning over my outline beneath the covers.

I pull the blanket up a little higher. "I'm fine."

He tosses a paper bag at Lucas, who catches it easily and grins at what's inside. "Thanks," he tells him as he pulls out our phones and his wallet.

Grant rubs his jaw, seeming to weigh his next words. "People are starting to gather at the house. They wanted to hear the news for themselves. They want to see you." He looks at me.

"People?" Lucas asks.

"Yes, *our* people," he stresses. "Nothing to worry about."

"They already know?" I ask.

"Ken, the bodyguard, went upstairs and started blabbing. He seems to think you did something to John. He believes you traded Lucas's life for John's. I told him your story. That it was a heart attack, and that he must be mistaken."

Lucas looks at me, and I look away. I can't discuss the details of what happened in that room. I just can't. The words would cut too deeply.

"Do we need to worry about him?" Lucas finally asks.

Grant shakes his head. "He won't talk to outsiders. We take care of things ourselves. I cleaned up the room, put John in his bed upstairs, and told Nyla to call an ambulance."

My nerves jump at the sound of her name. I'd forgotten about her.

"They came and took him away. No one suspects anything but

natural causes." Grant grins. "It's all good."

I shake my head at his good cheer and nonchalance. Grant is obviously pleased with the outcome and not trying to pretend otherwise.

"How is Nyla?" I ask. If anyone is going to miss my father, it's her.

Grant's smile falters. "She's actually not so good. But she won't make any trouble."

"What about Shane and Apollo?" Lucas asks, and at the sound of Apollo's name, I tense. I can hardly believe how wrong I was about him. He saved my life, but then he nearly helped to destroy it.

Grant shrugs. "I'm not sure. They must know something's up because I can't get a hold of either of them. Apollo isn't one of us, and now that John is gone, he has no ties to us. If he's smart, he'll go back to his life and take himself out of the picture. And Shane, well, without John behind him, he's not much of a threat. I wouldn't worry about him."

Grant focuses on me. "I'd like you to come back to the house with me. Meera will be arriving later. She's anxious to see you." He steps farther into the room. "Everything is different now, Raielle. You made it different. I want you to know that we're your friends. We could be your family, too, if you'd let us be."

I'm ready to refuse when Lucas speaks up. "Could you give us a minute?" he asks.

Grant's gaze travels uncertainly between us before he nods his head. "I'll be outside."

Once he's gone, I wait for Lucas to say something, figuring he wants to run whatever excuse he's come up with by me. He comes over to the bed and sits down. "Maybe we should go with him."

My eyes nearly bug out of my head. "What?"

He turns, resting his forearms on his thighs and looking down at the floor. "You can't just dismiss what he said. You have a gift and—"

I shake my head, cutting him off. "It's not a gift."

"Yes, it is," he insists. "The way you would use it, it would be."

Leaning forward, I try to see his expression. "Are you saying that you think I should stay here? Go back to that house and pretend like I'm one of them?"

He looks at me over his shoulder. "I don't want you to pretend anything. I want you to be true to yourself. Grant told us how difficult it is to be isolated from others who are like you. I already saw you suffering from that when I first met you. You've been hiding your whole life. What I'm saying is that I'll understand if staying here is what you decide to do. I'll stay with you."

I can't believe what I'm hearing. "You almost died last night. That's what this so-called gift did to you."

"That was your father. No one else. And he's not a factor anymore."

My head is shaking, and I can't seem to stop it. After trying to convince me to leave so many times, now he doesn't want to? "Do you honestly want us to stay here? Please don't pretend that whatever I decide is completely fine with you. You must have an opinion. Don't you want us to go to New York together anymore?"

He pinches the bridge of his nose. When he lowers his hand, he levels determined eyes at me. "Yes. New York is still what I want, but it's selfish of me to tell you that."

"How is that selfish?" He's the least selfish person I know.

"Because of who you are. Look at what you can do. You've got a destiny that's bigger than me, and I won't be the one that you walk away from it for."

I find myself staring at him in complete disbelief. My throat is suddenly so clogged with emotion, I can't find the words to tell him how wrong he is. Pushing the covers off me, I stand and pull on my clothes with angry, jerky movements.

I can feel Lucas come up beside me. "Look, I just—"

My hand goes up to halt him. "Go get Grant." I yank my shirt over my head, and when he doesn't move, I tell him again.

Sighing, he leaves, and moments later he returns with Grant in tow. Grant is wearing a tense smile, and I wonder what Lucas said to him.

Dressed now, I turn to both of them. "I'm not going back to that house again. Ever."

Grant nods immediately. "I understand. I don't blame you. We can find somewhere else to meet."

"No. I don't want to meet anywhere. Lucas and I are leaving."

Grant looks like I slapped him. "You can't leave," he says as if it's a crazy notion, instead of the only sane one.

"Watch us," I reply, and my eyes shift to Lucas. He's looking at me, silently questioning me.

Appearing panicky now, Grant says, "You've been through a lot. I know that. Take some time to think about this. Don't make any rash decisions, because this is too important. This is your legacy, Raielle."

His words have the opposite effect of what he intends. They infuriate me. I think of Charlie cutting Lucas with her knife, and of Grant plotting to murder my father and involving Lucas. I think of Shane and Apollo with their hate and betrayal.

"You think this is my legacy?" I ask. "This legacy killed my mother, and yesterday it nearly took away the person I love most in the world. It's caused me nothing but heartache. This so-called legacy turns my stomach. It's dark and deceptive and teeming with bad intentions. I may be destined to do something with my power, but getting involved with you people isn't it."

Grant stares at me, gritting his teeth, but Lucas is finally revealing his true feelings. He looks utterly relieved. The grim determination on his face before when he was talking about staying was nothing but bravado. He wants to go even more than I do, but he was willing to put that aside because he thought I needed to be here. It's just another sacrifice he was going to make for me. But I'm not letting him make any more sacrifices.

"You need some time," Grant says, ignoring what I said. "You'll change your mind."

"I won't be changing my mind. Good-bye, Grant." My arms cross over my chest, and I don't so much as blink when his lips flatten into a tight, disapproving line.

"You will," he insists. "What you just went through has you running scared. That's understandable. But when you're ready to come back, you'll be welcome."

"Good-bye, Grant," Lucas says.

Grant's eyes bore into mine. He doesn't move.

"And thanks," Lucas adds, offering his hand. The gesture amuses me, and Lucas keeps his hand up, waiting, while Grant is still frozen in place.

After a few more awkward, silent moments, Grant seems to reluctantly deflate. He tears his eyes off me and ignores Lucas's hand before turning and walking out of the apartment.

TWENTY-TWO

Raielle

S I pull the brush through my hair, I hear Lucas turn off the shower in the bathroom. We're at an inn a few miles outside of Fort Upton. After we both withdrew from school, Lucas decided to buy a new truck and drive us to New York, stopping along the way to do touristy things like hike through Bryce Canyon and see Mount Rushmore. Apparently the truck I loved so much was stolen, but we've already made memories in the new truck, and now I don't miss the old one too badly.

Before we left, I asked if we could drive down to San Diego to visit my mother's grave. I'd still never seen it. There was a nervous flutter in my stomach as we drove up the hill to the cemetery. Kyle chose a beautiful spot for her with a view of the ocean in the distance. I nearly laughed at the irony of it. It was nicer than anyplace she'd ever lived, and it was a kind gesture on Kyle's part for a woman who abandoned him. I was afraid I'd find something closer to a pauper's grave. But instead, there was a simple headstone with her name and the pertinent dates. When I got emotional standing there, Lucas came up beside me, and I imagined that she could see him, and knew that I had someone in my life who loved me.

In total, the drive across country took us a little over two weeks. We stayed at motels along the way, and didn't worry about our route or how little sightseeing we were actually doing, because we spent most of our time in bed together.

Lucas was right about this trip. He needed it, even more than I did. He's undergone a subtle change while we've been on the road. The tension that once vibrated off him in waves has waned. He smiles more easily now—real, genuine, light-up-his-face smiles—and every time it happens, my chest grows tight at the beauty of it.

There's still an undertone of sadness about him. For as long as I've known him, it's been there. I suppose it will never go away, but it doesn't eat at him the way it once did, and I'm finding that this new lightness of his is contagious. My hope is that he sees a change in me, too. I'm still not great at telling him how I feel. That probably comes from years of not having anyone to talk to. But he seems to know my thoughts anyway. He knows every part of me, and he still loves me.

The bathroom door opens and he steps out with nothing but the white motel towel wrapped low around his waist. My eyes travel over his tall, muscled frame, and he takes my breath away. We've been basically living together since he came to Los Angeles, but I'll never get used to this. The butterflies in my belly still flutter away when he's near, and I hungrily crave his touch.

The muscles in his arm bunch as he reaches up to push the wet hair off his forehead, and his midnight-blue eyes smile at me, caressing me with the love that shines through them.

"Are you sure you don't want to call Kyle first?" he asks.

I shake my head and take a sip of the coffee I went out for earlier. "I'd rather see him in person. A telephone conversation would be too awkward."

"How do you know it would be awkward?"

I put the coffee down. "Because I have no idea what to say to him.

For all I know, he doesn't even want to talk to me."

"Ray." He walks over to me and bends down so we're at eye level. I can smell soap and the unique, spicy scent that's just him. "I know you want to see him. And I have a feeling he's going to be glad to see you."

He's so close and he smells so good that I forget my train of thought. One dark eyebrow arches knowingly at me, and his cocky smirk appears. I have to look away to unscramble my brain.

"I'll have to lie to him," I murmur. "I'll have to lie to everyone when they ask why I left Fort Upton so suddenly."

"So?" He shrugs. "You tell them a story. Then you move on. After everything you've been through, this part should be easy."

"Are you sure you won't come with me?" I thrust out my bottom lip in a pout.

His smile disappears. "I don't want to see him."

Lucas still holds a grudge against Kyle. "You can't blame him for—"

"Yes, I can." He stands abruptly. "I don't forgive as easily as you do, and I'm okay with that."

"But he didn't know—"

"He knew enough," Lucas says in a clipped, harsh tone. Then he lets out a frustrated breath, calming himself down and appearing apologetic. "And he knew it the whole time you lived there. He knows about Alec now, too, and he still sees him like nothing has changed. I understand that you don't blame Kyle for anything that happened, but I don't feel the same way."

I sigh and go for my coffee again.

Lucas rubs his hand over his face. "I'm sorry. I don't mean to ruin this for you. Kyle cares about you. I know that. And he was in a tough position, but I can't help how I feel. Especially when it comes to people who hurt you."

I nod with understanding because I'd feel the same way about anyone who hurt him.

When I stand to finish packing, he takes my hand and turns me to him. "Let's take another week. We could drive up to Maine. Have you ever been there?"

I cock my head at him. He knows I've never been there. Besides, he's bluffing, I think. "No." I smile.

His brows inch up. "Want to go?"

I nod, resting my hand on the warm skin over his heart. Its steady thrum beneath my palm reassures me. This has become a habit of mine and Lucas indulges me. He understands.

I have nightmares sometimes that I touch his chest and there's no rhythm beneath my hand. When I look up at his face, his eyes are glassy and vacant. Then I startle awake, my own heart pounding, and I shatter in relief when his strong arms pull me close.

Lucas has bad dreams, too, terrible ones that leave him shaking, covered in sweat, and reaching for me desperately. We don't talk about our nightmares. We lived them together, and we know what they are. During those quiet, dark hours, we hold each other until the last remnants of our dreams fade. One day, I hope they'll finally disappear forever.

"We can't." He frowns about extending our road trip, but I already knew that. His family is expecting him today.

I reach up and run my fingers through his damp hair. He groans, and then he starts to laugh, pulling my hands away. "If you don't stop, we're going to be late." When I turn away, I've barely walked a few steps before I feel his towel whip out and snap me on the butt.

"Hey!" I whirl around to see his gloriously naked form.

When he smiles wickedly at me, I know without a doubt that we're going to be late.

This is new, the easy way we have with each other. When I think back to when we first met and those heated exchanges, it's hard to believe how we are now. Lucas was infuriating at the beginning, ignoring me and then convincing me to give him a chance, only to ignore me again. Back then, I couldn't have imagined ever understanding him so well. But I do. He's still infuriating sometimes, but now I know how good and brave he is, too, and how his fiery reactions are a result of the passion he feels for the people he loves.

I'm very lucky to be one of those people.

WE'RE in the new truck, parked in front of Kyle's house. "They're home," I say, eyeing both their cars in the driveway. "I guess we're not late enough to have missed them."

Alec's sedan isn't here, which I also take note of. Running into him is something I'm hoping to avoid while we're in town. Actually, I'm planning on actively avoiding him.

I swallow against a sea of emotion churning inside me before glancing over at Myles's house, and at the place Lucas was standing when I saw him that first night. It's hard to believe all that's happened since.

"Look," Lucas says, "maybe you should do this tomorrow when I can go with you. I guess I could stomach being in the same room with Kyle for a few hours."

Smiling at his offer, I say, "No. I'm okay. I can do this." Then I pull in a deep breath. "Say hi to Liam for me."

"You can tell him yourself when you see him later. Call me when you're ready to leave. If that's in the next five minutes, it's no problem." He leans over and kisses me.

Then I turn and jump down out of the truck. Lucas remains there, watching me, as I make my way to the front door. Rather than hesitate on the threshold and prolong the anxiety, I ring the bell the moment it's within reach. Commotion sounds from inside, and I think I hear Kyle's voice just before the door swings open. His eyes go wide when they see me, and at the sight of him standing there, my heart seems to stop.

When I lived here last spring, I eventually got used to seeing his eyes, our mother's eyes, looking back at me. But now, they shock me all over again, and I have to glance away. Instead, I scan his tall, rangy form clad in jeans and a T-shirt. "Hi," I say to a spot in the middle of his chest.

He clears his throat, taking a moment to find his voice. "Hi." Then his gaze shifts over my head to Lucas's truck. I turn and give Lucas a small wave, letting him know I'm okay. He stares at Kyle for a beat before pulling away from the curb.

"Who is it, Daddy?" Penelope pokes her head out next to Kyle's legs. "Raielle!" she screeches. "It's Raielle!" Then she runs back inside, yelling to her mother.

Stepping out of the doorway, Kyle's shock is fading, and deep lines form on either side of his mouth. "You left without a word," he finally says.

"I know. I'm sorry." It isn't easy maintaining eye contact with him, but I do.

There's some commotion from within the house before Penelope and Chloe appear at the door. I can't help but smile down at Penelope. "You're so big," I tell her. Not only that, but her hair is longer and her face seems slimmer with less baby fat.

She beams proudly at me. "I had to go get all new clothes for school. Mommy says I'm growing like a weed." She giggles.

From behind Penelope, Chloe watches me. "How are you?" she asks.

I look at Kyle when I answer. "I'm good."

Penelope tugs on my jeans. "Can I give you a hug?"

I've barely nodded when she launches herself at me. Her arms come around my legs and she rests her head against my thigh. With tears blurring my vision, I bend down and let her arms move to my neck as I hug her close. "I missed you," I whisper.

"I missed you, too," she whispers back.

My eyes flick up to Kyle, and compared to Penelope, he feels so remote. The tenuous relationship we built seems like something I imagined. Kyle's a lot like me, slow to trust, and hard to get close to. Before I left, he made me feel like I was part of his family. But now, I'm not sure he wants that anymore. I straighten and smile hesitantly at him. "Is this okay? That I'm here, I mean."

He gives me a sad smile. "Of course it's okay."

I stare at him, and his words seem sincere. Right then, I make a decision. Before I go, I'm going to tell him the truth. I need him to understand why I left. Unlike Lucas, I know everything he did was to save his daughter, and I can't find it inside me to be angry at him for that. All he did was try to help everyone. It's not his fault that he couldn't help me.

"Maybe you could come inside?" Kyle asks, and I realize that he seems nervous, like I may turn him down. "Just for a little while?" he adds.

Smiling now, I nod as I step over the threshold.

I never thought I'd find myself back here again. Kyle once said that I should think of this as my home. I don't, though, and I never really did. But I'd still like to think of him as my brother.

Lucas

CHECK my phone again to see if I missed her call, even though the ringer volume is pinned to the top, and it's also on vibrate in my hand. To say I'm on edge would be a massive understatement.

"If you would stop fucking around and put away your phone, we'd be done by now," Liam gripes as he carries another box into Mom's new house.

"I could have hired movers," she calls to us from inside.

"No, it's fine. We don't mind!" I holler back, scowling at Liam.

"You mean *you* don't mind," he says darkly.

I give him a light shove. "You need to eat your Wheaties. I've already unloaded half the truck myself."

Following behind Liam, I hoist another box onto my shoulder, shoving the phone into my back pocket. "So how did she find this place?" I ask, handing him the box in my other hand and snickering at him when he grunts and nearly buckles under its weight.

He glances at me as he balances it. "Someone she met at the hospital told her about it."

"So, is this official? Have they talked to lawyers?" I ask, feeling mostly ambivalence about their breakup and wondering if that makes me a bad son.

"How would I know? They don't tell me anything. They probably don't want to traumatize me now that I'm going to be a child of divorce." He rolls his eyes.

He's being a wiseass to cover. I know he's upset. "It's the best thing for her if it's going to make her happy," I point out.

Liam shoots me a look. "You're an idiot. Do you really think it's a good idea for her to be living alone?"

I put down the box as I take in his rigid posture. "She says the memories in the house are too hard for her. So, yes, if this will help, I think it's a good idea. What's with the hostility? Are you pissed about something else?"

He scoffs. "I'm pissed about everything and everyone's reaction, including yours. I don't care what her doctors say, she isn't better. I don't think we should leave her here."

I walk over to stand in front of him, and it still shocks me that my kid brother is nearly as tall as I am. "She promised to keep up with her therapy. If she doesn't, I'll get a call. There's a visiting nurse that supposed to check on her every day. She also promised to take her meds, and short of turning into her full-time babysitters, we're doing all we can."

Liam gnaws on the inside of his cheek, and I hate how much responsibility for her he's taken onto himself in the past few months.

"Stop worrying yourself to death," I say. "Just worry a normal amount. That's what I'm trying to do."

He snorts out a laugh and shakes his head, like I'm asking him to do the impossible. But I don't know what else to say to him to make him feel better. There is nothing to say. It's just going to take time.

Liam's gaze shifts beyond me. "That looks like Myles."

When we spoke earlier, Myles said he might stop by. I turn to see him pulling into the driveway. He and Zack step out of a brand new silver Prius. "Nice wheels," I comment as they walk up the lawn.

"They're his." Myles points to Zack, who's one step behind him. "He bought it new. He's been working since he was like sixteen and saving all his money. Can you believe that shit? Who does that?"

Zack's forehead furrows between his thick eyebrows. "Responsible people?"

Myles ignores him, waving at Liam before clapping me on the back. "So Raielle's dad, who she just met, died of a heart attack?" he asks with disbelief. This is the story we're telling everyone, and technically, it's not a lie.

"Yeah. But look, if you see her while you're here, don't bring him up too much. It's still kind of raw." The lie rolls off my tongue mainly because it's so much more believable than the truth.

"No problem," he says. "That girl has had some bad shit happen to her. The poor thing is an orphan now."

I hate hearing her described that way, like she's to be pitied, because I know how much she would hate it herself. "Definitely don't say that to her."

"The poor thing is here now." Liam mimics Myles as he lifts his chin toward the road.

I shoot him an annoyed look. "Cut the *poor thing* shit."

"What? She can't hear us?" Liam argues.

"But I can hear you."

"Whatever." He rolls his eyes again at me. "What crawled up your butt today?"

"He gets this way when he's worried about her," Myles explains to Liam, and he's right. I was supposed to be picking her up.

She's on the passenger side of Kyle's car, and a sliver of fear cuts at me. I'm down the driveway, already at her door as she pushes it open. "Are you okay? I thought you were going to call me when you were ready to leave."

She grins. "I'm fine. Kyle insisted on driving me here so he could see you."

Kyle is walking around the car, coming toward me. "I wanted to thank you for taking care of Raielle, for changing your school plans and going out there to be with her. If I'd known what was going on, I'd have been there, too."

Confused, I look at Raielle.

"I told him the truth," she says.

I lean in closer to her. "The truth? All of it?"

She hesitates and then nods.

That wasn't the plan, but I guess I'm not really surprised. Raielle isn't much of a liar.

Kyle's lips press together. "Raielle tells me she's staying with you while she's here."

I nod my answer, my expression daring him to disapprove. After spending every night together for weeks, she belongs in my bed. Besides, she's not staying at his house again as long as Alec is a part of his family. And I don't see that changing anytime soon.

"And your mother's moving here?" he asks, looking around.

I nod again.

"How is she?" Kyle's tone is casual, but his shoulders are tense.

"She's good. We'll be staying at my father's house, though," I tell him, knowing that's the information he's fishing for.

Kyle appears relieved. Then he turns to Raielle and places his hands on her shoulders. "I'd like to see you again before you go."

She smiles up at him. "That would be nice." She has a serious soft spot for this guy. I wonder if she told him that he's not her only brother anymore.

As he looks at her, he seems to get emotional. "I'll call you then. You'll answer?"

She tells him she will, appearing to feel guilty for not having answered his previous calls.

He pulls her in for a quick hug before getting back into his car.

Watching as he drives away, she says, "I really need to transfer my phone into my name. I can't believe he's still paying for it."

"We can do it tomorrow." I put my arm around her shoulder and turn her toward the street so I can talk to her before she notices Myles is here. "Why did you tell him?"

She lets out a breath. "It was his expression when he first saw me. He looked so hurt. Now that I won't be staying there like he wants, he deserves to know why."

I feel a surge of annoyance. "He doesn't get to be hurt. You did nothing wrong."

"But he didn't know that. He didn't know any of it."

The truth is, I'm glad she told him, and I hope hearing what she went through made him feel like shit. "So, how did he react?" I ask.

She hugs her arms around herself. "I think he's shocked and confused. When I explained about my father and what he tried to do to me, Kyle looked like I'd said aliens came and took me. Then we talked about Alec. The police already told him everything I did, but he doesn't believe his own father is responsible for our mother's murder. Or he doesn't want to believe it."

I move in front of her to better see her expression. "Alec will probably never pay for what he did."

She glances down at her feet. "I know."

"Can you be okay with that?"

Exhaling, she says, "It doesn't matter since I don't have a choice. Besides, I can't think about revenge or justice anymore. I want to put it behind me. Does that make me a bad daughter?"

I look at her, wondering how she could think that. Placing my finger beneath her chin, I make her look at me. "If your mother could see you now, she'd be very proud of you."

She smiles sadly. "You think so?"

I nod, watching her expression change as she lets this possibility sink in.

"You two done yet? I've been waiting patiently over here for my turn."

Her eyes widen as she peers over my shoulder. "Myles!" She brushes past me, meeting him halfway across the front lawn.

He pulls her into a hug. "California girl, you're slumming it again."

Raielle laughs, tossing her head back when he picks her up, and my chest feels heavy because I've seen her this way so few times. She should always look this happy. Once he releases her, he introduces her to Zack, who surprises her with a hug. She's saying hello to Liam as I come up beside her.

"Sorry about your dad," Myles says, his eyes moving to me to make sure that simple statement wasn't out-of-bounds.

She glances down at the grass. "Thanks."

"I hear you're a couple of college dropouts," Zack jokes, trying to lighten the mood, and I cut him a grateful look.

Raielle shakes her head. "Not Lucas. He's starting at Columbia in January. He registers for classes soon."

"What about you?" Zack asks her.

"I'm going to work for a while and apply to school for next summer or fall."

"Gwen is at NYU, isn't she?" Myles asks.

She nods wistfully, missing her friend.

"Will you and Lucas get a place together?" Zack asks.

I say yes at the same time Raielle says umm...

Zack and Myles give me a curious look while I stare at the side of her head, since she's avoiding making eye contact with me. "Ray?"

She shifts self-consciously from one foot to the other. "We'll talk about it later. Okay?" she asks quietly.

I get a sinking feeling in my stomach. "What's there to talk about?"

"Finances," she replies. Then she sighs. "Later."

I see the stern set of her jaw, and I'm not sure what she's thinking, but this isn't going to be a quick fix. Now I don't want an audience either. I drop it for now, but my eyes stay on her. Finances? Why are finances a problem? She just completely blindsided me.

Myles clears his throat. "Hey, we should all go out tonight."

Raielle accepts enthusiastically, and Myles and Zack take off after we make plans to meet them later . When Liam heads back into the house, I don't waste any time asking her about it. "What's going on?"

She tenses. "I wanted to go in and say a quick hello to your mom."

My hands go to my hips as I try not to growl in frustration at her. "I wasn't sure if you'd want to see her after what she did to you," I reply, giving in to her subject change so we can get this over with and get back to the conversation she wants to avoid.

"She wasn't herself. I don't hold that against her, Lucas."

Of course she doesn't. She couldn't hold a grudge if it were glued to her hand. "Sure," I answer. "We'll go see her after we talk."

When she sighs again, I can feel my blood pressure skyrocketing. "Are you kidding me, Ray? I thought everything was decided. I deserve an explanation."

Her lips tighten into a straight line. "You decided. We started looking online together, but then you took over the apartment search and figured I'd just go along with things."

"I didn't take it over. I asked your opinion."

"But you didn't listen to it." She takes a step toward me. "Who's going to pay the rent?"

"What?" My eyes narrow in confusion.

"Those places you were finding, there's no way I'm going to be able to afford them, no matter what kind of a job I get."

Shit. Now I get it. "Well, I figured—"

"You figured you were paying. That you would be supporting me."

Her face tenses with righteous indignation, and I feel the need to deny her accusation. "Just until you get school figured out and get your financial aid in place."

She laughs. "No financial aid package is going to be enough to pay for those places."

I try not to roll my eyes at her extreme reaction to a simple problem. "Then we'll look at other places, cheaper places."

"I was looking at cheaper places. You didn't like any of them, and why should you? You can afford to live in a nice place. Why would you want to live in a dump with me when you don't have to?"

Now I'm laughing. "Come on. You don't have to live in a dump. And why can't I support you? I'm able to, and I want to. I want you with me."

She crosses her arms. "I can't be dependent on you. I wouldn't be comfortable with that."

I just stare at her, wondering how I can feel both proud and irritated at the same time. "I understand what you're saying. But living apart isn't an option. We'll look for less expensive places. It doesn't matter to me where we live."

"But you're used to a certain way of living." she says, her tone softening.

I cock my head at her. "You've been upset about this for a while. Haven't you? Why didn't you say something?" She doesn't deny it, and a familiar frustration wells up inside me. "What happened to talking to me? I thought we were past this?"

Her lips press together. "I'm talking to you now. Aren't I?"

I can't hide my disappointment. "After I practically forced you to. We haven't made any progress, have we?"

She looks hurt. "Don't say that. It's not true. I've been trying. You know I have. This time I just wanted to avoid an argument."

"Why would you expect an argument? I'm not argumentative." Once the words are out, I nearly crack a smile, realizing that I'm arguing about not being argumentative.

She narrows her eyes at my claim, obviously disagreeing.

"Look." I cross my arms. "You shouldn't avoid talking to me if you have something to say. If you don't think I'm listening the first time, tell me again. Okay?"

At first she doesn't answer, chewing on her lip instead. But finally she says, "Okay." She still looks defiant, though, like she thinks I'm picking on her. "I'm going inside now to say hi to your mom," she says, turning on her heel.

"Wait a minute." I reach for her hand, halting her before she can walk away. "This isn't settled yet. We're going to look for an affordable place together. We're going to live together. Agreed?"

She nods once at me. "Agreed."

I release her, along with an exasperated breath as she walks away from me, heading toward the house. Then I make a decision that will surely come back to haunt me. I'm going to find a way around this apartment agreement we just made.

She's spent most of her life living in poverty, whether it was crowded foster homes or run-down apartments with her mom. But she's with me now, and those days are over. My father may be a prick, but he's a generous one. I'm sure he thinks that money makes up for his lack of parenting skills, and who am I to contradict him? I just have to find a way to give her all the things she deserves without ticking her off too badly.

TWENTY-THREE

Raielle

WE find Lucas's mother in the kitchen, arranging the silverware in a drawer beside the sink. The house she's moving in to is compact and cozy with one large open space on the first floor, sectioned only by furniture into separate dining and living areas. Lucas tells me that a stairway directly in front of the door leads to two bedrooms upstairs, and I think how different this is from the large Tudor house she came from.

According to Lucas, when he informed them of our plan to bring Liam to New York City with us, neither of his parents had much to say about it. Liam actually complained the most. He wanted to go, but he was afraid to leave his mother, just as Lucas predicted. Lucas is anxious to get him away from here, afraid he's spending too much of his time worrying about her. Since Lucas left for California, Liam quit the basketball team and his grades have started to fall.

"Hey, Mom. Look who's here?" Lucas calls to her.

She turns and her dark blue eyes, the same color as Lucas's, find mine. "Hello, Raielle." Shyly, she smiles at me.

I notice that she still looks thin and pale, but her chestnut-brown hair is neatly brushed, and her gaze is steady and clear. She grips her hands tightly in front of her, and she seems nervous to see me.

I return her smile and approach her slowly, making sure it's okay before reaching out to give her a hug. As her cool cheek brushes mine, I feel a familiar pull inside me. My stomach hollows as I try to home in on what I'm sensing. But she releases me too quickly and steps back. "Can I get you anything to drink? Are you hungry?" she asks.

I try to shake the feeling off. "No, thank you. Your new place is nice."

She nods politely and glances around, looking a little lost. When she raises her hand to push her hair behind her ear, I notice that it trembles slightly, and I feel uneasy.

"We're going to head back to the house to get settled in, but we'll stop by again tomorrow," Lucas says.

"Sure, sweetheart." She grins and almost seems relieved that we're going, but then she adds, "Come by whenever you like."

"Nice to see you again, Mrs. Diesel." I reach out for her hand, wanting to touch her again. When I squeeze her fingers, I feel it, and I'm stunned.

Lucas's appraising eyes are on me as we walk out the front door. "What is it?" he asks.

I'm surprised he noticed, and dismayed, too, because now I have to explain myself. He watches me expectantly, but I can't seem to get the words out. I'm not sure I want to. Wasting time, I watch Liam sitting in the truck bed, playing with his phone, and I know I have to tell Lucas. This is too big to keep from him. I stop chewing on my lip long enough to say, "I felt something when I touched her."

His forehead creases.

I bunch the bottom of my shirt in my fist. "I don't feel that way unless there's something I can heal."

I see the shock on his face as he pulls in a breath. Glancing back toward the house, I wonder if I was wrong to tell him. I'm probably stirring things up that are better left alone. I can sense his thoughts racing behind his uneasy eyes.

"Is it something physical?" Lucas asks quietly.

I shift my weight restlessly. "I don't know." I hesitate. "But I don't think so."

He gives me a confused look. "Are you talking about her depression? I thought mental illness was out-of-bounds for you?"

His questions make me feel worse because I don't have answers for him. I couldn't help with his mother's depression before when I reversed the damage my grandmother had done, and I made no difference with Leo either. He still killed himself. But I do know that my ability has grown stronger since I last saw Lucas's mother. When I healed Leo, my power wasn't fully within my control because of what my father had done to me. I sigh in frustration. "I don't know what my limits are anymore," I finally tell him.

He stares at me. "Are you saying that you can help her?"

"I don't know. I only know what I feel. But yes, that's what I'm thinking."

Running a hand through this hair, he takes a small step back from me. "What then? Are you asking for my permission?"

He almost seems angry now. I shake my head and shrug at the same time. "I hadn't thought it through that far, but I guess I'm asking your permission to ask her permission."

His gaze shifts above me before returning again and looking even more conflicted than before. "I have to think about it."

I nod, standing apart from him, hating how tense I've made him, and how my power keeps throwing a wrench into any peace we manage to achieve. "I'm sorry."

Lucas's eyes close. Then he scrubs a hand over his face. When he looks at me again, the intensity has cooled. "You don't have to be sorry. I'm glad you told me."

I study his face for the truth, but I only see confusion there. I try to give him a reassuring smile, knowing that if he seems this upset on the outside, then he must be churning with emotion inside. But as much as I hate making him feel this way, I can't deny the whisper of excitement inside me. If I could help his mother overcome this once and for all, I know how much I'll be helping him and Liam, too. How could I not tell him? How could I not want to try?

LUCAS is quiet beside me. He seems remote, locked inside his own head. We're on our way back to his house after meeting Myles and Zack at a pub in the next town over. It cheered me to see Myles so happy. He and Zack are good together. I hadn't wanted to ask Myles if he talked to his parents or if they know about Zack. We were having such a nice time, I didn't want to bring up a potentially touchy subject.

But I asked Lucas once we were back in the truck. He told me that Myles came out to his parents just after school ended, and their reactions were what he'd expected. Despite that, they haven't done what Zack's folks did, which was to cut him off completely. They simply don't want to discuss Zack with him, like if they don't talk about it, they can pretend Myles never told them. My chest aches at that news, and I decide that I should go visit him on my own before we leave.

We arrive back at Lucas's house just after midnight. His father's car is parked in the driveway. I met him earlier, very briefly, when we came back from Lucas's mother's house. His father was pretty much what I expected based on everything I'd heard. He was brusque, in a hurry, and on his way out. Even though he'd never met me before, I know he disapproves of our relationship, thinking Lucas was in California "throwing his life away" because of me. But I don't hold that against him since I agree. I could see that Lucas was embarrassed by my chilly reception, but I shrugged it off, and tried to reassure him that I wasn't bothered.

Lucas got his height and his broad build from his father, but his good looks come from his mother. His father's coloring is paler, and his hair is a lighter brown. Both Lucas and Liam resemble their mother, who used to be striking based on the few family pictures I've spotted throughout the house.

"Will your father be okay with my sleeping in your bedroom?" I ask when we walk into his room.

"He won't even notice," he says dismissively. "Don't worry about it."

His back is to me as he rifles around in his bag that he didn't bother to unpack earlier. We're not sure how long we'll stay here. I like the idea of going to the city soon and getting settled, but Liam can't start at his new school for another month. That's how long the paperwork is going to take, and I don't think Lucas wants to leave him here alone again. So, I haven't brought it up.

I come up behind him and run my hand up and down his back, feeling his muscles shift beneath my touch. From his bag, he pulls out my beat-up copy of *Jane Eyre*. I let him borrow it while we were on the road. He mostly read it when it was my turn to drive, and when he wasn't too busy making comments about my lead foot and how far above the speed limit I was going.

"Did you finish it?" I ask.

"Last night."

Lucas hands it to me, and I trace the familiar creases on the cover.

"I can see why you're so attached to it," he says offhandedly.

I tilt my head at him curiously, and he turns to face me.

"You obviously relate to Jane in the story. Despite everything she's been through, she didn't break. She got kind of badass instead, but in a quiet way. The main guy falls in love with her, and even though he's a dick sometimes, she loves him back. But then that fucked-up situation with the secret wife comes out, and because of her, Jane believes she has to leave him. But when his place burns down and he's hurt, she comes back and she heals him with her compassion and shit."

It takes a minute before I can comment without laughing, which I'm pretty sure was his goal. He's got a teasing glint in his eye. "Very eloquently put. You know, I read *Jane Eyre* long before I met you. And if you think you're Mr. Rochester in the story, you just called yourself a dick."

A ghost of a smile turns his lips. "You called me a dick first. Remember?"

"I remember what inspired me to call you that." I place the book in my own bag, pulling out the warm pajamas I bought while we were on the road.

"You quoted from it when you left me that voice-mail message."

I turn to face him again, but his back is to me now. There's no question what message he's referring to. I lick my suddenly dry lips. "Yes."

He glances at me over his shoulder. "You didn't finish the quote in your message. I didn't much like the rest of it, about being exiled forever. You really believed I wouldn't come looking for you, didn't you?"

His gaze zeroes in on me, and I acknowledge him guiltily because at the time, I didn't. I had no idea the lengths he would go to.

He faces me. "You understand me now, though."

I swallow at his sudden intensity. Then I nod.

"You're not gonna need those," he says, pointing to the pajamas in my hands.

I hesitate at the odd mix of emotions in his eyes. "We should talk, Lucas, and I'd rather not do it naked. It's freaking freezing in your house."

He approaches me and pulls the pajamas from my hands. "I'll keep you warm."

"You don't want to talk about it?" I can hear the accusation in my voice. I know he's thinking about it, but he's keeping his thoughts to himself.

Shaking his head, he's either ignoring my tone or trying to erase it when he slips his finger beneath the bottom of my shirt and starts to inch it up.

"Because you're the one doing it now. Not talking to me."

Sighing, he lowers his forehead to mine. "You're killing my mood here."

"Lucas…"

"I'm not doing it," he says softly. "I talk to you. It takes me time, though. I tell you everything. Just not always when you want me to."

Exhaling heavily, he sits down on the bed and watches me with a bleak expression. I lower myself beside him and wait. The air in the room feels thicker than it did a moment ago.

"It's not up to me," he finally says. "It's her decision. But I don't want to get her hopes up or scare her, and there's no way to do this without one or both of those things happening."

My fear is the same as his. I don't want to get her hopes up only to dash them again. But I can't help feeling that it's worth trying, even if the end result is disappointing. "It surprised me," I say, trying to explain it to him. "I've gotten pretty good at blocking it all out again, but with your mom, it just kind of hit me."

He eyes me curiously.

My lips press together. "I was trying not to be my usual standoffish self so she wouldn't be nervous around me. I want her to like me."

He reaches over and pulls my hand onto his lap. "She already likes you. She thinks you walk on water."

I can't help laughing because I find that hard to believe. She seems so wary of me.

He smiles at my reaction, but it fades quickly. "If you could help her, it would be…" Shaking his head, he can't seem to find the words.

I turn, looping my arms around his neck. "I would never hurt her, not even by mistake like my grandmother did. You know that, right?"

His gaze travels over my face, like he's looking for the answer there. Then he turns with me, gripping my waist, and laying us back on the bed with my body beneath his. He presses me down into the mattress and says, "I think you should try. I'll talk to her."

I smile, and a nervous flutter starts in my stomach at the thought of it. But then I worry that I've talked him into this. Looking into his eyes, I try to gauge the thoughts behind them. "Are you sure?"

He traces his finger down my cheek to my lips. Then he skims over them softly. "Yes," he says, his gaze on my mouth. "But the final decision will be hers."

Keeping this possibility from her wouldn't be right, and I knew this would be his decision. But I still hated putting him through this. He's been through too much already.

I shift my body beneath his, moving my leg out from under him. Then I hook it around his back and press down, placing him right where I want him.

His eyes fall closed, and he hums low in his throat. "See?" he says. "You're not gonna need those pajamas." Then he reaches a hand between us and begins to strip off my clothes.

TWENTY-FOUR

Raielle

I HATE this.

Waiting.

I'm leaning against Lucas's truck, and letting the cool fall wind whip my hair around. Blazing red and orange leaves decorate the trees and litter the ground. It's beautiful, like a postcard. In town, the stores have Thanksgiving decorations in their windows, cardboard cutout turkeys and pumpkins. I used to greet this time of year with such cynicism. The holidays felt like an elaborate play being put on around me. They weren't real to me since I'd never experienced them firsthand.

But this year, things are different. Kyle hasn't asked me to join them for Thanksgiving yet. But I can see he's building up to it. I won't spend it with them, though, and I think Kyle realizes that. I'll be with Lucas. Knowing that gives me a sense of security that I never imagined I'd have. From now on, I'll be with Lucas for everything. He's my center and my new beginning. He makes it all okay, even when it isn't.

Smiling to myself, I push away from the truck and watch as a gust of wind picks the leaves up off the grass and carries them along the ground toward the stone wall that lines the edge of the yard. There they gather and fall together in a colorful pile.

A moment later, the front door opens and Lucas waves for me to come inside. I take a deep breath. *Here we go.* The wind wants to blow the leaves in through the door with me, but Lucas closes it quickly behind me.

"What did she say?" I ask anxiously, shrugging out of my coat.

"That I want to do it now," Mrs. Diesel answers.

Surprised, I turn to see her standing just behind him, watching us. I look at Lucas.

"She trusts you," he says.

My gaze travels between them, and I pick up on the jumble of nerves coming from both of them.

She takes a step forward. "Lucas explained things to me. I'll be okay if it doesn't work. You don't have to worry about that." She gives me a shaky smile, and I doubt she's telling the truth about being okay. "I'm sorry, but I don't remember much from last time. How do we start this?" she asks, appearing anxious to begin immediately, when I thought she'd need a little time to get used to the idea.

Her reference to the night she attacked me catches me off guard. My heart starts to knock against my ribs because I recall every detail. I look to Lucas, and he nods encouragingly at me.

"Um. We could sit on the couch," I suggest, cranking up my smile to cover my nerves.

I watch as she moves forward slowly but deliberately, and then lowers herself onto the seat cushion. Lucas whispers in my ear, "No speeches or explanations. Just start. Okay?"

When my eyebrows shoot up at him, he adds, "She's nervous. I don't want a big buildup if it's not going to work."

I dart a look at her, noticing how stiff she's sitting and how her gaze is on the carpet rather than us. Nodding my understanding to Lucas, I sit down beside her. He takes the chair across from us, and I can feel his tension ratcheting up in time with my own. This is Lucas's mother. The stakes couldn't be higher. I want this to work so badly, I'm already dreading the devastation my failure could bring to both of them.

Mrs. Diesel is watching me intently now, and I can see her chin is wobbly, like she's on the verge of tears.

"Try to relax," I say, taking one of her hands and clasping it in mine. I notice right away that the sensation is still there, a calling to my energy from someplace deep inside her. But her skin is ice-cold, and I try not to visibly shiver. Lucas is right. I have to start this now before she shatters right in front of me.

I close my eyes, making my breathing steady and even. Soon I feel my stomach seem to flip inside me as the energy grows and swirls. It surprises me, how easily I can command it now.

Once the power reaches a peak, I gradually send it toward her, not wanting to overwhelm her with the sensation. I know she feels it when her fingers relax in my hand. Then I send out more, letting the entire coil unfurl and flow to her. When the concentration is high enough, saturating her system, it acts instinctively, knowing exactly what to do. It all moves upward to the same place, and I hold my breath, wondering what it will find. The energy begins diffusing rather than focusing. It seems to be stimulating certain sections of her brain, mostly in the front.

When her fingers squeeze mine, my eyes open.

"Mom?" Lucas is out of the chair now, hovering over her.

But the healing isn't done and I keep going, watching as her gaze gradually focuses on me. I know I'm not hurting her, but I hope I'm helping. Her expression gives nothing away, though. She watches me calmly, her face relaxed, her nervousness a memory. Soon the energy fades, slowly drawing down before it dissolves completely.

I turn my hand in hers. "Mrs. Diesel?"

A smile curves her lips. "That felt nice."

I let out the breath I'd been holding and look for Lucas's reaction, but he's aiming questioning eyes at me.

"I just changed some brain chemistry," I explain.

His eyebrows quirk up. "*Just* changed some brain chemistry."

When I shrug, unsure, I can see he wants to know more, but he's too concerned about his mother, who's still sitting quietly. He bends down in front of her. "Are you okay, Mom?"

Her eyes are wide and unfocused. "I feel good, I think. I'm not sure."

"It might take some time," I offer, because I have an optimistic but strange feeling about what just happened. I don't think what I did is permanent. Over time, I'm afraid her brain may change back to how it was before, although I'm not sure how I know this.

"I feel good, Lucas. I do," she says, her voice stronger now. "I feel different, but more like myself. Does that make sense?"

He puts his hands on her shoulders. "Actually, it does. Everyone always feels good after Ray does her thing. That's part of it. Give it some time, like she says. You might not see a change right away."

She nods her agreement, but I can see an undercurrent of hope in her eyes.

I want this to have worked so badly that I can't help myself. I reach out and hug her because she looks like she needs it. Without hesitation, her arms come around me, and she holds on tight. From the corner of my eye, I notice Lucas watching us with a strange emotion on his face.

"Thank you," she whispers, pulling back and wiping at her damp eyes. Then she laughs, seeming embarrassed as she stands and self-consciously smoothes the wrinkles in her skirt. "I have a doctor's appointment this morning. I should change, I think." She glances down at herself before turning for the stairs. "I'll be right back," she calls to us, looking more like she wants to conceal her tears than change her outfit.

"What do you think?" Lucas asks once she's out of earshot.

We can hear her moving around above us, and all I know is that the pull I felt from her before is gone now. So are the shakes she always seems to have. "If it worked, it's temporary," I say softly. "Like a megadose of antidepressants or something. If the depression is really gone, I think it will eventually come back, but I also think I can fix it again when it does."

When I walk over to him, Lucas wraps his arms around me and squeezes me tight. "I love you," he says. When I hear the hitch in his voice, I know he's choked up.

"I love you, too. But I don't think you have any idea how much," I whisper beside his ear, and I feel him pull an unsteady breath into his lungs.

THE café isn't too crowded tonight. Since Lucas is almost out of the pricey coffee he likes so much, I decided to stop for more on the way home from Kyle's house. I pay for the freshly ground beans and turn for the door, smiling as I picture the mess Penelope made with the chocolate cake I brought over. She probably ruined Kyle and Chloe's dining room rug when she dropped her whole slice on it frosting side down. *Oops. Sorry, Chloe.*

Glancing up, my smile disappears. I squint, not wanting to believe my eyes when I see who's standing just inside the doorway. But he doesn't go away. He's really there, and he's looking right at me. I'm glued to the spot as he approaches with a hesitant expression.

"Hi," Grant says in a far too intimate tone.

My spine stiffens. "What are you doing here?"

He looks down at a manila folder in his hand. "Can we talk?"

My heart starts beating a path all the way up to my throat. "There's nothing to talk about."

His fingers grip the folder tighter. "Yes, there is. Please, Raielle. I've come a long way to see you. Give me ten minutes." He nods toward an empty table and eyes me hopefully.

I take a step back from him. "You waited to get me alone."

His expression turns sheepish. "Lucas has a well-known temper. I wanted to avoid it. Can you blame me?"

I waver, my eyes on the door.

"I have information you'll want to hear. Ten minutes. That's all I ask."

Despite my better judgment, I find myself giving in. Somehow I knew I hadn't seen the last of him, and we're in a public place. I may as well find out what he wants. I precede him to the table, sitting down and watching as he settles in across from me, folding his long legs beneath the short table. I angle my chair so that our feet won't touch. "You came almost three thousand miles to talk to me for ten minutes?"

Grant places the folder on the table in front of him. "What I have to tell you is too important for a phone call, even if I thought you'd pick up when you saw it was me." Sighing, he leans forward. "I hate the way you've cut yourself off from us."

My jaw tightens. "Is this how you want to use your time?"

He sits back in his chair and eyes me with frustration. "I'm here because I promised Kaylie's family I would come. They want to thank the person who saved her life."

He watches me closely for a reaction, and I work hard not to give him one, even though my head and heart are racing. When I don't respond, he explains further. "She's the girl from the clinic. The one who—"

"I know who she is," I snap, wondering what he's up to with this, and if he would lie about something so important to manipulate me into coming back. I push out of my chair.

"Wait." His hand shoots across the table to grab my arm. "It's true. She's cured."

My eyes narrow. "I didn't cure her. My father stopped me. You know that."

"You're right. You didn't cure her then," he agrees. "But the healing you started continued even after you stopped. You initiated a process that didn't end until it was complete. And now it is. She's cancer free. I'm telling you the truth."

I stare at him, not knowing what to believe. Then I sink back into the chair. "She tried to run from the room that day. She was so scared. When we saw that the clinic was empty, I was afraid she'd died."

"She's very much alive, and John took all the credit and the money for it. When I found his notes, I visited her myself. All I had to do was touch her, and I knew what happened. I felt your energy inside her." He releases my arm. "I've never heard of a healer's power working this way, but yours does. Somehow you did it. Do you know what this means?"

Grant's eyes are wide with excitement, and I notice a trace of the same awe I saw in them when I drained his energy at Meera's house. Could he be telling me the truth? A lump starts to form in my throat as I stare down at the table.

"Come back with me," he pleads. "Don't turn away from us. We need each other. We all want the same thing. What good does it do to cut yourself off this way? You're only hurting yourself."

As badly as I want to believe that Kaylie is well now, his obvious agenda taints his news. I raise my eyes to his again. "I don't trust you."

His lips part. "How can you say that after what I was willing to do for you? I risked everything for you."

His words only show me how misguided he still is. "You expect me to be grateful for that? For nearly getting Lucas involved in a murder?"

He looks around at the surrounding tables before leaning in close to me. "I never meant for that—"

I interrupt him. "I know what you meant. You were excusing your actions because you told yourself that you were helping us. But they don't excuse you. You're reckless and self-serving, and I haven't changed my mind about anything."

His face falls. He seems truly surprised that this is what I think of him.

Pulling in a deep breath, I try to calm my racing pulse. My mind is filled with thoughts of Kaylie. If what he's telling me is true, the rules of life and death we all live by don't apply to me any longer. What are the boundaries for me now? Do I even have any? "Is that it?" I ask, anxious to be away from him.

"No," he says quietly.

Of course it isn't. I cross my arms and wait for him to continue.

Grant seems confused, like my reactions haven't been what he was expecting, and he's not sure what to think now. "John didn't have a will," he says, watching me closely. "He probably thought he'd live forever. And it turns out that he and Nyla were never legally married."

I bite my lip, and hope this isn't going where I think it is.

"That means his children inherit everything. You get half, Raielle. With Shane still missing, you might get it all."

My head is already shaking back and forth when he adds, "There's millions in property alone."

I know without a doubt that I don't want any of it, and I can see he correctly anticipated my answer this time. He's gearing up to persuade me. But I realize something and laugh. Grant eyes me with a mixture of concern and confusion. I take Lucas's coffee into my hands, ready to walk out. "I bet you all those millions his name isn't on my birth certificate."

His eyes widen.

"Do you know how much time I spent in foster care because they couldn't find my father? They didn't even know who he was. If it were as simple as looking it up on my birth certificate, they would have done it. Therefore, it's not there. It probably just says"—I use air quotes—"John." Then I dissolve into more laughter at the irony of it.

Grant doesn't even crack a smile. "I'll tell the lawyers about you. A blood test will prove who you are."

I pull in a deep breath and wipe at my eyes. "I'm not taking a blood test."

He leans forward, his eyes intent on mine. "Then it could all go to Shane and he certainly doesn't deserve it. If they can't locate him, the state of California gets it. You can't let that happen. I know you could use the money and so could the organization. I'm telling them who you are, Raielle."

"Go ahead. I'll deny it." I shift in my seat. "Besides, Shane will turn up. He wouldn't walk away from all that money."

"Maybe not. But he wasn't liked any more than your father was. Without your father's influence, he knows he's not wanted or welcome anymore."

"It doesn't matter. Either way, I'm not interested." My eyes go back to the door, wanting to be on the other side of it.

His face tenses. "There's one last thing. The notes on Kaylie I was telling you about, I found them in a safe where your father kept records. He had hundreds of files in there. It turns out that Kaylie was one of only ten patients he had at the clinic this year. His power had diminished, and he kept it a secret, passing the less complicated cases on to the rest of us. But the sickest patients, those like Kaylie, only he could heal, and he was too weak to do as many as he used to. He still took money from clients, though, and he made promises he couldn't keep. He gave them excuses to buy himself time. He was in trouble, Raielle.

"When you gave yourself that disease last spring, he canceled all his healings. Then he stored up his power so he could cure you when you arrived. That's why he wanted Apollo to drive you to California. He was stalling for time but he didn't want anyone to know. Then he had you at the house on life support while he waited even longer. He wanted to be as strong as possible for you. He thought if he could save you, you would save him."

I sit there listening as the bile burns inside me. I didn't think I could despise my father any more than I already did, but I was wrong. He saved my life, but just barely. *Life support?* I hadn't known that. And he did it for himself, not for me at all.

"He kept files on all of us, including you," Grant continues. "This is yours. I thought you might be interested in what's inside." He pushes the manila folder toward me.

I stare at it, hesitant to pick it up.

I startle when he grabs my hand, gripping it so tightly I can't pull it back. "I read your file," he says, his eyes intent on mine. "I knew about your niece and what happened when you tried to cure her. But I didn't know your mother's own husband had her murdered. I didn't know that John and Apollo helped him to cover it up."

My eyes widen, and I stare at the file again like it's a poisonous snake about to strike me.

"Alec Dean hasn't paid for what he's done, Raielle. I can fix that for you."

My gaze flies to his.

Grant leans in close. "He could get sick, like he was supposed to in the first place. If you'd been successful, he'd be gone by now and you'd have justice for your mother."

My throat grows tight. "No," I answer, pushing the word up from a raw place deep inside me.

"Why?" His brow knots in confusion. "Let me make this right for you."

I tug hard on my hand, glaring at him until he finally releases it. Then I push to my feet. "You're not that different from him. You like to think you are, but you're more like my father than you know."

He stands, too, placing himself in front of me. "You're wrong. I'm more like you. I just lost my innocence a long time ago." When his hand comes up to touch my cheek, I blink and flinch away.

Disappointment washes over Grant as his hand slowly falls back to his side. He looks like he wants to say more, like he doesn't want to leave things this way. But then his jaw clenches tight, and without another word he turns and walks out of the café.

TWENTY-FIVE

Lucas

LIAM wants to stay in Fort Upton. He told us this afternoon. He's moving in with Mom, and I think it's a good idea. It's been a week, and she's changed. But she's also the same. She's the mother I remember from when I was a kid.

I told Dad that she was better, excited to give him the news, even though I couldn't tell him how or why. He gave me a strange look, like he's too tired of all the drama to care anymore. A part of me doesn't blame him after everything she put us through, but another part of me loses the little respect I had left for him. He's one hundred percent checked out now. I know he's having an affair. It started before Mom moved out, and it's probably not the first one.

Glancing at my phone, I realize Raielle should have been back already. She's at Kyle's having dinner. I was included in the invitation, but I passed. I wouldn't be great company if I had to sit there and pretend I didn't still hate them just a little bit. Raielle doesn't have to hold grudges. I'm perfectly capable of holding both hers and mine.

I'm debating whether to call her when I hear my truck pull into the driveway. My nerves cool, and I smile. She loves driving the new truck even more than the old one. I'm going to miss it when we leave, but it's too complicated keeping a vehicle in the city.

"How'd it go?" I call from the kitchen when I hear the front door open.

She walks in and drops my keys, her bag, an envelope, and some coffee on the kitchen table.

My smile widens at the sight of the coffee. "Thanks, babe."

She's wearing dark pants with a sweater, and I'm glad to see that she's gained back some weight. She fucking scared me to death when I first laid eyes on her back in LA, all pale and thin and lost-looking.

"How was dinner?" I ask.

She gives me a strange look and wraps her arms around her middle.

Shit. "What happened? Did Chloe say something to you?"

Without answering, she grabs a kitchen chair and drops down onto it. "Sit," she says, using her foot to push another chair out for me.

As I lower myself onto it, my muscles tense up.

"I just saw Grant," she says flatly.

"What?" I wasn't expecting that. "Where?"

"At the café while I was getting the coffee." Then she looks down, and I see that she's digging her fingernails into her palms so hard her knuckles are turning white.

"He waited to get you alone. He's been watching you," I say, certain of it, and angry at myself for not expecting it.

Her eyes shift up to meet mine, and my breathing catches at the anguish I see there. I reach out and lay my hand on her knee. "What did he want?"

She rolls her eyes. "So many things, I hardly know where to start." Then she releases a ragged breath and proceeds to tell me about their conversation. She explains about the girl in the clinic, and the fact that she may have actually healed her. She talks about a possible inheritance, and her unwillingness to accept it. My emotions bounce all over the place as I grow angrier with each word, feeling the tension inside her, and despising Grant for coming here to dredge all this up again.

Then her eyes slide over to the envelope on the table. "And he found a file. One my father kept on me. Grant says he had them on everyone. I read it in the truck. Some of it is just factual stuff that he probably lifted from my social services records. But then there are reports that start from when we moved to our last place in San Diego. He began watching me more closely then." Her eyes well with tears. "It talks about my mother's murder," she whispers. "It confirms what you said, that my father knew about Alec's plan, and he let it happen. It also says that Rob Jarvis told Alec he was going to expose me and my whole family if the police arrested him for my mother's murder. So my father had Apollo kill him to keep our secret."

When she finishes, her shoulders are rolled forward and she looks completely defeated. I lean in close and take her hands in mine, wanting to give her comfort, but also knowing I probably can't make a dent in how she's feeling right now.

"There's more," she whispers. Her throat works as she tries to get the words out. "I know who my father used to save my life. I know who died for me." Her voice breaks.

Curses spill from my lips, and I can see she's struggling not to break down. What the fuck was Grant thinking giving this file to her?

She pulls in a deep breath and manages to hold herself together. "Her name was Emily. He paid her one-hundred and fifty thousand dollars. She told him she was giving the money to her granddaughter to help pay for college." She turns red-rimmed eyes up to mine. "I feel like I should do something. I should find her family and apologize or thank them, but I don't think they know what she did for them."

I squeeze her hands, not sure what to tell her. Although I think approaching this woman's family is probably a bad idea.

"At least I know now," she says. Then she sits back in the chair, reclaiming her hands, trying to show me that she's okay. "I finally know everything."

But she had to walk through fire to learn it. She had to nearly die. We both did, and every time I think it's over, it's not. Even now, as we're sitting here, her phone dings with a text message. She looks at me curiously because I'm still the only person who texts her. Kyle always calls. Nikki hasn't talked to her since she told her she was withdrawing from school.

Since I'm closer, I reach for her bag on the table and pull out her phone. She takes it and looks at the screen. Then she sucks in a harsh breath.

"Who's it from?" I ask.

She doesn't move. She's still staring at it.

I pull it from her hand and see that it's a Los Angeles area code. *It's done. No one gets to hurt you without paying for it.*

When I look back at her, wide and fearful eyes stare up at me. "It's from Grant," she says. "He did something to Alec."

AFTER seeing the text, Raielle wanted to call the police, or even Kyle, but I convinced her not to. Grant's text said it was done. If Raielle was right about what that meant, there was no point in exposing ourselves and what we knew. All we could do was wait.

The next morning, after being up all night, Raielle finally called Kyle's house. She planned to pretend it was a casual call to say hello, although I doubted she could pull that off. She didn't have to, though. Chloe answered and said Kyle couldn't come to the phone because he was at his father's house with Linda. After being missing for hours, Linda had discovered Alec in the garage this morning, lying on the cold concrete floor. She swore she looked in the garage earlier and saw no sign of him. But this morning, there he was, lying dead, and the reason wasn't immediately apparent. They think it was probably natural causes, though, maybe a stroke or a heart attack.

Only we know differently.

We're certainly not mourning him, but we are shocked, walking around in a daze wondering what exactly Grant did to Alec, and if Alec knew why his life was ending. I can see that Raielle is struggling to figure out how she feels. Guilt and remorse for Penelope and Kyle's loss, combined with justified satisfaction for herself, make for a dense and confusing jumble of emotions.

We stay away from the funeral. We stay away from everyone for a while. Knowing how much Raielle hates deception of any kind, I spend a lot of time convincing her that there's no point in telling Kyle the truth. She seems to agree with me, but I feel her hesitance. I doubt Kyle suspects anything. From what we hear, foul play hasn't been raised as a possibility. Grant doesn't appear to have left any evidence of the truth behind.

The strange thing is I feel like I understand Grant. Now that I've had time to think about it, I get why he gave Raielle the file and took care of Alec for her. If I were a different kind of person, one more like Grant who thought the normal rules of society didn't apply to me, I might have done the same things. But sometimes his attempts to do good are so extreme, he ends up inadvertently doing bad things, and he doesn't seem to understand that.

Two weeks have passed now since Grant showed up and turned everything upside down, and it's been rough, but we've been through worse, and we're slowly getting our equilibrium back. At some point during that time, I decided we should leave sooner rather than later. It's easier for us to get lost in a city than it is here. I don't think Grant will come back again, but Raielle's been found in Fort Upton too many times, and although she hasn't said anything, I know she's anxious to go.

"My mom wants us to come by in the morning so she can say good-bye," I call out to her.

Raielle walks toward me, bringing the last of the dinner dishes to the sink. She's made us dinner several times since we've been here, and she's a good cook. Although true to her word, she hasn't cooked dinner for me naked yet.

A smile plays on her lips, and she seems pleased that my mom wants to see us.

My mother is better. There's no question about it. The darkness has lifted. She complains about how closely I watch her, looking for cracks, wondering if she's pretending for my sake. But I don't think she is pretending. I honestly believe her depression is gone, and so does she.

Mom and Raielle have gotten close over the past couple of weeks. They talk nearly every day, or at least my mom talks. Raielle smiles and listens. Could be she's telling embarrassing stories about me. Who knows? But they seem to genuinely like each other, and I completely love that.

I figure the dishes can wait as I pull her to me and plant a kiss on her unsuspecting lips. She sighs and leans into me the way she always does when I touch her.

"What do you want to do tonight?" I ask, since it's still early. I'm wondering if she wants to go out for a change, even though I'd rather keep her all to myself again. "Want to catch a movie?"

"I don't really feel like going to the movies," she says, eyeing me. "Maybe we could watch something here?"

I easily agree, taking her hand to lead her into the family room. Leaving her by the couch, I walk over and open the cabinet of DVDs Liam and I have collected. "What do you feel like? Comedy, drama… porn?" I waggle my eyebrows on the last one.

She tilts her head at me. "You keep porn in the family room?"

"Doesn't everyone?"

She laughs and crosses her arms. "Does it really matter what we watch? We haven't finished a movie yet. Last time the opening credits were still on when you started mauling me."

I narrow my eyes, acting offended, but the band around my chest loosens because she's teasing me. She's being playful. Something she couldn't have managed only yesterday. I give her a stern look. "Did you just use the word *maul*? You think I maul you?"

One of her shoulders lifts, and there's a dim but visible gleam in her eye.

I take a step toward her. "Mauling is for horny kids copping a feel for the first time." With my eyes glued to hers, I take another determined step and she straightens, her playfulness changing to awareness.

"Mauling is for unskilled amateurs." My next step brings our chests into contact, and I try not to grin arrogantly when she pulls in a soft breath. I raise my hand to her cheek as her eyes flutter closed. Then I lower my mouth to her ear. "I don't maul you, Ray. I play you like an instrument."

My fingers massage the back of her neck as I nibble on her ear. "Strumming your strings." Slowly, my hand moves down to palm her breast through her shirt while my thumb brushes over her nipple. "Caressing your keys."

Her fingers grip my shoulders for support as her breathing turns shallow.

Next I trail my hand down over her stomach to the juncture of her thighs, which I know must be throbbing by now. "And banging your drum." I apply pressure.

She moans and falls against me.

"Want to start that movie now?" I whisper into her hair. She shakes her head, and I laugh softly. "I didn't think so."

TWENTY-SIX

Raielle
Three Months Later

CAN see it coming, the cab and the bike messenger about to collide. I yell out a warning, but I know there's no chance of anyone hearing. Beside me, a tall girl, almost as tall as me, turns her head to see what I'm looking at. Her hand travels up to her open mouth just as the front fender of the yellow cab swipes the back wheel, jerking the bike and its rider up into the air. All around me, heads tilt upward watching the shocking ascension and then the crushing landing of first the rider and then the bike onto the curb, just in front of where I'm standing. Everyone stills in silent disbelief for a moment before the shock gives way to panic, and people start pushing toward him.

I hover at the periphery, watching as his helmet is removed. His blond hair is plastered to his forehead, and his face is crumpled in confusion. Around me, onlookers offer advice.

"Don't move him."

"I called 911. You'll be okay. Just lie still."

"Excuse me. I'm a nurse," says the tall girl who was standing beside me. When she cuts a path through the crowd, I now have a clear view of the bike messenger. Since I'm barely four feet away, I can sense his pain.

I watch as the girl checks his pulse. When she takes his hand and asks him a question, he starts to panic, his eyes widening and his mouth turning down with fear. Inadvertently, I've been inching closer. When I look down, my foot is nearly touching his bent leg, which is half on and half off the curb.

"It's going to be all right. Help is on the way," the girl says soothingly. She seems too young to be a nurse with her messy dark bun and ripped, artfully patched jeans. Sirens sound in the distance and the crowd starts to back away. That's when I decide to touch him. I can't help myself. The moment my fingers find the exposed skin at his wrist, I understand that life as he knows it is over. His neck is broken. He's paralyzed.

It's been months since I used my energy, and it's begging for release. As the ambulance sirens blare, trying to part traffic, I check to make sure no one is paying attention to me. Then I close my eyes and breathe out slowly, letting the power inside me flow into him. The energy snakes throughout his body, finding the damage and repairing it, regenerating what's broken. I finish just as the paramedics arrive, loudly shooing the remaining onlookers away. I step back while still watching. A smile blooms on my face because the usual high is kicking in, and I no longer feel any pain coming from the bike messenger.

When he suddenly sits up and smiles, the nurse gasps.

The paramedics are beside him now, asking him what hurts. He replies, "Nothing," and tries to stand, but they tell him to remain down until they can check him over.

When I glance over at the nurse, her eyes are wide and they're pinned on me. I avert my gaze and turn away, trying to push through the people blocking the sidewalk. Once I break through, a hand lands on my shoulder. The girl places herself in front of me. "He couldn't move or feel anything," she says accusingly. "Then you touched him."

I don't meet her eyes when I say, "I'm glad he's okay." I try to move around her.

She steps in my path. "You made him okay."

I mumble something incoherent as I push past her and continue down the street. I speed up when I hear heels clicking rapidly behind me.

"Please stop," she calls to me. "I know what you did. I know about people like you. I've been looking for you."

I halt abruptly as the back of my neck prickles. "Excuse me?" I ask rudely, knowing I'm being stupid, that I should just keep moving.

She gets in front of me again. "It's my father. He's sick and no doctors can do anything for him, but maybe you can."

My mind starts to flip through the possibilities. Is this a trick? Did Grant send her? Does she know who my father was? I'm about to put as much distance between us as I can, when she places her hand on my arm. My eyes flick up to her face. Her expression is pleading and desperate, but I don't miss the sheen of hope in her eyes.

"He has amyotrophic lateral sclerosis. Do you know what that is?" she asks, seeming to sense my indecision as her fingers grip me tighter.

I shake my head, and I can't make myself move. The anguish in her voice is holding me still.

"It's Lou Gehrig's disease. He was diagnosed a year ago." Her lips press together tightly, like she's trying not to break down. Then she sucks in a breath and staves off her emotion. "I can see that you're suspicious. I understand." She releases my arm and reaches into her bag to pull out a business card. Then she roots around for a pen. With both in hand, she presses the card against the building behind me and writes something on the back of it. Instead of handing it to me, she holds it close as she steps toward me again.

"I've met someone like you before," she says. "At the hospital where I work, there was a volunteer who used to spend her time in the children's cancer ward. Those children adored her. I don't think she had any family of her own. But she would sit there and play games with them and read them stories. Then she would tell them good-bye, and you'd find her crying in the lobby, heartbroken over those sick kids. One morning, she spent her usual time with them and after she left, they started telling us she'd cured them. As you can imagine, we were all upset, wondering what she could have said to make them think that. We didn't know how to tell them it wasn't true. But as the doctors made their rounds that afternoon, they knew something had changed with the children. Little by little, tests were run and no signs of cancer were found in any of them. The doctors tried to explain it using some far-fetched medical logic none of us believed. Because we knew it was her. We watched for that woman every day after that. But she never came back again."

I hug myself as chills travel through me. If she was a healer, I can imagine all too well how that woman must have felt sitting there among those sick children.

"Please. My father is dying. He's only fifty-five years old. I promise you, he's a good man. He used to be a police officer." She holds her hand out to me. "This is my card so you can verify who I am. I wrote my brother's information on the other side. He's a cop, too. You can check him out. We're good people. My father doesn't deserve what's happening to him. He doesn't deserve to suffer this way."

I glance down at the hand holding the business card. She's shaking, and I can just make out the words *Registered Nurse* on it. When I look up, her eyes are filling with tears. I take the card from her and she smiles tightly. "Please don't walk away without telling me you'll think about it."

Slipping the card into my pocket, my heart is hammering, and I feel sure she can hear it. "I will," I tell her. Then I turn and walk away quickly, not knowing if I lied to her or not.

As I make my way to the subway, my heart won't slow down and I feel breathless. I dash into a shoe store, quickly heading toward the back where I sit down and try to calm myself, hoping the girl didn't follow me, hoping I haven't done something foolish. As I'm sitting there, the story of that volunteer haunts me. I can so easily picture her going back to that hospital day after day, struggling with what she knew she could do, but wasn't sure if she should. I wonder if she was on her own like me, or if there are groups of healers here in the city.

When a salesperson approaches me, asking if I need help, I shake my head and walk back to the front. After waiting a few more moments and not seeing any sign of her, I rejoin the moving mass of people on the sidewalk.

I need to talk to Lucas, but finding time to be together isn't easy these days. I have to work tonight and tomorrow night. Lucas doesn't get back from class until after I'm already gone. Sometimes he stops into work to see me, but other times he's racing to and from his internship at the paper. I didn't know freshmen could have internships. But now that my life is no longer a catastrophe that takes up all his time, his overachieving ways are evident.

Back in Fort Upton, I knew he must have worked his ass off to get into Columbia early, but I never saw him crack a book. I see it now, though. He's driven and ambitious, and I'm proud of him. I just wish we had more time together. I would never tell him that, though. This is his time to get back on track, and I'm completely on board with it. No clingy girlfriend here. Not me. But I really do want to talk to him now.

I run through his schedule in my head, and I think I can get to campus in time to catch him before he leaves for the newspaper. With that thought, I turn and head in a different direction. Forty minutes later, I'm dialing him as I walk through the doors of Lerner Hall, the huge glass-and-concrete student center where we meet for lunch sometimes.

"Hey," he answers, a smile in his voice.

"I'm here on campus. Have you got a minute to meet me?"

He's quiet.

"Lucas?"

"Is everything okay?" he asks cautiously.

Crap. He's worried. "Everything's fine. I just wanted to see you."

"Yeah?" The smile is back.

"I'm sitting in the first-floor café. Right by the door." I hear static as he starts moving.

"Be there in five," he says.

It's crowded in here, and the vibe is different from UCLA. The clothes are darker and the smiles are fewer. Lucas felt like a fish out of water in Los Angeles, and now it's my turn. Glancing down at my light blue sweater, which matches my necklace perfectly, I'm like a beacon of color among the grays and blacks.

"This is a nice surprise."

His voice breaks into my thoughts. Then it happens, like it does every time. The Lucas effect. My body temperature goes up, my tummy flutters, and my skin tingles with awareness.

I grin like an idiot, and he leans down to kiss me before sliding into the seat across from mine. And I don't miss the attention he's getting from the girls in the room. He stands out in a crowd, even one as dense and jaded as this. It's not only his good looks that get him noticed, it's his charisma. You can feel it. People are both attracted to him and intimidated by him. Just like in high school.

"How's your day going?" I ask.

"It was good before. But it's better now." His eyes narrow on me. "There's something different about you."

I blink, confused. Nothing's different as far as I know.

"It's a good different, like you're more rested or something." He lays his hand palm side up on the table. As soon as I place mine within his, it's enveloped in his firm grip. He turns our hands, and his thumb starts to rub circles along the inside of my wrist as his eyes hold mine. My desire for him is strong and immediate, and he's looking so smug right now I can't decide if I want to smack him or kiss him.

"You're starting something you can't finish," I point out.

"I'll finish it later tonight," he says.

My eyes close, and I groan. "I came here to talk to you, but you're making my head all fuzzy."

He chuckles low, but his thumb stops moving. "Okay, talk. I'll be good."

I peek at him and the bedroom eyes are gone. He's just watching me with amusement now.

When I open my mouth to start, two guys appear beside our table. The taller, lankier of the two starts talking. "Hey, Diesel. Party at Kenny's tonight. You going? They'll be plenty of sorority chicks there and if you give it some time, they'll all be wasted."

The shorter guy elbows the tall one, and when he has his friend's attention, he looks pointedly at me.

"Oh." His eyes widen. Then they travel over me. "Nice. Bring her with you," he adds without missing a beat.

Now it's my turn to shoot Lucas an amused look.

"Dumbass, that's his girlfriend," the other guy whispers.

Lucas's expression turns wry. "You've met Ray."

His face is a mask of surprise. "Oh, right." Then he laughs. "Sorry about that. No offense." He glances nervously at Lucas. "Um, well, maybe we'll see you both later."

"Let me guess. Freshmen," I mutter dryly once they're gone.

Lucas laughs and squeezes my hand.

I've gone to a few parties with him, and I've seen how girls throw themselves at Lucas. But I trust him. And I've perfected the death glare that sends them scurrying away. The one thing I do worry about is him missing out on stuff like parties because of me. "You can go if you want," I say. "You don't have to blow it off because I'm working."

He looks at me like I suggested he go for a swim in the Hudson. "Let me think about this," he says, releasing my hand and leaning back in his chair. "Get drunk with those idiots or come home to be with you. That's a tough one."

"What about the slutty sorority chicks?"

"Actually, he promised me wasted sorority chicks. I think the slut part was implied." His fingers tap his chin. "And you've got a point. I forgot about them. I may have to rethink my plans for the night."

"Screw you." I laugh, kicking him lightly under the table.

He leans forward. "Screwing you is my plan, and I'm not changing it." The bedroom eyes are aimed at me again. They erase my smile, and have me gulping back any lingering comments.

"So." He nudges my hand. "What did you want to talk to me about?"

I exhale and give myself a little shake, trying to switch back to serious mode as quickly as he somehow does. "I healed someone today."

He stills, completely alert and focused now.

Nerves creep in, and for a moment, the hard way he's looking at me makes me feel like a child who's been naughty. We haven't talked about this. I know he assumed I'd put my power on the back burner. When we left California, I was determined to never put Lucas at risk again. At the time I wasn't sure if that meant suppressing my power, but even then I knew that wouldn't be possible, and I can't pretend anymore. "I was right there when a cab hit a bike messenger. It was bad," I explain.

Lucas still hasn't moved or spoken.

"I reached over and touched him," I continue. "I didn't think anyone saw."

"But someone did," he says evenly.

I nod. "She said she was a nurse. She was helping him, too. She knew what I'd done right away. She asked me if I would heal her sick father. She gave me her card to call her."

His brow furrows. "What do you mean, she knew what you'd done?"

Then I tell him the story she told me about the children at the hospital and the volunteer. He's quiet as he listens, never interrupting. When I finish, he surprises me by saying, "That's what's different about you." There's an edge to his voice. "You healed someone for the first time in a while. It does something to you."

I bite my lip, realizing he's right. Since it happened, I do feel different, like I have more energy. And I feel something else that's hard to describe, like a missing piece of me was put back into place, like I'm more whole than I was when I woke up this morning.

"Do you want to help her father?" he asks, and the edge has dulled. I can tell he honestly wants to know the answer.

When I don't respond right away, he nods once to himself. "You do. Give me the card." He holds his hand out for it, but I don't move.

"What are you going to do with it?" I ask suspiciously. I can't read his expression, but I won't let him throw it away, if that's what he's thinking.

He sighs. "I'm going to check her out. I can use the paper's resources. If she's telling the truth, I'll find out. Then we can decide what to do."

"Really?" I was expecting more resistance. Actually, I was gearing up for an argument, and I don't know what I would have done if he were dead set against this.

I hand the card over to him. He studies it for a moment before slipping it into his jacket pocket.

"Are you sure you want to open this can of worms?" he asks.

My hands rub against my jeans as my nerves continue to jump.

He reaches beneath the table and settles his hands over mine, stilling them. "Ray."

"Yeah?"

His eyes lock onto me. "Are you sure?"

"Are you?"

After a moment's hesitation, he says, "No."

I swallow. "Neither am I."

His gaze softens. "But we're doing it anyway, aren't we?"

"Yes," I whisper.

Lucas

'M in Midtown, pushing through the office doors. Someone calls out a greeting to me, but I don't stop. The trip here was a blur. I have no idea how I got here. The card Raielle handed me is burning a hole in my pocket. My only thought is to get to Adam. I did him a favor a couple of weeks ago, and now I want payback. He's a rookie reporter, just out of school. But he has well-placed friends, and he has access to information. If I don't like what he finds, I'm tempted to take Raielle and disappear for a while. There's no way Grant or his friends are getting near her again if that's what this is about.

As I exit the elevator, Cassie's there. "Hey, Lucas. I'm taking a break. Come hang out with me."

It's the same thing every time with her. She doesn't take my unfriendliness at face value. She thinks I'm being coy. Without stopping, I tell her, "Sorry, I can't."

"Sure you can." One of her shoulders hitches up. "It's a slow news day."

"Not for me." I walk into the bull pen, where all the reporters sit. They call this place a newspaper, but the actual paper circulation is low and diminishing each day. It's mostly online now, and it's all the time. Nothing waits for the next issue. The story happens. It gets written, and it goes on the Internet. Sometimes all within an hour. Everyone grumbles about the pace and the subsequent lack of quality, but everyone does it. And Adam does it 24–7 because he's hungry. That's why I wanted him to owe me. I knew he'd be useful.

He's here, like always, sitting at his desk, hunched over his laptop. There's a pen stuck in his frazzled puff of hair. It's teetering toward his nose, about to drop onto the desk. It slides that last millimeter past the point of no return when I stop beside him. He whips around, and the pen hits me square in the chest.

"What do you want?" he asks impatiently. "I'm on deadline."

I retrieve his pen and place it on his notebook. "You're always on deadline." Then I slide the card from my pocket. "I need you to check out some people for me. I want to know who they are and if there's anything shady about them."

He squints at me now, giving me his full attention. "Is this for a story?"

I shake my head slowly. "It's personal."

Adam turns back to his laptop. "Leave it. I'll do it later."

"I need it now." Leaning against his desk, I lay the card down over his keyboard.

His hands hover above it. "What part of later don't you understand? That bomb threat at your school wasn't worth missing my deadline today."

"It got you the lead story. First time that ever happened." I bend toward him. "This is important to me. Don't fuck me over, Adam. I don't forget shit like that."

His jaw clenches as he tries to stare me down. "Fine," he finally bites out. "Let's go find an empty office." He disconnects his laptop, slams it closed, and tucks it under his arm. I follow him to one of the many empty offices that line the wall, meant for meetings or private phone calls.

He grabs a chair and doesn't spare me a glance when he says, "Give me the card. But we're even after this. Don't ask me for anything else."

I shrug. "Okay. If I catch a lead, I'll give Cassie a call next time."

Now he looks up. "You're such an asshole."

"Takes one to know one."

This earns me a sliver of a smile before Adam gets down to work. I make myself comfortable as he punches keys and starts navigating through systems he really has no business accessing.

Kevin, the managing editor of the paper, walks into the office and starts looking around. I watch him through the glass. "Diesel," he says when he spots me.

Jumping up, I stick my head out the door. "Yeah?"

Kevin reminds me of Humpty Dumpty with his huge belly, and skinny arms and legs. But for a small guy, his voice is surprisingly loud, kind of like a natural bullhorn. He points a pen in my direction.

"Manhole fire downtown. A transformer blew. Some tourists got hurt. You're with Sheila. The address is on your desk. Grab a cab and wait for her." Then he disappears back down the hallway.

Adam chuckles behind me. "Covering a fire with Sheila? That's like descending into the pits of hell with Satan himself."

"She's not so bad." I've been to a couple of fires with her. Fires are always news, and Sheila almost always gets assigned to them.

He winces, disagreeing with me. "Try sitting next to her when a story breaks, and doesn't stop for three days. When she can't get home to eat or shower, she chain-smokes and drowns herself in perfume. That combination is toxic when it reaches certain concentrations. I was ready to call in a hazmat crew." He shudders. "Go. I'll have this ready when you get back."

"Thanks, man." I clap him on the back.

"And you'd better not fucking call Cassie next time!" he yells after me.

I throw him a wave over my shoulder, grab the address off my desk along with my bag, and head downstairs. I'm waiting in the cab for less than five minutes when Sheila comes running out of the building with her luggage-sized purse bouncing against her hip, and a cigarette hanging from her mouth. She's somewhere in her forties, I think, and thin as a rail. Her voice is a deep, phlegmy baritone; I assume from all the smoking.

She slides in beside me, tossing her bag in my lap. "Did you give him the address?" she asks, slamming the door.

"You can't smoke in here," the cabbie says, eyeing her in the rearview mirror.

"Yeah, no problem. I'll put it out," she tells him, but she doesn't. "Have you got cash for this, Lucas? I left my wallet inside."

I nod at her. She does this to me every time, even though she's the one with an expense account.

We sit in silence as the cab pulls out into traffic. Then she turns to me. "You'd love my niece. Blonde, built, and she's a smart cookie, too." She blows smoke in my direction. I shift toward the door and crack open the window.

"I know. You've got a girlfriend." She nods dismissively. "But if you ever find yourself single, you'd love Stephanie. I'm telling you."

Smiling politely, I turn to the window and inhale the traffic fumes instead of her secondhand smoke, wondering which toxin is more likely to kill me first.

"So, what kind of a reporter do you want to be when you grow up?" she asks.

I just look at her, not sure if this is a serious question or not.

"A strapping young man like yourself?" Sheila waves her cigarette around, gesturing at me. "You probably want to travel the world or go to war. Cover the big stories that get you the syndicated headlines."

I don't bother responding, but she's right. When I thought about being a reporter, that's how I imagined it, going where the important stories were, uncovering the truth and writing about it.

"Is your girlfriend up for that? Saying good-bye to you every time she turns around and watching you fly off to dangerous places. It takes a strong woman to deal with that."

I grin because she has no idea. My woman is as strong as they come.

"But you're only nineteen. You've got time to figure all that out. You'll probably change your mind ten times before you graduate. A reporter, a baker, a candlestick maker." She laughs at her joke. The sound is a wet cackle before it changes into a deep, hacking cough.

But I imagined that career before I met Raielle, when leaving was all I wanted to do, and a potent mix of numbness and anger were all I ever felt. Things are different now. A long separation from her is not something I can think about.

I glance out the window while Sheila chatters on. My thoughts return to the possibility of Raielle exposing her abilities to a stranger, and what the consequences could be. When I first saw her at Lerner Hall today, she took my breath away. She had a glow about her, and every person in that place was throwing glances her way. She's a beautiful girl and she always attracts attention, but today was different. She shined, and everyone wanted to catch a glimpse of her. That alone should be enough for me to put a stop to this. It would be better for her to be inconspicuous. But how can I stop it when she looked so excited at the possibility? Unless I find a very good reason to tell her no, I just don't think I can.

Meanwhile, Sheila is having an entire conversation with me, and I haven't had to open my mouth once. I don't understand why Adam doesn't like her. She's easier to be with than a lot of women I've known.

TWENTY-SEVEN

Raielle

"**D**o you want anything to drink?"

I get no response.

"Lucas!"

"Yeah, I'll take one of those iced teas," he calls from the other room.

Reaching into the refrigerator, I easily find the blue can he wants because its only company is a bag of apples I bought on the way home last night. After tossing away the wrappers sitting on the counter from the takeout Lucas had for dinner, I make my way down our narrow hallway to the end, where it opens up to the sunken living room.

Sitting on the black leather couch, Lucas is sorting through a stack of printouts he brought home with him. We've been house-sitting the empty apartment of a friend of Lucas's father since we got to town. It's on the Upper West Side, a few blocks from Central Park, and the owner is working overseas in Europe for the rest of the year. Apparently, we're doing him a favor by staying here.

At least, that's the story I've been told. And no, I'm not an idiot. I'm sure Lucas somehow scammed us into this great apartment with an excuse he thought I would buy. I don't think he's outright lying, since there are pictures of this friend around the place and a closetful of his clothes, but I also don't think we were asked to house-sit. And now Lucas is avoiding looking for our own place by saying that he doesn't have time, and that this arrangement is good until the end of the year. So, why bother.

I must be getting soft because I haven't pushed it. I figure if he went to so much trouble to get this setup for us, he must care about it more than I thought. He has offhandedly mentioned that he wants me to live in a safe building with a doorman too many times for me to miss his point. So, I'm letting this one go and saving the money he won't take for rent, since he claims we're not paying any. His intentions are good, and it's hard to dig in my heels when he seems so happy right now.

When I got home from work a half hour ago, he grunted a hello to me, barely looking up from his reading material. Somehow, he's already managed to pull together everything there is to know about the nurse I met this morning and her family. He has public and not-so-public records on them, and he's been reading these documents for hours.

"They're on Facebook and everything." Lucas smirks at me as I plop down beside him, place his drink on the glass coffee table, and curl my legs beneath me. "Thanks, babe," he says. He has the television on mute, tuned to a basketball game.

"Her name is Samantha Miller and her brother, the cop, is Dominic. So far, I can't find anything suspicious. Everything she told you checks out." His voice is flat, sounding almost disappointed, like he wanted to find a reason for me not to help them.

"She used Facebook to try to find healers," he says, glancing up at the TV and then back down at the sheet in his lap. "She had a post on her page a few months ago." He starts chuckling. "You should read some of the responses she got. Nothing but crackpots."

I guess she never found her way to my father's network. She probably wasn't rich enough to attract his attention.

"He got an award for bravery," Lucas says, still reading. "Her father saved a kid from a building fire. Ran inside, right through the flames. It also says that he started a mentoring program for underprivileged children." Putting down the papers, he slaps his hand on the pile beside him, indicating that he's read it all. Then he turns to me. "I can't find any red flags. He's a good guy, Ray. He seems worthy of your help."

His statement rubs me the wrong way, and I sit up straighter, placing my feet on the floor. "This isn't about his worth. It's about making sure they're being honest with us. It's not my place to sit in judgment of anyone."

He gives me an amused once-over. "That was predictable," he says, reaching for his drink.

"What?" I scowl. "The fact that I don't want to judge people?"

When he picks up the can, I notice a ring of condensation on the table. "Crap," I mutter, wiping at it with my hand and reaching for a coaster to set down in front of him.

"Ray," he mutters, disliking the way I try to keep the apartment as clean as we found it when we arrived. He takes nice things for granted, using an obviously expensive coffee table the same way he would a cheap one from a bargain store. But I can't seem to do that. I walk on eggshells around here. This apartment is modest compared to the condo in LA, but I've learned that it's practically luxurious by Manhattan standards, and it's filled with nice things that don't belong to us.

"I didn't mean that you're predictable in a bad way," he says, tilting his head back to take a sip, and wincing when it hits his mouth. "This is the lemon-flavored one," he complains, turning the can to inspect it.

"You don't like lemon?"

"Not the artificial-flavoring kind." Lucas puts it back on the table, resting it on the coaster this time. "I must have bought the wrong ones."

I reach for the can and take a tentative taste. Then I try not to make a face. He's right, it's awful. "I'll drink them." I shrug.

"You like it?" He looks at me like I'm nuts.

"It's fine."

Shaking his head, he says, "No, it's not. You just don't want me to throw them out. That issue you have with being wasteful is rearing its head."

I roll my eyes at him.

"See?" He points a finger at me. "Predictable again. And you're not drinking that shit either if you don't like it."

I give him a disapproving look. "I won't call you spoiled because I know better. But you'd be in for a very rude awakening if your father ever cut you off."

He surprises me by grinning. "You think so?"

I nod, but now I'm not so sure as I take in his smug expression.

"Between you and me," he says. "If my dad cut me off tomorrow, we'd only have to tough it out for a little while, until I turn twenty-one and get access to the trust fund my grandfather set up for me."

Shaking my head, I laugh. Of course he has a trust fund.

"So you don't have to drink crap you don't like, and you don't have to worry about messing up this apartment or damaging anything because I can have it all cleaned or replaced. My dad used to warn me about women wanting me for my money, but he never told me what to do if the woman I wanted refused to take a dime from me." He leans forward, his expression turning serious. "Money is one worry I can easily erase for you. Please let me."

Swallowing hard, nerves skitter beneath my skin. I don't know how the conversation took this turn, but I have to ask the question, "Whose apartment is this?"

He looks at me for a long moment before answering. "Ours."

My eyes close briefly because he tricked me, or maybe I let him. "What about the clothes and the pictures?"

"Staged," he replies.

"You lied." I pull in a breath, waiting for the hurt to find me.

"Yeah." His eyes turn wary.

Leaning back against the couch, I realize that I don't feel hurt, not really. I know why he did this. Lucas didn't lie to make a fool of me or to be purposely mean or deceptive. He only ever lies when he's doing it to protect me. That's how he justifies it to himself.

He's tense, waiting for my reaction. I can't tell him it's all right, because it's not. He still lied. But without saying anything, I shift so that I can lay my head on his shoulder. He's not going to change, and I don't want to make him feel as though he has to.

His hand spreads across my thigh, and he leaves it there. We sit quietly this way for a while until he finally asks, "Are we okay?"

I nod and he exhales, his shoulder relaxing beneath my cheek. I think we understand each other.

"What about the nurse?" he asks. "Do you still want to help her father?"

Glancing at the stack of papers beside him, I say, "Yes. I'll call her tomorrow and tell her."

Lucas's fingers squeeze my leg. "Let me do it. I want to talk to her before we agree to anything."

I can't see his face from this angle, but his tone sounds determined. He probably wants to vet her personally, despite everything he's already learned about her.

"Okay," I reply. If I'm doing this, he needs to feel comfortable with it. He wants to take care of me, and I'm starting to understand that maybe I should let him sometimes.

T'S mostly students who come in after nine to order double espressos. That or people who work the late shift. Thankfully, I don't work the late shift, and I'm pulling off my green apron just as Gwen comes strolling in.

"Hey, party people!" she calls out to us far too loudly.

Behind me, Mitch rolls his eyes. Gwen grins at him as she plops her elbows down on the counter. She's had flaming red streaks in her hair since January and it was jarring at first, but I'm used to it now. She also has on a yellow scarf tonight, breaking up her otherwise all-black ensemble. With Gwen, yellow means happy. Since she and Mitch are celebrating their seven-month anniversary, I think that must have something to do with her sunny flash of color.

"Where's he taking me?" she whispers, glancing up at him to make sure he's not listening.

"I don't know where he's taking you!" I answer loudly. Gwen scowls at me as Mitch starts to chuckle.

I have my friend back. Gwen seems to be thriving here at school. She has a ton of new friends, and she has Mitch. They met during freshman orientation, and she tells me that they've been inseparable ever since. She even helped me get my job, since Mitch already worked here and put in a good word.

I was a jumble of nerves when I first called her up. Once Lucas and I had been in the city for a few weeks, I finally worked up the courage. Yes, she was pissed at me. But thankfully, she forgave me. My story about discovering my father and then having him die from a heart attack pretty much jerked her heartstrings the same way it did for Myles. It's a ridiculous story. I hate telling it. But I had to explain things some way.

"Before I forget, there's a party tomorrow night," she says. "The cousin of my roommate's friend has a loft near Columbus Circle. Everyone's going."

I eye her skeptically. "The cousin of your…"

"Roommate's friend," she finishes, her eyes wide with excitement. "There's going to be a live band."

"I'll think about it." I grab my bag from beneath the counter and give a little wave to Heidi, my manager.

Gwen's gaze follows me as I move around next to her. "What's to think about?" she asks with a frown. Then her finger points at me. "You and Lucas are practically shut-ins. You need to get out a little. I mean, I know you two are constantly going at it, but come up for air once in a while… What?"

She angles her head at me, trying to see beneath the curtain of hair I let fall over my flushed face. She wasn't exactly whispering, and now it feels like everyone in the place is staring at me.

Mitch catches my eye and winks, making my cheeks burn even hotter.

"Don't get me wrong. I like Lucas. I've been rooting for you guys from the beginning," Gwen persists. "All I'm saying is you shouldn't make your boyfriend your whole world. If it doesn't work out, what are you left with?"

Mitch comes up beside her, pulling on his coat. "She's right. We're dumping you soon if you don't start paying more attention to us. We're needy that way."

Gwen turns to him, her mouth hanging open. "That's not what I'm saying. You know that's not what I'm saying. Right?" she asks me.

"Actually, you were saying she has a lot of sex," Mitch supplies helpfully.

"Oh my God, you two," I mutter, giving them the evil eye before I make a beeline for the door. As I walk through it, I hear them laughing behind me.

Huddling close to the building, I shove my arms into my coat, finding myself grinning, warming at the way they tease me, like good friends do. I should have thought of a witty comeback to toss at them. They're not exactly celibate. But I'm not used to the banter, and all my responses seem to come to me long after the conversation is over.

The sidewalk is teeming with people. Most have their heads down against the cold as they move quickly to their destinations. I grew up in a city, but New York City is different, and I'm finding that I like the constant noise and movement, the hum of activity that resounds even in the wee hours of the morning.

The door opens and they walk out together, looking for me. When Gwen spots me, she smiles. "You know we love you."

"Otherwise we wouldn't bother embarrassing you," Mitch says.

I nod, being a good sport. "Yeah, I know. Love you guys, too."

"We're headed this way," Mitch says, pointing to his left. "Can we walk you somewhere?"

Thanking them for the offer, I beg off. "I'm meeting Lucas this way." I point in the opposite direction. "Have fun and happy anniversary."

Gwen pulls me in for a cheek kiss before moving back beside Mitch and grinning up at him when he puts his arm around her. The lead singer from her favorite band, Disturbed, is in a new band, and they're playing in town tonight. She's going to flip out when she discovers that Mitch is taking her to see them.

I glance at my phone to check the time again, and yelp when it rings in my hand. "I'm leaving now," I announce when I answer.

"Stay put. I'm a block away, heading in your direction," Lucas says.

He wanted to pick me up at work, but I told him not to bother since it was out of his way. But as usual, he didn't listen. He never does when it comes to this chivalry stuff. He takes it very seriously.

Tonight we're meeting at the hospital where Samantha works. She told Lucas she could get an empty exam room, and we could meet them there. Lucas thinks she chose the hospital in case anything goes wrong. We like it because it's a public place and therefore less threatening.

I turn the corner and spot Lucas walking toward me from the other direction. His long legs, wrapped in dark jeans, eat up the sidewalk. He has on his leather coat and there's a red scarf around his neck. His unruly locks are pushed back off his forehead with visible trails left behind from his fingers. That tells me he's worried. His expression may give nothing away, but he can't stop his fingers from continually slicing through his hair.

There are still about twenty yards between us when I break into a run, closing the distance, grinning hugely at him as I leap into his arms.

He laughs as he catches me and spins me around. "God, you're gorgeous when you're all amped up like this."

"Amped up?" I ask as he puts me down.

"It's like the power inside you knows what you're about to do, and it's busting at the seams to get out. I can feel the electricity coming off you. And you smell like coffee. You know how much I love coffee."

I'm still smiling because I can feel it, too. I feel alive and hyperalert, like I decided to chug some of those double espressos I've been making all night.

We turn together, heading back in the direction Lucas came from, going toward the hospital. He takes my hand and uses his free one to put his phone to his ear. "We're going in now. Give us an hour. Then call me."

When he disconnects, he notices my curious look. "I told Liam about tonight. Someone needs to know where we're going and what's happening. If I don't pick up when he calls, he'll know we ran into a problem."

My eyebrows draw together. "Then what?"

He shrugs. "Then nothing, but at least we won't fall off the radar with no one the wiser."

My stomach does a flip.

His arm comes around me. "I'm just being cautious."

I lean into him, and I know he's right. My eagerness may be clouding my judgment, but I feel better knowing it's not clouding his. And despite his calm exterior, the arm he has around my shoulder tightens as we near the hospital. It's lit up brightly in the darkness with ambulances parked by the Emergency door. The main entrance is bustling, too, with the constant whooshing sound of the doors sliding open and closed automatically as people continually trail in and out of the building.

A few feet short of the entrance, Lucas abruptly stops walking. "Hold up a minute."

I glance at him and his expression is serious.

"If you're healing this guy and you sense that you should stop, then do it. Don't make me stop you. I need to be able to trust you on this. I need to know you won't let yourself get hurt, even if it means not being able to help him."

Even though I knew this was coming, I'm surprised it took him so long to say it. "I won't," I tell him truthfully, making sure to maintain eye contact with him so he'll believe me. "I have too much to lose now. There's no way I would do that to you or to myself."

Lucas studies me for a moment. Then he nods. But before I can turn back toward the building, his hands land on my shoulders and he seals his lips to mine. His mouth opens as he kisses me hungrily right in front of the busy hospital entrance.

I begin to understand what this is costing him. If he thought he could get away with forbidding me to do this, he would. Instead, he's swallowing his fear, and he's supporting me because he knows this is who I am. I didn't think I could love him any more than I already did, but my heart swells, and I kiss him back with all the emotion I'm feeling. When we finally break away, breathless and flushed, a small crowd has gathered around us. They quickly disperse when we notice them, and my cheeks grow even hotter at the attention. But Lucas just looks satisfied. "Come on," he says, turning me back toward the door.

We're barely inside the bright main entrance when she steps in front of us. Samantha's smile is frozen on her face as her big brown eyes travel between us. Something in her expression tells me she saw what we were just doing out there.

"You must be Lucas, and you're Raielle, is it?" she asks, pronouncing it hesitantly but correctly. I haven't spoken to her since that day on the street, but Lucas has. I'm sure he grilled her, but she's showing no side effects of it now. Unlike the day we met, today she actually looks like a nurse. She's wearing pink scrubs with white clogs, and her long black hair is secured in a barrette at the base of her head.

I nod at her as my eyes dart around, watching the people moving past us. Beside me, Lucas is doing the same thing. Samantha appears completely sincere, but we'll always have suspicions, and I know how rude and standoffish that must make us seem.

When my eyes land on the crowded lobby area, I think about the volunteer sitting there weeping over the sick children, and I wonder if she knew about my father's organization but decided to remain on her own. Based on Samantha's story, it seems like she was suppressing her power while she was here, until she finally couldn't hold it in any longer. Why would she volunteer in a hospital if it was going to affect her so deeply?

There was a time when I couldn't set foot in a hospital without being leveled by the need to heal, to the point of feeling sick myself. But the control I have over my energy now still surprises me. I can feel it, the way my body senses the subtle vibration of illness filling this building, but I'm not overtaken by it. It's like background noise that I can choose to focus on or not.

"You good?" Lucas asks, his hand on my back, his eyes searching mine.

I blink back to my surroundings and smile to reassure him. Then I look over at Samantha. "I'm ready."

We follow her through a maze of brightly lit hallways. The deeper she takes us into the hospital, the quieter it becomes, with patients and hospital workers thinning out along with the noise. Then she comes to a set of double doors and hits a button on the wall that causes them to slowly slide apart.

"This section has been cleared out for a renovation that's starting next month. No one will bother us here," she says as she moves toward the only open door along the narrow hallway. "This way," she says and gestures.

Lucas's hand runs over my back, helping to calm my nerves as I move forward. Samantha walks in first and Lucas grips my shirt, pulling me slightly behind him as he peers inside the room. Over his shoulder, I see a frail-looking man sitting in a wheelchair, and another man who looks like a younger, beefier version of the first one, standing beside the chair. Lucas steps to the side, seeming to decide there's no immediate danger. When I walk in, all eyes lock on me.

Samantha clears her throat. "This is my brother, Dom, and my father, Thomas."

Both men look me over, and it's hard to miss the skepticism in their expressions. I get the feeling they were coerced by Samantha into being here.

"Thank you for coming," her father finally says, offering me a small smile that doesn't seem genuine. He has thinning white hair, and you can tell that he used to be handsome. The brother is a whole different story. He's scowling so hard, I wonder if that's his expression or if his face actually looks all pinched like that.

"Good to meet you, sir," Lucas says, taking the initiative and offering the older man his hand to shake. We all watch as Thomas slowly lifts a trembling arm a few inches before stopping, unable to go any farther. Lucas leans down, taking his hand and giving it a firm shake.

I don't reach out to shake hands; I don't want to touch anyone yet. "Nice to meet you, Mr. Miller," I say politely.

His mouth hitches up again stiffly. Then he clears his throat, and with introductions out of the way, the atmosphere starts to turn awkward. "I should probably say that I don't really believe what Samantha's telling me about you. I'm sorry."

Samantha comes and puts her hand on her father's shoulder. "You don't have to believe it. You only have to let her do it." She smiles apologetically at me.

"You travel light," Dominic says, speaking for the first time. "No scarves or crystal balls?"

I try to suppress a smile, but it's hard. I've never been in a situation like this before. Usually, I'm hiding what I can do, not trying to prove it. I've never experienced this kind of skepticism, and it's doing the opposite of what Dominic expects. Rather than intimidating me, it's making me feel more at ease as my residual suspicions disappear.

Lucas notices my reaction, and he winks at me before saying, "We left the Ouija board and the animal sacrifice in the car. Want me to go get them, babe?"

Their eyes widen, and I elbow Lucas. "He's joking." I point toward the chair behind Dominic. "If I could just sit there beside you and hold your hand, that's all I need."

"Of course," Samantha says too brightly, nudging her brother out of the way.

As I make my way to the chair, Dominic holds up his hand. "Wait a minute. I need to know exactly what you're going to do to my father."

I try to be reassuring. "I need to get a sense of his illness and what it's doing to his body. Then I'll know if there's anything I can do to help." I turn to their father. "You might feel kind of a giddy sensation, but that's all."

"Give her some room and stop being a jerk," Samantha says to Dominic. His lips press together before he relents, taking a step back but still staying close, and leaning against the wall behind me.

I notice that Lucas moves beside him, seemingly casual, but his eyes are narrowed and his shoulders are tight, ready to step in if Dominic tries to interrupt or do anything that Lucas perceives as a threat. He's got my back, like always.

I sit down and smile, trying to put Samantha's father at ease. Lou Gehrig's disease is not something I've encountered before, and I'm not sure what to expect. I know it's fatal. I know I hold their hopes in the palm of my hand, or at least Samantha's hopes. She maneuvers the wheelchair so that it sits directly beside my chair.

"Can I take your hand," I ask him.

Thomas's eyes are a dull brown color, and lines of red shoot through the whites. They reveal a hint of fear, but I don't know of what, me or the possibility of hope.

"Yes," he says quietly, lifting his hand in my direction.

When I loosely grip his fingers, his skin is cold, and it feels paper thin in my hand. I close my eyes and take a deep breath, releasing the hold I have on my energy. It sparks immediately, growing quickly, swirling inside me. It recognizes something in Thomas and reaches out to him. I let it go, no longer restraining it, and feel my stomach dip as the energy flows into him. It doesn't take long for understanding to seep back toward me. The disease is in his nervous system and it's moving slowly, like a shallow wave lapping at the nerve cells inside him, doggedly carving away at them.

I breathe out slowly, knowing that I can stop the disease from progressing any further, but not sure if I can repair the damage that's already been done. Thomas gasps, and my eyes open. In my peripheral vision, I can see Lucas urging a tense Dominic to stay back. But my attention is on Thomas. His eyes flutter closed and a subtle smile appears on his face. It's not too difficult, extinguishing the momentum of the disease. But there are strands of damaged nerves that are resisting me, and I push harder, trying to fix them. Behind me, Samantha whispers, "Oh, my God," as the room grows brighter.

The nerves that have experienced the most recent damage seem to be responding. I pass through those one by one, but the older damage that began at the start of his decline, I can't seem to fix. There's nothing I can do there. I close my eyes again and begin to bring the energy back to me. The light fades, and I settle back into the chair, releasing his hand.

My eyes open and go directly to Lucas, who's apprehensive, but smiling warmly at me. I give him a nod before looking back at Thomas. In an instant, Samantha is on her knees in front of her father.

"Is that it?" she asks me. Before I can answer, she's lifting her father's hands. "Dad? Are you okay?"

He stares at her, only blinking, but still smiling. The smile on his face never went away. "I think…" He hesitates.

Dominic steps forward. "You think what?"

Thomas's smile grows as his gaze moves to me. "I think I am." He laughs, still giddy from the healing. Then he raises his right arm easily with no hesitation, and the left arm moves, too. His children stare at him, shock apparent on their faces. But when he looks down and tries to move his legs, they only shift slightly.

"There are some nerves that I couldn't repair," I explain. "I'm not sure you'll ever regain strength in your legs. But the disease is gone. It won't do any more damage."

Samantha covers her mouth, and she starts to cry.

Dominic has no reaction, standing there quietly watching his father.

Thomas is quiet, too, though his eyes are wide as his attention shifts between me and the limbs that are within his control again. Even his head seems steadier on his shoulders as he purposely cranes his neck, testing his mobility. When he touches the top of his head with his fingers, he laughs in disbelief at that accomplishment.

Samantha bends down to wrap her arms around him, and she begins to sob.

My own eyes water as I push myself up from the chair. Lucas comes to stand beside me.

"He's cured?" Dominic asks, seeming unwilling to accept it. "This thing won't kill him now?"

"No, it won't," I reply. "I'm sorry I couldn't do more, though."

"You're sorry?" Dominic exclaims, rearing back in disbelief at my words, then looks again at his father.

"Thank you so much," Samantha whispers, her voice thick with emotion.

Thomas's arms go around his daughter. When he meets his son's wide gaze, Dominic's mouth is tight and he says, "We should make you an appointment while we're here. I need a doctor to tell me it's really gone."

Lucas shifts uncomfortably beside me. Then he clears his throat to get their attention. "You can't tell anyone what just happened here. I don't know how you're going to explain this, but the truth isn't an option. You could be putting Raielle at risk if you say anything, and that would be a really shitty way to pay her back."

I give him a sharp look before turning back to them. "I'm sorry for his bluntness, but he's right. You can't tell his doctor or anyone else about this."

Samantha brushes away her tears and takes a step toward us. "It's obvious that…you've been through something. But you don't have to worry. I told Lucas on the phone, and I'm telling you now. We won't say a word. You have my promise."

"We'll keep your secret," Dominic agrees. "But what if…" He breaks off, his gaze shifting between Lucas and me. "What if I know someone else who could use your help?"

Beside me, Lucas sighs heavily and gives me a wary look. I can't help asking Dominic the obvious question. "You have someone in mind?"

He nods.

Lucas's eyes close, and they stay that way for a beat before opening again.

I didn't think past this one time, but I should have. "I'll have to think about it," I reply, but it's hard to imagine turning him down.

Dominic looks at Lucas when he nods his understanding.

"I should get Ray home now," Lucas says.

Samantha and Thomas want to hug me and thank me again, and as usual, this makes me uncomfortable. I still don't like this part, the gratitude, the overwhelming smothering gratitude for doing something I know I should be doing so much more of. I should be helping as many people as I can, not selfishly hiding myself away.

After we finally manage to break free, we're making our way out of the hospital when Lucas says, "That looked like an easy one. Did it tire you out at all?"

I'm shaking my head, thinking I feel the exact opposite of tired, when his phone rings and he answers, assuring Liam that we're fine.

On the way home, we stop at a deli to grab some dinner. We're quiet as we sit across from each other. My leg is bouncing beneath the table, and my skin is still tingling. Lucas notices my restlessness, but he doesn't comment. He seems tense and solemn, and I'm too lost in my own thoughts to ask him what's going on in his head just yet. Besides, I know what he's thinking, and I'm pretty sure he knows what I'm thinking.

When we get back to the apartment, I shrug off my coat, ready for him to dive right in and try to persuade me to his point of view, which is probably that exposing my power to more people could be dangerous. But I hardly have time to prepare myself when he stalks toward me and says, "Not yet."

My argument stalls in my throat as he wraps his arms around me and presses his mouth to mine. Our tongues brush against each other. I feel his hands wander. My need for him takes over, and soon we're pulling each other's clothes off while we stumble toward the bedroom.

He has me stripped first, and I lie down on the bed, watching him as he finishes undressing. Then he stands there looking at me while his eyes darken with desire. When he walks toward the bed, gone is the urgency he showed before. He moves over me slowly, placing his arms on either side of my head and dipping down to kiss my lips before moving down to my neck. Next he pays attention to my breasts, before going lower. After that, I'm lost to him.

Lucas knows how to play my body, just like he said, and build it into a frenzy of want. He uses his tongue and then his fingers. Next he makes me talk to him. He needs to hear how much I want him. Once I tell him, he grips my wrists, pushes my arms over my head and slides inside me. Then he teases me, bringing us to the edge, only to pull back, stilling himself above me. He does it again and again until I'm writhing beneath him, begging him to satisfy me. When he does, we climax together, and he bites out my name like it hurts for him to say it. But as his breathing slows, he whispers my name again like he's savoring the sound of it.

Later, with our limbs tangled in the sheets, his expression is tender as he traces a finger down my cheek. "Been a while," he says. "We needed that."

I laugh, and his brow quirks up. It hasn't even been twenty-four hours, but I know what he means. I miss him and want him constantly, too.

"What?" he asks.

He's leaning over me, and my fingers wander over the bunched muscles of his shoulder. "Want to talk now?"

He sighs heavily and drops down onto his back. "When you start school, we're going to have even less time together."

I push up and look down into his eyes, which are starting to turn stormy. "Is it really my time management skills you're worried about?"

His gaze tilts up to the ceiling as his hand scrapes over his cheek. "You've been hurt so many times. The possibilities for how this could go bad are too many to list."

I rest my head on his shoulder as he wraps his arm around me, pulling me against him. This is the place where I feel safest and most content, in our bed with him holding me. We've had an incredible and disaster-free few months. Do I really want to risk this?

When we first got here, we did all the touristy things Lucas promised we'd do in the city. It was unbelievably romantic when he kissed me at the top of the Empire State Building. Then we celebrated his birthday on a snowy winter night. It was low-key, just dinner out and some quality time at home. That's all he wanted. It was simple and beautiful. Then I gave him his present, tickets to the Yankees home opener in April. I spent more than a few paychecks on them. His reaction took my breath away. He was so excited, like a little kid, picking me up and spinning me around the room. I loved seeing him that way.

Now our lives have fallen into a hectic routine, becoming what I imagine is normal for most people. We see less of each other, but when we do come together, it's desperately perfect. And now I'm throwing a wrench into it…again. But as happy as we've been, I put aside a big part of myself. I've tried not to let Lucas see that my happiness has a small dent in the middle of it, but he knows me too well. He must sense it.

"I'll be honest," he says. "I trust them. Samantha and her family." His fingers absently brush over my arm. "She's a nurse and they're both cops. They're good people. I've been thinking about the way you met her that day. And I can't believe I'm saying this, because I don't generally buy into this shit, but maybe it was fate."

My lips curl up. "That occurred to me, too," I say. Just like sometimes I think my meeting Lucas was fate, but I've never told him that. There's too much pain behind the events that put me in his path. I guess fate has been both cruel and kind to us.

He kisses the top of my head. "I'd like to keep you all to myself, protected inside a bubble. But I know you need this. I'm not sure you can live without it, not happily at least. We'll just be careful. We'll find a way for you to do what you're meant to and still stay safe."

Wanting to see his expression, I lean up on my elbow, and he turns to face me. The dark blue of his eyes reminds me of the ocean tonight, pouring out so many emotions—hope, fear, and bittersweet acceptance. But beneath it all is love.

"You deserve to be happy, Ray."

My gaze locks on his. "You deserve that, too. You deserve everything."

Before I met Lucas, happiness was unfamiliar, and dreams were a luxury I could never afford. But the moment we came together, it all changed. He makes me want to dream now. Then he makes my dreams come true.

I let my gaze trail down from his eyes, over the curve of his strong chin, down to the smooth planes of his chest. My hand reaches out to trace the ridges of his stomach before shifting up over the warm skin above his heart. The rhythm I feel beneath my palm reaches out to someplace deep inside me, a once hollow spot that he fills completely.

I shift on top of him, stretching myself over the length of him so that each part of my body is touching a part of his. Lucas smiles at me as I reach up to smooth a hand over his hair. I feel his thigh muscles flex beneath me. His chest expands as he pulls in a breath, and he starts to want me again. I can feel his every movement. I know his thoughts, and I know his body.

He's mine.

He's my home.

Thank you for reading *To Have and to Harm*.

If you enjoyed this book, why not take a minute or two to leave a review? Reviews are a valuable resource in helping readers find other books they may enjoy.

Connect with Debra:
www.Facebook.com/AuthorDebraDoxer
www.twitter.com/debradoxer
debradoxer@gmail.com

ALSO BY DEBRA DOXER

Keep You from Harm
Sometime Soon
Wintertide

This paperback interior was designed and formatted by

www.emtippettsbookdesigns.com

Artisan interiors for discerning authors and publishers.

81602256R00187

Made in the USA
Columbia, SC
23 November 2017